THE DORSET SQUIRREL

'At the first scent of burning heather on the breeze, Oak had scrambled to the highest branch of the fir. He could see the billowing smoke-clouds, lit from underneath by the red and orange flames, coming downwind towards them on an ever widening front. Coming too fast to race away from, particularly with Old Burdock unable to move quickly. There was a chance that if they stayed in the tree the flames might not reach them, but he had once seen a burning tree and was not going to risk that. There was only one other option…'

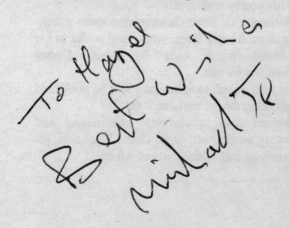

To Hazel
Best wiles
Michael Tye

By the same author
A Curlew's Cry   (Poetry)
Dolphinsong   (March 2000)

Novelist, poet and philosopher Michael Tod was born in Dorset in 1937 where these stories are set. He lived near Weymouth until his family moved to a hill farm in Wales when he was eleven. His childhood experiences on the Dorset coast and in the Welsh mountains gave him a deep love and knowledge of wild creatures and wild places, which is reflected in his poetry and novels.

Married with three children and three grand-children, he still lives, works and walks in his beloved Welsh hills but visits Dorset whenever he can.

His next novel, Dolphinsong will be published by Cadno Books early in 2000.

Michael Tod is currently researching and writing another eco-saga, God's Elephants, set largely in the wilder parts of Africa.

THE
DORSET
SQUIRRELS

Michael Tod

Cadno
Books

The Silver Tide was first published by Cadno Books in 1993
and by Orion in 1994
The Second Wave was first published by Orion in 1994
The Golden Flight was first published by Orion in 1995

The Dorset Squirrels was first published by Cadno Books in
1999.

www.michaeltod.co.uk

Published by Cadno Books
cadnobooks@btinternet.com

Michael Tod has asserted his right to be
identified as the author of this book.

Cover illustration by Kevin Tweedell.
Maps by Barbara Anne Knight.

ISBN 1-89822503 6

Printed and bound in Great Britain by
Cox & Wyman Ltd, Reading, Berkshire.

Dorset
New America

The White Horse

Water Barrow

Barrow of the Ferns

Barrow of the Flowers

ABBOTSBURY
The Swannery

WEYMOUTH

White Nothe   Lulworth Cove

Worbarrow Tout

The Fleet Lagoon   Weymouth Bay

The Dragons Teeth

Portland Harbour

N

Chesil Bank

THE ISLE OF PORTLAND

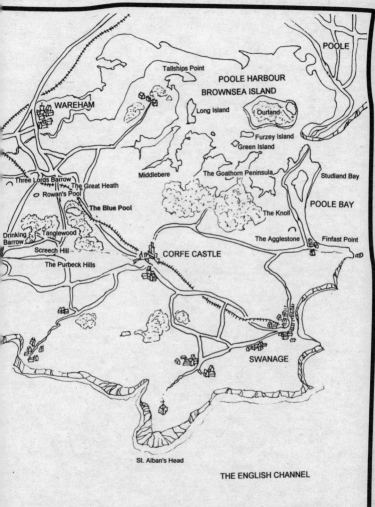

POOLE

Tallships Point

POOLE HARBOUR

BROWNSEA ISLAND

Long Island

Ourland

WAREHAM

Furzey Island

Green Island

Three Lords Barrow

The Great Heath

Middlebere

The Goathorn Peninsula

Studland Bay

Rowan's Pool

POOLE BAY

The Blue Pool

The Knoll

Drinking
Barrow

Tanglewood

The Agglestone

Finfast Point

Screech Hill

CORFE CASTLE

The Purbeck Hills

SWANAGE

St. Alban's Head

THE ENGLISH CHANNEL

BOOK ONE

THE SILVER TIDE

Chapter 1

The year was nineteen sixty-one. Humans symbolised this as 1 9 6 1 but, as all humans know, such symbols are meaningless to lesser creatures.

Marble sat on top of the World. Actually it was a fence-post with slack strands of rusting wire joining his post to those on either side of him, on one of which his companion and acolyte, Gabbro, was sitting, tearing the limbs off a fledgling with his sharp yellow teeth.

The World around them was Dorset, in the south of England, or New America as his kind liked to call it.

A male grey squirrel in the prime of life, Marble licked the blood from his lips and looked out across the Great Heath to the hills of Purbeck beyond. Out there was Adventure, Advancement and Achievement!

He flicked his tail at the blackbirds, the parents of the babies he and Gabbro had just taken from their nest in a hawthorn bush and killed, annoyed at the way they flew at his head in protest, shouting "Chit, chit, chit. Chit, chit, chit."

"Chit to you too," he shouted back and Gabbro, sworn to silence for the journey, grinned over at him.

Marble had invented the "Vow of Silence" on the second day out as noisy, inquisitive youngsters learned more if they kept their mouths shut and their ears and eyes open.

"Tomorrow we probe Purbeck," Marble called across, proud to be an Explorer, Missionary and Disturber of the Peace.

There had been patches of snow on the ground under the trees when Marble and Gabbro had left Home-Base at Woburn Park, moons before. Having received his instructions from the Great Lord Silver, he had wasted no time in leaving; better to be out adventuring than hanging about in idleness with the plotters and the hangers-on.

He had chosen a promising youngster with the name of Gabbro to be his acolyte and, when they had set out together, he had only glanced back once at the cluster of dreys forming the New America Base. These dreys were almost completely hidden amongst the branches, each round, woven mass of twigs and leaves the retreat of one of the senior governing families. Each so high and well concealed that human Visitors passing underneath seldom noticed them.

Ever since the first grey squirrels from America had been released there, in what the humans called the eighteen nineties, Woburn had been the centre of their operations.

The toughest, meanest Grey in that first batch had taken charge and called himself Lord Silver. It had seemed to him that grey was a drab sort of colour and it *was* true that in certain conditions, the light-coloured guard-hairs projecting through the squirrels' fur made them look silvery. Anyway, he was chief and could call himself by any name he wished.

Lord Silver had soon become Great Lord Silver and there had been a Great Lord Silver at Woburn ever since. When one died, others fought for his rank and position. The winner, if he survived his wounds, would then impose his ideas and prejudices on the others.

Marble had been glad to be away. He hated the intrigue and the plotting of the Oval Drey, and the current occupant was far too permissive in many ways for Marble's taste. Maybe, when he, Marble, had made a real name for himself he might . . . No – get on with the job in hand! Purbeck was a real challenge. Somewhere where he could prove himself.

His training had finished with his return from that trip to the west, keeping north of the Great River and penetrating as far as the Ford of the Oxen, though the name of the place, once given to it by the native red squirrels, seemed inappropriate.

It was an honour now to have been given the chance to explore and soften up this place the natives called Purbeck. Very little was known of it and he and Gabbro would be the first Silvers to probe there.

On that first day out he had hopped along, Gabbro chattering excitedly at his side.

"No – I don't know why it's called Purbeck! Yes – it is a long way. No – I haven't been there before." An acolyte was all very well, they could be useful at times, and every ambitious youngster had to learn, but . . .

Marble had scented an acorn under the leaf litter, probably buried by a fellow squirrel, or perhaps a jay, the previous autumn. He had dug it up and eaten it rapidly while Gabbro had searched around until he too had found one. Marble then moved on, Gabbro following, awkwardly holding the acorn in his teeth, snatching a bite whenever Marble stopped to choose a route. Gabbro clearly had a mass of questions he wanted to ask but, with an acorn in his mouth, he had been forced to keep them until later.

Spring had come and passed as the pair made steady progress towards the west and south. They had passed through Silver country all the way, meeting no native red squirrels. Marble had thought how satisfying it was to see the success his kind had at exploiting the countryside, and with the population pressure behind him building up inexorably, more land *was* needed. What was that term that the Great Lord Silver had used? "Leaping-room!" That had summed it up precisely.

He, Marble, had been chosen personally for this mission. He might not agree with all that Woburn stood for now, but if the chief had sent him, it was up to him as a loyal Silver to do his very best.

There were Reds still holding out in parts of southern New America and there were reputed to be Reds still skulking in this place they called Purbeck, who might never have heard of the Silver Tide sweeping irresistibly their way. They were not dangerous, more of a nuisance really, but they did cling on so to what they called their Guardianships. Such primitive ideas! How could they be so naïve? And the Sun business that he had heard tell of – well!

They had lingered a little in what the colonists called the New Forest, though it was obviously very old. Had he not had a mission, Marble might have been tempted to stay on and fight for a territory there. Even he had been moved by the beauty of the place when the sunlight, striking through

4

the new green leaves of the gnarled oak trees, had lit up the forest floor and shone on the dappled coats of the fallow deer that passed below.

It was here that he had shown Gabbro the Stone force.

Each night, before finding a suitable sleeping place, Marble had instructed his now silent acolyte to collect stones and lay them out in the square patterns, and how to activate the force by his body power.

Marble enjoyed watching the concentration and concern showing on Gabbro's face as he made squares with four stones on each side and then when Marble told him to, reached out apprehensively to place his paw on one of the corner stones. The invisible Earth force could be whisker-sensed as it was drawn from the ground and diverted upwards to treetop height in the shape of a toadstool. Any creature getting too near was paralysed, although, as Marble himself had learned in his training, a certain degree of immunity could be acquired.

Gabbro had quickly become adept at laying out the Power Squares and bracing himself for the drain on his body energy as he started the force going. Marble knew that the energy to start a four by four square would be restored by a night's sleep but, even so, he preferred Gabbro to be the one to supply it. He had expended enough of his own energy during *his* training.

Between the New Forest and Purbeck they overtook colonising groups also pressing south and west, each group dealing with the few remaining Reds in whatever way they chose, harassing them until they moved on, leaving the best woods to be taken over and settled by the Greys.

Now Marble and Gabbro had come to the edge of the

heathland which was as far as the earlier explorers had penetrated. They had not reported how hot it would be here, but maybe this heat was exceptional. New America was noted for the vagaries of its weather!

Somewhere across the heather, beyond the birches and the pines, was Purbeck – his challenge!

Gabbro had finished eating the fledgling, so Marble flicked the "follow me" signal with his tail and leapt to the ground.

The youngster followed, and the blackbirds, still scolding, flew to the fence-posts and perched there, calling after the two strange creatures as they hopped away along the dusty path through the heather stems.

Marble ignored their calls. He knew that the birds could not harm him and there were other real dangers to watch for. But most of all, he was alert for signs of native Reds. Their presence would mean good squirrel country – country suitable for colonisation!

Rowan the Bold was lost. Not the heart-thumping, stomach-twisting feeling of being lost that hits a dreyling when it first looks around on the ground and cannot see its parents, but the "Where, in the name of the Sun, am I now?" sort of being lost.

It was bad enough to be on the ground amongst all this heather, where he felt vulnerable, but he must get his bearings or he could wander around lost for hours and that would be a poor way to finish his climbabout.

Standing up to his full red squirrel height, he could just see over the tops of the heath plants and he looked for a tree, as a shipwrecked sailor on a raft searches for an island and the security that this implies. The only tree that he could see was a stunted birch about the height of a Man, growing out of a bank of whitish-grey clay further along the path. The peaty dust from the parched soil tickled his throat as he hopped towards it, glancing over his shoulder from time to time to make sure that no hungry fox or playful dog was following. "Come on," he said to himself, "don't be a squimp, remember your tag. You're Rowan the Bold."

He scrambled up the bank and climbed the tree, feeling the comfort of being off the ground and the joy of his claws biting into the smooth bark. He climbed until the tree started to sag sideways with his weight, then paused to enjoy a tiny breeze which ruffled his fur and fluffed out the hairs of his tail.

Now, where am I? he wondered, peering around as he clung to the swaying stem. Through the heat-haze he could see a line of pine trees but not in any familiar pattern, and turning his head he could see the ridge of the Purbeck Hills. Studying their outline, he knew that he had come too far west. He was about to drop to the ground and head off eastwards towards home, when he caught the faintest whiff of water-scent on the air.

Rowan turned his head slowly, testing the scent and trying for a direction. It seemed to be floating to him from just beyond the pine trees. His mouth was dry and the idea of a cool drink drove thoughts of home into second place. Dropping on to the clay bank, he headed towards the pines.

The line of trees formed, vanished and re-formed in the haze ahead as he followed a twisting path through the heather, bracken and furze in the shimmering desert of the Great Heath.

Reaching the trees, he was tempted to rush down to the water and slake his thirst, but instinct and training had taught him to proceed more cautiously.

In a strange country,
Be careful. Time spent looking
Is seldom wasted.

He climbed the nearest tree and ran out along a branch to look down on to the pool below. It was not quite as big as the one at home, the Blue Pool, and certainly not as dramatically coloured. This one was a delicate orangey brown, but the water was clear enough from above for him to see the white of the clay bottom, well below the surface. It was surrounded by a low sand-cliff and in one place, where the clay must have been of too poor a quality for the long-dead quarrymen to have bothered with it, an over-grown mound remained, surrounded on all sides by water, and topped by three well-grown trees. Across the pool where the cliff had collapsed in places, the quartz particles in the sand caught the rays of the sun, now quite low in the sky, making them sparkle and gleam.

Air smelling of warm damp moss rose from the water's edge to mingle deliciously with the resin-scent of bark on the hot pine trunks. Huge pink and white flowers set amongst dark green circular leaves fringed the pool, leaving a large clear area in the centre.

Rowan watched a green dragonfly alight on a lily pad to rest for a moment, curl its tail under the leaf and lay an egg before rising and circling away. There were many damsel-flies flitting over the water, smaller than the dragons, some flying in mating pairs.

8

From high above, the pool was the shape of a hunched animal, perhaps a rabbit with his ears down, thought Rowan, the hump of land above the water being just where its eye would be. There was no scent nor sense of danger but he went slowly down the trunk head-first, looking about him as he did so.

A watchful squirrel
Survives to breed and father –
More watchful squirrels.

He drank at the water's edge, glanced at the sun to measure its angle and decided to stay there for the night. He could be home in one or two days at the most. There was plenty of food about, no sign of other squirrels having foraged there, and he ate until comfortably full, then chose a tree to sleep in. It was too warm to think of making even the most rudimentary drey for shelter, so he made himself at home in a fork of one of the tallest of the pines and fell asleep; to dream of the beautiful pool below him, with its sparkling sand, water-flowers, dragonflies and the "Eyeland" at the far end.

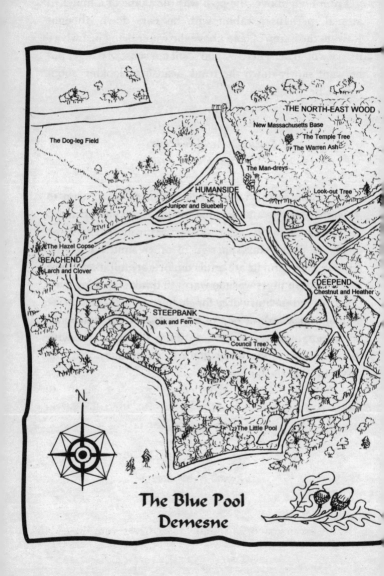

THE NORTH-EAST WOOD

New Massachusetts Base
The Temple Tree
The Warren Ash

The Man-dreys

The Dog-leg Field

Look-out Tree

HUMANSIDE
Juniper and Bluebell

The Hazel Copse

BEACHEND
Larch and Clover

DEEPEND
Chestnut and Heather

STEEPBANK
Oak and Fern

Council Tree

The Little Pool

N

The Blue Pool
Demesne

Chapter 2

Old Burdock, the Tagger Squirrel, sitting in a tree above a lake of sapphire blue water, watched the dreylings at play, the bright early morning sunlight glowing on their ruddy brown fur. Soon it would be her job to give them a tag which would stay with them for their lifetime. Unless, that is, they earned another, better tag through some outstanding act or impressive behaviour. Then a special Council Meeting would consider her recommendation for a change.

Ambitious squirrels were always hoping and working for an up-tag. This was good for the community. Not so pleasant was when she had to propose a down-tag for unsquirrel-like behaviour or worse.

She must always remember the code by which she worked, taught in the pattern of words used for all the symbolic and cultural traditions of her race.

> *Tagging a squirrel*
> *As reward or punishment*
> *Is a weighty task.*

This arrangement of sounds, five, then seven, then five

again, had a special authority and all squirrel lore was embodied in Kernels like this.

Only recently the Council had had to downgrade Juniper and Bluebell, the Guardians of Humanside, for scrounging food from the Visitors who came to the Blue Pool and who ate at the stone Man-dreys in that Guardianship. Since then Juniper and Bluebell, now tagged the Scavengers, had kept to their own side of the pool, lowering their tails in shame when they saw other squirrels, but there was no evidence yet of them mending their ways. Burdock knew how powerful the effect of a bad tag could be. A squirrel carrying the burden of a denigratory tag would have low self-esteem and be unable to mate, thus ensuring that only squirrels conforming to acceptable standards of squirrel behaviour would produce and raise youngsters. It was Old Burdock's burdensome task, as Tagger, to keep an eye on the behaviour of the whole community, and to allocate "True Tags" without favouritism.

On the winding Man-paths below her, human Visitors would soon be strolling, admiring the views glimpsed between the trees, most not giving any thought to the possibility of their being watched by squirrels from above.

These Visitors would come all through the summer, arriving in cars and coaches to park in the field which was a part of the Humanside Guardianship. They would wander under the pines, their cameras clicking in an attempt to capture the beauty and the "blueness" of the famous pool.

The size of a small field, this pool, like Rowan's, had once been a clay quarry, providing high quality blue ball-clay to make tobacco pipes and Wedgwood pottery and for use in refining sugar as it was made into sugarloaves, those cone-shaped blocks after which so many mountains have been named all across the world. Now, nearly a century after the workings had been abandoned, some unique combination of suspended clay particles and concentrated minerals in the rainwater trapped there gave it the name by which it was known. The Blue Pool was now on the itinerary of all Visitors to Purbeck.

Burdock looked out over the water, then resumed her watch on the dreylings. One, her own granddaughter, was outstanding – Marguerite, the only dreyling this year of Oak the Cautious and Burdock's daughter, Fern the Fussy, who were the current Guardians of Steepbank on the opposite side of the pool to Humanside. Oak combined this role of Guardianship with that of Council Leader and was inordinately fond of Marguerite.

Intelligent, active and charismatic, definitely a youngster to watch. Could be Council Leader herself one day, thought Burdock. Not common to have a female for leader but there is no taboo. If not Leader, then she may take over my job when I am Sun-gone. A mixed batch the rest, though.

Soon it would be time for Rowan the Bold, Marguerite's brother from the previous year, to be home from his climbabout. She was looking forward to hearing about his exploits. Sharing the active experiences of the youngsters seemed a fair repayment for the time she had spent in passing on the lessons her years had taught her.

Some of them, knowing that she was watching, showed off, leaping from branch to branch and demonstrating their developing prowess in any way they thought would impress.

Earning a good tag
Is each squirrel's ambition –
Then to retain it.

She envied them their youthful energy and remembered with a sigh just how it felt to test oneself by leaping greater and greater distances and the excitement and relief of landing safely in the branches beyond. Now, even a small jump across a modest gap tired her and she often found it easier to go down one tree trunk and up another. She felt she was too old to risk a fall.

Burdock cocked her head, listening. Across the pool came the sound of the metal gates at Humanside being unlocked, the signal for the squirrels to retreat into the upper branches and lie out on the resinous bark, enjoying the sunshine and any light breezes filtering through the treetops. They were safe there from foxes and the dogs of human Visitors, and no hawks big enough to be dangerous had been seen for many years. The once dreaded pine marten was now only an ancestral memory and a bogey to frighten unruly youngsters with marten-dread. Burdock recalled the old Kernel:

Pine marten's sharp teeth
Bite off the ears and the tails
Of naughty dreylings.

She moved to the highest branch of the tallest tree on Steepbank above where the sand-cliff dropped almost sheer to the water's edge. Not only was there the best chance of catching any breezes, but from there she had the finest view, and it was her job to watch and report on any unusual happenings. She looked across towards Humanside and the Man-dreys. The Red-Haired Girl was there. No danger from her – never has been – almost one of us, she thought.

Nothing was moving at Deepend to her right paw side: the guardians there would already be resting and no Visitors had arrived so far. She looked at Beachend to her left, all quiet there too, the sandy beach gleaming in the sun, curving round beyond the blue of the water. Sun, how she loved this place! Burdock stretched out and closed her eyes, reflecting on the part she had taken in building this happy community.

There was now a clear recognition of the place the Sun played in all their lives. She had gradually got rid of that old concept of worship. Respect was a much better term. The Sun could surely not want worshipping, it was far too all-wise for that.

The selection of Leaders and the establishment of the Council for the Demesne had largely been her idea. After a disastrous run of First-borns taking automatic control, regardless of their abilities, she had at last been able to get the demoralised squirrels to give her ideas a try. The worst that any squirrel could complain of now was boredom.

Old Burdock drifted off to sleep as the first pair of humans strolled along the path round the deep end of the pool, the male fanning his face with his summer straw hat.

At two o'clock, the Red-Haired Girl who was the waitress at the Tea Rooms was clearing the tables, the lunchtime rush over.

That pair of squirrels was hanging around again waiting

for any scraps to be thrown to them. She had noticed that one seemed particularly fond of salted peanuts and she idly wondered what it thought of the unusual taste, and was about to fetch a packet from the display of snacks when a visitor called to her, asking for another cup of coffee.

The squirrels were forgotten.

Chapter 3

Precisely at five o'clock, Tom, the caretaker, swung the big metal gates shut, collected his litter-bag and walked away to pick up the cigarette packets and ice-cream wrappers that somehow had not found their way into the waste-bins.

Burdock stretched one leg after another and looked down on to the network of paths. The Visitors had all gone, the Human Who Picked Things Up, now down at Beachend, was a part of the landscape and quite harmless, so it was safe to come down and forage for pine cones and early fungi. Halfway down the tree she stopped and stared.

Two creatures were coming along the path. They moved like squirrels but were much bigger than any squirrel she had ever seen – and grey!

Burdock watched from the tree trunk as the unfamiliar animals advanced. They progressed in a series of short dashes, pausing between each to look round. The leading one saw Burdock, stopped and sat up.

"What place is this?"

"You are in the Guardianship of Oak the Cautious, in the Blue Pool Demesne. I am Burdock, the Tagger."

"Greetings, Burdock," said the Grey. "I am called

Marble. This is my companion, Gabbro. We bring salutations from the Great Lord Silver, to whom we all owe allegiance." He held his right paw diagonally across his chest.

"Are you squirrels?" asked Burdock.

"We are. Squirrels of the Silver Kind. Our ancestors came from the Great Lands far away over the water beyond the sunset, but we are now bringing enlightenment to this land." He raised his tail proudly.

Burdock considered his action unmannerly. It was not proper to raise your tail until you had been greeted by the local guardian.

> Stranger, show respect
> You are the alien here.
> Teach us to trust you.

"What is your business?" asked Burdock, her voice sharp.

"Are you the Senior Squirrel in this precinct?" asked Marble coldly.

The word was new to Burdock but she understood its meaning. "No, I'm the Tagger, Oak the Cautious is the Council Leader."

"Take us to his drey," commanded Marble.

"As you wish," said Burdock and, holding her tail as high as possible, she set off in the direction of Oak's drey in the Council Tree.

Other squirrels had watched the confrontation and followed Burdock, Gabbro and Marble along the path. Burdock suddenly climbed a tree to see if the strangers could climb. They could. She forced herself to race along a branch as fast as she could and then leap to another tree. The Greys followed effortlessly. They *were* squirrels!

By the time they reached Oak's drey there were half a dozen more squirrels following them. Oak heard the movements in the branches before he could see the cause and moved higher for a better view. He was as surprised as Old Burdock had been to see the grey creatures which now approached, their tails low. "Greetings, strangers," said Oak, looking at Burdock for an explanation.

"Greetings, Oak the Cautious," said Burdock. "These strangers of the Silver Kind have come with 'salutations' from *their* Leader." She paused uncomfortably, still resenting the ill manners of the Greys and the high-handed way Marble had spoken to her. Taggers were second only to Council Leaders and should be treated with respect.

Oak looked with interest at the two Greys. They were larger than any of the Reds, more heavily built, and their ears were round without any trace of tufts on them. Their eyes were different too, seeming not to look straight at him. He did not feel he could trust them.

"So, you can speak our tongue," said Oak.

"After a fashion, Cautious Oak," said Marble. "We bring salutations from the Great Lord Silver and, as you are the local chief, seek your permission to teach the power of numbers to your subjects."

"I have no subjects, Marble the Stranger, these are all Respecters of the Sun, Guardians of the Land. I am just their chosen Leader. What are these numbers of which you speak?"

"In due course, in due course," replied Marble

dismissively, looking round to see if the other squirrels were listening. They were. "First I wish to learn of your local customs and then to rest from my journey." He held his tail low in a gesture of deference, during which display no reasonable request can be refused.

A submissive stance
And a request, presumes help –
Give it if you can.

"What do you wish to know, Marble the Stranger?" asked Oak.

"I suppose you consider the Sun to be the provider of everything, like the other natives who inhabited the middle lands?" said Marble.

Oak nodded assent. Could there be any doubt about that? This he had been taught by his Tagger when he was a dreyling and the evidence was to be seen everywhere. Plants started to grow when warmed by the Sun. The squirrel dreylings were born after the warmth of the spring Sun had aroused their parents to courtship. It was obviously the Sun that ripened the nuts and pine cones in the autumn to provide their winter food stocks.

The life-giving Sun
Provides all we need. Father
Of all the squirrels.

"Yes," said Oak positively, "that is our belief."

His mate, Fern the Fussy, was only half listening. An obstinate blob of resin was sticking to the hairs of her tail.

She combed it with her claws, then tried to lick off the residue. In the end she had to bite away a few hairs. She combed again to cover the gap. After all she was the Council Leader's life-mate and would be expected to look her best, especially when there were important visitors. She nipped off a twig which was sticking out of a branch at an untidy angle.

"What number comes after eight?" asked Marble.

"There is no number after eight," replied Oak. "We only have eight front claws to count on. After that there are 'lots'. "

"Great Lord Silver," Marble said quietly, glancing at the silent Gabbro and fighting to keep his tail from rising with superiority. "It seems you still practise guardianship instead of possession?"

"This word – possession – is unknown to me," said Oak.

"Possession, ownership, what's mine is mine, what's yours is yours, for as long as you can keep it. The only civilised way to behave, everybody knows where they are. Surely you can understand that?"

Oak tried, but the concept was beyond him. It was like trying to think about how far the land stretched away from the Blue Pool. Beyond it was the heath, or fields or woods, and beyond them, more. What was beyond those? They must stop somewhere, but where? He had heard about the Sea but had never seen it. What was beyond the Sea? He had often puzzled over this engima but had had to give up, unsatisfied, and other duties had prevented him ever having gone climbabout as some of the more adventurous squirrels did when they were young.

This concept of ownership was the same. A squirrel

couldn't "own" a tree or a path or a glade! The idea didn't make sense. *Guardianship* was clear. From the treetops, squirrels could watch out for anything that might be harmful or unnatural. Not that they could always do anything about it, he thought ruefully. At least some of the humans must feel the same. One of them, the Human Who Picked Things Up, did keep the whole of the demesne free of other humans' litter.

"Any special customs or rituals?" asked Marble.

By now virtually all the squirrels of the community were listening. News of the strangers' arrival had quickly spread through the demesne.

"Nothing that comes to mind," said Oak after a pause, "unless you mean the Sun-tithe, where we dig up and eat only seven out of every eight nuts we hide. We've always done that."

> *One out of eight nuts*
> *Must be left to germinate.*
> *Here grows our future.*

Marble was disappointed; he had learned about native behaviour from his mentor the previous year, and there appeared to be nothing dramatically different here. No natives ever understood the importance of ownership. "Just another lot of thick Reds," he would have to report to Woburn. It was all so boring. They all seemed obsessed by this Sun idea, as if the sun would care about any of them! Take and hold was the only way. The sun's there, always has been, always will be, and that's that, he thought superciliously. But the area is good, plenty of food and the surroundings are attractive.

If the Great Lord Silver was pleased with him he might put in a claim for this precinct for himself when he reported back.

"We will rest now," he said. "Tomorrow I'll teach you something about the power of numbers, and indeed Stone force. With your permission," he added, looking at Oak and keeping his tail lowered with difficulty. These natives were so naïve!

Oak looked round, saw his daughter, Marguerite, and said, "Please escort our guests to the Strangers' Drey, Daughter, and see that they have food."

The dreyling skipped about. "I am Marguerite the Bright One. Please follow me, Marble the Stranger, Gabbro the Companion."

She led them to the drey kept for squirrels passing through and checked that the supply of nuts and other delicacies was adequate.

"Is there anything else you would like?" she asked innocently.

Marble looked her over. Only a first-year chit. Anyway he was tired and didn't really approve of the way some of his kind used the red females. "No," he said, and went into the drey, followed by a disappointed Gabbro. In fact, he was not happy about the way most of the younger squirrels of his kind behaved nowadays. Since the change of leadership back at Woburn, all the old moral standards seemed to have been thrown out of the trees. Okay, he'd been a bit of a lad in his time, maybe even sired a litter or two, but now – now anyone mated with anyone, at any time and in any place! He shuddered.

He shelled and ate a nut and thought of the natives they had just met. He knew what would happen now. They would hold a Council Meeting. First there would be a discussion on who these strangers were and where they came from, then demands from some that they be sent on their way.

Others, however, would want to hear what he had to say and finally there would be a decision to hear him out and, if they didn't like what he said, they would ask the two of them to leave the area. But by then he would have sown the demoralising seeds, and when the Silver Tide reached Purbeck the Reds would be swept away easily.

And so it was. Old Burdock the Tagger, still upset at what she considered to have been shabby treatment, was all for sending them on at once. But the phrase that Marble had used, "the other natives who *inhabited* the middle lands", had stuck in her mind and she felt she needed to know more. Also she had to agree that, as hospitality had been offered, it could not now be withdrawn.

> *All passing strangers*
> *Must be accommodated*
> *At whatever cost.*

Most of the demesne, especially the younger ones, were intrigued by the talk of 'numbers' and 'Stone force' and wanted to hear more. The decision reached was exactly as Marble had predicted. He was already asleep.

Chapter 4

A fox wandered under the pine trees of Steepbank as the sun peered over the distant horizon. Fingers of pale light had touched Poole Harbour away to the east, making the colours of the anchored boats glow and reflect in the water. Then these same rays, reaching westwards, lit up Brownsea and Furzey Islands, the Goathorn Peninsula, Middlebere and the Great Heath.

At the Blue Pool the light touched the tops of the tallest pines and the squirrels stirred in their warm dreys, most anticipating an exciting day learning the power of numbers that the stranger had promised to tell them. What could that be?

Below, the pool was still in darkness, the fox could smell squirrels all about but knew that they were out of his reach. He scent-marked an anthill and moved away towards Humanside. Sometimes there were scraps of Man-food to be found near the Man-earths. If not, he would trot along the deserted road to see if any rabbits had been killed there in the night. Anything for an easy life.

A pair of jays screeched with the sound of tearing linen to express their displeasure as he passed through what they considered to be *their* territory.

As the light grew stronger and the sun cleared the pine trees of Deepend, the pool began to change colour from a soft green to a deep blue, mirroring the sky. Wraiths of mist twisted over the surface and vanished. A moorhen called to her young and paddled out from under an overhanging bush, followed by five tiny black chicks pecking at insects on the surface, ripples from their frantic activity disturbing the still water. The fox looked down from the bank, sniffed the air disdainfully, having found nothing near the waste-bins; thought to himself that, if there had been, it probably wouldn't have been worth eating anyway, and slipped away towards the road.

Oak poked his head out of the drey, which was built from a mass of carefully intertwined twigs, honeysuckle bines and leaves in a fork of the Council Tree. He sniffed the air, smelt fox, the scent too faint now to inspire the paralysing fox-dread, looked carefully down, whiskers twitching to sense air movement, sniffed again to judge exactly how long it had been since the fox had left, then pulled his head back into the drey. Fern was curled up in the warm lining of moss, feathers and rabbit fur, still half asleep.

"Been a dog-fox through but he's gone now. It's going to be another hot day. We've got to listen to that grey fellow soon so you'd better stir yourself, Fern-Mate. I'm going down for a bite."

He went head-first down the scaly tree trunk, pausing now and then to look around for anything unusual, any pattern that was unfamiliar, any shape that was different from the night before, anything which could spell danger to him and his community.

"Sun, that fox stinks!"

Moving away from the urine-sprinkled anthill, he searched for early fungi and was soon joined by others from Beachend and Deepend. Even Juniper and Bluebell, the Scavengers, had arrived from Humanside to hear the words of the grey strangers.

Fern had followed Oak out of the drey on to her look-about branch and was grooming herself in the sunshine. She wanted to be extra smart today, with visitors there, and it was up to her to set an example. Some of those youngsters had no sense of what was important! She combed through her fur with her claws, fluffed out her tail and felt her ears. No tufts yet – hurry up, winter!

Marble watched the activity through the entrance to the Strangers' Drey, which he had found cramped and smaller than those his kind built. He was invisible to those outside, and he waited until he judged the time was exactly right.

"Now," he said, then exploded through the entrance hole and swung down through the branches of the tree, followed closely by Gabbro, frightening the Reds on the ground and causing them to freeze, then scatter and instinctively leap for the safety of the nearest tree trunk. He dropped to the ground and bounded up on to a stump in the centre of the clearing, Gabbro staying on the pine-needle-littered earth nearby. The smell of fox was strong but Marble ignored it. He had watched that animal pass underneath him an hour ago and it would be far away by now. The scent would unsettle these stupid natives and make them more susceptible.

The Reds came down out of the trees and approached the stump, glancing around warily. Oak looked up at Marble and greeted him, thought briefly of climbing on to the

27

stump himself, but he felt he needed to keep a suitable space between him and the grey creature, as otherwise it might appear that he was endorsing what the Grey might say. On the other hand it gave Marble an increase in stature to be above him. This stranger was no fool! He thought of the Kernel:

> *Let others look up*
> *To see where the Leaders are.*
> *Reach down to help them.*

When the chattering had died down, Marble stood on his hind legs so that he looked even more dominant.

"Form a circle," he commanded. The Reds jostled and nudged each other into a ring around him.

"Today," said Marble loudly, "I will show you some of our Ways. I will begin with numbers. It is this knowledge of numbers that makes our kind so superior." He raised his tail proudly. Oak resented this remark and glanced at Old Burdock who was clearly fuming.

The Grey looked round. "Bright Marguerite, take some dreylings and collect 'lots' of stones and bring them to me."

Marguerite skipped away, proud to have been selected and named in front of the others. With other young squirrels she found a number of stones which they rolled and carried into the circle.

Then, watched in silence by the Reds, Gabbro selected four stones of equal size and laid them out in a square on the ground. He placed a forepaw on one of the stones. Oak noticed at once that all the wood-ants foraging nearby scurried from the square in confusion.

"That is the smallest square," said Marble. "It has the number Four which you know. It has a little Power, but not much. We show it as a symbol like this." He nodded to Gabbro who then put a twig on the ground near the square with two small pine cones next to it.

The Reds tried to understand what he meant but with little success. Larch the Curious and Chestnut the Doubter climbed up into the branches above to get a clearer view.

Gabbro selected more stones and made a square with four rows of four stones. Marble said, "We symbolise this so." Gabbro added another two cones to his symbols.

The audience was mystified. They watched him pull a piece of dead bark from the tree stump, select a large black beetle from it, drop it into the square and stand with a forepaw on one of the corner stones. The beetle, which had been scrambling away, stiffened, and rolled over on to its back. Its legs contracted slowly, and it died.

"Power," said Marble, "Power." His tail rose but no one noticed, their attention was directed to the stones and the dead beetle. Gabbro's paw was still on the corner stone. Oak reached out to disturb the arrangement of the stones. He did not like this, it felt unnatural. As his paw neared the square his claws tingled and itched, and his whiskers

*Humans would call this sixteen in binary.

vibrated painfully. Then his muscles locked with cramp and he could not move.

"Stay quite still," Marble said to Oak in a commanding voice. Oak was unable to do anything else and realised that the stranger must appear to be able to command obedience from him, the Leader.

In the silence that followed there was a thump, then another. Larch and Chestnut had fallen from the tree to the ground, unconscious.

The squirrels backed away from the square of stones. Oak stayed where he was, still unable to move.

He remained there, as if petrified, for a full minute. Then Marble motioned to Gabbro who suddenly lifted his paw and scattered the stones. Oak unfroze, and the natives chattered in relief.

"If you think this is powerful you should see the effect of a square this size." He added another two cones to the line.

 *

Oak advanced stiffly on Marble. "We do not care for your Ways, Marble the Stranger, and request that you and your companion leave at once."

"As you wish, Cautious Oak," said Marble with the hint of a sneer in his voice. "But remember what you have seen when the Silver Tide comes."

Holding their tails high and twitching them insultingly, the two Greys left, heading back the way they had come. The seeds of demoralisation had been sown!

*Humans' binary sixty-four.

Chapter 5

The sound of the gates opening rang across the pool but instead of dispersing as usual, the squirrels sat in small groups in the trees, discussing the disturbing events they had just seen.

"What was the Power in the stones?"

"What is the Silver Tide?"

"When will it come, whatever it is?"

Oak felt it to be his duty to rally the squirrels and dispel this foolish talk, but he was stiff and sore and his mind was in a turmoil. The roots of his whiskers hurt. The Reds looked towards him for leadership and explanations but, when none was forthcoming, they drifted away, puzzled and dispirited.

Warily, Oak picked up one of the stones and examined it closely. Just an ordinary stone. He thought of remaking the square pattern, then dismissed the idea, it was all so unnatural. After scattering the cones that Gabbro had laid out in the line next to the twig, he climbed slowly and painfully back up to the security of his drey.

Unknown danger near –
Lie high, wait, watch and look out.
Trust in the Sun's light.

None of the squirrels noticed that young Marguerite was not in any of the groups. Even the normally sharp-eyed Burdock was somewhat befuddled by the pace of events in what was usually a quiet and perhaps even a dull demesne, and had not seen the youngster leave to follow the Greys. The old Tagger had felt portents of doom and had returned to her own drey to dredge her mind for appropriate Kernels to encourage and support her companions.

The Greys had left along one of the ground-paths and, once she was out of sight of the others, Marguerite took to the trees and raced along, jumping even quite wide gaps in her efforts to catch up with them. These strangers had some special knowledge that had created a great curiosity in her. If she didn't see them again, the chance of satisfying it might be gone for ever.

Marble heard the rustling in the branches above and behind him and waited, Gabbro silent at his side. Marguerite dropped to the ground near them, breathless.

"Excuse me, sir," she panted.

Marble held up his paw. "Wait, there is no hurry. We have all day." His face was stern yet Marguerite was aware of just a trace of warmth in his voice. She held her tail low, as was fitting for a youngster addressing a senior.

"Please, sir," she said at last, "I would like to know more about the numbers."

"What about them, Bright Marguerite?"

"Are there any numbers after eight?"

Marble looked at Gabbro. This is a bold one, he thought. Most natives are terrified when they have seen the Power demonstration and here's one wanting to know about numbers!

"Show me eight," said Marble.

She held up both paws, extending her claws.

"Show me again," said Marble.

Marguerite repeated the action.

"So there must be, Bright One," said Marble, turning away and signalling to Gabbro to follow. He wanted confusion behind him, not understanding. Understanding would give power where it was not desirable.

Marguerite stood on the path, mystified, tail low, wondering if they were laughing at her, before creeping back unnoticed to join the other unhappy Reds.

Whilst all this was taking place at the Blue Pool, Rowan the Bold had woken and stretched his stiff limbs, one by one. His fur was bejewelled with dew in the first rays of the sun. He shook himself and looked out over the water below the tree where he had slept. Down at the Eyeland end of the pool a heron was wading in the shallows, stabbing at an occasional frog. No danger about; if there had been, the heron would have been off at once with a harsh squawk and a sweep of those huge grey wings. No dragonflies were active yet, they needed sunshine to loosen up their wings after the chill of the night.

As Rowan made his way down the tree trunk, the heron paused at the sight of movement, then resumed its feeding, satisfied that the little animal on the tree at the other end of the pool was not dangerous – for the present. Rowan fed slowly, enjoying the increasing warmth as the sun rose higher and the rays lit up the trees on the Eyeland. In the mellow light, they formed a pleasing group and he felt a great urge to experience them and feel their crisp bark under his claws, and so, watched by the wary heron, he made his way along the shoreline towards that end of the pool. Finally the tall grey bird decided that perhaps the Swamp was a better place to be and flapped away out of sight, legs trailing behind him.

Rowan half circled the pool before realising, what he later told himself he had known all along, that unless he could fly like the heron, the Eyeland and those tempting trees were out of his reach. No thought of swimming had entered his head; water to a squirrel was as alien an element as the treetops would be to a mole. Eventually he gave up the dream and, with one last look at the pool where the great pink and white water-flowers were beginning to open, he turned towards the sun and home.

Chapter 6

It was early evening when Rowan, tired but elated, crossed the unmarked boundary of his home demesne. As he did so he was aware that something had changed. There was tension in the air, a foreboding of change, unwelcome change. He climbed slowly up to his parents' drey but before reaching it met his younger sister, Marguerite. She greeted him warmly.

"We've got so much to tell you, Rowan," she said. "You'll never guess who was here today!"

Rowan was full of his own news. It was customary for a squirrel returning from climbabout to be the centre of attention, as others asked about the world beyond their trees. Now, even as his parents came out to greet him, he could see that their minds were on other things.

"Rowan-Son," Oak called down to him, "welcome home. We've had some odd visitors here. Come up and we'll tell you."

Rowan decided that it was not the time to relate his adventures and listened to a recital of the events of that morning.

"Did you see any of the grey creatures?" asked Oak. He could not yet bring himself to call them squirrels.

Rowan shook his head. "I met some friendly red ones like us over beyond Screech Hill, where the barn owls live, Oak-Pa," he replied, "but none like those you say were here."

Marguerite wanted to tell him about her later meeting with the Greys but decided to leave that for another time and they sat comfortably side by side, brother and sister together again, watching the sun go down. They were still sitting there enjoying each other's company long after their parents had withdrawn into the drey for the night.

Eventually Marguerite said, "I like numbers," hoping for an interested response, but her brother's thoughts were concentrated on how to get across the water to an Eyeland surrounded by pink and white water-flowers, and he did not reply. As the moon rose they joined Oak and Fern in their drey.

As they entered, their mother started to tell of her plans for building a new drey so that the youngsters could take over this old one, but Oak cut her short.

"We can discuss that again, Fern-Mate," he said. "I'm trying to work out what all this business with the grey creatures could mean for us."

The visit of the Greys was the main topic of conversation in each of the dreys around the pool.

Juniper and Bluebell, the Scavengers, in their home high in an oak tree on Humanside, were not too concerned. They had gone to the Man-dreys after the Greys had left and had done their usual begging routine for the Visitors. Lots of food-bits had come their way, thrown from the tables on the terrace, and a good number of their favourite salted peanuts. Life was good, life was easy, tomorrow there was bound to be more.

"What did you make of those grey fellows, Bluebell-Mate?" Juniper asked sleepily.

"Here yesterday, gone today. Don't suppose we'll see them again. Did you bring any peanuts up with you; the salty ones?"

At Deepend, Chestnut the Doubter was trying to recall exactly what he had seen before he fell from the tree.

"What was the name of that Grey, the senior one, Heather-Mate?" he asked.

"Marble. Funny sort of name, I thought."

"Probably not his real name, wouldn't trust him for a minute," said Chestnut.

"I didn't like him either, arrogant sort of character, no breeding," Heather Treetops agreed. "Glad they've moved on. What do you make of this Silver Tide business?"

"Unbelievable!" Chestnut replied.

In the Beachend drey Clover the Carer was more concerned.

"Larch-Mate," she asked, "what did it feel like before you dropped out of the tree?"

She had attended to Larch the Curious and to Chestnut after the Greys had gone. It had been some time before either of them was fully conscious again and Oak had clearly not been himself after that funny business with the square of stones. She needed to know more in case something similar should happen in the future. As Carer for the community it was her task to provide relief and comfort when squirrels were not fully fit and well.

37

"All I remember," Larch replied, "was looking down with Chestnut and seeing that Marble fellow put his paw on one of the corner stones. Then a sort of wave hit me, coming upwards from the stones. My whiskers hurt like crazy, then I can't remember any more until I woke up with you licking my face. I'd like to know just what caused it. I still feel sick."

"Try nibbling this, Larch-Mate mine," said Clover, reaching into the mossy lining of the drey and pulling out a pawful of a sweet-scented herb. "That might help." She passed it to Larch, trying not to wake their dreyling, Tansy Quick-Thought.

The following day dawned with the same clear sky and promise of heat to come, and a brilliant sun shone down with growing intensity throughout the long morning and early afternoon.

The squirrels dozed or slept through the time of greatest heat, most of them forgetting briefly their worries about the Silver Tide, ignoring the constant passing of humans on the paths below, and only rousing themselves to feed when they heard the big gates close.

"Come and look at this," called Tansy to Rowan. "What in the name of the Sun is it?"

Below, a large red rubber beachball, left by a visiting child, was lying in a hollow below a tree. Rowan the Bold climbed down for a closer look.

"It smells like the scent Visitors' feet leave on the paths," he called up. "But I don't think it's alive." He poked it with a forepaw. The ball moved slightly and he jumped back.

The other young squirrels came down and joined him in

pushing it about, watched from above by the older ones, some of whom were still uneasy after the visit of the Greys. Was *this* something to do with the Silver Tide? What was it?

Old Burdock looked at the round red thing, thought how much it looked like the Sun and was about to call to the others to show respect, when Rowan, living up to his tag, climbed the tree, ran on to a branch, dropped on to the top of the ball and bounced into the air to land several feet away, to the amusement of the other youngsters. Then they were all at it. Squirrels racing up the tree trunk, out along the branch and dropping on to the ball, grinning and chattering with excitement at this new game.

Squirrelation took over, the infectious revelry enticing all the squirrels of the demesne to join in the fun.

The Scavengers from Humanside hopped over and, before long, with the exception of Burdock, who watched apprehensively, even the staidest of the elders were enjoying the sport.

No squirrel ever admitted to being the one who had aimed badly and, in an attempt to stay on top, had dug its claws into the red skin. Each subsequently blamed another but shortly afterwards the ball sagged and, with a gentle hiss and a sigh, "died" in a circle of contrite red squirrels. The game was over.

Later, the caretaker, on his litter round, picked up the deflated ball and stuffed it in his bag with the other rubbish, watched by the squirrels peering down from behind a screen of pine needles.

Great anvils of cumulus clouds had been building up during the early evening and now towered in the western sky, and although the setting sun was hidden, the oppressive heat remained. The squirrels were listless and uncomfortable.

> *A storm with thunder*
> *Follows three hot summer days –*
> *Then clear air again.*

So ran the old Kernel. But it had been "lots" more than three days of unusual heat. Burdock wished the storm would come soon.

Oak visited her drey to ask about the red thing that had looked like a Sun.

"It can't have been the Sun down here," she said to Oak. "That was still in the sky when I first saw it."

"It was round and red just like the Sun," replied Oak. "Smaller, though, perhaps it's the Sun's child. Does the Sun have youngsters?"

"I don't know, but it *was* like a little Sun. Why would it come here?"

"Maybe it was about to tell us before we caught squirrelation and some Sun-damned dreyling scratched it and it died."

"We won't ever know now," Burdock said slowly, dredging an old saying up from deep in her memory.

> *The Sun will prevail.*
> *Greyness eliminated then.*
> *Even a little Sun.*

"I never knew what that meant. Do you think the Greyness could be referring to those grey animals that were here yesterday? And that round thing could have been 'a little Sun'?"

"Perhaps you're right," Oak replied, with his usual caution. "It was just like a little Sun."

Burdock said hopefully, "Maybe the Sun sent its youngster to tell us not to take any notice of the Grey Ones."

"Maybe," said Oak, mentally clutching at a leaf.

The squirrels drifted apart to forage, each occupied by their own thoughts and fears. Only a pensive Juniper knew whose claws had done the fatal act.

The storm, so long in coming, broke over the Great Heath soon after nightfall, the wind raging in the tops of the pine and fir trees, whistling through the needles and penetrating into the usually cosy, warm centres of the dreys to chill the uneasy squirrels huddled inside. Flashes of lightning tore open the night sky, each branch silhouetted blackly against the intense light beyond. Squalls of rain lashed the heather and churned the surfaces of the pool into a confused mass of rings, ripples and bouncing droplets.

By morning a new Kernel was circulating, though none could say where it had originated.

> *The Sun sent its child*
> *To protect us from the Greys –*
> *And we all killed it.*

The Sun's-child Legend had been born, sending a sense of collective guilt throughout the community.

Chapter 7

When the sun rose the next day over the damp and storm-damaged woodland, causing the bracken and pine needles on the ground to steam in the early rays, a group of bedraggled red squirrels, who had obviously spent the night without proper shelter, appeared at Humanside and asked the resident guardians of that area, Juniper and Bluebell, for permission to pass through.

Throughout the morning "lots" more squirrels appeared, some singly, some in couples and some in small family groups. Most bore bite-marks on their legs, some had patches of fur missing and many were limping, unable to leap from tree to tree and having to travel, fearfully, on the ground.

They were all escorted by Juniper and Bluebell to meet Oak and Burdock, to whom they told harrowing tales of their homes being taken over by advancing waves of Greys calling themselves the Silver Tide and claiming possession of whichever areas took their fancy. Any Reds who resisted had been savaged and harassed until they gave way to the larger and more aggressive invaders.

Oak offered hospitality to the refugees but they would

not stay and, after sharing a quick meal, they moved on westwards, urging the locals to get out before it was too late.

"Leave while you can, they'll be coming here soon, Oak-Friend."

Oak replied that he and his community had been Guardians of the Blue Pool for longer than any squirrel could remember and he could not desert his trust. He would talk with the Greys when they came and ask them to move on and look for uninhabited territory to settle in.

"They won't listen," he was told. "They just take what they want. You mustn't stay. Come with us while you can. Didn't you have a visit from some missionaries?"

"Do you mean the two who showed us what they called Stone force?"

"There are lots of missionaries, they all use different methods. The ones who came to us told us all about the Sunless Pit and how we would all go there if we didn't obey their instructions. When we said we didn't believe them, they attacked us with their teeth."

Oak and Old Burdock conferred and decided that the threat had probably been exaggerated and that it was their duty to remain at the pool.

A Guardianship
Means responsibility.
Defend at all cost.

Oak, however, remembering the effect of Marble's Power Squares on him, was apprehensive, and he was relieved when night fell with no further alarms.

Early next morning another party of "lots" of squirrels arrived and were offered hospitality. Their Leader, Alder, had a broken tail, the result of a "lesson" from a Grey.

With the exception of Bluebell and Juniper, who were entertaining the human Visitors, all the squirrel community gathered to greet and assist the refugees.

Clover looked at the mud-caked remains of Alder's broken tail, which was obviously causing him considerable pain as it dragged along the ground, his suffering evident in his drawn features and the way he winced whenever he moved his rump.

"That's going to have to come off, Alder-Friend," she said gently, "or it will go bad. Would you like me to do it?"

Alder considered for a moment. A squirrel without a tail would feel like half a squirrel, but his tail was worse than useless as it was, and without it he could lead his party away from the danger faster.

"Yes, please do, but spare my whiskers," he said, trying to make a joke of it. A tail is important to a squirrel but without whiskers one becomes a bumbling idiot.

Clover passed him a large pine cone. "Hug this," she told him. "Shut your eyes and count to eight."

Alder gripped the cone and started to count. At "two" Clover severed the tail quickly and cleanly with a single bite. Alder hardly felt a thing and went on counting, "three, four, five . . . "

"Works every time," said Clover, slipping away to bury the scraggy tail in a disused rabbit hole.

When she came back, Alder, surrounded by the rest of his party, was licking away the blood oozing from the stump. His life-mate, Dandelion, whose skin had several

44

bald patches and the signs of recent scars, was comforting him.

"It'll stop bleeding soon," Clover told Alder, "but lick it clean several times each day and I'll give you something to put on it. Now you must rest."

A youngster, Tamarisk, already tagged the Tactless, kept asking Clover what she had done with Alder's tail, until Heather led him away.

Alder wanted to press on with his group, but Clover and Dandelion persuaded him to stay for at least half a day and to make the others with him rest too.

"He'll get the shivers in a few minutes," Clover told them. "We must help him to the Strangers' Drey."

Dandelion took charge and, despite Alder's protests, led him away to rest.

Clover slipped off to find a plant of woundwort, whose healing properties had been known to Caring squirrels since the days of the first squirrels in the world, Acorn and Primrose.

Rowan had been watching one of the younger female squirrels, a yearling like himself. She seemed not to have a mate with her and was looking tired and forlorn. He introduced himself. "I'm Rowan the Bold."

"You are that," she said, smiling. "I'm Meadowsweet. Alder is my father."

Rowan asked about their journey and their home Guardianship. "It is . . . it was, a place called Wolves-barrow, Rowan-Friend," she told him. "We've been following the Leylines."

Rowan briefly wondered what a Leyline was, but was more interested in the fascinating way she twitched her whiskers at him and used her paws and tail to emphasise what she was saying. This is a very special squirrel, he thought to himself and, to prolong their meeting, he took her to view the pool. He thought that he had never seen a squirrel leap with such style and grace.

Later, returning to the rest of the group, she thanked him. "I really forgot our situation for a few hours," she said. "I feel much stronger. We are leaving now – I must go and help my father. Perhaps we shall meet again some day."

"I hope so, Meadowsweet-Friend," said Rowan.

Rowan sat on a high branch, eyes moist with the tears that squirrels cannot shed, flicking the "fond farewell" signal with his tail. So engrossed was she with her father that Meadowsweet did not look back until the very last minute before they disappeared from sight. Although by then they were a long way apart, Rowan was sure that she returned his signal and he turned sadly away. He would have followed had he not felt that he was needed here at the Blue Pool.

That night he dreamt of living on a beautiful Eyeland in a lovely pool with an even lovelier Meadowsweet beside him as his life-mate.

Love conquered duty.

At first light he left without even telling his sister or his parents of his intentions, and hurried off in the direction of the Clay-Pan, only to find that a shower in the night had washed away any traces of footprints or scent. By High Sun he was forced to give up the search and return to his family.

If only I'd asked about those Leylines, I might know which direction they had taken, he thought ruefully.

Chapter 8

Over the course of the next three days the flow of refugees slowed to a trickle, then died to nothing at about the time of High Sun on the third day. Late that afternoon, just after the last of the human Visitors had left, the first squirrels of the Silver Tide arrived at the Blue Pool Demesne.

Two male and two female Greys appeared at Humanside, found Juniper the Scavenger living up to his tag, and demanded that he take them to see the Senior Squirrel. With arrant discourtesy they marched through the Humanside, Deepend and Steepbank Guardianships, tails high, ignoring the watching natives as they followed Juniper to where Oak was waiting, warned by the turmoil in the community that something was amiss.

Oak greeted them formally.

The male Greys introduced themselves as Flint and Quartz, the females as Chert and Granite. Oak thought that the foursome looked as hard as their names sounded.

"We have come to arrange territories for our use," said Flint.

"I'm sorry but this demesne is fully guardianed," said Oak. "You must seek elsewhere."

"I said – we have come to arrange territories for our own use," repeated Flint, slowly. "Marble, the missionary whom you have met, has told us that the humans' side of the pool would be very suitable. We'll take that. From now on it will be known as New Connecticut."

The four Greys left, tails high.

Oak was bemused and angry. Nothing in his experience, nor in any of the Kernels he could recall, fitted this situation. He followed the Greys to protest, but they were gone, heading in a group back through Deepend, watched from a distance by other anxious Reds.

On reaching Humanside the Greys located the guardians' drey in the oak tree and destroyed it twig by twig, ignoring the furious protests of Juniper and Bluebell. The four built two new dreys in a beech tree nearby and one pair moved into each.

Juniper and Bluebell spent a cold night in the open, watching, until the Greys emerged at dawn to forage on the ground. It was then that Juniper, his tail raised defiantly, climbed the beech tree on the side away from the Greys and began to dismantle one of their dreys, throwing the twigs to the ground.

His gesture did not go unnoticed for long.

Together the four Greys climbed the smooth-barked trunk and surrounded him, then just sat staring at him as though he was the slimiest piece of fox-dropping ever seen. Soon his tail sagged and hung limply over the branch on which he sat.

Flint lunged at him and he drew back startled, only to flinch again as Quartz made a similar move from his other side. "Look out, Brown Job," called a female voice from behind him and he turned to face Chert, who crept forward menacingly, then sat grinning at him.

Juniper looked around desperately for a way of escape, saw a chance and dropped on to a branch below. Quartz and Chert followed. He ran along a limb and leapt into the next tree, then the next and the next, the Greys effortlessly staying a few squirrel-lengths behind him.

In his anxiety to escape, Juniper did not plan his route and, perhaps because he was looking over his shoulder frequently, he found he was back in the tree from which he had started, face to face with Flint and Granite. Every breath was hurting him and there was a painful pounding in his chest.

He turned along a side branch and leapt into another tree. When he next looked over his shoulder there were the faces of the two rested Greys close behind. He caught a glimpse of Quartz and Chert sitting in the beech tree, grinning as they watched the chase.

Juniper was tiring rapidly and making ill-judged leaps, but the Greys seemed in no hurry to catch up with him. His progress became more and more clumsy and soon he was having to pause before each leap to gather his breath, while the Greys also paused and called insulting remarks at him. He leapt again and realised that once more he was back in the beech tree.

Quartz ran at him and he lost his hold and fell to the ground with a bone-shaking impact, too tired to turn gracefully in the air as he would normally have done.

Sick and tired, he lay there panting and terrified as all the Greys came down the trunk head-first, sneering at him.

"We're not finished with you yet, Brown Job," Flint

hissed in his face. "Get up and run." He nipped the exhausted squirrel's tail painfully.

"Now. Run, I said!" He nipped again.

Juniper ran, the Greys keeping pace on either side of him, nipping at his legs and tail. The harassment continued, his retreat being cleverly guided along the ground under low bushes towards a tall tree, its upper branches overhanging the pool.

Here the Greys allowed him to climb before following, biting at his tail and forcing him ever further out along a branch which spread over the water.

Juniper turned to face his tormentors but was driven back down the thinning branch in mounting terror.

An uncontrolled fall and deep water are two of the things a squirrel fears most.

The Greys paused to let Juniper feel the full horror of his situation. Then, slowly and deliberately, they began to gnaw at the branch, tearing off great splinters and letting them drop, to splash in the water below. Juniper hung on desperately as the bough began to sag downwards. The Greys paused again, prolonging his agony. They knew other Reds were watching and that this was to be a lesson to them all, one they would never forget.

Juniper clung to the branch, now hanging only by a strip of bark. He was paralysed by water-dread, his eyes swivelling around in terror searching for a safe place to leap to, yet knowing he had no strength to make such a leap.

Then Flint bit through the last strip of bark.

The branch fell, Juniper clinging on, chattering with fear.

Hitting the water, the branch was submerged, dragging

the squirrel down with it. Then it rose slowly to the surface. Juniper, coughing and spluttering, held tight to the wet bark, his body racked with spasms of pain, until the breeze eventually blew the branch to the shore.

He crawled on to the sandy beach, bedraggled and sodden, and lay there gasping.

The Greys went off to forage as though nothing had happened.

Later, much later, Juniper and Bluebell sought refuge with the Deependers.

"Greetings to you Chestnut the Doubter, and to you Heather Treetops," Juniper began formally. "We, Juniper and Bluebell, tagged the Scavengers, seek sanctuary in your Guardianship. As I am sure you have seen, the Greys have taken over Humanside. Temporarily," he added, with unconvincing bravado.

Chestnut looked at the forlorn squirrels on the trunk below him, then at Heather. He had no cause to doubt what he had been told, as he had witnessed the chase himself. Heather flicked her tail as if to say, "You decide if you want *these* two in our area," and went into their drey.

He looked again at the pathetic pair, pictured himself harried and homeless, and said, "Yes, my friends, choose a tree, I'll get some others and we'll help you build."

Soon, in a show of community spirit, a new and comfortable drey had been assembled in the fork of a Deepend pine, Heather herself collecting the moss for the lining, and Fern ensuring that, even if it was for the Scavengers, it was tidy and respectable.

*

That evening, an emergency Council Meeting was called.

Greetings were quick and formal and the Protection Kernel was said for the first time that most could remember.

Great Guardian Sun
Giver of all life and warmth
Protect your squirrels.

The Bright One wondered if the Sun included grey as well as red squirrels, but did not ask.

"Do we just let them take what they want?" Heather Treetops asked scornfully.

Marguerite had once asked her mother how Heather had earned that tag.

"She is very proud of the fact that her grandfather was the last of the hereditary chiefs of this demesne and believes that places her above all of us," Fern had told her. "It is one of Old Burdock's best and truest tags. I wish I could have a new tag, I'm sure that 'the Fussy' isn't really appropriate to me."

She had smoothed her tail as she had said this and Marguerite had turned away to hide her smile.

Oak looked uncomfortable. There was a big difference between being Leader in a stable, year-to-year cycle of seasons, with comforting Kernels from a wise Tagger to guide you in decision-making, and being Leader now with unprecedented things happening in one's demesne.

"I doubt if there is anything we can do," said Chestnut and turned away to avoid the withering look his mate gave him.

Burdock intervened to cool the debate.

"We were warned what would happen by the other squirrels who passed through here, though some of us didn't believe them." She glanced at Chestnut. "Or didn't want to."

Avoid illusions.
Reality must be faced.
Be down-to-earth now.

Marguerite played with the words. She knew that squirrels were at home in the trees and that down-to-earth was what Old Burdock had taught her was a figure of speech, but it was so easy up in the branches to lose sight of all the things going on below in a world which did affect them, even if they sometimes felt above it all.

Larch was speaking now. "I wonder what it is they want. Are they intending to stay here? Will there be more of them? Will they want to take more of what they called territory?"

Oak held up his paw. "One question at a time. But none of us knows the answers anyway. Time will tell us more."

If mists hide the view
All will be revealed to us,
In the Sun's good time.

Finally, a decision was taken to abandon Humanside to the Greys, in the hope that they would be content there. Juniper and Bluebell were given permission to stay on at Deepend. Then Juniper, realising that the easy pickings from the Visitors would not be his that summer, asked if he could have a new tag.

Old Burdock the Tagger looked at him coldly. "The one that comes to mind is Juniper the Diver. Would you like that?"

This raised the only laugh of the day. Juniper turned away. Any new tag would have to be earned.

Chapter 9

Seven days and nights had passed since the Greys had arrived. Marguerite had watched the event, especially the humiliation of Juniper, with interest. Now well grown, she was living up to the early promise that Burdock had recognised. The tag she had been given, the Bright One, was ambiguous. She puzzled over it and wondered if it referred to her glossy brown fur or her eyes. Or was it because she seemed to understand complicated things better than others of her year? It was against custom to ask about your tag, as this would be an insult to the wisdom and observation of the Tagger.

Now she was concerned as to how only four Greys, admittedly bigger physically than the natives, could intimidate a group of squirrels who outnumbered them many times over.

Bluebell was concerned about far more mundane things, like how to get some of the salted peanuts she craved. She hung about the edge of Humanside watching the Greys scavenging at the Tea Rooms, which they called the Eating Man-Drey. Each day she ventured nearer, apparently unnoticed, until one day a peanut, sparkling with salt, thrown by a Visitor, rolled past the Greys towards her. She ran forward, grabbed at the nut and dashed away with it, not daring to look back in case the dreaded Greys were coming after her.

Safely back at Deepend she ate the peanut slowly, relishing the exquisite saltiness. She was hooked. She must have more, whatever the dangers. Early the next morning, before the human Visitors arrived, she returned, planning to be hidden ready to be the first to have any salted nuts that day.

As she came down a tree near the Eating Man-Drey and was about to drop over the bank behind the buildings she saw Flint, apparently waiting for her. She turned to avoid him, her whiskers twitching nervously, and thought of running back towards Deepend. Then a harsh screech sounded from above her and a grey body dropped from a branch.

She instinctively jumped sideways and Quartz landed where she had been a moment before.

"Missed you that time," he said, striking out at her with his paw.

Bluebell, terrified, leapt away and scampered off through the trees, pursued by the mocking laughter of the two Greys.

When she realised that she was not actually being chased, she slowed to a hop and then stopped – the salt craving still on her! She turned; there was no sign of the Greys now and she started back again. Near the Man-dreys she heard the mocking laughter again, but could not make out where it was coming from. Cones were dropped on her and mysterious rustlings came from the bushes, but no squirrel seemed to be there.

Her fur stood on end when a stone rolled down the bank and she had to jump clear. Then she found a square of four stones where she knew none had been a few moments before.

Only the salt craving held her – every instinct told her to climb and run through the treetops to safety. She kept telling herself that it could only be Flint and Quartz playing tricks to scare her and she hesitatingly called their names, "Flint, Quartz, please. I only want some nuts!"

Mocking laughter came from above and behind her, but she could not see her tomentors. Then, hearing the clang of the metal gates being opened, she scampered down the bank and into the area in front of the Eating Man-Drey, confident that the presence of humans would protect her. She stayed in the open, waiting for Visitors to arrive and be brought their food by the Red- Haired Girl, other Greys arriving and also waiting expectantly. Flint and Quartz were amongst them, leering at her and bumping into her as they scurried about.

Then she saw it. A peanut, salt-encrusted, was thrown to her. She caught it, dropped it, then ran after it as it bounced down the steps towards the pool. She caught it again and sat up breathlessly, holding the nut, only to be bowled over by Flint who had bounded down the steps behind her. The nut flew from her paws, bouncing and rolling, to splash in the water.

By the time she had evaded Flint and scooped the nut from the shallow water, it had lost its appeal and tasted like the other peanuts which were more easily begged from the Visitors.

She waited all day, enduring the threats and abuse from

the Greys until, when the last Visitor had left, she scurried away and ran back to Deepend and the security of her drey.

Juniper had missed her, knew that she had been at Humanside and guessed that she had been overcome by the salt craving. It took *him* sometimes, and he knew how hard he had to fight within himself to resist it.

He decided not to speak of it that night. He could explain how he could help her in the morning, when she would be calmer. They slept restlessly together, but while he was still asleep she slipped away from the drey and although he searched until the gates clanged he could not find her. Then he saw her near the Man-dreys submitting to every kind of abuse from the Greys.

Bluebell returned to the drey that night, but refused to speak to Juniper about what he had seen.

She was gone again in the morning and it was inevitable that a report on her behaviour reached Old Burdock. To Juniper's disgrace, as well as her own, she was summoned to appear before the Council and account for her behaviour.

She told how she *needed* the salty nuts and could only get them at the Eating Man-Drey. Yes, the Greys did treat her badly, but she *must* have the salted nuts. Bluebell could not lie, she did not know what a lie was, but she made the various incidents of abuse and humiliation seem almost routine.

No member of the Council could conceive of the idea of an urge so irresistible that it would lead a squirrel into such behaviour, except perhaps Juniper, who remembered the taste from his scavenging days. His mouth watered at the recollection.

A denigratory tag was clearly justified and Burdock thought long and hard for a suitable one, hampered by a lack of words for such an alien action. Bluebell was sent out of listening distance during the discussions. Then, after much debate, she was called back and given the down-tag Who Sells Herself for Peanuts, and with this she crept away from the Council in disgrace, tail low.

Juniper tried to follow but she turned on him, snapping, "Leave me alone," and later, when he expected to find her at their drey, she was not there and did not return. She had gone to Humanside to live amongst the Greys, totally dependent on a supply of the salt-encrusted nuts.

Chapter 10

Some days later, Bluebell watched the arrival of another posse of Greys which included a confident male whom she recognised as Marble. He was accompanied by his companion Gabbro, whom she remembered as having been strangely silent on the last visit but now chattered constantly.

Marble showed his surprise at finding a Red living among the Greys and greeted her curtly but, as the salt-dominated days passed, she was relieved to find that he always treated her in a civil enough way. By picking up snatches of the Greys' conversation she learned that Marble had guided this group of colonisers to the Blue Pool and was resting there for a time before returning to Woburn, where it was hinted that he had great expectations. She noted that he was frequently accompanied by a grey female known as Sandstone and once or twice she overheard him address her affectionately as Sandy.

One afternoon, hearing sounds of violent conflict near the Eating Man-Drey, Bluebell was drawn by curiosity to climb on to the wood shingle roof and peer over. Below her, tables were being pushed back, people were standing up, some were shouting and one woman was slashing with a dog lead at a whirling black, white and grey mass on the floor. From her viewpoint she could see that a fight was in progress between a Visitor's Jack Russell terrier and one of the grey squirrels.

The whining dog, bitten about the nose and ears, was whipped off and dragged away towards the car park, leaving a squirrel, who she could see was Marble, unconscious on the ground. An elderly man with a kind face stooped to pick up the limp animal. Another man, whom she recognised as the Human Who Picked Things Up, shouted at him and he drew back.

This man knelt and called to the Red-Haired Girl who came out of the Tea Rooms and gave him an old towel in which he wrapped the body of Marble. He stood up, holding the squirrel, and turned to her.

"A vet should see this," he said.

"The vet's here now, over at the paddock with the horses, but I don't know if he'll bother with a squirrel. You could try," she suggested.

The caretaker went off towards the paddock, carrying the wrapped-up squirrel, and found the vet just as he was packing up to leave.

"Hello," he said cheerfully, recognising the caretaker. "What have you got there?"

"It's a grey squirrel, had a fight with a dog down by the Tea Rooms and got chewed up a bit. Helen, the waitress, said you were here so I brought it over."

"Let's see the little fellow," the vet said, reaching out to take the bundle, which was now showing blood on the white towelling. The squirrel was beginning to stir. "I'll

61

just give him a small injection to keep him quiet while I look at him."

The vet lowered the back door of his estate car to make a platform, laid out a rubber sheet, then prepared a syringe. When he was sure that the squirrel was safely under, he cleaned the blood from its fur and examined the limp body.

"His right front paw is badly bitten, but there doesn't appear to be any other serious damage – one can't be sure, though. I'll have to take off that paw if he's going to have a chance to survive. Even then he may have internal injuries. Would you rather I put him down?"

Tom shook his head. "No, give the poor beggar a chance."

The vet reached into his bag for instruments and operated swiftly and cleanly.

"I'll be interested to know how he gets on," the vet said. "Animals can do surprisingly well with one paw missing, but sometimes the others will turn on it and drive it away. Let me know if you see it again, I'm over here quite often."

Tom cautiously rewrapped the squirrel in the towel.

"He'll be okay in a few hours," the vet told him. "I suggest you leave him in an open box to recover. When he's up to it he'll go off on his own."

Then, as he wiped and put away the instruments, he asked if the other squirrels seemed healthy. "There was an article I saw in a journal about some mysterious disease affecting grey squirrels in some parts of the country. No one knows how it is spread, but the squirrels seem to go into a decline, lose their natural resistance and then die from any small infection they would normally resist. There's research into it being done at Norwich. They're calling it Gradual Decline Syndrome, 'Grades' for short."

"The grey ones have only been here a few weeks," Tom replied. "Prefer the red ones myself, but don't see so much of them now. Except that scruffy one who's mad on peanuts."

The vet raised an inquisitive eyebrow.

"Oh, yes, do anything for a peanut that one, got to be salted, though."

"Well I never," said the vet, closing the rear car door. "How many Reds are here?"

"Hard to tell," Tom replied. "About fifteen or twenty, I suppose. Can't say I've ever tried to count them."

Tom walked back to the Tea Rooms, carrying the squirrel, and found the waitress. "The vet fixed him up, but had to cut one of his paws off, and said I should leave him out in a box under the trees until he comes round."

"Poor little thing," Helen said sympathetically, and reached out to stroke the squirrel's head. Seeing the sharp teeth exposed where Marble's lips were drawn back, she paused, then turned and went to find a box.

An hour later, curious to know if it had gone, Tom went over to the box, saw the squirrel still lying there with its eyes closed, and went to pick it up for a closer look at what the vet had done. He instantly regretted this. At his touch the squirrel turned its head and sank its teeth deep into his fingers. He danced about, shaking his hand and shouting, "Let go, you little beggar, let go, damn you." Eventually Marble did so and, as fast as he could in his drugged state and with a front leg that no longer seemed to reach the ground, made for the nearest tree, trying to dodge Tom's boot as he kicked savagely at him.

"Ungrateful swine," shouted Tom at the squirrel, wrapping a dirty handkerchief around his bleeding finger.

Marble felt very sick indeed. Nauseous from the anaesthetic, with a cruel pain where his paw had been and wishing now that he had not teased the terrier, he crouched behind a tree trunk watching Tom depart, grumbling.

When Marble did eventually get back to the Man-dreys that evening after the humans had left, the other Greys crowded round sniffing and peering.

"Marble's lost one of his paws," said one, not known for his diplomacy. "Where did you see it last, Marble?"

A grey youngster, carefully keeping out of sight behind the other larger squirrels, cruelly chanted, "Marble, Three Paws," before receiving a cuff from Gabbro. The name, however, as persistent as a red squirrel's tag, was to stick to him all his life.

That same evening, across the pool, the Reds were discussing the incident involving Marble and the dog. Juniper, from his new drey in the Deepend Guardianship, had witnessed the fight. He often watched the Man-dreys, hoping that Bluebell would see him, tire of the way the Greys treated her, abandon the peanuts and come back to him.

"That dog really got him," said Juniper. "But he fought back well, no trace of hound-dread." Juniper was torn between admiration for the way a fellow squirrel, even if a grey one, had defended itself, and pleasure in having seen one of those he now blamed for Bluebell's downfall savaged.

"What happened then?" asked Oak.

"The Sun-damned Grey was lying there, not moving, and the Man Who Picks Things Up took him away. Later on I saw him put the Grey on the ground near the foot of my old drey-tree in one of those things that people carry fodder in, and leave him there." Juniper was enjoying being the centre of attention, and this time not for his misdemeanours.

"What happened then?" Oak asked again.

"Nothing for a bit," said Juniper. "Then the human came back and the Grey bit him and after that he went to join the others, but was falling about and couldn't walk very well."

"Serves him right," said Heather. "Damnation to them all."

Chapter 11

Juniper lay in his drey, listening to the crackling and rustling of dead leaves as they twisted and settled into new positions. The dew which had soaked the outer leaves in the night was drying rapidly in the sunshine. He stretched luxuriously, then felt a pang of regret as he once more realised he was alone. Bluebell was somewhere away in Humanside with those grey creatures.

He was stretching himself again, guiltily enjoying the extra space, when his whiskers started to buzz and tingle painfully. He pressed them with his paws but the buzzing continued, then stopped as suddenly as it had begun. He felt a little sick.

Poking his head cautiously through the side of the drey, he looked down and counted eight Greys at the foot of the tree. He counted again. It was eight, the same number as his claws. Four he recognised, but the others were strange to him. More new arrivals? Another wave of the Silver Tide? What were they doing down there?

His queasiness increased and he had some difficulty in focusing his eyes. When his vision cleared he saw that the Greys were arranging a square of stones at the base of his tree. There were "lots" of stones, certainly more than eight. He tried to count again. For some reason, it seemed to be important to know how many stones there were.

He counted four on one side of the square and four on the other side; in fact there were four on every side. He tried to work out how many that made but still came up with the answer "lots".

The Grey, Quartz, came forward and put his forepaw on one of the corner stones. Juniper's whiskers instantly buzzed and tingled, much worse than before, and his body started to shake uncontrollably.

The Grey lifted his paw and the buzzing and shaking stopped. Juniper hung limply out of the drey coughing and retching, his head aching intolerably.

Quartz called up to him, his voice faint and distorted by the ringing in Juniper's ears. "Had enough yet, Brown Job?"

Juniper couldn't move. He felt weak and ached all over.

Again Quartz put a paw on the corner stone. The Powerwaves hit Juniper and his body contracted and shook, spasms of pain rippling along his muscles. His back arched from the invisible force and, unable to make his claws hold on, he slipped out of the entrance of the drey and fell to the ground, landing amongst the stones and scattering them, his limbs twitching feebly. The force had gone, but he was lying, limp and winded, in a circle of savage grey faces. He had never felt so bad nor so scared in his life. It was worse than the fall into the pool.

Quartz leant forward, pushing his face close to Juniper's. Even in his present position Juniper resented the intrusion. This was *his* space! He tried to draw his head back.

Always give others
The space they need to live in.
Squirrels respect this.

He was unable to move. The Grey pushed his face right up to Juniper's. Didn't the Grey know the Kernel?

"Listen, Brown Job," hissed Quartz, "we've had orders from the Great Lord Silver to expand this colony, so we're taking over this precinct, the one you lot call Deepend. So get out and tell the others; unless you want more Stone force, that is."

Not waiting for a reaction, he signalled to the other Greys, and together they turned and left, not one of them looking back.

Later, when he had recovered sufficiently, Juniper made his way along to the drey-tree of Chestnut the Doubter, Guardian of Deepend, and attracted his attention by scratching on the bark of the tree. He was still unfit to climb. Chestnut came down to investigate.

"Oh, it's you, Juniper the Scavenger," he said. Even now Juniper winced at the derogatory tag. "You're in a mess. Did you find yourself a bag of peanuts?"

"No," said Juniper weakly. "Some Greys came, eight of them." He twitched his front claws at Chestnut as if to validate what he was saying. "They made a pattern of stones under my drey-tree and I fell. Like *you* did when that first Grey, Marble, came. Sun, I feel bad."

"Are you sure you didn't dream it?" asked Chestnut, true to his tag. "How many did you say there were?"

"Eight. For the Sun's sake go to Steepbank to tell Oak, we're all in danger. I can't climb. I'll go down by the Little

Pool and hide. Get him to come down there, I must talk to him. Urgently!" he added, as Chestnut hung about indecisively, his mate and their two dreylings behind him. "Go now."

"Are you sure it really happened?" Chestnut asked again.

"Yes. Go *now*." Juniper turned and, stumbling and rolling in places, painfully made his way towards the Little Pool. Here he found a hiding place in a clump of rushes, glad that it was now too late in the morning for foxes to be about.

Oak was in his drey with Fern, upset and fretting because he felt aware of some serious danger but could not yet sense exactly what it was. When he heard rustling and scratching outside, he poked his head crossly out of the drey and was taken aback to find the entire Deepend family on his look-about branch.

Chestnut was flicking the "Urgent" signal with his tail.

"What is it? What has happened?" Oak asked, as Fern tried to wriggle past him through the entrance.

"Shusssh," said Chestnut, looking over his shoulder. "Danger! It's the Greys." He explained what they had done to Juniper and told Oak that the sick squirrel was hiding on the ground down by the Little Pool.

"I must go to him," Oak replied. "On the ground, you said?"

Leaders help squirrels
Regardless of the dangers.
Duty demands this.

69

He looked around. There was no sign of the Greys, the gate-noise hadn't come yet, so it was a safe time for him to go and find Juniper. Relatively safe, his cautious mind added.

"You lot stay here," he told the Deependers, glowering at Fern so that she knew that her place was to remain with them.

He found Juniper easily. An odd vibration emanated from his hiding place, causing Oak's whiskers to tickle gently even when he was some distance away. By turning his head from side to side he knew exactly the direction and how far from him Juniper was. It was uncanny, and unnerving, but he was soon amongst the rushes hearing the events of that morning from the sick and dishevelled squirrel.

"Oak-Leader," Juniper gasped, wanting to say "Oak-Friend" but aware, even in his present state, that over-familiarity would be resented from one with a denigratory tag. "Oak-Leader, we are in danger. The Greys are planning to take more territory. Sun, my whiskers hurt." He rubbed them with his paws as he spoke. "They're going to take over Deepend. They told me."

Oak was about to say, "Over my dead body," but checked himself, afraid that it might come to that.

"We'll see, we'll see," he said, and then went off to find Clover the Carer to ask if any of her herbs might help Juniper recover.

Chapter 12

The Guardians of Beachend, Larch and Clover, decided, with the approval of the Council, to move temporarily into the Steepbank Guardianship. They felt exposed and vulnerable so near the Greys occupying Humanside. They had noticed how more Greys were arriving every day and were foraging all through Beachend without any reference to Larch or Clover at all. If the guardians dared to approach, they were either ignored or insulted, and after the incident with Juniper they stayed well away from the intruders.

Juniper, able to climb again, although still having bouts of nausea, was living in the Strangers' Drey at Steepbank.

Chestnut and Heather, the Guardians of Deepend, had differing views on the situation. Chestnut suggested to her that they might consider following the example of Larch and Clover, and move on to Steepbank "just in case".

"Don't be such a squimp," she said. "It'll take more than a bunch of tree-rats to move *me* out of *my* home!"

"We've got our youngsters to think of," he said. "It's not just us. If there's any truth in what Juniper said about those stones it could be nasty for them. Let's see what Oak thinks."

The Council, now meeting at least once a day, decided that it would be prudent for Chestnut and Heather to build a new drey, still within their Guardianship but much closer to Steepbank.

Larch and Clover, not so brave, built near Oak and Fern's drey at Steepbank, and satisfied their Guardianship duties by making daily patrols through the Beachend treetops.

Each day the Greys encroached further, foraging far into both the Deepend and Beachend Guardianships. They had effectively taken over the hazel copse which all the Blue Pool community normally shared in the autumn. Larch and Clover were powerless to do anything other than report back to the Council.

"There are so many of them, and they are all so big," said Clover. She proposed to an early morning meeting of the Council that perhaps they should consider moving to a safer area, away from the Blue Pool altogether. "The dreylings are all strong enough for a journey now."

Larch the Curious backed her up. "All those other squirrels who came through here last moon had decided to move on. It might be exciting to explore and find a new home. I'm prepared to give it a try. The weather's good for travelling now."

Oak looked at Fern. He knew that she hated change and had just got their drey the way she had wanted it to be. "We can't just give up our Guardianships like that!"

A Guardianship
Given, is a sacred trust.
Hold and protect it.

"That's all very well," said Juniper. "But how can we do anything? Not only are they bigger, and there are more of them, but they know how to use those stones. And their teeth," he added.

"Can't we learn to use the stones too?"

The adults looked round to see who had spoken. It was Marguerite. "I saw how Marble did it."

"Hush, dear, while the Council is meeting," said Fern.

Youngsters were encouraged to attend Council if they wished, once they had been tagged, but were not expected to speak at meetings until after their first winter.

"I don't think we should play around with things we don't understand," said Chestnut.

"Perhaps we should just stay here and see what happens. We can leave later if we have to," Juniper said, for he was still hoping that Bluebell would give up those wretched peanuts and come back to him. Each day he ventured as far into Deepend as he dared, to watch her at the Man-dreys. Each day his hopes were dashed as he saw her humiliated and abused by Grey after Grey and watched her fawning on the Visitors at the tables.

"I agree, for now. We'll meet again this evening," said Oak, and the families dispersed.

Juniper waited until he heard the gates open, then, staying in the treetops, crossed Deepend until he was close to the Man-dreys. He was almost sure that the Greys would not dare bother him while there were Visitors about. He could see Bluebell hopping about expectantly under the tables, but then, as he watched, he heard grey-squirrel-chatter below and had to retreat to avoid being seen by a party of foraging Greys.

Back at Steepbank he climbed a tree to where he could look out and see the Man-dreys across the pool. He stretched out on a branch and watched, a dull ache in his chest.

The younger squirrels, aware of the tensions and uncertainties felt by the elders, stayed close to their parents' dreys, but Old Burdock still got them together once a day for their training and the recitation of the Basic Kernels that each was expected to know.

Ignorant squirrels
Not knowing all their Kernels
Will act foolishly.

Marble's stump of a forelimb healed quickly. He had managed to climb to his drey with only one forepaw and Gabbro brought him food but no other Grey visited and he was bitterly disappointed that Sandy had also stayed away.

When he felt fit enough, he came out and carefully lowered himself backwards down the trunk, the loss of his paw hampering him considerably. He fell the last few feet to the ground and hopped over to join the other foraging Greys. Sandy was with them but although Gabbro came over at once and greeted him, Sandy kept her distance and Marble soon realised that she had transferred her affections to a large Grey with an exceptionally bushy tail and strong-looking limbs.

He approached Flint and Quartz but they continued to talk to one another as though they could not see him and, when a chit of a young Grey called out, "Marble, Three Paws," he turned and went towards the hazel copse and the

74

Dogleg Field. Here Gabbro helped him build a drey in a spruce tree that had once been taken indoors and used as a Christmas tree by humans, before being replanted in the woods. The disturbance had stunted the tree and it had failed to grow to its normal height, but the dense mass of twigs around the lower trunk was ideal for a three-pawed squirrel to use when it had to climb up or down.

Here Marble was to live in virtual exile, visited occasionally by Gabbro who brought news of the increasing number of Greys arriving at the Blue Pool Colony, and passing on all the news from Woburn. Marble listened with interest and when Gabbro had gone, would lie in his drey reflecting, "If only . . ."

Rowan often took his sister Marguerite on short expeditions along the "safe" side of Steepbank, teaching her the names of the plants and the trees and showing her the different creatures that shared the heath and woodlands with the squirrels. Recently, at the Little Pool, he had shown her a dragonfly larva as it crawled up a reed-stem out of the water and together they watched for an hour, any danger from Greys or foxes totally forgotten, as the ugly insect clinging to the stem split open along its back and another, apparently quite different, one climbed out of the empty case. The sun dried the four shimmering wings as they unfolded, the huge eyes brightened and the colour of its tail intensified to a brilliant blue. One by one the gaudy insect flexed its legs and tested its wings until, with a whirr and a clicking, it rose, circled over the pool and flew away, breaking the spell that had held them for so long.

They also visited the Clay-Pan, which in winter was a

shallow pool, but in summer dried out to become a favourite place for lizards to bask in the sun, the surface of the pan breaking up into hard grey-white cakes. Overhanging the greater part of the Clay-Pan was an ancient fir tree, its gnarled roots reaching into and over the bank which surrounded the pan and the trunk leaning at an angle which cast a welcome shadow when the sun was at its highest.

On one of these explorations Marguerite sat in this shade with Rowan, scratching the surface of one of the clay cakes with her claws. She was trying to explain something to him. Something that had been growing in her mind but which she could not yet formulate precisely, even to herself. Rowan indulged her, listening intently, trying to follow.

"You remember what I told you about Marble and Gabbro and the Power Squares?" she asked him.

"Yes," said Rowan, although the memory was not clear.

"Well, I think the way Marble showed the numbers with the pine cones was clumsy. What do you think of these?" She scratched some symbols on the clay.

"This is for one." She held up one claw, then pointed to a mark in the clay: **1**

She indicated the angle at the top of the figure and said, "Here is a corner to hide one nut in, so this is for *one*.

"And this is for *two*: **Z**

"See that *two* has *two* corners. It's really quite easy. Here is *three*:" **3**

Marguerite showed him **4 5 6 7** and **8**

Rowan, watching a grass snake on the other side of the Clay-Pan, wasn't now giving her his full attention. What was the use of this obsession with numbers? But then, sensing how important it all seemed to his sister, he turned back and studied the scratches in the clay.

"I don't like the eight," he said. "This would be a more elegant shape and still have eight corners to hide your imaginary nuts in." He drew

4

"I like that!" said Marguerite. "It's a four with another four underneath it but upside down – eight *is* two lots of four."

"What comes after eight?" he asked. "Do you have a sign for 'lots'?"

"I haven't got that far," admitted Marguerite, "but I will soon." She scratched X to show that they were *her* marks and turned to follow her brother as he chased after a grasshopper.

Heavy clouds covered the sun as they returned to Steepbank but, as they passed through a copse of hazel bushes, a single ray of sunshine broke through and shone on just one of the saplings. Marguerite had often come this way but had never before noticed *this* stem, now lit brilliantly against the gloom of the leaves under the overcast sky. It had a bine of honeysuckle twisting around it, which in growing had strangled the sapling, forcing it to grow into a curious spiral of tortured wood.

Then, as suddenly as it had appeared, the ray of light

died and the twisted stem became as inconspicuous as before.

She ran on to catch up with Rowan.

Chapter 13

Bluebell was having a bad morning. Not a single salted nut had come her way and she was feeling desperate; she could not get the taste from her mouth. It was there, but it wasn't, and it had to be. She had tried every trick she knew to entertain the Visitors but none of the special nuts was thrown to her. Maybe she could find some around by the bins. It was a forlorn hope as there had never been any there before, scraps of food, yes, but nuts, no, but she still went to look, feeling awful. Her limbs were stiff and her mouth was dry and uncomfortable.

There were Greys talking behind one of the tall metal dustbins. She listened to hear who it was, ready to leave quickly if they were any of the ones who plagued her.

But then, there might be a nut for her. "Salt, salt, salt. Oh, dear Sun, I need that salt." She stayed.

It was a stranger's voice that she heard. "New orders from the Great Lord Silver. Get rid of *all* the Brown Jobs, kill them if need be. We need more Leaping-room. Do whatever you have to. There will be big territories for the most active."

"No constraints?"

Bluebell recognised Quartz's voice.

"None. Do whatever you have to!"

"Right," said Quartz. "We'll soon sort out that decrepit bunch of savages across the pool. I fancy that precinct. We'll get them before sundown. I'm looking forward to this. Yes, sir. Thank you, Stranger."

Thoughts whirled in Bluebell's head. It was Juniper and all her old friends they were talking of killing – that evening!

Her mind cleared suddenly. What a fool she'd been, consorting with these ruthless creatures all this time, just for those nuts. No, she mustn't even think of those; her duty was to warn the others.

Learning of danger
Leap, scramble, climb, hop or run,
Warn all the others.

She turned to go. She would cut through Deepend and reach Steepbank that way. Her claws scratched on the concrete as she moved.

"Quiet." It was Quartz's voice. "Who's there?"

Bluebell froze.

A whispered voice. "You go round that way, I'll take this side."

Bluebell leapt for the top of the bin, her claws scrabbling on the smooth metal lid, and from there to the wood-shingled roof.

"It's the Red – 'Bell. She must have heard the plan – after her!"

Bluebell raced up the grey shingles, her claws biting into the soft cedarwood. She ran over the ridge, jumped across a gap into a tree and scrambled along a branch in the direction of Deepend. She felt dizzy, unused now to climbing and running and, badly out of condition, missed a hold and fell. The Greys behind her were catching up, calling to others on the ground to head her off. Deepend seemed full of Greys, but maybe she could make it around Beachend. She must warn Juniper, her Juniper, she must, she must. The Greys ran too. Stronger, bigger, fitter, they cornered her on the shore below the Man-dreys.

"Sneaks and eavesdroppers don't deserve to die quickly," said Quartz. "Death by nipping, I think. Me first."

Bluebell closed her eyes as she felt his sharp teeth pierce the skin of her left thigh. Then her tail – excruciatingly painful – her ears, forepaws, her nose, her tail again, her back. Her head swam with the pain, the colour faded out of the sky, her legs no longer supported her and she slumped to the ground, kicked spasmodically and then was still. Blood oozed from her nose and dripped on to the sand of the narrow beach.

"That's one for a start," said Quartz as the Greys trooped excitedly up the bank. "More will join her by tonight."

Juniper had watched all this from the opposite side of the pool. He knew that the Red he had seen being chased and attacked must be Bluebell and that it was her limp body on the shore.

They had killed her, killed his Bluebell and just left her there. He burned with anger. Who *were* these squirrels who could do this just so as they could take over the area for themselves? He set off around the head of the pool, through

Deepend, to get to Bluebell. The woods there were teeming with Greys, so he tried to go round by way of Beachend. More Greys; he turned back again along the shore below Steepbank.

Looking to where Bluebell lay in the sun across the pool, he stopped and listened.

"Juniper, Juniper."

A faint voice was calling, some freak of nature carrying the sound along the surface of the water. "Juniper."

Bluebell wasn't dead; she was calling him. His Bluebell – still alive and needing him.

He was frantic. He ran up and down the shoreline. There was no way he could get to her. No way.

But there *was* a way, he realised, and it terrified him. He would have to *swim*.

"Juniper, *Juniper*." Bluebell's voice came again.

Juniper looked at the expanse of water between him and the tiny body. He dared not swim. Memories of being in the water when he had been chased by the Greys overwhelmed him, and he cowered on the beach shivering with fear.

The calls came again: "Juniper, *Juniper*."

He stood up, shook himself, waded into the pool, cold in the shadow of the Steepbank trees, and set off to swim across. He felt the change in the temperature as he swam from the shade into the sunlight, finding it easier in the warmer water. He kept on, guided by Bluebell's calls. "Juniper, *Juniper*, come to me." His bedraggled tail, as thin as a rat's, acted as a rudder, steering him towards her voice.

Then, feeling the coarse sand below his feet, he crawled out, shook off some of the water, waved his tail in an attempt to fluff it and went to where Bluebell lay. Flies rose lazily from her wounds as he approached.

Juniper licked her face and she opened her eyes.

"You came," she said and the lids dropped again.

Juniper waved his tail over her, the sun drying his fur rapidly. He was not sure what to do next. At least he could keep the flies off.

Bluebell opened her eyes again. "The Greys are going to attack Steepbank. This evening. You must warn the . . ." The sentence was never finished. Her tail twitched convulsively. Bluebell the Scavenger had gone Sunwards.

"Well, look at this, then, here's another one. Where did he come from? He must have crept through the pickets." A Grey was looking down from the top of the small bank. "Come on, we'll give *him* the treatment. Down here. Come on."

Juniper turned back to Bluebell but knew it was useless. She was Sun-gone now for sure. He put his paw on her shoulder, looked upwards and said the Farewell Kernel.

Sun, take this squirrel
Into the peace of your earth
To nourish a tree.

The Greys were streaming down the bank. Quickly, without thinking, he entered the water again.

Chapter 14

Rowan and Marguerite returned from the Clay-Pan to find the community in a state of alarm. Juniper's news had spread rapidly and all the squirrels were converging on the Council Tree for an emergency meeting. Oak and Burdock were trying to calm them, but it was apparent to all that the period of indecision must now be over.

When they were all assembled, Oak addressed them.

"My friends, we have lived here together under the Sun for longer than even Old Burdock can remember, and I had hoped to spend the whole of my life in this most beautiful of places, and be able to pass on our traditions to generations yet to be given life. Now, though, the Silver Tide has come, and threatens our very existence. Bluebell Who Sold . . ." He paused. "Bluebell is Sun-gone after an assault by these savage creatures but not before warning us, through Juniper, that they intend to attack us all this evening. None of us knows how to fight and the Greys are bigger and stronger than we are; they also have the Stone force and we have no counter to that.

"It is clear that we must, however reluctantly, give up our Guardianships here and move away to a safer place, if only for the sake of our youngsters."

The squirrels nodded in agreement, but said nothing.

"So," Oak continued, "we must now decide just where. Does anyone have any idea where we might go?"

Again there was silence, each looking at the others for inspiration.

Eventually Chestnut said, "I don't suppose anywhere is safe. Anywhere *we* can go, the Greys can follow, but since they came from the east, clearly we must go westwards."

Rowan said, "If we go west there is a pool with an Eyeland in it. If we could get on to that we would be safe."

"What's an Eyeland?" asked Larch, who had missed hearing Rowan telling of his climbabout adventures.

He described the Eyeland; the perfect proportions of the trees and the pink and white water-flowers, making it all sound so attractive that several wanted to start out for it at once.

"Wait, steady everyone," said Oak. "How big is this Eyeland, Rowan?"

Rowan told him.

"It's a fine idea, but there are 'lots' of us, far too many to live on an Eyeland of that size, even if we could get across the water to it." He looked around forlornly, reluctant to let the idea go. "Does any squirrel know of a bigger Eyeland?"

"Yes," said Heather Treetops, and the other squirrels turned to look at her, for she seldom spoke at meetings. "Sometimes, when I wanted to be alone, and before the Greys came, I would go up to the top of a private Look-out Tree on the other side of our Deepend Guardianship. From there, far away to the east, I could see a huge pool with these 'Eyeland' things in it. Big ones," she added.

"You never told me," said her life-mate, Chestnut.

"Didn't I?" Heather responded innocently.

"How far away?" asked Oak.

"Must be several days' journeying," said Heather, remembering her time on climbabout a few years before.

"Were there trees on these Eyelands?" asked Larch the Curious.

"Covered in them, lots!" said Heather.

"That's the place to go, then," said Oak, thankful for a positive suggestion, then, thinking of the difficulties, added, "assuming we can get there, that is."

They discussed the practicalities. First they would have to go through an area probably now held by Greys, then find a way to cross the water to reach safety on one of the Eyelands.

They all agreed to risk the first danger but no squirrel had a suggestion for the crossing. Finally Old Burdock quoted a Kernel which had not been called on for many generations in their community.

Exiles in danger
Trust in the Sun. Help will come
When least expected.

"We must trust in the Sun," she said, and plans were made to hide from the Greys near the Little Pool that evening and leave the area finally at first light.

Then Burdock said, "Before we go to prepare, I have another subject to discuss. Juniper, will you leave us, please?"

Juniper looked up. A squirrel was only asked to leave a Council Meeting by the Tagger when a tag change was being discussed. Surely he hadn't done anything wrong now? Tail low, he left and waited out of ear-twitch of the Council.

Burdock then said, "I know it is not a custom to give new tags to squirrels after they are Sun-gone but in the case of Bluebell, she gave her life trying to warn us. This was a 'noble' act." Burdock realised that she had used an archaic word from the days when Leaders were born to the job and not "selected" as now, but on glancing round could see that every squirrel understood her meaning. Even Heather Treetops was nodding agreement.

"I don't think we should remember her as Bluebell Who Sold Herself for Peanuts. I am proposing a new tag – Bluebell Who Gave All to Save Us. Any objections?" Burdock looked around. There were no objections, just a murmur of approval.

"Now, Juniper – the Scavenger. For some time this tag has been inappropriate and I have been watching for some action on which to base a new, truer tag. Today, as we know, it happened. Juniper swam the pool to get to Bluebell and then swam back to warn us. Both of these were worthy deeds and I propose that he is now tagged – the Swimmer. To a stranger this may not mean much, but to those of us who recognise his good qualities it will mean a great deal. Any objections?" Once again there were none.

When Juniper was called back and told of his new tag, he was delighted and his tail rose for the first time in moons, mitigating to some extent his sorrow over the loss of Bluebell.

The Reds busied themselves with preparations to leave,

before they all assembled near the Little Pool. Old Burdock suggested to Oak that a whole series of confusing scent-trails be laid and squirrels ran from tree to tree and off along the paths in various directions.

Guards were posted to watch for any Greys, but all the mature squirrels were aware that they had no real plans for defence, and waited apprehensively as the light faded.

Marguerite, observing the preparation of what were clearly inadequate defence plans, thought that it was important to know exactly how many squirrels there were. She counted, reached eight and then stopped. "Lots" came next and that was much too vague. She tried again and still reached "lots".

She counted each family separately. There was her own, consisting of Old Burdock, her grandmother; Oak and Fern, her parents; Rowan, her elder brother and herself. That was five.

Then the Deependers, Heather and Chestnut with their two youngsters, one of whom, Tamarisk, was growing out of the dreyling stage, but was very immature in the way he behaved.

She looked round for the Beachenders and saw them in the next tree. Clover was with her daughter Tansy, and her son. She could not see Larch the Curious, he must be one of the guards. Marguerite counted these on her claws – four more.

Then there was Juniper, he must be on guard duty too.

She tried to work out how many that made altogether. Five and four and four and one. It was "lots" once again!

Tom, the caretaker, was on his rounds with the litter-bag.

He was much later than usual; the sun had been so hot earlier that he had slept most of the afternoon and now had to make up for the time he had lost. He walked along, pausing occasionally to transfer the sweet papers and cigarette packets from the end of his spiked stick to his bag, grumbling to himself and cursing the thoughtlessness of people who just threw their rubbish down anywhere.

Seeing the body of a red squirrel on the beach near the steps, he picked it up by the tail, wrinkled his nose as the flies rose in a cloud, put it in a rabbit-scrape at the foot of a pine tree, covered it over with soil and pressed it down with his foot.

Don't want to upset the visitors, he thought.

At the deep end of the pool he surprised a large party of grey squirrels hopping along the path towards the steep-banked side. There was a kind of menace in the way they were moving. He waved his stick at them and shouted, "Get off with you, you nasty little beggars!"

The squirrels scattered and ran back past the Mandreys.

With dusk closing in, he was collecting the last few pieces of paper on the path above the beach when he again saw the phalanx of Greys heading for the steep-banked side and chased and scattered them once more.

"What in hell are you lot up to?" he shouted.

Chapter 15

The Reds had spent a sleepless night in the trees near the Little Pool waiting for an attack that never came. Now, they were ready to move off even before the sun was over the horizon. They were tense and chattered nervously among themselves in small family groups.

Oak, though, was calmer now. Although unhappy about abandoning the Guardianship which had meant so much to him, sad at leaving the lovely pool and concerned about the hazards of the journey ahead, a decision had been made and he could at last lead them in some action.

Indecision kills.
Act positively and lead.
Action is the Key.

"Right," he said clearly. "If the Greys *are* planning to attack us and find we have gone, they will expect us to head west and follow. So we will start off by going that way and when we pass the Clay-Pan we will turn south, then go east and cross the Great Heath towards the Huge Pool and safety on the Eyelands. No turning back, eyes forward. We leave *now*."

He leapt into the next tree, the others following in an undignified scramble which disentangled after a few trees were passed, until there was an orderly column of squirrels running and leaping in single file through the branches. Fern, preoccupied with grooming her tail, was the last to leave.

Old Burdock leapt with the others but her joints ached and she soon fell back to the last position, behind even Fern, to be joined there by Clover the Carer, who asked if she was all right.

"You may have to leave me behind, Clover-Friend," she panted. "I'll catch up with you later."

Clover ran after the leaders, passing squirrel after squirrel until she was just behind Oak. "Slow down!" she called. "Some of us can't keep up at this pace."

Oak stopped and waited until all the squirrels were together again, then, aware of the differences in ages and fitness within the group, he led off more slowly, looking back frequently for signs of pursuit. Their speed was slowed by Old Burdock who often had to stop for breath and insisted each time that they leave her behind, "to catch up later".

Oak would hear none of this and, by the time they reached the Clay-Pan, the sun was high in the sky and the heat was getting unbearable. All was quiet behind them, and as Old Burdock looked worn out, Oak ordered a halt. They all climbed into the shady branches of the ancient fir overhanging the Clay-Pan to rest, each busy with their thoughts.

Chestnut was having doubts about the wisdom of leaving the area they knew for the unknown. "Are we doing the right thing?" he asked Heather.

"We had no choice," she reminded him. "I hate the idea of just clearing out and leaving my ancestral home to the Greys, but we can survive – and prosper. We'll get to one of those Eyelands and we'll all be safe there. We can start a new life for the youngsters then."

"I hope you're right. I must admit I have my doubts."

Larch, further down the sloping trunk with Clover and their youngster Tansy, was more cheerful. "This is like being on climbabout again, only with company. I'm dying to know what those Eyelands are like. Do you think they will have any pools on them?"

Clover's mind was on other things. She was watching Old Burdock who was dozing fitfully near her.

Larch said, "Do you?"

"Hush, Larch-Pa," said Tansy, indicating Old Burdock with her paw. Larch nodded and shut his eyes.

Oak was worried. The responsibility for the group's safety lay heavy on his shoulders. If they were to survive and reach the Eyelands it was going to be up to him to lead them through unknown country and he had never even been on climbabout. Was he really fit to be Leader? He shook himself.

> *When the cones are down,*
> *Even if you doubt yourself,*
> *Hide all your concerns.*

That was a Kernel the Tagger taught to newly elected

Leaders. It was important not to let fear show. Make decisions – lead! Even if the decision should subsequently be proved wrong, action could then be taken to correct and recover. *Action* was the *Key*.

Should he be doing something positive now? More doubts assailed him, but he only had to look at Old Burdock slumped across the branch below to know that if he wanted her wisdom for the journey and on the Eyeland, they must wait until she was fit to travel again.

Fern was unconcernedly grooming herself on a nearby branch.

Marguerite and Rowan were together, looking down at her numbers, still visible where she had scratched them in the clay surface the day before. "There's the eight that you drew." She pointed it out to him.

A pair of lizards ran across the hot dry clay. Rowan wanted to chase them.

Juniper had climbed to the very highest part of the tree and was looking back at where he knew the Blue Pool lay sparkling in the sun. Farewell, Bluebell-Mate, he was thinking, I wish I had been able to bury you under a tree, but at least you are free of the grey monsters now. He came down slowly and settled on the trunk where there was a patch of shade. He yawned and closed his eyes. Oak would wake him when it was time to go.

Just after High Sun Oak woke up from a doze and looked down. "Lots" of Greys were fanning out across the dry white clay below, following the footprints and the scents left by his party.

Rowan was also awake. He glanced at Oak, then slipped

down the upper side of the trunk, ran along the top of the bank, showed himself on the skyline and shouted.

"Flea-ridden tree-rats," he called. "Sun-damn you all!" and he disappeared into the heather and bracken, heading westwards.

The Reds, all awake but silent in the leaning tree above, watched the posse of Greys chase after Rowan as he ran along the bank and off into the heather. The squirrel-chatter faded into the distance.

Oak turned to Fern. "A son to be proud of," he said, his tail high.

Rowan raced on along the dusty heath path, the sun beating down on him. At a crossways he ran a little way along each track, then leapt over a clump of heather to confuse and delay the Greys. He could hear them behind him now and ran faster, leading them away from the vulnerable group in the tree above the Clay-Pan. Then suddenly he felt an inexplicable urge to turn aside and stop. Something, a sensation in the base of his whiskers, had said, "Turn and stop here."

He hopped sideways off the path, knocking over the base part of a broken bottle as he did so, and crouched down to wait.

The Greys had paused at the crossways and were arguing amongst themselves, some saying the Brown Job had gone one way and some another. Then he heard an urgent, confident shout. "This way, this way."

Rowan crouched lower, convinced that his hiding place had been found out, then, smelling the terrifying scent of smoke, he turned his head and saw how the rays of the sun were being focused by the bottle-base on to a wisp of dry moss in which a tiny flame was already showing. He crawled backwards away from the miniature fire. The flame grew, caught the bone-dry heather and suddenly and explosively leapt from clump to clump, fanned by a westerly breeze which seemed to have come from nowhere.

The fire, spreading ever wider, swept down on the Greys and he could hear their shrieks and screams as it overwhelmed them. Then there was just the crackling of the burning heather stems.

Rowan waited upwind of the flames, then, as they moved away over the ridge between him and the Clay-Pan, he tried to follow the fire back the way he had come. In his haste he burned his paws badly and, despite repeated attempts, was unable to walk more than a few steps until the following morning.

At the first scent of burning heather on the breeze, Oak had scrambled to the highest branch of the fir. He could see the billowing smoke-clouds, lit from underneath by the red and orange flames, coming downwind towards them on an ever widening front. Coming too fast to race away from, particularly with Old Burdock unable to move quickly. There was a chance that if they stayed in the tree the flames might not reach them, but he had once seen a burning tree and was not going to risk that. There was only one other option.

He called down, "Every squirrel. Drop out of the tree and crouch in the centre of the Clay-Pan. The fire can't reach us there. It has to feed on plants!" Squirrels fell from the tree like rain and huddled together on the dry clay beneath it as the fire roared past, small pines and birches flaring up as their needles and leaves scorched, shrivelled and burnt. The leaning tree above them, although enveloped in smoke, escaped the flames and gave some protection from the hot embers falling out of the smoke-clouds.

They crouched there for what seemed hours, coughing the smoke out of their lungs, until the air cleared enough for them to look around. They felt very vulnerable in the open, but they had nowhere else to go until the ground cooled. There was no sign of Rowan or the Greys; they must all have died in the fire. But these were unspoken thoughts.

Oak kept testing the ground on the eastern side of the Clay-Pan until, just before dusk, he judged it cool enough for them to cross. Even so there were some scorched paws before they were through the burnt area. They returned part of the way they had come and were relieved to find that the fire had passed to the south of the Little Pool and missed the Blue Pool altogether, but Oak would not let them venture too near. That morning's posse had contained only a small number of the Greys, and others might be waiting for them.

They passed over an area of open heath dotted with small pines and birches but none within leaping distance of the others, and so the whole party had to stay together on the ground, fearful of being caught in the open by a fox. They need not have worried; the resident foxes had slipped away at the first scent of smoke.

The squirrels passed clumps of gorse, dark and menacing in the fading light, and, in the small boggy places where marsh gentians flowered, they cooled their paws on the damp moss.

It was when they came to the two metal lines across their route that Oak finally called a halt. These needed careful examination. He was not going to risk crossing whatever these were, in the dark.

They climbed a tree and tried to sleep, Marguerite finding sleep especially evasive as she grieved for her lost brother.

Rowan had spent a sleepless, painful night in the open. In the morning, soaked by a shower of rain which also put out the last remnants of the fire, he found he was able to hobble back to the Clay-Pan, passing the burnt bodies of the Greys on the way. Except for the leaning tree, everything there was scorched and black, and, finding no sign of his companions in the tree and all scent obliterated by the overwhelming smell of the damp burned foliage, he searched for their bodies, feeling sick with the horror of it all. It was hopeless; too vast an expanse. Hopeless, hopeless. His paws throbbed with pain.

Somewhere out there must be the charred remains of his family and friends, but he might search for days and then never find them.

He thought of his water-flower pool with the dream Eyeland and turned sadly away westwards, alone.

A skylark sang incongruously above the blackened heathland and in the distance a curlew circled over the site of its nest, mournfully bubbling its loss.

Chapter 16

After the shower had passed, Oak looked at the railway lines in the grey dawn light, unable to comprehend their purpose, then, seeing how they continued into the distance to either side of them, touched one cautiously. It seemed harmless enough, so he clambered over one slippery rail and then the other, before encouraging the others to follow him. The youngsters and elderly squirrels were helped over and the party of exiles went on along the side of a field, hearing dogs barking from a Man-drey, but too far away to inflict hound-dread on even the most nervous. Then through a hedge, down into a ditch, up the other side and they came to a roadway, smelling of oil and rubber, familiar to them from the car park at Humanside.

There was no traffic to be seen in the early light and they crossed in single file, wriggling under a gate on the far side into another field with a wood to their right, behind an earthen bank riddled with rabbit holes. The rabbits, nibbling their last mouthfuls before lying up for the day, ignored the squirrels who passed them silently through the cool dewy grass.

The group were moving more slowly now, resting

frequently for the sake of Old Burdock and those with sore paws, convinced that there was now no immediate pursuit and intent only on getting to the Huge Pool and finding, with the Sun's help, some way to cross to the Eyelands and safety.

By evening, after a long rest in a lone pine tree at High Sun, they had reached a stream with willow and alder trees on either side. In the hollow they lost sight of the familiar outline of Screech Hill behind them, and a small wood hid the view ahead. Oak and Juniper climbed a tree to plan a route, the others keeping watch below. They could see the Huge Pool in the distance and how the stream widened into a series of marshy pools with spear-grass growing around the edges.

A woodpecker, glowing green and yellow in the light of the setting sun, flew in to land on its favourite rotten alder, saw the squirrels and turned away, rising and falling through the air with its strange undulating flight. It seemed to be laughing at them in a high-pitched human voice.

In the swamp below were unfamiliar rushes with brown furry flowers which reminded Oak of the tail of the cat that had once lived around the Man-dreys at the Blue Pool. A wave of homesickness hit him and he turned to look back, but there was nothing to see but the grass-covered rise in the ground and grazing cows on the skyline.

> *If it hurts too much*
> *Thinking of what cannot be,*
> *Put it out of mind.*

He shook his head violently, turned to Juniper and said,

"We'll follow the edge of the swamp, keeping near the trees so that we can retreat into them if we need to. I'd like to go through the treetops, but Old Burdock can't leap for long and the gaps are too wide for some of the youngsters."

Cows looked up briefly from their grazing as the group passed, some of the squirrels pausing to eat the ripe blackberries and the hips and haws in the bushes around them. Sloes, black, but with a dusty bloom on the drupes, covered the twigs of blackthorn bushes, but the Reds, knowing the dryness these gave in the mouth, ignored them and hurried on. When it was nearly dark, Oak called a halt and they all climbed a friendly alder tree to huddle together in the darkness.

Each night was becoming a little colder than the last and there was a tang of autumn in the air at dawn. One morning there was another scent as well, one that Juniper recognised as salt, and he had to fight to keep the old craving from overwhelming him. He remembered his Bluebell and was determined not to let it dominate him again.

The squirrels fed uneasily on the plentiful food all about them. They saw where bark had been stripped off a number of young trees and there were cones lying about under a pine tree which bore the marks of larger teeth than theirs. The distinctive scent of Greys was there too. It was only an elusive hint in the air, but to those who had lived in close proximity to them for a while there was also something else, more sensed by whiskers than by nose, ear, or eye. A sense of arrogance, contempt almost, possession by right of might.

The Reds looked about them, feeling that this must be a

part of some Greys' territory, then scrambled through the scrubby trees, alert for danger, until they reached a shoreline of muddy banks with clumps of rushes. Water lapped on to the beach. Burdock went forward and tasted it.

"This isn't a pool!" she said. "This is the sea.

> *Pools have sweet water.*
> *Bitter water makes the Sea,*
> *You can't get round it.*

"That's a Kernel for squirrels going on climbabout. I never thought I would see it, though. We have come to a *Sea*."

"Now what do we do?" asked Chestnut, looking out to where the tree-covered Eyelands appeared to float on the rippling water.

"Trust in the Sun," said Burdock, after a pause. "We've got this far safely." Then, lowering her voice, added, "Apart from Rowan, that is."

The squirrels spread out along the shoreline, where the water jostled twigs and pieces of broken reed-stem at the very highest tide mark.

"I think the sea is going away!" said Marguerite a few minutes later. "Look, this stone was under the water when I came past it, and now the top of it is sticking out."

The squirrels gathered round and watched. Eventually even Chestnut the Doubter was convinced that the sea was indeed going away and soon they would be able to walk across to the nearest Eyeland. Marguerite realised that if they could, then the Eyelands would not be safe havens for them. She spoke her fears quietly to Burdock. "Trust in the

Sun," she was told and had to be content with that, as they watched the sea continue to slide away over the mud-flats towards the Eyelands.

They sat in the short grass along the shoreline, fascinated by the disappearing sea, until High Sun, most of them hoping that a dry path would appear to enable them to cross to the Eyelands. Even Oak forgot the possibility of danger from landwards, until Heather, who had looked over her shoulder, whispered to him, "Don't move suddenly, Oak-Friend, but there's a posse of Greys behind us."

Oak turned his head casually as though looking at the sky to judge the time, and saw the Greys, lots and lots, all watching them ominously.

"No squirrel turn around," he said calmly. "Just start walking towards the Eyelands where the sea has been. *Don't* look back."

The Reds did as they were told and walked out on to the slowly drying mudbanks, which got stickier and stickier under their paws as they neared the water.

Fern the Fussy stopped to lick some of the foul-tasting mire off her tail and saw the Greys following them menacingly, although keeping some distance behind. With their greater weight they were sinking further into the mud than the Reds.

Ahead, the sea appeared to have stopped going away and the fugitives waited there uncertainly, sinking in the cloying ooze at the water's edge.

The Greys, also picking their way carefully, were still trying to advance, but without their usual cockiness, their fur becoming covered in a grey slime until they also halted some yards back and stared silently at the Reds on the mudbank below them.

For several minutes both sides crouched, neither moving, the Greys apparently waiting for something to happen.

"The sea is coming back," wailed Tamarisk, "it's all over my feet."

The Greys laughed and nudged one another. "Time and tide wait for no squirrel," one of them called out and the others all laughed again.

The sun shone down from a cloudless sky on to the red and the grey squirrels, the heat drying the slime on their fur. It also shone on a discarded door floating along on the rising tide beyond the trapped Reds, touching the shore from time to time, then lifting and drifting on as the tide inexorably rose higher. The Leader of the Greys saw it coming and started to move forward but was unable to do so without sinking dangerously into the mud.

Oak, seeing the Greys watching something behind him, turned, saw the door himself and recognised that here was a chance of escape.

"Follow me," he shouted, leaping for the door as it touched against the mudbank, and the others leapt after him, although Old Burdock, spluttering and spitting salty water, had to be unceremoniously hauled aboard. The door, pushed from the shore by the impact of the leaping bodies, drifted away, turning slowly as it did so.

Tamarisk the Tactless, feeling safe now, put his paw to his nose and wiggled his claws at the frustrated Greys, who were retreating in disorder. The Reds did not see the fate of the Greys as the door, its surface now awash with water, drifted around a mud-spit, and caught an offshore breeze. Each squirrel had to dig its claws into the soft wood and cling on for dear life.

Chapter 17

"The Eyelands are going away," Burdock reported to Oak
as they drifted along. The squirrels were getting used to the
strange way the door moved on the water; some had even
started to scramble about, their bodies adjusting to the
movement as they did in wind-tossed treetops. All were wet
from the wavelets that sloshed over the door from time to
time, but the sun was warm and none was seriously chilled.
Unfamiliar long-necked black birds flew heavily past and
gulls, normally seen only rarely by the squirrels when
storms forced seabirds inland, were everywhere, looking
down with cold yellow eyes on the door and its unusual
passengers, and squawking their disapproval.

Marguerite the Bright One was oblivious to all of this
and to the rocking motion under her feet. Painted on the
wood where she sat was one of *her* numbers and one she
didn't know. There was a 4 and then a number with no
corners in it at all – 0. What could this last number mean?
No corners meant that there was nothing to record. A
number for nothing? That did not make any kind of sense.
She scratched at the figures as if this would make them
reveal their true meaning, but the flaking paint came off

Ourland
Brownsea Island

Woodstock Bay

Ruined Man-dreys

The Pier

Palm Tree Valley

Lagoon

Man-track

The Bunker

The Zwamp

New Council Tree

Man-dreys

The Wall

Beech Valley

CHURCH

Royal Tree

CASTLE

The Island Screen

Pottery Point

N

South Shore

Furzey Island

under her claws, broke up and floated away on the next wave to wash over their raft.

Old Burdock was repeating to herself, "Trust in the Sun. Trust in the Sun." Marguerite joined her and soon all the squirrels were chanting in unison.

Oak stood precariously, swaying with the motion under his feet. "The Eyelands are coming back," he said and the chanting stopped as every squirrel turned and looked in the direction he was pointing. They all agreed that the Eyelands were indeed getting nearer as they watched, the door drifting in towards the shore of the largest.

Finally, to the huge relief of every squirrel, the door grounded and, glad to be on land again, they were able to walk ashore over wet but firm, gravelly sand, from which strange half-buried round and rectangular objects projected. They clustered together amongst the flotsam at the top of the beach.

It was Larch the Curious who made the first move. "Come on," he said, "let's go look and see what there is to see."

"But we don't know where we are," replied Chestnut.

"We never will if we stay here!" Heather pointed out.

Oak, though still feeling slightly queasy from the unaccustomed movement of the door, felt it was time to assert himself.

Firm Leadership shown
Provides other squirrels with
A common purpose.

"We will go carefully, all staying together. No squirrel is

to go off on their own. We don't know what dangers might be lurking here."

The beach and the foreshore where they had come aground were littered with broken drainage pipes and misfired bricks, the debris from a pottery which had once occupied the site. Broken shards were everywhere, many overgrown with herbage, and even the large pines behind the foreshore grew out of mounds and banks of soil covering old scrap heaps. The whole area had an unreal and disturbing sense for the tired animals.

Tansy looked unhappy and whimpered, "I don't like it here, let's go home."

Clover went over to her and said, "The Sun has guided and helped us to get here, I don't think we *can* go home. Don't forget those Greys are there now."

The mention of the Greys made all the other squirrels look around but there was no sense of danger even after the most vigorous sniffing and whisker-twitching. Certainly there was no scent of fox or grey squirrel although Juniper and Oak thought they could detect just a whiff of strange Reds. However, with the breeze blowing from behind them and the salt smell from the sea, neither could be sure.

Tamarisk the Tactless was snuffling at an old crab shell on the beach. "This place stinks," he pronounced loudly.

Keeping together, they climbed the bank of soil-covered, broken pipes to the grass under the pines and sensed the air again. Now there was nothing but a benign and even slothful feeling, not the slightest hint of danger of any kind.

The squirrels spread out a little and, staying on the ground, made their way through the coarse grass and bracken to the top of the next bank. There was still no sign of any animals other than harmless rabbits and, with the sun setting behind them, they prepared for their first night in the safety of an Eyeland. Food was everywhere. The squirrels ate well and started to relax in the peaceful atmosphere, later sleeping in family groups in the upper branches of a large pine.

"We will explore in the morning," Oak told them.

There seemed to be no reason to hurry when the sun first showed itself through the trees to the east, and after an especially thankful morning prayer the party foraged in a leisurely way, before moving further inland in a loose group on the ground, to find out exactly what the Eyeland had in store for them. Passing through clumps of rhododendrons and crossing several overgrown Man-paths, they came to a place where these tracks passed below some magnificent mature pines, their high branches forming a canopy over a light brown carpet of fallen needles. Above they could hear squirrel sounds. The exiles crowded together and waited expectantly.

Red squirrels came down the trees and stared at them. None spoke, and Oak, knowing that *they* were the strangers, signalled to his party to keep their tails low.

The Eyeland squirrels circled the newcomers suspiciously, led by an elderly and dignified Red who kept his tail high.

"Who are yew, and from whence have yew come?" he asked.

"Who are these funny foreigners?" Marguerite whispered to Burdock.

"Shush. We are the foreigners here. Keep your tail down," replied Burdock.

No lands are Foreign
It is those who pass through that
Are the foreigners.

Oak replied, "I am Oak the Cautious, Leader of this party, and this is Burdock the Tagger, this is Fern the Fussy – my life-mate, this is . . ." He introduced each member of the exiles in turn, down to and including every tagged youngster, as is proper. Each raised and lowered his tail in the traditional manner. "We have come from the Blue Pool." He could explain more later. Then, remembering the tradition, he added, "We greet you . . ." and paused, not yet knowing the name and tag of the Leader.

The distinguished-looking squirrel stepped forward and bowed to Fern, who looked sideways at Oak and fluffed her tail proudly, hoping that there were no tangles visible.

"Uz iz King Willow the Third, zon of King Azpen the Fourth, zon of King Cyprezz the Won and Only, zon of King Willow the Zecond, zon of King Poplar the Fifth, zon of . . ." The Leader went on and on through a poll-list of ancestors, his tail high with evident pride, then turned to a female at his side and introduced her.

"This is Kingz-Mate Thizle the Zecond, daughter of Rozebay, daughter of Cowzlip, daughter of Groundzel, daughter of . . ." This list, too, seemed to go on for ever.

Burdock listened with interest. The naming pattern was the same as her community used, tree-names for males, flower-names for females, but the tags, if one could call them that, told one nothing about their characters, and after one generation or, at the most two, parentage gave no guide as to what to expect from *that* individual.

King Willow then turned to one of the younger squirrels. "And thiz iz my zon, Next-King Zallow." He indicated a narrow-chested squirrel with a slight squint.

The exiles braced themselves for another string of names and sighed audibly when he passed straight on, introducing another, more handsome son, Poplar, and a nephew, Fir. Then a daughter, Teazle, and lastly two nieces, Voxglove and Cowzlip, who together would have weighed as much as one healthy squirrel.

The half-dozen or so other squirrels who sat with lowered tails he did not introduce, but with a wave of his paw said, "And theze are zome of the zervantz."

"What is the name of this land?" Oak asked, when he realised that the formal greeting was not being returned.

'Thiz iz *Ourland*," replied King Willow. Then, seeming to lose his suspicion, he and each of his family passed along the line of exiles, brushing their whiskers with their own, in a special and rather pleasant form of greeting. The exiles felt free to raise their tails and relax, mixing with the Ourlanders and making friends, the youngsters from each party romping and playing together in the pine trees and running wildly about in the grassy glades.

Oak, cautious as usual, asked King Willow if they should not go up into a tree for safety and was asked why.

"To be safe from surprise by a fox or a dog."

"What is voxez and dogz?" asked King Willow. "There'z nothing here to harm uz."

Burdock was talking to Kingz-Mate Thizle, asking about Ourland.

"There iz water all round it, no other zquirrelz can come here, and that huz been our problem. There'z no choize of maytz now. Brotherz have to mate with their zizterz or cloze couzinz, even if it feelz the wrong thing to do."

Burdock was appalled. One of the most important Kernels said:

> *Never mate with kin.*
> *Seek new blood for strong dreylings,*
> *They are your future.*

"Why don't they chose mates from other families?" she asked.

Kingz-Mate Thizle looked round sadly. "There aren't any good wonz now. Only the zervantz' familiez, and uz *obviouzly* can't mate with thoze." She wrinkled her nose disparagingly. "Uz are all that are left and uz don't have many dreylingz now. Mozd of the wonz that are born each year are zickly and are Zun-gone afore their firzt winter. Perhapz that'z why the Zun zent all of yew. Welcome to Ourland."

Burdock was pleased that these strange Reds shared their respect for the Sun even if some of their other customs were different. She acknowledged the welcome with a lowering of the head and a sideways flick of her tail.

Chapter 18

Burdock and King Willow were lying out in the upper branches of the Royal Macrocarpa Tree which grew near an abandoned church. From here they could look out over the meadow where the humans obligingly fed the peacocks which strutted about between the Royal Tree and the grounds of Brownsea Castle.

This magnificent multi-trunked tree stood proudly on a high bank, and the resting squirrels could see over the castle to the Poole Harbour entrance and the open sea beyond. They could watch the car ferry as it shuttled back and forth between Sandbanks and South Haven Point, but the squirrels were no more concerned with this than with the sailing boats dotting the harbour, part of a strange Man-world beyond their shores and of no interest to them.

The autumn harvest was in full swing, and so plentiful were nuts of every kind that only a few hours of gathering and hiding each day were sufficient to ensure a well-fed winter. King Willow never gathered nuts. "Let the zervantz do that," he had said, even offering their services to Oak, Fern and Burdock. There were plenty of them to do so, all apparently just there to make life easy for the Royals.

The exiles politely refused, preferring to make their own provision as they had always done.

> *Save for the future,*
> *Store plentiful nuts safely,*
> *Prepare for lean times.*

Somehow it did not seem right to let others do this for them.

The two elderly squirrels often lay out on fine days swapping legends and traditions. Many of the Ourland customs were quite unlike those practised on the mainland and at first Burdock had been appalled to learn that the Sun-tithe, which was such an essential part of their mainland life, had deteriorated here into a mere ritual. Although the Ourland squirrels still stored nuts for the winter days and for the leaner times of early spring, they had forgotten the reason for leaving some undisturbed.

> *One out of eight nuts*
> *Must be left to germinate.*
> *Here grows our future.*

King Willow could not remember the whole of that Kernel. He had mumbled something about "eight nutz being left" and described how each autumn they buried eight nuts together, which were never to be dug up, and then forgot about them until it was time to do the same thing at the next harvest.

"But what about future trees?" Burdock had asked.

"Never zeemed to be a problem," replied King Willow

listlessly. "The deerz eat zum new zeedlingz and the rabbitz eat zum but there alwayz zeem to be enough each year. Maybe it only matterz where yew com'z from."

Burdock was interested in the absence of tagging. With the Ourlanders there seemed to be no sign of any system of reward or punishment. The Ourland Royal youngsters had, at first, appeared to be a spoilt lot, pampered by their parents, but in fact, now that they were maturing, she had grown fond of them. They seemed willing to learn and had joined in with the newcomers when she taught "Kernels, Traditions and Manners", although most of the elder Ourlanders ignored her teaching sessions.

"Have you never had punishments?" she asked King Willow.

"Oh yez, when uz wuz Next-King we had a zquirrel who wuz called The Nipper. He wuz a half-brother of my father the King, zo muzt have been a zort of uncle to me. Pure white he wuz, with funny pink eyz. Nazty fellow him; if zomeone upzet the King he told The Nipper to bite that zquirrel'z whizkerz off. Have yew ever zeen a zquirrel without whizkerz? Totally lozt, yew don't realize how important they are until yew haven't got any. Lozt mine once. Zun, it wuz awful!"

"What had yew – you done?" Burdock asked, fascinated.

"Uz fanzied a female, a couzin of mine, won of my year, but my father, old King Azpen, had hiz eye on her too. Zo he zent The Nipper to teach me a lezzon. No mating for me that year, uz could hardly climb and didn't dare jump until uz'z whizkerz had grown again. Yew juzt feel zick all the time, zort of out of touch with what iz going on around yew."

"What happened then?" asked Burdock, trying to imagine a whiskerless world.

"Old King Azpen went Zunwardz that winter and uz became King, zo uz bit off The Nipper'z whizkerz uzzelf and zent him off to live in the Zwamp. Put him under a taboo. No zquirrel wuz ever to mention him again and he huz not been zeen zinze. Gone Zunwardz himzelf long ago uz exzpectz, good riddanze too. When uz wuz dreylingz uz uzed to zcare one another in the duzk by calling out 'The Nipperz behind yew'." He chuckled. "Zcared uz all rigid, he did! Nazty old fellow.

"Uz got that female too. Her'z Kingz-Mate Thizle now. Zeemed odd mating with won of my father'z fanzy femalz but with zo few of uz now, uz have got uzed to that kind of thing."

Burdock shuddered. Kin-mating was abhorrent, every Kernel she knew in that area spoke against it, yet she understood the dilemma in which the Ourlanders had found themselves. Ultimately the urge to mate would overcome all taboos. No wonder they were glad to greet the newcomers.

"Was that the only punishment?" she asked.

"If any of the zervantz hurt a Royal, he lozt hiz tail. Another of The Nipper'z jobz. He told uz wonz that he wuz really a kind old zoul and knew how much it would hurt if he bit it all off at wonz, zo to make it hurt lezz he would bite off only an inch each day. Uz never knew if he wuz joking."

Old Burdock said nothing, she just looked at the King, sprawled on the branch laughing quietly to himself, then out to sea. Soon she would go and do some more harvesting.

"That granddaughter of yourz – Marguerite," King Willow said, unexpectedly. "In the zpring uz will mate her with Next-King Zallow. Her may not be a Royal but uz can't be too choozey nowadayz. Her iz a chief'z daughter and a good looker too."

Burdock did not know how to reply. They were still regarded, and regarded themselves, as strangers in another's Guardianship, and had accepted that they must try and live by the local rules, but her knowledge of the ancient Kernels still provided the basis for all her decisions.

> Not even parents
> Can choose a squirrel's life-mate.
> The Sun guides self-choice.

This Kernel was clearly applicable here. She would need to think of a way round this which would not antagonise the King. She excused herself and slipped away down the trunk.

Later she spoke to Oak, and told him what King Willow had suggested. He was appalled. "Next-King Zallow is a *squimp*," he said. "Marguerite would never want *him* for a life-mate."

"I'm not sure that that is exactly what was being suggested," Burdock replied. "There was no mention of 'life', but so much is different here I could not be sure. Do we tell Marguerite what is being planned?"

"Oh yes. You tagged her well with 'the Bright One'. I'll tell her what the King said and see what her reaction is. Sometimes I think she's cleverer than all of us."

Chapter 19

Marguerite had other things on her mind. She kept thinking of the painted figures she had seen on the door as they were floating over to Ourland. One was clearly a four, almost exactly as she had invented it, with four corners in it to check against one's claws. But the other number had no corners at all. It had been round like a pebble or a bird's egg. Who would want a number for nothing? A number for nothing, there must be some other meaning. Sitting at the top of the beach she drew her numbers with her claws in the damp sand.

1 2 3 4 5 6 7 4 and then 0

Was "0" the number that came after eight, instead of "lots"?

She glanced Sunwards as though for guidance, then back at her figures. A tiny piece of glass, polished by the sand and waves, was glinting in the centre of the 0, reflecting the sunlight. The answer must be in that 0, she thought, and as she studied the symbols, a seagull, passing overhead, emptied its bowels and the stinking white guano splattered

down on to the line of figures, obliterating most of the 4
and leaving only enough showing to read as a 1 .

1, 2, 3, 4, 5, 6, 7, 1 0, she now read, and in a flash the
answer was with her. After seven, there was *one* lot of eight
and NO more.

If there was another it would be 11, one lot of eight and 1
more, then 12, one lot of eight and 2 more. It was so
obvious, but the Sun did have strange ways of enlightening
the Seeking Squirrel! She skipped up and down the beach
joyfully, needing to tell someone. "There *are* numbers after
eight!" she wanted to shout and rushed off to find Old
Burdock, who always had time for her.

In the open ground above the beach she saw her father
hurrying in her direction so she ran to him and breathlessly
started to explain about her discovery.

Oak held up a paw to check her. "Just a minute, just a
minute, Marguerite-Lass, listen to me first. Old Burdock
has just told me that King Willow wants to mate you with
Next-King Sallow in the spring. I thought you should
know," he added lamely, realising as he said it that he had
acted out of character. Spring was a long way off and he
should have spent more time thinking the implications
through, before blurting it out to his beloved daughter.

Marguerite hardly heard him, her mind full of magical
numbers. After one lot of eight and 7 more – 1 7 – would
come 2 0, two lots of eight and NO more, then . . . Her
mind raced away: 21, 22 . . . 2 7, 30, 31, 32 . . . Numbers
could go on for ever!

Oak tried to listen and understand as she described it all
to him. He would have to tell her about King Willow's

plans when she had calmed down and would heed him.

This took some time. Marguerite would spend hours on the beach, trying out numbers in different combinations: 12, 21, 23, 43, 34, 33, 6 7, 66 . . . and having finished a session, signed the symbols in the sand with her special mark – X.

Several times Oak and Burdock had told her about King Willow's plan to mate her with Next-King Sallow in the spring but she would only reply, "Him, he's a squimp!" as though this would end the whole matter. Oak and Burdock were not as sure.

An air of estrangement was building up between the two communities. King Willow had expected his proposal for the mating to have been eagerly agreed to, but it was apparent that Marguerite was not, to say the least, overjoyed at the proposal. "Who did her think her wuz?" he remarked one day to Kingz-Mate Thizle. "The whole Sun-damned lot of them huz come unazked to Ourland and iz eating away az though it belongz to them! They'z even burying uz nutz to eat in the zpring and now rejecting uz zon and heir. If only The Nipper wuz alive, he would teach won or two of them a lezzon."

Kingz-Mate Thizle was not really listening. Her mind was full of pictures of healthy young grandchildren leaping around in the branches of the Great Macrocarpa. "Yes, uz'z zure yew iz right," was all she said.

King Willow summoned Oak to come, alone, to a meeting at the Royal Tree.

"Uz have dezided," he said imperiously, "that yew and yewr party are being too free with uz harvezt and taking advantage of uz generozity. In future yew will reztrict yewr-zelvez to the weztern end of *Our*land." He put a heavy emphasis on "Our".

"That iz all," he said, dismissing the stunned Oak with a wave of his paw.

Oak returned, tail low, to summon a Council Meeting of the exiles. He described his session with King Willow.

"He may be King," said Heather. "Even so we should ignore him. He speaks from under his tail. He can't hurt us. There are as many of us as there are of them and, if hop comes to leap, the zervantz would be on our side."

This was probably true. Two of them, a female called Woodlouze and a male, Zpider, were now regularly attending Old Burdock's training sessions, as were the younger Royals with the exception of Next-King Sallow, though it was unlikely that King Willow was aware of this. Some of the other zervantz visited at quiet times to talk with the exiles. Zpider had realised after one such visit that for the first time in his life he was walking with his tail raised. He lowered it quickly before any of the Royals saw him.

"It's not as simple as that," said Burdock. "We are still the foreigners here. Remember how *we* felt when the Greys came and ignored *our* wishes?"

"But all the Kernels are on our side," said Chestnut. "Aren't they?" He looked at Burdock.

"There are no Kernels regarding Royalty," she replied, "only on how chosen Leaders should behave. There are plenty of them and none gives the right to force-mate a female against her wishes."

"I haven't said I won't take Next-King Sallow yet," said Marguerite, and the squirrels looked at her in surprise.

"Let's leave that issue until the spring, and talk about living in the west of Ourland apart from the others until then."

A swaying sapling
Survives the storm. Stubborn trees
Often get blown down.

Chapter 20

It was not a good winter. Although there was plenty of food, the winds blew cold and rain was so frequent that it soaked into the dreys, chilling the squirrels inside.

On rare sunny days they would come out and run around on the ground and through the trees, enjoying the sunshine and the feel of the blood flowing through their veins. Then, resting, they would discuss what was likely to happen in the spring if King Willow insisted on pursuing his plans for a mating of Marguerite with Next-King Sallow. Marguerite seemed the least bothered of them all. "I can handle that squimp," she would say, but Oak and Old Burdock especially were concerned about the consequences for the Westerners if the Royals had cause to take umbrage.

Fern was not so sure that the proposed mating would be a bad thing.

"It would make our Marguerite the next King's-Mate," she said to Oak one evening. "That would be something!"

"I'm going to pretend I didn't hear that," said Oak sternly. "The only one of that bunch worth a nutshell is Poplar, and the King doesn't even seem to notice that he exists. I'd rather she chose Tamarisk than Sallow!"

"Tamarisk the Tactless? She'd never choose him."

"I know that. All I'm saying is that it has to be *her* choice, I'm not having my – our daughter force-mated with any squirrel. Especially Sallow."

Marble was not enjoying that winter either. Alone for most of the time in his drey in the stunted spruce, he had ample time to reflect on his changed circumstances. Hope of power and influence at Woburn was clearly gone for ever. His ambitions of becoming the Great Lord Silver seemed ludicrous to him now.

His lifeline was Gabbro, who hopped over every time news was brought by passing Greys. This happened often as the Silver Tide swept on through the south-west of New America.

"There is a whole new batch resting up on their way through to some place the natives know as the Wall of Corn. Sandy says she is going on with them, and would I let you know? No hard feelings, she said, but these are a vigorous lot and you know how she likes Lustees."

Marble rubbed the stump of his missing paw and looked out of his drey, to where a cold mist swirled past the entrance.

"When are they going?" he asked.

"Today I think, could even be gone by now. There's not much daylight for travelling in winter and they've got a long way to go!"

Marble said nothing but Gabbro noted the forlorn look on his friend's face.

"Seems it's all bad news today," he said. "There are rumours of some kind of illness about. The Lustees did not know much about it, but it's bad down near the Bright Stone area. Hope it doesn't come here!" Gabbro looked out of the drey. "I'd better be off, the mist is thickening up. See you in a few days." He scrambled down through the scratchy dead twigs of the spruce and was gone.

Gradually spring emerged, heralded by the greening of the hawthorn bushes. The squirrels on the island tasted the fresh buds and combed the hazels for pollen-laden catkins, a welcome change from stored nuts. Marguerite was at this pleasant task when Next-King Sallow came courting, finding her sitting in a hazel bush with yellow pollen around her mouth and on her whiskers.

She hardly noticed him. She had been counting as she ate, seven lots of eight and six more, 76. Seven lots of eight and seven more, 77. She stopped. What came next? Since she had been Sun-inspired to abandon the figure 8, she could go no further. Was this as far as numbers could go?

Next-King Sallow called up to her. "Hello, my pretty one."

Marguerite looked down at him. He was pale and his tail was scraggy and thin. "Are you speaking to me?" she asked, peering around as though to see some other squirrel that he might have been addressing.

"Yez. Yew my pretty," he said, her scent floating tantalisingly down to him in the warm spring sunshine.

Marguerite assessed his strength and likely stamina. "If you want me, you'll have to catch me," she called teasingly.

She leapt for the nearest tree. "One," she counted, ran through the branches and leapt into the next. "Two."

At "six lots of eight and seven more", 67, she looked

back and was amazed to find that Sallow was still following. She glimpsed other squirrels watching the chase from trees or from the ground.

Innocently unaware of the mating-scent trailing behind her which was whipping Sallow into a frenzy of unaccustomed activity, she ran and leapt on.

At seven lots of eight and seven more, 77, Marguerite found that either by accident or by Sallow's design she was in a tree on the edge of the wide Man-track with him close behind her. She would have to try a leap greater than she had ever attempted before or submit to Sallow and mate with him, and this was tree number 77.

Was the Sun saying, "There are no more numbers after 77, your destiny *is* to be mated with Sallow?"

She turned, looked into his leering dog-like face, saw the red foam bubbling around his mouth and felt a kind of hound-dread trying to paralyse her body, but, with a massive effort of will, she suppressed the hound-dread, gathered her strength, ran down a branch and leapt into space.

She cleared the Man-track, scrabbled for a hold on the very tips of the branches of the tree opposite and hung there, repeating, "I beat the hound-dread, I beat the hound-dread, the hound-dread, hound-dread," and as her brain cleared and her breathing slowed, a new and beautiful figure formed in her mind – 100 – and she knew then that numbers went on for ever and ever!

Below her, bruised and bedraggled, Next-King Sallow crawled from the puddle in the Man-track into which he had fallen, and, shaking off the proffered paws of Woodlouze and Zpider, limped back to the east, coughing and spitting out the blood which bubbled up from his strained lungs and consigning all Westerners, and especially Marguerite, to the Sunless Pit.

Marguerite thanked the Sun for her escape but Oak and Old Burdock could not believe this would be the end of the affair.

The Bright One had recently taken to scratching numbers in the smooth bark of birch trees, 100, 101 . . . 123, 321 . . . finishing each session with her mark – X, until Burdock pointed out gently that as the trees grew the numbers would get bigger.

"Larger," Marguerite corrected her grandmother, equally gently, and tried to explain the difference when applied to numbers.

"Either way they disfigure the trees and that isn't done, my dear."

> Squirrels protect trees.
> They have enough enemies,
> Treat them as our friends.

So Marguerite went back to scratching in the sand on the beach, but if any piece of driftwood offered a clear surface it soon carried the marks of her claws and teeth. 123 X. 654 X. 666 X.

Chapter 21

A week had passed since the chase. The days were warmer, buds were breaking and leaves opening all over the island. Most of the western squirrels were out in the sunshine and many, led by Fern, were replacing the linings of their winter dreys or contemplating building lighter summer ones. There had been no word from the east, and none of the Royals, nor any of the zervantz, were coming to the teaching sessions any more.

A Council Meeting was held but there was little to discuss. There was an air of expectation, but none could think of any action that they could take to heal the breach between east and west. They would just have to wait and see what would happen. It was as if an invisible wall had been built from north to south across the middle of Ourland, the Royals and the zervantz rigidly confining themselves to the eastern end and leaving the exiles to their own devices in the west.

After the meeting, Marguerite was on the beach scratching figures in the sand, watched at a distance from downwind by Juniper. She moved to a clear patch, away from the scratch-marks she had just made, and found a most curious piece of driftwood washed up by the sea. It was almost the same size as herself and the sand-smoothed wood was twisted into a spiral where some creeper had once grown tightly around it. The creeper itself had been worn away by the action of the waves and the sand that had smoothed the wood. She bit the end to try and identify the wood. It looked to her like hazel and the taste should confirm this, but the expected nutty flavour had been leached out by the sea and replaced by salt. She spat out the bitter wood and rubbed her whiskers that were tingling in a strange way.

Digging into her memory Marguerite recalled the hazel sapling, strangled by a honeysuckle bine, that she had seen in the shaft of sunlight when she had been with Rowan at the Blue Pool so long, long ago. She looked across the water at the mainland and sniffed. Juniper moved a little closer.

Enough of this squimpish nostalgia, she thought and reached out to scratch a number on the smooth wood. As she touched the spiral, her whiskers tingled again as though the wood held some hidden power, and she pulled her paw away. The tingling stopped. She tried again, producing the same effect. Juniper crept a little closer, his nostrils twitching.

Marguerite reached out boldly, held the stem firmly with her left paw and cut 123456710 X deeply into the wood with her teeth, her whiskers buzzing wildly with excitement as she did so. Juniper hopped closer still.

There was still room for more figures on the smooth grey driftwood so Marguerite lightly scratched a 3 after the X.

She felt the surge of power that spiralled out of the end of the woodstock and twisted across the beach, bowling

Juniper over, before it dissipated above the sea, leaving him groaning and clutching at his face.

"Sun, my whiskers, Sun, my whiskers," he kept saying.

Marguerite ran to him and pulled his paws away. His whiskers were curled into spirals as tight as those on the twisted stick. She tried not to smile at his ludicrous appearance as she attempted, unsuccessfully, to comb them straight with her claws.

An hour later, at Juniper's insistence, Clover bit away each whisker, to stop the spinning feeling in his head.

Several more days passed with no word from the Easterners.

Juniper was recovering slowly as his whiskers started to regrow but he could not climb and was living in a ground-drey hidden in the bushes near the shore.

The Woodstock, left on the beach while Juniper was being attended to, had evidently floated away on the next tide. Marguerite searched for it each day, trying beach after beach all around the western end of Ourland.

"Why is it so important, my dear?" Old Burdock had asked.

"I don't know. I just know that I must find it. Will you help me?" They searched together in vain. Then, one evening, as the tide was going out, Marguerite, alone this time, was rummaging through the flotsam in a bay on the north-west corner of the island when, to her delight, she found the Woodstock again, lying half buried in the drying seaweed. She approached cautiously, reached out and touched it. Her whiskers tingled, and with mounting excitement, she again scratched a 3 after the 123456710 X.

The force spiralled out along the beach and she felt it fade away and die just beyond the water's edge. She tried a 6 and out over the sea in the line the force had taken, a group of seagulls rose in a twist from the water, calling angrily. A 1 produced no result at all, and the force produced by a 2 did not even reach the shoreline.

So intent was she with her experiments in the gathering dusk that she did not see the ancient, dingy-white squirrel hobbling towards her on the sand.

He called to her, "Yew, Yew."

She looked up in panic, pulled the Woodstock towards herself in a defensive gesture and scratched a 6 on the wood.

The surging, spiralling power caught the old squirrel and threw him on his back.

Marguerite ran from the beach as though all the foxes, dogs, martens and hawks in the world were after her.

In the calm of the morning she led others down to the shore, disturbing a pair of herring-gulls who had just pecked the pink eyes from The Nipper's body. No squirrel wanted to approach the corpse too closely, but despite their protests, Marguerite rolled the Woodstock to a place well above the tideline and then insisted that the body was decently buried under a tree, as was proper for any Sun-gone squirrel.

Chapter 22

Remembering the disparaging way in which King Willow had spoken of The Nipper, Burdock saw an opportunity to reinstate Marguerite in the King's favour and perhaps end the artificial partition of the island. She went off alone later that day to see him.

She was coolly received. Like herself, the King was ageing rapidly and Next-King Sallow was now always at his side. Both were seated high in the Royal Macrocarpa Tree, with its many great trunks, as she described what had happened at the North-West Bay.

The King listened with interest; he was really quite fond of this knowledgeable old Tagger as she called herself, and was about to say, "Fanzy The Nipper ztill being alive," when Next-King Sallow, his thin face cold with fury, said to Burdock, "Are yew telling uz that yewr granddaughter huz killed a Royal?"

"You could put it that way," she replied, "but . . ."

"No butz about it," said Next-King Sallow. "By yewr own admizzion her huz, and her muzt be tried for it." He turned to the King. "Tomorrow uz tryz her; uz – Zallow – will prozecute."

The King, with some reluctance, agreed, and said to Burdock, "Thiz iz the Law and at High Zun on the Morrow, Marguerite the Bright One muzt appear before the Royal Court. Her will be charged with 'Taking the Life of a Fellow Zquirrel, Knowing Him to be a Member of the Royal Family, the Punizhment for Which iz Tail-docking'."

Next-King Sallow slipped away through the branches, his skinny tail even higher than usual, knowing that once the Court had been declared it could not be cancelled.

A shocked Burdock tried to speak about it to the King. "But this is a nonsense," she started to say.

Embarrassed, the King cut her short. "Uz can't discuzz it with yew. That'z the Law," he said. "Yewr Marguerite muzd be here at High Zun. Her can have won other zquirrel with her, no more iz allowed."

Burdock was "dismizzed".

At the Westerners' Council Meeting she related what had happened.

"It's that Sun-damned squimp Sallow trying to get his own back," said Heather.

"That's obvious," replied Clover, "but what can we do about it?"

"Tell them to go to the Sunless Pit," said Tamarisk the Tactless, now a handsome yearling, though as quick with his tongue as ever.

"What are these trials like?" asked Larch the Curious. "I'd like to go to one."

"You can't," Burdock told him. "Only one other squirrel is allowed by their Law. We must decide who it is to be."

The choice came down to Oak, as Council Leader and Marguerite's father, or to Burdock as the Tagger, and because she had a greater knowledge of squirrel traditions than any of the others. Although, as she readily admitted, the Ourlanders' customs were different from those she knew so well.

Burdock skilfully guided the meeting to select her. She was thinking ahead.

At mid-morning on "the Morrow", Fern was trying to groom Marguerite's tail. "Appearances *are* important, my dear," she said as Marguerite pulled it away.

All the Westerners accompanied Marguerite and Old Burdock to the west–east boundary where Oak took Burdock to one side and pleaded with her. "Look after Marguerite, she means a lot to all of us."

"I know that," she told him. "I'll do all I can."

"Sun guide you both," they called after the Bright One and her grandmother as they watched them hop off down the Man-track to the trial. It seemed unfair to them that all the Easterners were allowed to attend, even the zervantz.

Clover slipped quietly away to look for a woundwort plant.

The Court was held in the upper branches of the Royal Tree. King Willow and Kingz-Mate Thizle each held a feather from one of the peacocks that strutted around the meadow behind the castle and Next-King Sallow held a white seagull quill which he waved in the air to emphasise any point he wanted to make. It all seemed somewhat bizarre to Burdock and Marguerite who were both used to more simple proceedings.

"Zilenze," said the King, waving his gaudy feather.

"It huz been reported to uz" – he glanced at Burdock, who shifted on the branch uncomfortably – "that yew, Marguerite, known as the Bright One, huz killed a Royal. Iz thiz true?" He pointed the feather at her.

"Yes, what happened was this – "

Next-King Sallow raised his quill to stop her.

"Yew admit killing Nipper the Royal?"

"Yes. But – "

"No butz! Yew are clearly guilty by yewr own admizzion. Yew knew it wuz wrong to kill a Royal?" He pointed the quill at her.

"It is wrong to kill any squirrel. What happened – " Marguerite started to reply, but Next-King Sallow cut her short with a wave of the quill.

"Thiz wuz not *any* zquirrel. Anzwer the queztion."

"What happened was this – "

She was cut short again. "Yew knew it wuz wrong to kill a Royal?"

Marguerite was getting angry. "Please. Will you listen to me? Please?" she shouted.

"Zilenze in the Court," ordered the King, waving his feather.

Burdock tried to intercede.

"Yew are only allowed here to zee, not to zay anything," Next-King Sallow told her and turned back to Marguerite.

"Do yew admit that yew killed Nipper the Royal and that yew knew it wuz wrong to kill a Royal?"

"Yes," she replied.

He spread his paws wide and said, "Yew have all heard her confezz," he said. "And by Ourland Law that iz the end of it. A confezzion completez the trial. Uz demandz that the penalty iz paid. Tail-docking iz the decreed punizment." He turned to his father expectantly.

King Willow was looking out over the harbour, thinking, then, making up his mind said, "Killing any Royal iz a heinouz offenze and muzd be punizhed according to the Law. Tail-docking at dawn."

Burdock, who could not believe what she was hearing, leaned over to Marguerite and whispered, "When I say go, run. Hide by Pottery Point. There is no justice here." She turned to King Willow and eyed him coldly.

"What I have seen here today is a disgrace to Squirreldom. I demand the right to speak before any sentence is pronounced."

The King looked away towards the castle. "Yew are only here to zee. The Court iz over, zentenze huz been pronounzed. Tail-docking at dawn. However" – he paused and looked at Marguerite – "the prizoner iz allowed by our Law to make won ztatement, and won only." He signalled to her with the feather.

Marguerite looked at the distraught Burdock, drew herself up to her full height, raised her tail and spoke the Understanding Kernel.

If you could know all
Then you could understand all
Then you'd forgive all.

She looked expectantly at the King. He could not meet her eye and got up to leave with Kingz-Mate Thizle behind him, both awkwardly carrying their peacock feathers. As the other Royals and the zervantz lowered their tails in deference, Burdock leaned over to Marguerite and said, "Go. Go now!"

Somehow Old Burdock, despite her age, seemed to be everywhere and in every squirrel's way, jumping from one of the tree's many trunks to another and then another and back again. In the ensuing confusion Marguerite launched herself out of the Macrocarpa and into a chestnut tree. "One," she counted.

By the time pursuit had been organised she was six trees in front of the nearest chasers, the zervantz Woodlouze and Zpider, heading, as Burdock had suggested, for Pottery Point.

"7, 10, 11 . . . 65, 66, 67, 70 . . . " she counted as she jumped from tree to tree.

At the boundary she glanced back. She was still ahead of Woodlouze and Zpider by some 7 trees but, not far behind the two zervantz, she could hear the excited chatter of a mass of pursuing squirrels, with Next-King Sallow's high-pitched voice urging them on.

Then she heard Juniper's voice calling up from the ground below. "Go to the Woodstock Beach," he called. "I'll try and divert the others." He hid himself under a bush as Marguerite changed course. "532, 533, 534 . . ."

"Her'z heading for Pottery Point, her'z zinking fazt, uz'll catch her zoon," Juniper called up as the first two squirrels passed above him.

Woodlouze and Zpider ignored him, they had seen her alter course and ran on in hot pursuit.

Juniper was more successful with the mob. They heard the first lie he had ever told and headed south-west.

*

Marguerite was in fact "zinking fazt". Her energy, already drained by a sleepless night, the tension of her trial and the run through the trees in the heat of the day, was virtually exhausted.

"775, 776, 777." There was one more tree – and there was no number for it! She leapt for the tree, a pine, missed and fell to the beach. The Woodstock was somewhere ahead and she knew that she could get to it if she could only keep going through the sand, through the sand. She struggled on, "Through sand, through sand, throu'sand, th'ou'sand, thou'sand . . ."

Thousands of grains of sand scattered behind her as she made one last scrabbling attempt to stay ahead of the zervantz and reach the Woodstock.

Her sight was failing, her limbs were no longer obeying her brain and she knew then that she could not reach it before the zervantz caught up with her. But, as she lost consciousness, her last thought was that, if she had to lose her lovely tail, at least she had found the number which came after 777 – 1000. One thou'sand, one thousand, how beautiful it sounded.

She awoke to find Woodlouze and Zpider licking her face and paws and was surprised at their evident delight when she opened her eyes.

"Oh, ma'am, yew are awl right. Uz are zo pleazed," said Woodlouze.

"Yewr Juniper led the otherz away. Uz recognized hiz voize," added Zpider. "Yew're safe with uz for a bit."

Chapter 23

On a beach on the far side of Poole Harbour, the human holidaymakers were complaining about the heat. The scent of suntan lotion hung heavy in the sultry air. Instead of lying on their towels, people were holding them above their heads to act as sun-shelters. The temperature rose ever higher. Little whirlwinds raised spirals of dry sand which chased each other about the beach, stinging skin and eyes.

Some people were beginning to pack up and leave, although it was only mid-afternoon. Then, as though directed by some co-ordinating force, the little whirlwinds joined to make one big one which whooshed across the beach, filling the air with flying towels, sunhats and paper bags. A child's rubber dinghy was lifted high in the sky and dropped far out in the harbour to float away on the tide.

The holidaymakers, strangers until then, gathered in friendly groups to discuss the phenomenon and to sort their own belongings from the heaps scattered across the sand. Above the chatter a little boy's voice wailed, "Daddy, my boat's gone!"

When Juniper knew that the pursuing Easterners were at

Pottery Point, searching for Marguerite amongst the broken shards, he went as fast as he could with his half-grown whiskers, through the tangled rhododendron bushes, past the ruined Man-dreys of Maryland and on towards Woodstock Bay. He had to make sure that she had been able to use that weapon to deal with the two zervantz.

On the way he met Tamarisk.

"What's going on?" he asked.

As they ran together through the bushes, Juniper told Tamarisk of the trick he had played on the Easterners. Then, dropping down on to Woodstock Beach, they were very surprised to find Marguerite being cared for by the two zervantz who were tending her with every sign of affection.

They went across the sand to them, to ensure that she was safe.

We must get her off Ourland, Juniper was thinking, but it was Tamarisk who saw the red rubber dinghy drifting past. "Frizzle my whiskers," he said, "the Sun's-child is back."

Juniper looked up. "So it is," he said. Then, clutching at a leaf, "Maybe it's come to take Marguerite to safety."

"It's not coming in," said Tamarisk. "You're the Swimmer, you'll have to swim out and fetch it."

Juniper looked at the water, calm and blue under the bright Sun, took a deep breath, waded in and swam out strongly to the rubber boat. He gripped a rope that was hanging over the side with his teeth, and towed it ashore. Digging his claws into the sand, he tugged until one end of the boat was resting on the beach.

"Quick, get in," he told Marguerite, who had recovered

her composure. She started to climb the rope, then dropped back on to the sand.

"I'm taking the Woodstock," she said, "it's up there behind those stones." Together they rolled it down the beach and, by piling up other pieces of driftwood to make a ramp, they got it over the side and into the boat. Thinking that she might need it later, she asked them to throw the rest of the wood in after it.

Marguerite climbed the rope, followed by Woodlouze and Zpider.

"Uz can't ztay now," Woodlouze explained. "Next-King Zallow would have uz tailz. Or worze!" She shuddered.

Together Juniper and Tamarisk waded out, pushing the new Sun's-child into deeper water, then as a breeze caught it, Juniper climbed up the rope.

"Are you coming too?" Marguerite asked.

"Of course," Juniper answered.

"Help, help me, someone," called Tamarisk, and Juniper looked over the side to see him hanging on to the rope and being towed through the water as the new Sun's-child responded to the strengthening wind.

Together they hauled him aboard and he collapsed, spluttering, amongst the driftwood.

"It looks as if you're coming as well," said Marguerite.

"In for a hazelnut, in for a walnut. I've always wanted to go climbabout but there's nowhere new to go on that Sun-damned Ourland. So, what's to be seen?" He climbed up the pile of driftwood and peered towards the land. "Look at this," he called.

They were being blown along past Pottery Point. The

squirrels there had abandoned their search and were grouped on the beach, as Next-King Sallow, once again coughing up blood after the exertion of the chase, was giving orders for them to spread out through the trees and try to locate Marguerite by her scent-trail.

Tamarisk, balanced on the edge of the Sun's-child, thumbed his nose at the group, as he had once done at the Greys on the mud-flats, and called out across the water, "Who'z a zilly zquirrel, then?"

Next-King Sallow turned, saw the rubber boat carrying the fugitive Marguerite, that creep, Juniper, who always seemed to be wherever Marguerite was, another squirrel who was being openly insulting to his Royal Personage and, worst of all, two disloyal zervantz, all laughing at him.

He spluttered in fury, unable to find words. The sunlight was sparkling on the water, the reflections hurting his eyes. Uz'z not feeling well, he thought. The damned zun iz too hot. Uz *muzd* get into the zhade.

He started to move backwards, slipped on a shard covered in sea-slime, and fell, blood gushing scarlet from his mouth.

The fugitives were, by then, too far away to see this happen or to notice that no squirrel went forward to help the stricken Next-King; they just stood round in a circle and watched him die. When a bottle-blue fly, heavy with eggs, landed on the face of Never-to-be-King Sallow, and proceeded to lay the eggs in his mouth, no squirrel moved forward to flick it away.

They all looked at one another. *Someone* was going to have to tell the King.

Chapter 24

It was strange that no boats had come near the Sun's-child with the squirrels aboard. Each time a boat with its tall mast and bright sails had looked as though it *was* coming near, there had been a shift of the wind and it had turned about and sailed away again. The Sun's-child itself had been blown up and down the harbour but had never come near to land.

As the sun slipped below the western horizon, the wind fell away entirely and the light rubber dinghy bearing the five squirrels, the Woodstock and the pile of assorted driftwood was carried on the falling tide out towards the harbour entrance and the open sea. Brownsea Island had appeared to drift past them again in the near darkness, but they could see no sign of squirrel life on shore. Waves slapped against the boat's side as they were drawn along, the sounds magnified by the inflated rubber ring.

Then the Man-lights of the car ferry crossed in front of them, carrying the day's last load of vehicles and, feeling the lift and surge of the open sea, they were out into the swell of Poole Bay.

The squirrels did not sleep much that night. Marguerite

repeated an old Kernel to encourage them, suddenly feeling the weight of responsibility for others.

> *Have faith in the Sun*
> *His ways are mysterious.*
> *Faith can fell fir trees.*

Faith. Just have Faith. There was nothing else she could do. Just wait, watch and have Faith.

"Where are we?" Juniper asked, climbing up the driftwood to join Marguerite as the top rim of a huge red sun showed above the horizon. Around them gulls floated on the gently undulating sea, watching the dinghy with its unusual passengers.

"Sunknows," she replied. "Certainly not where I expected to be."

A light breeze ruffled her tail, held high so as not to convey her concern to the others below. She had been "sensing" the breeze to try and find which way it was blowing but it seemed to move about. Sometimes it came from the east, sometimes from the north and even on one occasion briefly from the south.

When the swell lifted them, land was visible far off to the west but hidden when they sank into the next trough, the movement leaving an uncomfortable feeling in Marguerite's stomach.

Woodlouze woke from a brief doze, nudged Zpider awake and apologised to Marguerite. "Uz be zorry, ma'am," she said, "uz haven't zeen to yewr breakfazt." Then, realising that there was no food on board, bowed her head in confusion. Zpider put his paw on Woodlouze's forearm.

Marguerite hopped down from the woodpile to where the two zervantz stood together.

"We have no food, but we are all well fed and can go for days without it if need be. We do in the winter, remember. And you mustn't call me ma'am. I am Marguerite. We are all friends here."

"Yez, ma'am," said Zpider and they all laughed.

"We must do something about *your* names too," she said, then added, "unless you like to be called Woodlouze and Zpider, that is."

"Zervantz iz alwayz called after creepy-crawliez," said Woodlouze.

"You aren't zervantz now, you are our friends and companions. Would you like new names?"

"Yez, pleaze, ma'am," they replied together.

"*Marguerite*," she corrected them. "Zpider, how would you like us to call you Spindle; that is a lovely tree to be named after. It has pink fruit and the leaves turn bright red in the autumn."

"Thank yew, ma'am, Marguerite ma'am, uz would like that. Zpindle, Zpindle, Zpindle," he said.

"And for you, Woodlouze, I would love to call you Wood Anemone. It is one of my favourite flowers; anemone means 'Flower of the Wind'."

'Oh ma'am, Marguerite uz meanz, that iz a nize name. Pleaze do alwayz call uz that," she said, her tail rising for the first time that she could remember.

After High Sun, Juniper, who was on watch on the driftwood pile, called down to Marguerite, "The land is getting closer!" and they all climbed up to see. To the west of them were white cliffs and they could see that some had been eroded by the sea to form high pillars of chalky rock.

By evening they were amongst these, being tossed about very uncomfortably by waves breaking around the bases of the rock columns. Above them cormorants and other seabirds were flying in to roost for the night.

"It's like being in a stone forest," said Tamarisk. "These are like great stone tree trunks."

"Hold on," shouted Juniper, when an especially large wave nearly tipped them over as it smashed against the foot of one of the pillars and, turning over backwards, soaked the squirrels with spray. He eyed the sharp-pointed barnacles under the seaweed apprehensively, knowing how easy it was to pierce a Sun's-child's skin. If that happened it would be the end of them all.

"Trust in the Sun. Trust in the Sun," Marguerite kept telling the frightened squirrels in her care, but as the sun itself disappeared behind the cliffs, and the frail craft was tossed about in the surges, even she was losing a little of her faith. "Trust in the Sun. Faith can fell fir trees," she told herself, wishing that she was in a snug drey high in a fir tree right now. Calling to Tamarisk to take over the watch, she dropped down to comfort Wood Anemone and Spindle below. Juniper, with his short whiskers, was having a bad time balancing and was feeling very sick.

Marguerite was with the ex-zervantz, whispering, "Trust in the Sun," to each squirrel, when she became aware of something quite outside her experience.

Her ears heard whistles, grunts and clicks coming through the water which reverberated in the hollow air-filled rubber tube of the Sun's-child, but her mind heard something quite different. Two voices, one clearly male and the other female, were debating an issue in voices as soft and as sweet as breezes in high pines.

"I think we will have to modify that ancient Great Explosion theory. Since the South Atlantic Right whales found those strange holes in the atmospheric ozone it is much easier for them to pick up the signals placing the Black Holes. Thinking about the Universal Origins, now I believe that matter has *always* existed. It's more logical for the Universe to be expanding and then contracting in waves over enormous periods of time; from a Great Explosion and an outward wave, then a slowing-down of expansion, then an ever-increasing contraction, then another Great Explosion and off we go again. I never could accept that everything suddenly came into existence in one flip.

"That would make us now, as a mere planet in this Universe, be swimming outwards on a wave from the centre . . ."

The voice stopped. Then –

"Malin, some mammal is praying, we must help."

"You're right, Lundy. Near Finfast Point amongst the rock pillars. Mammals – I sense them to be squirrels, like the ones we saw down the coast – in danger. Turn and follow!"

A minute later, with the clicking and grunting now audible to all the squirrels, the heads of two dolphins broke the surface, one on either side of the Sun's-child.

Marguerite and Juniper had joined Tamarisk on the woodpile and looked with amazement at the strange creatures in the water.

In her mind Marguerite heard one dolphin say to the other, "Underneath and nose away."

An air of great peace and protection came over them. The dolphins' blowholes closed, their black polished heads slid below the surface, and the Sun's-child moved effortlessly away from the rocks and into the safety of the open Sea.

The heads popped up again. "Where are you going?" the soughing sound in her head asked, more or less in time with the movement of Malin's mouth.

Anywhere safer than this, Marguerite thought, but before she could speak the words, the dolphins seemed to understand.

"We know a place where other squirrels live. By the Sea. Would you like to go there?" a voice in her head asked.

"What colour are they?" Marguerite did not have to speak.

"An animal's colour means nothing to us, but their shape and size is the same as yours."

"Are their ears round or pointed?"

"The same as yours."

"Then we would like to go to them."

Marguerite realised that she had not opened her mouth and the other squirrels were looking at her with puzzled expressions on their faces.

The dolphins slid down and under the Sun's-child and propelled it gently southwards, taking it in turns to rise for air, all the time soundlessly conversing with Marguerite.

"We can't take you all the way, but we can put you into currents that will. We will put you at the end of the

Current ✣ 3* and that will take you to 3 ✣ 3 then 3 ✣ 33. Current ✣ 4 will take you ashore."

The dolphins read Marguerite's incomprehension. "Don't worry, trust in your Sun. You will be safe."

"How can you be sure?"

"Some of us have learned to 'Look Forward', but we don't often do that, it makes us sad. We learn to 'Look Backwards' even before we are born. We know the history of our race, back as far as when we lived on the land as you do still. Then we learn to 'Look Round' and find out all we can about Now and Here. Malin and I are studying 'Look Out' – searching way, way beyond this our planet 'Water'. It is most interesting but can be brain-exhausting. We are on our way to meet others near the Goodwin Sands to share our ideas. We often school there together."

"Can you count numbers?" Marguerite asked.

There was a pause. Then, "Count yours to us."

Marguerite started, "1, 2, 3, 4, 5, 6, 7, 10, 11 . . ."

"Ahhhh, yes, Base Eight, humans use Base Ten now. When we first taught the Phoenicians they used Base ✣ like us. That would be 60 in human numbers and" – there was a momentary pause – "74 in yours."

"Do *you* teach humans?"

"We used to, when they would listen. We had high hopes for them. They still use our ✣ for counting their time and 6 ✣ for dividing up circles, but they have probably forgotten where they learned it. With ten digits on their hands, Base Ten is easier for most of them."

"Don't they listen now?"

* ✣ is pronounced Zix-T

"Sadly no, they have been conceit-deaf for more than ⋈ of our generations."

The soughing in Marguerite's head died away, and the Sun's-child slowed to a stop. The dolphins' heads appeared above the water.

"We have brought you to Current ⋈ 3. You will be with the others of your kind by dawn on the day following tomorrow. We must leave you now. Dolphins must always be on time!

> *Punctuality*
> *Is vital. Other's time wasted,*
> *Is stolen by you*
> *And can never be returned.*
> *Lost minutes sink for ever.*

"Farewell, our friends, we are glad we heard your prayer."

They dived, then leapt together in a glorious arc through the air and swam off up-channel in the gathering darkness, followed by the unspoken but received thanks of Marguerite.

After the dolphins had gone, she felt unutterably lonely despite the presence of the other squirrels, who seemed not to have understood any of the conversation. She tried to explain to them what the dolphins had told her.

Chapter 25

The circle of silent zervantz surrounding the body of Sallow widened to allow Next-King Poplar through. He ordered them to carry the fly-blown corpse of his brother back to the Royal Macrocarpa Tree, following the cortège himself at a distance.

Poplar, attending the Court at High Sun, had listened to the proceedings with dismay. Everything that he had heard and seen had been contrary to what he had been taught by Old Burdock during the previous year, when he had studied Squirrel Lore and Traditions with the incomers.

> *Squirrels have the right*
> *To explain their own actions,*
> *Fully – in silence.*

Marguerite had not been allowed to do this. It was plainly unjust. Then there was:

> *Punishment through pain*
> *Degrades the one who gives – more*
> *Than the receiver.*

His brother had been spared this degradation, thank the Sun. Now it was going to be up to him to tell the King – and the Kingz-Mate.

These low-tailed zervantz were having the distasteful job of carrying his brother's body the full length of Ourland because he, another squirrel like them, had ordered them to do so.

Each squirrel is Free
To choose its own root through Life –
Guided by Kernels.

Sallow's corpse was laid at the foot of the Royal Tree and Next-King Poplar climbed up to tell his father of the circumstances of his brother's death, as told to him by the zervantz who had been present.

The King was silent for a while. He looked tired and old, all his pride and arrogance gone. He stared at his youngest son, sitting, head bowed and tail low, on the branch before him. For the first time in his life, he saw that Poplar was a fitter and better squirrel than Sallow had ever been.

He looked out over the sea, then, appearing to have come to some great decision, called for his and the Kingz-Mate's peacock feathers to be brought to them, together with one more. He stood to his full height, a Royal and dominating figure again, held his tail high and announced, "Uz *lazt* Decree iz thiz – uz giv'z up uz Kingz-zhip irrevocably and pazz thiz Name, the Dutiez and the Privilegez on to uz zun, King Poplar the Zixth. Long live King Poplar."

He bit through his peacock feather and let the pieces fall

through the branches to the ground far below, then looked expectantly at the Kingz-Mate, who, with just a hint of reluctance, did the same with hers, watching the blue and green feather, gleaming bright in the evening sun, drift away on a light breeze.

The Ex-King lowered his tail, handed the new feather to King Poplar the Zixth and turned to leave. His head was aching and he wanted to lie down, away from the excited chatter that had followed his announcement.

"Wait," commanded the new King. "Uz *firzt* Decree iz thiz. All zervantz are free," and, before any squirrel could realise the significance of this, he declared, "And uz zecond, and *lazt* Decree iz to abolizh for ever in Ourland the pozition and rank of King." He bit through his feather and let the pieces drop.

"In future uz am to be known az Poplar; not King Poplar, not even Ex-King Poplar, juzt Poplar."

In the chill of the following morning, Juzt Poplar crossed the west–east boundary, abolishing it with a flick of his tail to the cheers of a gaggle of adoring ex-zervantz who were busy trying to keep their tails in unaccustomed upright positions.

Behind them came Ex-King Willow playing hide and seek in the bushes with the dreylings of the ex-zervantz, and a slightly huffy Ex-Kingz-Mate.

"Uz haven't enjoyed uzzelf zo much for yearz," he told her.

Oak, Burdock and the rest of the exiles were in the trees above Woodstock Bay, looking out over the harbour.

Tansy had seen the Sun's-child leaving on the tide, and they were hoping it would return, unaware of what had taken place at Pottery Point, or later at the Royal Tree. They were now huddled together awaiting events when they heard the joyous group approaching.

"Will *you* be our Leader?" Juzt Poplar called up to Oak.

"That depends," Oak replied cautiously, and came down the trunk to learn from Poplar of the unexpected and dramatic events that had occurred at the eastern end of the island.

Old Burdock went across and brushed whiskers with Ex-King Willow and Ex-Kingz-Mate Thizle.

"Long live a united Ourland!" she said, and each squirrel repeated the words.

Chapter 26

Marguerite suggested to the squirrels below that they come up and lick some of the condensed dew from the Sun's-child's skin before the sun rose and dried it up. The sky was clear and it was going to be another hot day with no more water for them until nightfall.

Just before dawn a sleek warship had passed at a distance, leaving her wondering what the straight horizontal branches were that she could see silhouetted against the sky. She marvelled too at seeing some of *her* numbers painted hugely on its side: F126. The F puzzled her, but the numbers were hers.

The rubber dinghy was too small to show on the ship's radar but the pinging of its Asdic transmissions, as it sensed for hidden submarines, was picked up by the squirrels' sensitive whiskers, the pulses amplified by the inflated ring of the Sun's-child.

If it is trying to talk to us, thought Marguerite, I understood the dolphins better. Perhaps it's a special language these great ships use to each other when they are offering help.

*

Throughout the long day, the land to the north slipped past as they were carried along on the sea's currents. Now and then the flow would appear to stop and the Sun's-child would circle aimlessly for a few minutes, then they would be caught by another current and drawn off in a slightly different direction, sometimes close to the cliffs, sometimes well out to sea, but always westwards.

Another night crept up on them from the east and the squirrels settled down to try and sleep. The Sun had dried up the Sea-water that had splashed into the Sun's-child before the dolphins came, so they were dry and more comfortable now, although very hungry. All of them, including Juniper, had adjusted to the rising and falling motion of the sea.

During the night a wind from the south-west started to blow, gently at first, then growing in strength until, by midnight, it was driving them rapidly towards the shore. A fitful moon came out from behind the clouds and showed Marguerite the dangers that lay ahead. On Ourland she had often heard waves rushing at the shore and watched them curling over in a mass of white froth and bubbles. She knew that this was happening now, somewhere in front of them, and as the sounds were getting louder, she also knew that soon they would be in the breakers. "Trust in the Sun."

She turned to warn the others and found herself saying in a strong, confident voice:

> *Be ready to swim*
> *Keep together. Fear nothing.*
> *We will all be saved.*

Juniper added, "Trust in the Sun," as a giant wave lifted the Sun's-child, tipped it over in the surf and tumbled the squirrels into the cold water. Tamarisk, Spindle and Wood Anemone scrabbled and clutched at pieces of the driftwood thrown into the sea with them, while Marguerite swam directly to the shore.

Juniper, struck on the head by the Woodstock as the craft overturned, sank, and then, when he had struggled to the surface, found that he was trapped under the upturned Sun's-child, paddling round and round with no way of escape. In the blackness he felt the floating spiral of wood and grabbed at it in panic, his paws scratching and clawing at the smooth surface. He never knew which of Marguerite's numbers he unwittingly drew in the confusing darkness, but a powerful burst of energy shot out of the Woodstock, ripping the skin of the Sun's-child apart with an explosion that was heard by the other squirrels, now huddled together on the wet shingle further along the beach.

Coughing and spitting salt water, he climbed through the hole in the wet rubber and, as the current drew the remains of the dinghy along the shore, he swam through the breakers to the land, guided by the weak moonlight.

Chapter 27

Juniper was lying exhausted amongst the seaweed on the high-tide mark. Near him were the remains of the Sun's-child and at his side was the sodden Woodstock. A red squirrel with only a stump of a tail was shaking his shoulder. "Wake up, my friend, wake up," he was saying.

He rolled over in the soft light of the early dawn. A herring-gull was calling from a rock and the sound of the breakers was faint in his ears. He could just make out a sucking sound as the waves of the ebbing tide drew the shingle back after the rush up the beach.

Juniper coughed, tasting the salt in the fur around his mouth.

"Where are the others?" he asked.

"Don't worry, they are all safe, further along," the stump-tailed one said. "That bossy female sent me to find you."

Juniper smiled to himself, then looked ruefully at the remains of the Sun's-child. The stranger was nosing at the Woodstock. "Don't touch that!" Juniper called to him.

"Poisonous?" asked the stump-tailed one.

"No. I'll explain later," he said.

"Could you take me to Marguerite, please?"

"I think we've met before," Juniper said, as he limped stiffly along the beach. "Didn't you come through our Guardianship with a group of refugees last summer? One of us, Clover the Carer, bit off your broken tail for you."

"Where was that?" asked Stump-Tail. "My memory of that terrible journey is all mixed up in my mind. We came through many Guardianships to end up here."

"Mine was Humanside, at the Blue Pool."

"Not that beautiful place with water the colour of a summer sky? Your Council Leader asked us to stay but we came on. I remember it now. How is Clover? I didn't see her with the others."

They joined Marguerite, Tamarisk and the ex-zervantz, who were sitting grooming themselves in the sunshine and talking to the refugees. They had washed away the salt and drunk deeply from a stream which ran down the valley before disappearing under the shingle at the top of the beach. Now their fur was nearly dry.

Marguerite hopped over to Juniper and brushed whiskers with him. "Are you all right?" she asked.

Juniper looked around guiltily, lowered his voice and said, "I killed the Sun's-child."

"You'd better tell me about it." Marguerite led him away to the stream and, as he washed and drank, she listened as he told her what he could remember of the incident in the surf.

"I heard the noise as I came ashore. I wondered what it was, there was no thunder in the sky. That was the Sun's-child dying?"

"Yes," said Juniper. "It was an accident. I touched the Woodstock by mistake in the darkness. I would have drowned if I had stayed under there much longer."

> *You are forgiven*
> *The Sun's-child died to save you*
> *Your life is needed.*

Marguerite looked around, as if to see who was speaking, then apologised to Juniper. "Sometimes it is as if someone else is speaking through my mouth."

Juniper looked at the bright-eyed squirrel with awe.

Stump-Tail and his party were exchanging stories of hazardous journeys with Marguerite and her companions.

Marguerite had counted the refugees. There was one lot of eight and four more – 14.

"What are your plans now?" Stump-Tail's life-mate, Dandelion, asked.

"We'll rest for a while with you if we may, and work out what to do next. We didn't *plan* this journey."

> *To make the Sun laugh*
> *You tell it, in detail, your*
> *Plans for your Future.*

They all smiled at this Kernel. Then she told the incredulous refugees of all that had happened on Ourland, culminating in their departure from there, and their arrival here, at what they learned was called Worbarrow Bay.

In turn, they heard of the adventures of the refugees when they had followed the Leylines to the coast.

"We must get the Woodstock," said Tamarisk after they had finished, and he started off along the beach.

"Wait," called Juniper after him, "I'll do that."

A crestfallen Tamarisk came back to the group and Juniper went to fetch their weapon, circling around the skin of the Sun's-child cautiously before returning, dragging the Woodstock in his teeth and keeping his paws well clear of the twisted section with the incomprehensible "numbers".

"Where are your dreys?" Marguerite asked Dandelion.

"We don't have any," she replied. "When we got here, at first we thought we were safe and built homes in the trees up the valley where the empty Man-dreys are. Then the Greys came and we were forced to leave."

"What are these empty Man-dreys?" asked Juniper.

"Where humans used to live, but they are like our old dreys now, falling to pieces."

"Perhaps other fierce humans came and drove out the humans who lived there," said Juniper.

"I don't think humans are like that," said Marguerite, remembering the Red-Haired Girl, the Human Who Picked Things Up and the Visitors at the Blue Pool. "I'm *sure* that it couldn't have been that."

"Where *do* you live, then?" asked Tamarisk.

"Up there," said Stump-Tail, waving his paw at the towering grass-covered mound of Worbarrow Tout which projected into the sea, surrounded by water on three sides. "In old rabbit holes," he added, his tail stump dropping in shame.

"Rabbit holes?" said Tamarisk, tactless as ever. "*Rabbit holes?*"

"Up there and on the beach are the only places where the Greys never come, so that's why we live *there*. We scavenge along the beach. You can get quite fond of seafood," said Stump-Tail. "Can't you, Dandelion-Mate?"

"I do still crave a pine kernel," she said. "You didn't bring any with you, I suppose?"

"Sorry," said Juniper. "Never a one."

"When you've eaten, would you like to join us in our holes?" asked Stump-Tail, remembering the rules of hospitality.

> *All passing strangers*
> *Must be accommodated*
> *At whatever cost.*

"It is a long time since I heard that one," replied Marguerite, thinking of Marble's first visit. "Yes. We would be honoured, but please, we are old friends, not strangers," and she stepped forward and to their amazement brushed whiskers Ourland style with all the refugees. "Let's find food together."

As each of them moved away to forage on the beach, with Marguerite guiding them away from the remains of the Sun's-child, a pretty female squirrel approached her shyly. "I don't suppose you will remember me. My name is Meadowsweet. Where is your brother, Rowan the Bold? He's not with you?"

Marguerite turned her head away, then turned back and faced Meadowsweet. "It's rather a sad story," she said. "Can I tell you later?"

Chapter 28

A few days of recuperation followed, Marguerite and her party living amicably with Stump-Tail and the other coast-dwelling squirrels, but longing to get their claws into some tree-bark again. They felt safe enough living in the rabbit holes on Worbarrow Tout and all enjoyed the views over the sea, and of the white cliffs behind them, when on fine days they lay on rock-ledges in the sunshine, glad to be out of the dim burrow-light.

According to the coast-dwellers, humans only came there on two days each week and then they mostly stayed on the beach, very few climbing the steep path to the top of the Tout. The humans were easy for the squirrels to avoid, but it was not a life that any of them could see as a permanent arrangement. Squirrels *need* trees.

Marguerite sat in the sunshine thinking. Stump-Tail was obviously the Senior Squirrel, yet he was not now taking the lead in organising and guiding the group, and the lack of leadership was showing in many little ways – minor quarrels, a feeling of lassitude, morbid nostalgia and most of all a feeling that each day was somehow wasted. Yet he had brought his party safely to this place over the last year, so he must have the right qualities. Perhaps, through having no tail, he felt inhibited or insecure when it came to relationships with her party?

Then there was her own position to consider. Increasingly she wanted to spend time thinking; there was so much in the world that she did not understand and the day-to-day planning disrupted her contemplation. She would love to be a Tagger, she thought.

A good Leader needed a thinker behind him, one who had experienced real difficulties and had overcome them, someone who was respected as a "doer", as well as a "thinker", someone whose recommended tags would be recognised by all as fair and true, be they good or bad.

Was *she* up to this role? She was young for a Tagger and had not even mated yet. But then she seemed to command respect even from much older squirrels. The decision would not be hers anyway; all appointments had to be agreed by the group as a whole. But some squirrel would have to initiate the proceedings. *That* would have to be arranged.

Accordingly she suggested to Stump-Tail that they all get together that evening in Council to discuss plans for the future. He readily agreed and, as the day started to cool, the entire party gathered and sat in the sunshine amongst the sea-pinks and tufts of coarse grass on the top of the Tout, a pleasant sea breeze ruffling their fur and tails.

Marguerite waited for Stump-Tail to commence but he appeared reluctant to make the first move and looked towards her expectantly.

She glanced round, drew a deep breath and said, "*We* have called this meeting to draw up some plans for the future:

Squirrels without aims
Drift through life, vulnerable
To each passing whim.

"And for a group of squirrels to have no aims leaves us exposed to many kinds of danger. I would like to suggest that we choose who is to be our Leader and confirm *him* in that position, then discuss and select a Tagger from amongst ourselves. After that we can decide what our group aims should be. I propose that our friend without a tail be Leader of us all."

Marguerite turned and apologised for not having remembered his *real* name. Since they had been there he had always been called Stump-Tail.

"It's Alder," he told her. "Alder – with the stump-tail."

She recognised that he had said that to cover her embarrassment. It confirmed her belief that he had the sensitivity to be a good Leader, if only he also had the confidence.

"I propose our friend Alder Stump-Tail to be our Leader," Marguerite said again.

There was general agreement, shown by head-noddings and tail-twitchings from the squirrels.

Alder looked pleased, and, unable to give the tail-flick which says "I am willing to accept", bowed his head in an unmistakable gesture of acceptance.

Marguerite waited for Alder to propose a Tagger. In the silence that followed she realised that none of the coast-dwellers had tags; perhaps they had never had tags, and Taggers, at Wolvesbarrow. She glanced appealingly at Juniper the Swimmer.

Juniper drew himself up. "Not only does a group need a wise and steadfast Leader, it also needs a wise and thoughtful Tagger to advise the Leader, teach the dreylings and act as the conscience of the group by allocating tags to each, fairly and fearlessly. *We* have amongst us one such squirrel. I propose Marguerite the Bright One as our Tagger." He flicked his tail, and the others all followed.

Dandelion said, "We didn't have Taggers at our old home. We used to have a wise one whom we called the Bard, who acted as adviser to the Leader, but he was killed by a Grey just before we left and we haven't appointed another, what with one thing and another. I know that we'd all be happy to have Marguerite the Bright One as Bard and Tagger."

Marguerite raised her tail with the exact amount of speed and angle which indicated "I accept, with modesty, and thank you all for the trust you have put in me." There was no need to say it in words.

What she did say was, "Squirrels without tags are not complete squirrels. They have nothing to live up to, or master, and others do not know what to expect of them. If I may use our Leader, Alder, as an example?" She looked at him and he nodded. "While we call him Stump-Tail that will seem to be the most important thing about him and *he* will always be aware of it. Yet he led an entire party safely through many hazardous adventures to reach here. With the power you have given me I award him the tag Who Led His Party to Safety and we will call him simply Alder the Leader. Now it is up to him to take command and guide us wisely. I know that he will have the support of us all."

As she said this, Alder appeared to grow two inches in

height, and his lack of a tail faded into insignificance. He stepped forward, brushed whiskers with Marguerite the Tagger in the way she had taught him, and then confidently took over the meeting.

"Right," he said, "let's discuss what we should be doing, as self-respecting squirrels . . ." and the group, now united, discussed the options open to them.

It was agreed that they could not stay on the Tout. Spring was turning to summer, the flower heads on many of the tufts of sea-pinks were already brown and crisp. Speckled young gulls had left their cliff-face nests and were raucously demanding food from their parents as they sat on the rocks, beaks open to the sky. Yet no squirrel had felt the mating urge and this was a sure Sun-sign that things were not right for them there.

Inland were Greys who had forced them down from the abandoned Man-drey area to this treeless mound of Worbarrow Tout, where they had survived on seafood and by living in rabbit holes. If they were to hold their tails high again they must live, as squirrels, in trees. But where?

As far as they knew, the whole inland area was held by the Greys, and Ourland was a long way off and too dangerous for Marguerite and her party to return to, even if they could.

"We must remember that we have the Woodstock," she told them, "so the Greys won't have it all their own way. If we learn to use that effectively we could win back and hold an area for ourselves. With the Sun's help," she added.

"It would be a dangerous venture, we could all be killed," said Alder.

"That's true," said Marguerite, "and no squirrel should

167

be forced to join such an expedition, but to stay here means a degraded life with no future generations to follow."

Into her mind came a Sun-inspired picture of a lake of blue water sparkling in the bright morning light and she could smell the scent of warm pine bark and resin.

"Let's go and win back the Blue Pool," she said.

Chapter 29

The group, now working happily together, were resting on the top of Flowers Barrow, exhausted from the climb up the cliff-face.

Juniper had practised long and hard with the Woodstock, learning the numbers that had to be written after Marguerite's X to produce waves of different power and intensity. The beach below was littered with splintered pieces of wood that he had used as targets and the thistles on the bank behind were now trying to grow straight again. Having witnessed what it could do, all the other squirrels were now more confident of the success of their venture.

They had probed a little way inland along the stream from which they normally drank, and the only sign of Greys was a decomposing body in the stream itself. They each drank their fill, upstream from the body, watching, listening and scenting for the enemy, and then retreated up on to the Tout again. They would leave at first light and climb the Great Cliff to get to open ground where there would be less chance of meeting Greys. From the top, Dandelion, who was known to be the best at reading the Leylines, would guide them to the Blue Pool.

There had been almost a party atmosphere, a hint of squirrelation, as they had set off at daybreak along the beach to the undercliff, the older ones taking it in turns to drag the Woodstock. But, not being used to moving with a load, they had underestimated the time needed and it was High Sun before they were over the banks of fallen chalk and at the foot of the near-vertical cliff-face ready for the climb.

Juniper and Tamarisk had reconnoitred the face the previous evening, deciding that if they could find a path up, it would be safer than using the Man-track that led up from the valley to the Barrow of the Flowers, close to the edge of the cliff. A Grey attack there, with the cliff behind them and no known retreat route, would not be easy to hold off.

Juniper told Tamarisk:

> *In a strange country,*
> *Be careful. Time spent looking*
> *Is seldom wasted.*

"Not *exactly* appropriate for us now, but the message is right. That is one of the Kernels the Tagger teaches before you go on climbabout."

"This is much more exciting than climbabout," Tamarisk said to him as they had searched for a path to take them to the top.

The route they had found zigzagged up the face perilously, in places so narrow that the Woodstock had had to be dragged end-first with a danger that it might roll over the edge if they let go of it for a moment. Teeth and claws were aching from holding and pulling.

Squirrels ordinarily have no fear of heights up to that of the tallest tree, and they have sharp claws to grip fibrous bark, but climbing a cliff of crumbly white chalk while dragging the Woodstock was an altogether different experience.

They all found the great height brought on dizziness, and Marguerite advised them to keep their eyes on the path and not to look down. The sun, bright on the white chalk when they started their climb, obligingly hid behind a veil of thin cloud so they no longer had to half close their eyes, but seabirds, wheeling in to inspect the strange procession climbing up *their* cliff, screeched at them and sometimes nearly brushed the squirrels off the narrow pathway with their wing tips.

Where the ledge widened slightly near the top, they paused for breath. Marguerite ignored her own advice and peered over the edge to where the sea lay wrinkled far beneath them, patterned by darker stripes where currents ran. Her head swam and she felt dizzy. "Don't look down," she reminded herself. "Trust in the Sun."

Juniper was some way behind, helping Meadowsweet to pass a narrow place that sloped dangerously and where there were loose particles of chalk on the path.

"Can we rest here?" she pleaded when they came to a wider place.

Juniper stopped. The others were ahead but were still in sight, so would not be worrying about them. He was glad of the break too.

Meadowsweet looked at the older squirrel and said, "Would you tell me about Rowan the Bold leading the dreadful Greys away, and saving you all?"

Juniper smiled to himself. He had overheard Meadowsweet ask each of his party to tell her the same story whenever she could get one apart from the others. Having lost his own life-mate to the Greys he understood her feelings.

"Rowan the Bold was a hero," he told her. "There we were, up this fir tree which leant out over a clay-pan with 'lots' of Greys all around us on the ground. There was *no* way we could have escaped. Old Burdock, our Tagger, was exhausted, the rest of us were frightened, we had youngsters with us and no squirrel knew what to do. Then your Rowan crept craftily down the trunk so they could not see where he had come from, and shouted insults at the Greys.

"The whole horde of them ran off after him over the Great Heath, and he must have led them right into a fire, for they never came back. So we escaped and got away to Ourland.

"It was the bravest thing I have ever seen. I would have been proud to have had him for *my* son."

Meadowsweet looked proud herself, her bushy tail rising.

"Do you have any sons?" she asked Juniper.

"No," he replied, "my Bluebell and I were not Sun-blessed that way." He looked out over the sea to where the Isle of Portland lay low in the haze on the far horizon. "It's time we caught up with the others."

"What do you call this place?" Marguerite asked Alder.

They were enjoying the cool evening breeze which was blowing over the grass-covered hilltop.

"This is the Barrow of the Flowers," he replied.

"I can see the flowers," Marguerite said, looking around at the early harebells and the stemless thistles. "What's a barrow?"

"It's a place where the Ley forces start," replied Alder.

Marguerite looked puzzled. "Tell me more about these Ley forces."

"Don't you know about Leylines?" he asked. "How do you find your way about the country?"

"Until last year we had always lived at the Blue Pool and didn't need to. Will you tell me about them?"

"Not all squirrels can read the lines. I can, just, but Dandelion is very good at it. She grew up near the Barrow of the Wolves way up north of here in a big pine forest. There aren't any wolves there now but the name lingers on. I think that if you grow up near a barrow then you become extra sensitive. See if *you* can feel anything here."

He turned his head slowly. "There's a line," he said, "and there's another. There's the one we came in on last year." He pointed to the north. "There are a couple of others further round. Here's a very strong line. Try this one."

Marguerite sat up and turned in the direction indicated. She could see nothing nor sense anything unusual. The others of her party tried sensing in turn. Spindle, normally rather taciturn, called out excitedly, "Uz can feel it, uz can feel it. Uz whizkerz iz telling uz the line."

"How does it feel?" asked Juniper.

"Uz can't really dezcribe it, uz juzt knowz it'z there. And there, and there'z won there." He pointed to the north and then to the north-west.

Juniper tried, but with his whiskers still not fully regrown, he couldn't sense anything. Where he sat was a cigarette-end thrown down by a human earlier that day. The acrid scent was filling his nostrils, reminding him of the times when he and Bluebell had scavenged under the tables at the Eating Man-Drey. He hopped away and looked out over the vastness of the sea. "Bluebell," he sighed, "where are you now?"

Grasshoppers chirruped in the evening sunshine.

"Which way is it to the Blue Pool?" Marguerite asked Dandelion.

"Well, if you were to retrace the Leylines we took, you would go north to the Barrow of the Ferns, then turn away a bit to the Water Barrow, then north-east across a big heath to the Drinking Barrow and up to the barrow where we met the Three Lords."

"Who in the Sunless Pit are the Three Lords?" asked Tamarisk.

"We got to this particular barrow and I could feel a very strong force from the east, strong enough for several barrows together," said Dandelion. "We were going to go that way when three Greys appeared. They stopped us and wouldn't let us pass. The chief one called himself Lord Obsidian and the others were Lord Malachite and Lord Silicon. They said they were going to kill us but we pleaded with them and in the end they agreed to spare us if we turned south-west and didn't stop until we reached the sea. Mind you, we didn't really know what the sea was then. We do now, though!"

"Which way is it from the Three Lords Barrow to the Blue Pool?" asked Marguerite, her mind focused on their mission.

"South-east to the Icen Barrow, then pick up the force towards the mound where 'lots' of humans live. The one with the broken Man-drey on. That line passes right across your pool."

"We leave in the morning," Alder announced firmly. "We'll find shelter in a rabbit hole for tonight."

Chapter 30

When they were all huddled together cosily in the abandoned rabbit warren near the top of the Barrow of the Flowers, Marguerite asked Dandelion to tell them more about the Leylines. Dandelion knew lots of old legends and stories going back as far as the time of Acorn, the first squirrel, and loved to tell them to anyone ready and willing to listen. She only needed the slightest encouragement to launch into a story.

"And thereby hangs a tale," she would say. "Once upon a time . . ."

As the other squirrels jostled for position around Dandelion, Marguerite smiled as she recalled overhearing that "squamp" Tamarisk entertaining a group of yearlings one afternoon a week ago on the Tout below.

"Once upon a branch," he had started, mimicking Dandelion's Wolvesbarrow accent perfectly, "sat Acorn, the first squirrel in the world, holding a Council Meeting, all by himself, when he broke the first wind in the world. He looked round to see where it had come from. 'And thereby hangs a tail,' he said to himself."

There had been a snigger from his audience.

Marguerite had called to him quietly, but loud enough for the other yearlings to hear, "Tamarisk, when you grow out of being the Tactless I hope that I don't have to tag you the Rude Mimic."

There had been silence from the other side of the rock.

Now, with the whole group listening, Dandelion was in full voice.

"I think that the Leylines must always have been there, but my grandfather told me that *he* had been told that it was the humans who made them work many, many generations ago. They built the barrows on top of the hills and then smaller ones along the lines that appeared. Sometimes they made cones of soil which have since been flattened by the weather into low mounds; often they stood great stones up on end, sometimes they planted beautiful groups of pine trees on hilltops, but always on the Ley-force lines which are absolutely straight."

"Always?" asked Marguerite, fascinated by a subject so new to her.

"Always, absolutely," replied Dandelion. "Then, to move about the country through the trees, they followed the Leylines from marker to marker. In those days, my grandfather said, the whole country was covered in trees. A squirrel could go from the sea to the sea and never touch ground!"

"Do humans use them now?" Marguerite asked.

"I don't think so, they seem always to follow paths if they're walking, or roadways when they go about in groups in those smelly things. I think they've forgotten Leylines. I don't believe they even use them for sending messages now."

"Messages?" Marguerite's ears pricked up.

"That's another thing my grandfather told me. He was a wonderful old squirrel, what he didn't know wasn't worth knowing. I learned so much from him."

"Tell us about the messages," Marguerite said eagerly.

"When humans wanted other people to know something and did not want to walk there and tell them, they would go up to a high barrow and make special thoughts, facing along the Leyline the way that they wanted to send the message. A human at the other end would listen in another special way and know what the first one was thinking. Then if the message was not for them, they would turn and 'think' it along the next line until it got to where it had to go. The humans who did this wore long covers, the colour of snow, and would hold a bunch of mistletoe in their hands when they were 'thinking' the messages."

"Are you serious, or are you pulling our paws?" asked Tamarisk.

"Only passing on what my grandfather told me," Dandelion replied. "But the bit about following the lines is true, you saw it today. *I* can sense them and so can Spindle.

"The next thing my grandfather told me, even *I* find hard to believe. He may have been pulling *my* paw, he did sometimes." She smiled at the recollection. "He told me that at dawn, before the humans used the Leylines for messages, the squirrels did, in exactly the same way. Just face along the line the way you wanted to send a message and think. Of course there had to be a squirrel at the other end to receive it or it was a waste of time. I never knew whether to believe that.

"He also told me about Acorn, the first squirrel in the

world, and how he used to . . . But that's another story. I'll tell you that one tomorrow evening."

"Tell us now," demanded the squirrels, who loved a story.

Alder was about to check her but, on glancing at Marguerite, saw the tiny tail-flick indicating that a story might be good for morale. He nodded to Dandelion.

Chapter 31

"Once upon a time," Dandelion started, "there was Acorn, the first squirrel in the world.

"He sat in the First Great Oak, feeling lonely. All about him he could see other animals and birds and insects going about in pairs, mating and having youngsters or laying eggs and he thought, I'd like to have a mate like all these other creatures.

"So, that night he said a Needing Kernel to the Sun:

> *Oh Great Loving Sun*
> *What I need most at this time –*
> *Is another squirrel*

but that didn't work because there were six sounds in the last line, not five – so he tried again:

> *Oh Great Loving Sun*
> *What I need most at this time –*
> *Is a Mate.*

"But that only had three sounds, so he tried again:

Oh Great Loving Sun
What I need most at this time –
Is a loving Mate,

and the Sun, recognising the 5, 7, 5 sound pattern of a truly thought-out Kernel, arranged for Acorn to find a walnut in his drey when he woke up in the morning.

"Aha, he thought, the Sun is testing me; a walnut is not a mate, it's not even like a squirrel – but it's like a bird's egg. What's it like?" Dandelion looked at her audience seated round her in the dim burrow-light, listening intently.

"A bird's egg," they called back, enjoying the participation.

" 'Now what can I do with a bird's egg?' Acorn asked himself."

"Eat it?" called a voice from somewhere behind her and a laugh went through the audience.

"If he had done – none of us would be here now," Dandelion pointed out. She continued, "Maybe I can hatch it myself, Acorn thought, but then, as he sat outside his drey, he saw a woodcock come flying in through the trees below him to settle on its nest in the leaves on the ground.

"He climbed down and frightened the long-billed bird away. In the nest were three eggs which looked rather like walnuts, so Acorn carefully placed his special walnut egg in the nest, then climbed back up the tree and waited. Soon he saw the woodcock come jinking back through the trees to settle on the nest and brood, watching all about it with its eyes that are on the top of its head so that it can see in all directions at the same time.

"Every day after this, when the woodcock flew away to feed in the first swamp in the world, Acorn came down from his tree to listen at the nest. One day he heard the gentle tap, tap, tap of the woodcock chicks breaking out of their eggshells, so he carried his warm walnut up to his drey and sat there watching it. But nothing happened.

"He tried the What Do I Do Next Kernel:

Oh Great Loving Sun
You have set me a challenge
Help me to crack it,

and, as he said these words, he realised that all he had to do was to open *this* nut as he would any other.

"Carefully holding the precious brown nut, he split it open ever so gently and inside was – was – a tiny squirrel, all curled up and wet. He put down the empty halves of the shell and, holding the little red ball between his paws, he blew it dry, and as he did this it grew bigger and bigger, like a dragonfly does when it comes out of the water, until at last it was a perfect female squirrel.

"It was, of course, love at first sight. Acorn named her Primrose, which means the first of the flowers, as she *was* as pretty as a flower. Since then all true female squirrels are named after flowers, as all true male squirrels are named after trees.

"Acorn taught Primrose all he knew about foraging and drey-building and *she* taught him how to have fun and the joys of the mating chase. It was a very happy time for them both.

"Then one day, as they were playing in an oak tree,

Acorn picked an oak apple, young and brightly coloured green and red, and held it out to Primrose."

The squirrels nudged one another and giggled. They had all had that trick played on them, and in their turn had played it on others.

"Primrose took the beautiful thing and, trusting Acorn absolutely, bit into it.

"Not only was the oak apple bitter and nasty, but in the middle was a horrid little white grub, and to this day female squirrels never really trust males, *especially* when they bring gifts."

Dandelion looked round. The older females were nodding in agreement and the males were shaking their heads as if to say "That doesn't apply to me."

Marguerite slept little that night. As well as reviewing the first day's journey, she was wondering what the next day would have in store for them and was thinking through the implications of message-sending. How wonderful it would be if she could let her parents and her dear grandmother know that they were all alive and well.

At first light they set off northwards along the Leyline, heading for the Barrow of the Ferns, guided by Dandelion who stopped frequently to sense the direction of the force. They also needed regular rest periods as it was hard work dragging and pulling the Woodstock along. The older squirrels took turns to reconnoitre while the others rested, Juniper staying near to whichever pair of squirrels were in charge of the Woodstock, in case of a surprise attack by Greys.

As it happened, the precautions weren't needed. The country seemed empty of the enemy and each day's travel had been relatively uneventful. They had back-tracked on the refugees' route of the previous year, passing over the Barrow of the Ferns, the Water Barrow and the Drinking Barrow before turning almost due north towards the barrow where the three mysterious Lords had intercepted the fleeing party.

It was during one of the rest periods that Marguerite had another opportunity to talk to Dandelion about Earth forces.

The squirrels were, at this time, seated high in a tree looking out over the Army's tank and gunnery range, watching great brown and black patterned machines manoeuvring on the heath, distant and remote from them. They had seen the red flags marking the range boundaries but, as with so many of Man's structures and symbols, these meant nothing to the squirrels.

"What do *you* think makes the Greys' Stone force work?" Marguerite asked Dandelion.

These two females had come to respect each other's abilities in the time they had spent together and were now firm friends.

Dandelion looked around. The others were all out of ear-twitch. "They must tap one of Earth's hidden forces and focus it with the stone patterns. There are lots of forces we don't know much about. I know a little about the Leylines but my grandfather said that he believed that humans used an Earth force to find the north direction."

Marguerite looked puzzled. "Why would they need that? One only has to see where the moss on a tree grows to know which way is north, and on a clear night, if you poke your head out of your drey and look at the stars that make the Great Squirrel, you can see that its paws point to the star that is always in the north."

"Don't try and understand humans, my grandfather used to say. But they do know more about these things than we do. On our way south from Wolvesbarrow last year, we came to a line of huge metal trees that men must have made, with thin branches reaching from one to another. It was a wet day and some kind of force was blowing along those branches. We could hear it snapping and crackling and hissing and our whiskers were tingling and itching. We scampered under those, I can tell you."

Marguerite was silent, thinking of the force that made the Woodstock so powerful. Every squirrel knows the power of the Life-Force as it rises in the trees each spring. A sensitive squirrel can detect it moving upwards and outwards into every twig and leaf. She tried to picture the force rising in the hazel stem that formed the Woodstock *and* in the encircling honeysuckle bine, each trying to expand and outgrow the other. What a powerful but silent struggle this would be! The force would be trapped in the very fibres of the hazel, and held there in the form of a Woodstock, waiting to be released by *her* numbers.

A group of men were walking up the slope towards the tree, dressed in clothes the colour of ripe pine cones. The squirrels watched them through the leaves and saw them stop and stand in a group below where they sat. Occasionally one of the men would point across the heath and the others would hold black things up in front of their eyes.

Suddenly, from the straight branch projecting from one

185

of the machines in the distance, they saw a bright flash of light, followed by a loud crash. The squirrels ducked their heads instinctively. There was another flash and a crash from the hillside to their left and they ducked again.

"It looks as if humans have captured the thunder and lightning force," said Dandelion.

"I hope the Sun guides them to use it wisely," Marguerite replied. "It worries me sometimes, that if we tamper with forces we don't completely understand they may get out of control."

In all, two weeks on the march passed before they reached the Three Lords Barrow, which they approached warily.

There was no sign of the Lords, but they did find, under the furze bushes near the top of the mound, a squirrel skeleton with the remains of a grey tail attached.

"One less," said Alder, nosing at the remains disdainfully and, following the route pointed out by Dandelion, they turned south-west across a field and a roadway towards the Icen Barrow on the last-but-one leg to the Blue Pool.

Chapter 32

The squirrels crossed the roadway just before High Sun and passed through a small wood of chestnut and oak trees and were then on to heathland again.

"I can smell water. There must be a pool nearby," said Alder. "Although I can't remember seeing it on our way through here last year."

The scent was coming to them from somewhere south of the Leyline they were following, so the pool must be that way, hidden by the screen of pines on their right-paw side.

Tamarisk and Spindle, who were sent to find it, climbed one of the trees and looked down. The water was orangey brown and all around the edges were huge pink and white flowers set amongst dark green circular leaves. A heron was wading in the water near an Eyeland with three graceful trees on it.

If a heron was there, nothing dangerous was about. They slipped down the trunk and reported to the others.

"We'll break there," said Alder. "We could all use a rest and a drink."

Rowan was woken from sleep by a harsh squawk from his

guardian bird. The wary heron had just seen the party of strange squirrels appear on the top of the sand-cliff and, having vented his annoyance, had flown huffily away.

Something was about, thought Rowan, he must be careful, though he knew he was safer here on his Eyeland than on the mainland. He looked through a screen of twigs, then scratched himself to make sure he really was awake.

On the sand-cliff opposite stood his dear sister Marguerite, with Juniper, another squirrel without a tail whom he thought he had seen before, and "lots" of others; and, just behind them, he was sure he could see the face that had filled his dreams for a full year now. Could that really be Meadowsweet?

Now she had come to the edge of the sand-cliff and was looking towards the Eyeland.

"Meadowsweet," he called over the water, his voice breaking, "is it really you?"

"Rowan, my love!" she called back, oblivious of the stares of the other squirrels, and they all saw a squirrel leap from the upper branches of a tree on the Eyeland, to drop into the water and swim strongly ashore.

They all stood gaping as the wet animal scrabbled up the bank and hugged the slender female, their whiskers a-tangle. Then he turned to Marguerite who, realising who he was, had hopped nearer and was subjected to the same damp embrace.

"Rowan!"

"Meadowsweet, Marguerite! I thought I would never see either of you again."

"We thought you were caught by the fire . . ."

The excited squirrels chattered on, all talking at once,

until Alder interrupted, saying, "I greet you, Rowan, who I recall is tagged the Bold."

Rowan, remembering his manners, responded. "And I greet you . . . ?"

"Alder the Leader, father of Meadowsweet, whom you have soaked to the skin." He smiled at the handsome young squirrel as he said this, and Rowan grinned back.

". . . Alder the Leader, father of Meadowsweet, whom I have soaked to the skin and wish to have for my life-mate."

"You are well tagged, Rowan the Bold. If my Meadowsweet agrees, I would have no objection to such a mating."

The group foraged under the trees, drinking the sweet water and exchanging news. Rowan told how he had given up hope of finding the others alive after the fire and had crossed the Great Heath to this pool with his Eyeland, where he had learned to swim, so that he could live safely, surrounded by water, spending his time in celibacy and contemplation. Marguerite was intrigued to know that, despite all this time which he had been able to give to contemplation, he had not found out what came after eight, and she looked forward to explaining numbers to him later.

In their turn, they told him all that had happened to their parties in the past year, but how much Rowan took in, no squirrel could tell, for he did not take his eyes off Meadowsweet until the evening light faded.

They all climbed a tree near the shore of Rowan's Pool to sleep, having declined his offer to teach them to swim so that they could visit his magical Eyeland, but after it was dark, Marguerite was sure that she heard two soft splashes in the warm night. In the early dawn she saw Rowan and Meadowsweet licking each other dry on the shore below, but said nothing.

The party, now including Rowan, a little sorry to leave his Eyeland, moved off an hour later following the Leyline to the Icen Barrow where they disturbed a pair of deer lying up in a hollow under the vanilla-scented gorse that covered the mound. On the flattened grass in the sweetly smelling resting place of the deer, they held a Tagging Meeting, as Marguerite now felt able confidently to allocate meaningful tags to them all.

Dandelion was confirmed as the Ley Reader. Tamarisk's tag of the Tactless became the Forthright which he believed meant the same thing, but was pleased nevertheless. Spindle was tagged the Helpful because he always seemed to anticipate what other squirrels required and provided it, even before they realised their need themselves. Wood Anemone earned the tag of the Able because she could turn her paw to any task, no matter how great or small, and performed it without complaint. Both these squirrels were holding their tails high now.

Meadowsweet was tagged Rowan's Love as she seemed to have no life or interest beyond her love for him.

Juniper, to his great pleasure, was up-tagged the Steadfast.

Excitement was building when they left the Icen Barrow. They were nearing the Blue Pool area and although they did not expect to meet Greys in any numbers on the heathland, each knew that very soon they could be fighting against superior numbers of squirrels who would have the advantages of position, recent local knowledge, and, if they understood the term that Marble had once used to them, possession. Each was looking about nervously.

Dandelion reported with consternation that the Leyline from there to the great ruined Man-drey, which crossed the Blue Pool, was distorted and was behaving in an unusual way. "It's trying to curve away to the north and is breaking up," she told them. "Leylines don't do that. They are *always* perfectly straight. I don't know which way to go. We could miss your pool altogether."

The heat-haze over the heath hid any distant landmarks, even clumps of trees nearby were shimmering and insubstantial, so Alder called a halt and the senior squirrels got together to reformulate plans.

"We don't want to take on the Greys in unfamiliar countryside," Alder stated. "We must be in an area we know if we are going to surprise them. Remember, there are lots more of them than there are of us."

"Even more than when we left, they will have had a whole breeding year since then," Juniper added.

"*I* know this area," said Rowan. "I came through here on my way back from climbabout. At the end of the heath is a field, then a roadway, then a field shaped like a dog's leg, then it's the edge of the Beachend Guardianship. We need to go *this* way."

"Now for the Greys," said Juniper.

"Right," said Tamarisk.

Rowan was correct. That evening they reached the roadway, crossed the Dogleg Field and gathered together in the corner of the wood at the extreme western tip of the old Beachend Guardianship, whispering excitedly and watching for any sign of Greys.

"We should wait until morning before we go in," Marguerite advised Alder. "When we hear the big gates open it will be safer, as the Greys are less likely to attack us if Visitors are about."

Alder acknowledged her local experience and ordered a withdrawal back across the Dogleg Field to spend a watchful night in a hedgerow tree.

"My whiskers ache," Marguerite heard Tamarisk say in the morning.

"So do mine," said Dandelion, "I thought it was from the strain of following the Leylines."

The squirrels reported that they all had an unusual dull ache around the base of their whiskers, but none could suggest an explanation.

The sun was hidden by an early mist as they started off again, Marguerite hopping eagerly in front. Near the corner of the wood Alder called to her and she stopped. He told the others to position themselves some yards out in the field.

"You stay here in charge, Juniper," Alder instructed him. "When we hear that gate, I'll go with Marguerite to discover where the Greys are. Keep the Woodstock here. If you see any Greys, use it. *Don't* take any chances. You're responsible for the safety of this group. Keep the others behind you, mount the Woodstock on this mound – that way you can cover all the ground from here to the wood-edge – but *don't* power it at us by mistake when we come back!"

Having ensured that the Woodstock was on firm, raised ground, they waited for the sound of the gate, then, her heart thumping with excitement, Marguerite led Alder into the familiar woodland surrounding the Blue Pool.

Chapter 33

The mist had thinned out and drifted away and the sun was shining above them as the pair entered the trees, the shadows in the wood seeming unusually deep and sharp. Marguerite scented the air. This was her home! That was the water-scent, this was the home-pine smell, different in some subtle way from that of pines in all the other places through which she had travelled.

All around was the leaf-litter smell and on the paths the scents left by the Visitors from the day before stirred memories of happier days.

They climbed a tree, and then she and Alder moved cautiously through the Beachend treetops towards Humanside, watchful for any grey shapes in the trees, in the bushes, or on the ground below. None was to be seen and there did not even seem to be any scent of Greys. Nevertheless she led the way cautiously, startled at one point by a noisy rustling of leaves from the ground, but it was only a male blackbird searching for food. At last, they looked down on to the pool she loved.

It was no longer blue!

There seemed to be tiny vibrations disturbing the water,

hardly noticeable in themselves, yet enough to spoil any reflections, even on a day as bright as this one. The Blue Pool was just a dull grey colour.

Marguerite and Alder circled past the Man-dreys, seeing the Red-Haired Girl and the Human Who Picked Things Up talking on the steps, but with no sign of any scavenging Greys around the tables. Then on through Deepend to Steepbank where together they climbed up the old Council Tree. There were strange dreys there, but most were in a state of disrepair.

"I think the Greys have left," Marguerite whispered to Alder.

"Do you really?" he asked, hopefully.

"The Sun has been good to us. But . . ." She looked up through the pine needles, then down at the water. It should have been blue but it still wasn't. Something was seriously wrong. And her whiskers were aching intolerably.

Juniper was restless as he crouched behind the Woodstock waiting for hordes of savage Greys to come charging out of the wood to overwhelm him. Hot as it was, he struggled to stay alert, ready to defend his charges, should the enemy appear. As long as the Woodstock worked as well on the Greys as it had on The Nipper, they should be all right, he thought. The rest of the party dozed in the sun-warm grass behind him.

His eyelids kept closing in the drowsy heat and he forced himself to stay awake. *He* had been left in charge. He imagined Marguerite's contempt if she found him asleep at his post. What terrible tag would she give him then: Juniper the Dozy, or Juniper Who Risked the Lives of his

Friends by Sleeping? He stretched and walked around in a circle. "Sun, it's hot!" A movement at the wood-edge caught his eye and he scurried back to position himself behind the Woodstock.

As he watched, a grey squirrel hopped out from under the trees and scented the air. Juniper rotated the weapon so that it was aimed directly at the Grey and then reached forward to scratch a number as he had done a houndread times in practice on the Tout. His elbow locked. He could not move it forward. This was another *squirrel* he was about to kill in cold blood! That would make him no better than the Greys who had killed Bluebell at the poolside. He remembered Alder's instructions and went to reach forward again. Marguerite would be livid if she knew he had disobeyed the Leader's clear orders. She might even be watching, but still he could not bring himself to scratch the number on the grey twist of the Woodstock after the X.

The Grey hopped nearer, watching Juniper on the mound. He paused, stood to his full height and called out, keeping his tail low, "I come as a friend."

Juniper looked at him for a moment, then said, "Come forward slowly – very slowly. I only have to touch *this* and you're Sun-gone for sure. Are there more of you in the wood?"

"No. There is only me left now. All the other Silvers are gone. Grey Death has taken them. Every last one, but me," he added sadly, spreading his forelimbs as he said it.

Juniper saw then that the Grey had a paw missing.

The other squirrels had woken on hearing the voices and were gathering in a group behind Juniper and the Woodstock.

"A Grey, a Grey," shouted Tamarisk. "Get him with the Woodstock, Juniper, get him."

"No. Stay where you are and watch the wood-edge, I don't know if we can trust him. It may be a trick."

When Alder and Marguerite returned, soon after High Sun, to report the mysterious absence of any other squirrels, they were amazed to find the party grouped around a single Grey, with the Woodstock lying discarded on the mound. Marguerite looked sharply at Juniper, then at the Grey.

She recognised him. "Marble?" she asked.

"Yes, Bright Marguerite, it's me, Marble. Known to most as Three Paws," he added wryly. "The one who taught you the meaning of power when we first met. You were a dreyling then."

"Where are the other Greys?" she asked coldly.

"I was telling your friends how all the silver squirrels but me caught the Grey Death. Only your Sun knows how I avoided it. Even the biggest Power Square ever built couldn't protect them."

Chapter 34

Sure now that Marble was alone, they had all moved out of the heat into the cool of the wood and gathered round to hear his story. Marguerite had quietly told Juniper to stay at the back of the group with the Woodstock near him, "just in case".

Marble began. "At first, there were only a few sick squirrels. A new batch of colonists had just arrived from Woburn, travelling fast, and they had only taken about two moons to come all the way. They were what we call a 'randee' lot. No respect for the old moral standards, just mated with any squirrel they fancied at the time. But that's beside the point.

"They were allocated territories in New New England – you used to call that precinct Steepbank – and settled in well, but they would often go over to New Connecticut and mingle with the Silvers there. You remember Gabbro? He used to tell me what was going on. Such parties! As I said, they were a randee lot.

"Then a week or so later some of the local Silvers took poorly, nothing you could put your claw on, so to speak, they just looked a mite peaky and then within a few days they were, what do you so quaintly call it, Sun-gone?"

"What do you call it?" Marguerite asked.

"Zapped," replied Marble. "But call it what you like, they were gone. My friend Gabbro was one of the first to go. He loved those Randees.

"Then it started happening all over. There were squirrels falling out of trees like chestnuts in a gale. None ever recovered. The odd thing about it was that the Grey Death did not seem to get the very elderly, or the dreylings until they reached mating age. The old ones and the youngsters are usually the first to catch any sickness that's about. This seemed different. We called it 'Grey Death' because it made the silver fade out of our fur and just leave it dull. I went over to New Connecticut to help out but there was nothing much I could do.

"Then the Three Lords came through and gave orders that a giant Power Square was to be built on the dried-out Clay-Pan. They said it would protect us from the Grey Death. All Silvers, sick or well, were to collect and lay out stones. *Each side* was to have this many."

(Here Marble made this symbol with a stick and six fir cones.

"It took three weeks just to collect them. Many squirrels were so ill that they didn't survive this work, and collapsed and died while searching and carrying. I seemed to be the fittest, but with a paw missing I couldn't carry, so I was laying out the stones line after line after line. Sun, was I tired!"

*64 rows of 64 = 4096 total.

He paused to judge the effect his story was having on the Reds. They were spellbound. Feeling some of his old pleasure when holding an audience, he continued, "I had to leave out certain key and corner stones or I would have been overcome by the Power myself. A block of four larger keystones in the very centre, and the four corner stones, had to be added last. That was dangerous work. Finally I rolled in the keystones, positioned those and then had to run for my life down between two of the rows as the Power started to build up.

"At the same time four other squirrels had been selected to place the corner stones. The Lords had not told them that it was to be *their* body-power that would be used to start the force and not one of the four got clear."

"But you did, obviously," said Tamarisk.

"Yes, I was fit even if I was tired. I got away over the bank just in time. The Three Lords didn't. They wanted to stay and see it work. They were so proud of what they had had us make that they just sat on the top of the bank staring down. I watched them fall one by one. Then I ran away." He paused.

"So no Greys survived but you?" Alder asked.

"I am the only Silver left now," replied Marble, "so it was all to no avail and the Power Square will run for ever."

"Was it the square-thing that saved you?" asked Tamarisk.

"No. Grey Death has just passed me by, I think," Marble replied.

"Is it the Power Square that makes everything feel odd round here?" asked Juniper. "My whiskers have been aching all day."

"Mine too," said Dandelion. "And it was probably the Power Square affecting the Leyline and the colour of the pool."

"We must destroy it," said Marguerite.

"Impossible," said Marble.

"Nothing is impossible," responded Marguerite and her voice continued:

> *If you think you can*
> *Or if you think you cannot,*
> *Either way it's true.*

"Tomorrow we destroy that square," said Alder decisively.

"We must ask the Sun for help," said Dandelion unexpectedly.

"We will," replied Marguerite. "But also remember one of Old Burdock's favourite Kernels."

> *Your prayers alone*
> *Will not do. The Sun will help*
> *Those who help themselves.*

The lone Grey joined them as they prayed, closing his eyes and keeping his tail low.

Chapter 35

Marble had shown a marked reluctance to leave them as darkness fell. They were still discussing ways of destroying the Power Square until finally Alder told him that they were retreating for the night and if he was going to help, he could meet them here at the wood-edge just after dawn. With some hesitation, Marble left them and the Reds recrossed the Dogleg Field, taking the Woodstock with them.

Marguerite and Dandelion were together, talking, as Juniper and Tamarisk dragged it along through the grass behind them.

"Do you really think that all the Greys are dead?" Dandelion asked.

"You sound like Chestnut, who used to be one of the Guardians of Deepend," Marguerite said. "He was tagged the Doubter. But yes, I think Marble is telling the truth. Did you notice that he joined our prayers? It's strange to have come all this way fearing the Greys, only to find a different enemy."

Tamarisk, who had overheard the conversation, tapped the Woodstock and said optimistically, "With this we can zap Greys or stones."

"I don't know if zap is the right word for stones," Marguerite said, "but with the help of the Sun, tomorrow we'll find out."

Marble was waiting, as agreed, at the edge of the wood and he foraged with the Reds, his tail conspicuously low, and again joined in their prayers, before they all moved off towards the Clay-Pan, the aches in their whisker-roots growing more painful with every tree they passed. They went through woodland and patches of scrub familiar to Marguerite, Juniper, Rowan and Tamarisk, until they came to the edge of the area they had last seen devastated by the fire in the previous year. In place of the blackened, smoking mass of ash and charred heather stems, a forest of the tall, feathery stems of rosebay-willowherb waved in the breeze, releasing their fluffy seeds to drift away and colonise any other newly exposed ground before the native plants could re-establish themselves.

The squirrels moved through the stems, noting the new bright green shoots sprouting from the bases of the heather plants and the mosses and lichens beginning to cover the burnt-over ground.

As they neared the Clay-Pan and their whisker-aches grew almost unbearable, they saw how even the rosebay plants were stunted and the heather shoots weaker. The rim of the hollow containing the Clay-Pan was barren of vegetation of any kind.

They flattened themselves to the ground, wriggled to the edge and peered over. Just as Marble had described it, the clay surface was covered with line after line of stones, each one in perfect alignment, and in the very centre of the square were the four keystones, larger than the rest. Next to each corner stone lay the dried-up body of a grey squirrel.

Waves of sickening Power washed over the Reds and they moved back to crouch in the stunted growth, out of sight of the square.

"Look," said Marguerite, "all the needles on that tree are withered up."

She was pointing to the old fir in which they had hidden from the Grey posse the previous summer. It still leaned out over the Clay-Pan and had been exposed to the Power of the square ever since it had been activated by the deaths of the four Greys.

"Any ideas?" she asked the nervous squirrels.

"There might be one way," said Marble. "If I were to run out along that tree trunk and drop on to the keystones, I should be able to disrupt the Power for long enough for four of you to displace the corner stones."

"It'll kill you," said Marguerite, "and the other four."

"Probably the first and possibly the second," replied Marble. "Have you got any better ideas?"

"We should try the Woodstock," said Juniper.

The Woodstock was brought up and sighted first on to the keystones and then on to each corner stone in turn. Juniper tried first but, having scratched every number from 2 as far as 7 after the X, there was no noticeable effect. The spiralling power surged from the Woodstock as before, but was deflected upwards and lost in the withered needles of the overhanging fir.

He tried again and again and then had to retire, vomiting from the effects of the Stone force that he had been exposed to.

Marguerite tried but was no more successful, then Rowan, who, though unfamiliar with the weapon, insisted on trying until he too was forced back from the rim of the Clay-Pan.

Tamarisk tried, but he soon reported that the force from the Woodstock must be exhausted as he could get no response, whatever number he scratched.

"Are you really prepared to drop on to the keystones?" Alder asked Marble. "You'll be Sun-gone in an instant."

"I'll kick those stones out of line first," he replied. "I owe you this for the trouble we Silvers have brought you." There was a look of grim determination in his eyes.

Alder looked at him, then around the group and said, "Now I want three volunteers to help me deal with the corner stones."

"I'll be one," said Juniper the Steadfast and was immediately joined by Tamarisk the Forthright and Rowan the Bold. Meadowsweet put a restraining paw on Rowan's shoulder but he turned, brushed whiskers with her and moved over to where Alder was giving instructions.

"Act only when Marble has dropped, then we'll rush out of cover and kick away the corner stones. Don't miss. Trust in the Sun."

They moved off to get into position.

"The Sun be with you," Marguerite called to Marble and he acknowledged this by putting the stump of his paw diagonally across his chest, then crouched and wriggled to the base of the tree trunk. Here he paused, feeling the vibrations with his three good paws as the Power broke down the very fibres within the tree. He raised his head and watched the red volunteers get into their places.

"Now," he shouted, "now, now!" and ran awkwardly on his three paws, up and along the sloping trunk before launching himself through the air, to land, kicking and scrabbling amongst the stones below.

There was no change in the Power waves. He had missed the keystones!

Alder, crouched as near as he could to the corner stone he was to displace, watched in horror as Marble's kicking slowed to a spasmodic twitch. He ran forward, signalling to the other volunteers to do the same, but was repelled by the Stone force and rolled back, covered in dry clay-dust.

The other squirrels were having no more success. "Again," he called, "again." It was like leaping upwind in a gale.

After three more attempts, he signalled "retreat"; they crawled back to join the others sheltering beyond the bank and the volunteers lay in the dust retching and vomiting, hardly able to move.

"Is Marble Sun-gone?" Alder asked.

"Yes," said Marguerite. "A brave squirrel, despite his colour."

When they had recovered somewhat they sat in a circle, each trying to think of some new way to destroy the evil thing on the Clay-Pan. It was Tamarisk who spoke out at last.

"There's nothing else for it. One of *us* is going to have to scatter the keystones."

Rowan, without thinking further, started towards the leaning tree, saw Meadowsweet out of the corner of his eye, turned to give her a farewell hug and as he did so collided with Alder who was heading for the tree himself. Both squirrels, disoriented by the effect of their ordeal in the Clay-Pan, fell over and rolled in the dust which rose in clouds and blinded them.

Marguerite had been looking at the fir tree as Tamarisk was speaking, seeing its brown and sickly foliage, and thinking of the Power spreading out to destroy other beautiful trees. Would her pool ever be blue again? She stood up and moved deliberately towards the leaning fir trunk.

Juniper, who as usual was watching her, realised her intention and, sick as he was, gathered his strength, ran towards the tree, shouldered her roughly out of the way and leapt for the leaning trunk.

He scrabbled to hold on, a piece of rotten bark turning to powder under his claws as he dug deeper, searching for firm wood. It was as though the whole tree was punkwood and would give him no grip. Marguerite was on the trunk behind him. Juniper tried to kick her away.

Then, as though the tiny additional weight of the squirrels was too much, the ancient tree, rotten through from the continuous Power waves, with no sound other than the rustling of the dead and dying needles, collapsed and fell on to the clay.

Juniper and Marguerite jumped clear as the trunk shattered on the hard-baked ground, brittle branches breaking off and, in falling, sweeping away and destroying the pattern and the Power of the stones for ever.

The force died with a whimper, more felt than heard, and in the silence that followed a skylark sang high over the Great Heath.

Marguerite stood up, and embraced Juniper silently. "Now to the pool," she said, dusting the clay-dust from her fur. "Faith *can* fell fir trees."

Later, on the sweet-scented pine needles below the Council Tree at Steepbank, she spoke to the squirrels at a special meeting called by Alder, the pool a bright sapphire blue below them.

"We all have a job to do. We must repopulate this lovely land. Each pair of you can choose a Guardianship. Go now, there is some serious mating to be done."

She turned her rump to Juniper the Steadfast, who, scenting her readiness, needed no second bidding as she raced away through the treetops, closely pursued by him.

1, 2, 3 . . .

Chapter 36

On Ourland, Fern had wanted Oak to take over Ex-King Willow's drey in the magnificent Royal Macrocarpa Tree behind Brownsea Castle. Oak had refused, even though Ex-King Willow and Ex-Kingz Mate Thizle had moved out themselves to a more humble drey near the lagoon.

"It wouldn't be right, my dear," he explained. "All that kind of thing is past. We've quietly got to change things to a more sensible arrangement. But we *do* need a new drey in a more central position. Let's go and find a site near the pond in Beech Valley."

The Royal Macrocarpa itself, now abandoned by the squirrels, possibly just being over-mature, or perhaps sensing the shame of the injustice witnessed in its branches, was in decline and losing its foliage in showers with every breeze. By the Longest Day it was a bare skeleton of a tree.

Oak and Old Burdock were together in the new Council Tree near the Beech Valley pond. The tree was a full-grown beech, rooted on the very edge of the pool which, though smaller by far than the Blue Pool, still sent up a delicious water-scent on hot days. The clicking and whirring of dragonflies' wings below reminded them of home.

The water-lilies in the pond they had recognised as being the kind of flowers that Rowan had described as being at the Eyeland pool he had found while on climbabout, in those peaceful days before the Greys had come to spoil it all.

Burdock was a very old squirrel now.

"You have so many grey hairs I thought it was Marble come again," Oak had "pulled her paw", as she hauled herself breathlessly up the trunk to stretch out on the wide branch, shaded from the sun by the canopy of glossy green leaves.

"We must appoint a new Tagger," she told him, looking down at the water and the lilies, "I'll be Sun-gone soon."

"We'll all miss you," Oak told her warmly. "I can't imagine not having you about, with a Kernel for every occasion."

"My time is near and I'm ready for when the Sun calls me. To be honest I'm so tired nowadays I'm quite looking forward to the rest. It's nice to know that my old body will be feeding the trees that I have fed from for so long. It makes a sort of circle. A kind of fair deal."

She spoke slowly now and when a Kernel was needed, it seemed to come from way, way down in her mind.

"I must train a successor," she said, after a long pause. "I had been hoping that Marguerite would come back. She was a natural Tagger, but Sun knows where she is now." She paused again, looking round wistfully as though expecting to see the Bright One appear.

"Clover the Carer is my next choice; one learns a lot about squirrel-nature looking after the sick ones."

"Is there a lot to teach her?" Oak asked.

"Well, she knows all the Basic Kernels, but the skill is in recalling the right one at the right time, and saying it with just the degree of confidence for the others to be strengthened or guided by it. I think I've nearly got it right myself at last," she added with a modesty that made Oak, himself an elderly squirrel now, smile affectionately. "But I do wish I knew if Marguerite was all right."

"She will be," Oak assured her. "She's a survivor, that one. And she's got that old reprobate, Juniper, looking after her. She'll be fine. Probably made me a grandfather by now, if I but knew it." Oak, in his turn, looked wistful.

Oak was right. Marguerite, more to her own surprise than that of her companions, had accepted Juniper as her lifemate and they had destroyed the abandoned dreys in the Deepend Guardianship and together had built a new one where they could look out over the Blue Pool.

Juniper had a favourite lying-out place from which he could see the beach where Bluebell had died from her injuries the previous summer. Marguerite was wise enough not to resent this, and was pleased that he never ventured near the Man-dreys and the temptation of the salted nuts, though she could sense that even now he sometimes craved them.

She, in her turn, had a favourite lying-out place at the eastern side of the Guardianship, in a high Look-out Pine where she could see over Middlebere Heath to Poole Harbour and Ourland. She would lie in the branches for hours thinking of ways to send messages to her family there.

There *must* be a way. Dolphins could send messages into her mind through the air as well as through the water, she was sure that the great ship that passed them at sea had been sending messages and Dandelion had told how, long ago, men had sent messages along the Leylines. Even squirrels, if she could believe the legend, had once used the Leylines at dawn in a similar way.

She had asked Dandelion to sense for a Leyline which might lead from the Blue Pool to Ourland for there were dreylings stirring inside her and she wanted to tell her family.

Dandelion, herself heavy with young, was unable to find such a line, sitting in the Look-out Pine and turning her head slowly from side to side, sensing with the utmost concentration, aware of the intensity of Marguerite's desire.

"Trust in the Sun," she reminded her friend. "Faith can fell fir trees," she added, putting a comforting paw on Marguerite's shoulder. "We know *that* is true."

Marguerite gave life to two new squirrels a week later, one male and one female. Juniper had waited all night in the warm summer darkness outside the drey. Now as the sun rose, she called him in. "Names first," she said. "Tags when they're older."

In the dim light of the drey they looked at the bald pink creatures squirming blindly on the soft mossy lining, and saw handsome youngsters running and leaping with joy in the sunshine.

Juniper looked at the tiny female, opened his mouth to

suggest Bluebell, thought better of it and said, "Oak and Burdock?"

"That would be my choice too," said Marguerite.

On the same day Rowan came proudly and breathlessly over from Humanside to tell Juniper and Marguerite that his Meadowsweet had borne a female dreyling and that they would like to call her Bluebell to honour the squirrel who had given her life to save the whole colony from the Greys; and would Juniper mind?

Juniper looked as proud as he had earlier, when he had looked on his own first-born.

Soon afterwards, news came from Steepbank that Alder and Dandelion were also parents again, and the next day Spindle the Helpful came to see if he was needed for anything and after a while, casually told them that Wood Anemone had also borne twins on the previous day.

Tamarisk, unmated that year, raced around the pool visiting each drey as proudly as if he had been responsible for all the new lives. It was remembered as a High-Tail Time for them all.

Chapter 37

Marguerite's duties as a parent and as the Tagger kept her mind off the desire to contact the Ourlanders for a whole moon, but then the urge to communicate came back with even greater force than before. Her mind constantly reviewed everything she could recall about signals, messages and forces. She awoke one night with a picture of the Woodstock before her and at first light she slipped away to the Clay-Pan to find it.

She found the weapon, near to where they had discarded it, half sunk in a puddle of slimy clay from overnight rain, and dragged it out to dry. The sky was still heavily overcast but a light breeze eventually turned the slime on the wood to a smooth white covering through which her numbers were still visible, but as she had feared, there was now no power in it. Try as she would with any combination of figures following her X, no force of any kind was left. It *was* all expended when we used it against the square, she thought, and, abandoning the exhausted Woodstock amongst the scattered stones and the crushed branches of the fallen fir, she set out to return to Deepend through the hazel copse.

The green-fringed nuts were filling but were not yet ready to harvest, and, as she assessed the likely crop, the sun broke through the clouds as it had done for her once before, a single ray of sunshine again lighting for a moment the hazel sapling being strangled by the honeysuckle bine.

A new Woodstock! The message was clear. With her strong white teeth she cut through the bitter-tasting stem of the woodbine and then into the hazel bark, tasting tantalisingly of the developing nuts themselves.

When the distorted, tortured stem had been dragged to the ground, she trimmed it to the same length as the first Woodstock, feeling, as she did so, the power-tingle in her whiskers that she had always felt when handling that one.

Marguerite looked up through the leaves at the sun, now shining brightly from a clearing sky.

"Thank you," she said quietly, "thank you."

High in the Council Tree in Beech Valley the United Ourlanders were gathered for that day's study of Kernels, Traditions and Manners. Old Burdock was speaking slowly, "Every squirrel should know . . ."

She stopped, as though listening to leaf-whispers from far, far away, then in quite a different voice said, "Marguerite is talking to me . . . Marguerite is talking to me . . . She . . . and Juniper are life-mated and have borne two dreylings . . . they have named them . . . Oak and . . . and . . . Burdock . . ." (Her old face lit up.) ". . . Rowan is alive . . . as Bold as ever . . . he has life-mated with Meadowsweet . . . they have a dreyling named . . . named . . . Bluebell . . . Spindle and Wood Anemone . . . Zpider and Woodlouze . . . have borne twins . . . There are no

Greys at the Blue Pool . . . Tamarisk is on climba . . ."

Old Burdock's voice was failing, she was using every last remnant of her strength to catch the whisper in the air. Then as it faded, she turned towards the tiny clump of trees on the far-away skyline, focused her entire body-energy into one concentrated thought, magnified by the love she and all those around her felt, and sent it leaping out of her body and across the water to the distant heathlands.

"We have heard you, Marguerite. We *have* heard you."

Her body slumped exhausted on the broad grey-green branch of the beech tree and Clover moved forward to sit by her, a paw on the frail shoulder of her teacher and friend. She could feel the slowing of Old Burdock's breathing. All was silence except for a gentle breeze rustling the beech leaves about them.

At last Old Burdock raised her eyes to the sky, blinked at the bright light and said:

> *Sun, now let me come,*
> *Peacefully, to you. Your gift*
> *To a true Tagger.*

Clover reached forward and closed the lids of Old Burdock's vacant eyes. Fern combed out the last few hairs of her tail.

> *Sun, take this squirrel*
> *Into the peace of your earth*
> *To nourish a tree.*

Away over the water and the heath, Marguerite took her

paw from the New Woodstock and leant back exhausted against the trunk of the Look-out Pine.

"I reached them," she whispered to Juniper, "I reached them. The Key is 12345670 × *42*."

No wonder they called her the Bright One, Juniper thought lovingly, as he helped her back to the drey above the pool of sapphire blue where young Oak and Burdock were sleeping the sleep of the innocent.

BOOK TWO

THE SECOND WAVE

Characters

RED SQUIRRELS OF PORTLAND
Crag the Temple Master; his mate *Rusty*; their son *Chip*

RED SQUIRRELS OF THE BLUE POOL DEMESNE
Alder the Leader; his life-mate *Dandelion* the Storyteller
Juniper the Steadfast; his life-mate *Marguerite* the Tagger
Rowan the Bold; his life-mate *Meadowsweet* Rowan's Love
Spindle the Helpful; his life-mate *Wood Anemone* the Able
Dreylings and youngsters of the above
Tamarisk the Forthright

RED SQUIRRELS OF OURLAND

EX-ROYALS

Ex-King *Willow*; his mate Ex-Kingz-Mate *Thizle*; their
son *Just Poplar*; their daughter *Teazle*; their nephew *Fir*;
their nieces *Voxglove* and *Cowzlip*

EX-ZERVANTZ

Bug
Beetle
Caterpiller
Maple (was *Maggot*)

INCOMERS

Oak the Cautious; his life-mate *Fern* the Fussy
Larch the Curious; his life-mate *Clover* the Tagger and
Carer; their daughter *Tansy* the Wistful
Chestnut the Doubter; his life-mate *Heather* Treetops

GREY SQUIRRELS OF THE SECOND WAVE

Ivy, or *Poison Ivy* (was *Slate*)
Redwood (was *Basalt*)
Hickory (was *Chalk*)
Sitka (was *Shale*)
Bluegrass (was *Tufa*)
Yucca
Prairie Rose
Other unnamed survivors of the Grey Death

OTHERS

Blood the pine marten
Mogul the peacock; his harem of peahens
Malin the dolphin; his mate *Lundy*; their son *Finisterre*
Acorn and *Primrose*, the mythical first squirrels in the
world

Chapter 1

1962

Chip sat on top of the world. At least, that was what it seemed like to him as he looked down from the edge of the cliff. The wind was chill and he wriggled back into the shelter of a rock.

"Squimp!" called Crag, his father, in a voice as cold as the wind which tore at his fur. "Out from behind that rock. Now!"

Chip, a thin, first-year red squirrel, came out reluctantly and crouched beside his mother, Rusty, keeping as far away as he could from Crag, the Temple Master. He could never be sure of when he would get a cuff across the back of his head and it was as well to stay out of his father's reach.

He stood up and followed the gaze of his parents as they studied the panorama below, a gust buffeting him and tugging at his pointed ears where the first tufts were just beginning to show. The squirrels were on the very edge of the north-western cliff-top of Portland. Below him the white stone cliff-face fell away to terraces of tumbled rocks, against which the dark green, gale-driven sea fretted and gnawed. As he watched, a great wave crashed and tore itself to pieces in a weltering mass of foam and spray.

Looking further northwards, his eyes followed the golden sweep of the Chesil Beach curving away into the far distance, the September sun glowing on the myriad high-banked pebbles protecting the Fleet Lagoon which lay between the pebble bank and the land. Beyond his father, on his right-paw side, over the jostle of Man-dens on the lower ground, he could see the blue sheltered waters of Portland Harbour where battleships lay at anchor, but Young Chip had no idea what these were. A squirrel youngster has much to learn about the world, especially if he is the only one of his year on the great stone mass which is the Isle of Portland, so windswept that trees are rare, surviving only in hollows and a few other sheltered places.

He watched the blue of the harbour turn to grey as gusts of wind rippled the surface, then as the gold of the Chesil Beach darkened, he looked to his left. A bank of clouds had covered the sun and was racing towards the land trailing a grey veil below it. He knew that in a few minutes a rain squall would reach them, and again turned instinctively for cover. Crag glowered at him, so he turned back, to stare miserably out to sea, shivering. Even the comfortless stone of their den in the cave at the back of the quarry had been preferable to this!

Chip's world had suddenly changed with the death of his grandfather, Old Sarsen, five days before.

Chip had been with his parents in the Temple Cave, crouched near a mass of rusting scrap iron where the old squirrel lay, wheezing and coughing out his last instructions to Crag and Rusty.

2

"Remember your vows," the old squirrel had said. "*You* are nothing. The Sun is everything. Worship and serve it, or it'll be the Sunless Pit for both of you. For ever!"

Chip could still hear the intensity of expression in his grandfather's voice. "You there, you, young one, remember this – serve the Sun. The Sun is everything. Fear the Sun and *dread* the Sunless Pit."

Chip could recall the shudders of terror which had engulfed him. The thought of never seeing the sun again had terrified him, and even now his stomach churned with the thought.

"You will all have to leave Portland," his grandfather had told them. "The Sun punished all unworthy squirrels by denying them dreylings. They were too idle to collect the sacred metal as we all do, so the Sun in its wisdom denied them issue. There are only four of us left here now and the youngster will need to mate next year. Go to the Mainland. Carry the True Word. Serve the Sun."

"What about the Temple?" Crag had asked.

"You will have to leave it. It will still be here if you can ever return."

The old squirrel had scrabbled at the stone floor, his blunt claws slipping on the rock, worn smooth by the feet of generations of his ancestors, until with one last effort he had hauled himself to the top of the pile of metal, the rattle of empty tins echoing around the hollow of the cave. Then, in the silence that followed, he called,

> *"Sun, I've served you well.*
> *Take me to you. Save me from –*
> *That dread Sunless Pit!"*

3

An agonised look had crossed his face and his lifeless body had tumbled down the pile to sprawl at Chip's feet.

Showing no trace of emotion, Crag had ordered Rusty and Chip to help him drag the scraggy body up the rock face, to one of the drill holes left when the quarry was abandoned, where they had slid it, head first, down the hole, to join the bones of Old Sarsen's father and those of his father before him.

Death must be as uncomfortable as life if a squirrel was to avoid the Sunless Pit, the youngster had thought.

A seagull whirled past Chip's head, squawking as it was tossed on the updraught of the wind striking the cliff-face, and a kestrel that had been hovering turned away inland and dropped between the mass of rocks behind them. Out over the sea, the rain clouds were much nearer.

"We go down," Crag ordered.

Chip gave a last look at the wrinkled sea below and at where the waves twisted over themselves as they ran along the curve of the Chesil Beach, then followed his parents on to the vertical face of the rock.

The wind buffeted him, but he climbed down head-first, confidently finding claw-holds in the tiniest of cracks and crevices. As Mainland squirrels were totally at home in trees, so was he on rock; neither he nor any of his family had ever climbed a tree.

He had once seen a tattered sycamore in a sheltered hollow whilst searching for metal with his grandfather and had moved towards it, drawn by this exciting living thing which created such a strange craving within him, but Old Sarsen had ordered him to leave it alone. "Shut your eyes to

4

the temptation," he had been told. "We will search this way", and the old squirrel had led the youngster off between the rocks away from the sin-provoking tree.

These long-abandoned quarries, though eerie places to humans, were quite familiar to Chip and his family. Huge blocks of substandard rock had been stacked in heaps, or scattered about as though by the paws of some giant squirrel, and over and around these wild cotoneaster bushes trailed, their green foliage now covered by blood-red berries. Large snails, their grey shells banded with a darker whirl, grazed on the leaves, and grasshoppers, safe here from lowland farmers' pesticides, chirred and chirruped amongst the yellow-flowered ragwort and the purple valerian. Above the squirrels the spiky dry seed-heads of teazles had patterned the skyline.

In the quarry-waste they had found an old pick head, flaking into layers of rust, but, despite the combined efforts of the old squirrel and the youngster, they had been unable to do more than drag it to the bottom of the cliff below the Temple Cave. There they had had to leave it, lying amongst the hart's tongue ferns, a constant reminder of how feeble they were, compared with the might of the Sun above.

A moon or so ago Chip had asked his mother about the metal collecting. At first she had seemed reluctant to speak of it. Then, when just the two of them were out searching and had found nothing, she had spoken unguardedly in frustration.

"I'm sure the Sun doesn't want all this stuff," she had said. "It was your great-grandfather, Monolith, who started it all. He was the chief of all the Portland squirrels then, and a miserable old creature by all accounts. I never found out what sin he did that was so awful that he thought he had to punish himself this way. Metal collecting is a bore and it hurts our teeth and I hate the whole stupid business.

"Even worse, he taught your grandfather to do it and he taught your father. Now *he's* teaching you. When will it ever stop? Why in the name of the Sun do *we* have to suffer for something Old Monolith did that everyone has forgotten long ago?"

Chip had stared at his mother. She had never spoken like this before; he did not know what to say.

Rusty continued, the words tumbling out. "My brother, your uncle, said that the problem with living isolated on islands is that extreme ideas get more and more exaggerated."

Chip had wondered what "exaggerated" meant. He raised his tail into the query position and was about to ask, when his mother said, "He died last year with no dreylings to follow him. I do miss him."

Rusty had looked tired and worn, and Chip had moved across to comfort her, but she had waved him away.

"I shouldn't have said that," she had told him. "For the Sun's sake, and mine, don't repeat it. Come on, we must find *something*."

They had searched all day, quartering the stone slabs of the quarry floor, raking with their claws through every tuft of grass and peering into each crack and hole between the stones, but had returned to the cave with only a crown cap from a discarded bottle between them, to the disgust of Old Sarsen, the Temple Master.

Once Chip had complained that it hurt his teeth to drag

6

rusty tins along the stony paths of the old quarries, and the stern old squirrel had said, "That's one of the reasons why we do it. The discomfort is good for you."

Everything that felt uncomfortable, it seemed, was "good for you". The bundle of dried grass that he had once brought into the cave to make the ground less hard to sleep on had been thrown out, and he had been called "a self-indulgent squimp". He was *glad* the old squirrel was gone, but now his father seemed to be just as awful!

Crag, Rusty and Chip doggedly worked their way down the cliff-face, one paw searching for a new hold whilst the other three held on to whatever projection or crack their sharp claws could cling to. Crag and Chip moved confidently, heads down, but Rusty, never happy on high faces, descended slowly, tail first, feeling for holds and keeping her teeth clamped tightly together. It would not do to show fear.

Chip called out to her, "There's a good hold just below your left paw", but his words were lost in the splash and roar as the rain squall reached the land, drenching the squirrels on the rock face. In a moment their wet fur flattened to their skins and their tails became as thin as those of rats.

"Hold on," shouted Crag. "It'll pass in a moment."

They clung to the rock face chilled and uncomfortable, Rusty's teeth chattering audibly. Then, as suddenly as it had arrived, the squall passed on and the sun was visible again, though now so low that little warmth reached the cliff-bound animals. Crag signalled them to start down again.

*

The light was fading from the western sky as the three reached the tumbled rocks piled along the cliff-base. Here there was some protection from the wind, and the bedraggled animals hopped down from rock to rock, making their way towards the shore.

Chip could hear the crashing of the waves above the roar of the wind and a melancholy whistling as the gusts tore through the brambles and the shrubby bushes which grew between the fallen rocks. He shivered and kept close behind his mother, hoping his father would stop soon. He was cold and hungry, and this unfamiliar place frightened him.

As the last of the daylight died they came to a Man-den, a wooden hut built between two great rocks, where his father and mother sniffed the air for recent scents. Then, apparently satisfied, Chip's father wriggled into the darkness underneath the hut's wooden floor.

"This'll do for us," he called back, and Rusty and Chip crawled in after him.

Compared with the outside world, it was warm under the hut floor and the youngster licked himself dry; he could hear his parents doing the same. He was very hungry, but knew better than to ask for food, which plainly wasn't to be had that night. He would have to wait until morning, so he fumbled about in the darkness for a sleeping place. In a corner he found a pile of dry grass brought in by some other animal, and quietly and guiltily burrowed into it. He knew this was a sinful act, but he was *so* cold. No squirrel would know, but he must remember to be lying on the bare ground before it got light.

He heard his father start the Evening Prayer.

Invincible Sun,
Forgive us, your poor squirrels,
For always failing.

Tomorrow, we will,
If you will give us the strength,
Try to do better.

Try to do better at what? Chip wondered. What would the Mainland be like? Would they find other squirrels? Would they be like he was? There were so many questions that he dared not ask. He wriggled round in the grass and slept restlessly.

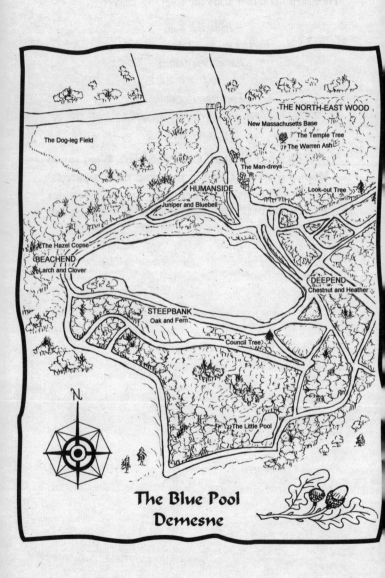

The Blue Pool
Demesne

Chapter 2

The rain and the wind had died away during the night and the red squirrels at the Blue Pool, on the Mainland fifteen miles to the north-east of Portland's great rock, peered out of their snug dreys at the pink glow in the sky that was the herald of a warm autumn day.

Alder the Leader had declared this day was to be a Sunday, devoted to fun and recreation.

Even as early as this the squirrels could sense the squirrelation that would spread from drey to drey and bring them all together to enjoy each other's company, with feasting, chases through the branches and, in the dusk, story-telling in the Council Tree on the steep bank overlooking the pool.

Each knew that the Harvest was in. Their weeks of frantic activity were over, and sufficient nuts were hidden and buried to see them through the hardest of winters and well into the otherwise hungry days of early spring.

The nuts had been hidden in groups of eight. By their ancient law, embodied as always in a Kernel, they would dig up and eat only seven of these.

One out of eight nuts
Must be left to germinate.
Here grows our future.

Marguerite the Tagger paused with her head outside and her body still in the warmth of the drey high in the Deepend tree. She sniffed the air and pulled her head inside. There was time for another little doze. Her two youngsters, Burdock and Oak, were big enough to fend for themselves. Together with the other squirrels born that year, they had been Tagged at her recommendation with an appropriate Tag to indicate their character, or to commemorate some worthy, or unworthy, achievement.

To be a True Tagger demanded a great deal of observation and concentration. An unfair denigratory tag could ruin a squirrel's life, though there would always be a chance to earn a better one. This year had produced a good-quality harvest of dreylings. One was her own son, Young Oak, who had earned his tag, the Wary, because he was always suspiciously alert for any sense of danger. Marguerite's father, Oak, Young Oak's grandfather, was tagged the Cautious, and some squirrels thought that the two tags meant the same thing, but, to a True Tagger, there was a world of difference. It was a good thing to have a "wary" son; it meant that there was a better chance of grandchildren. Being Wary was a good trait.

Her brother, Rowan the Bold, lived at the humans' side of the pool. His tag had been with him since he was a dreyling and suited him well, though now as a father of two he could not indulge in exciting climbabout journeys away from the Blue Pool any more. Marguerite was sure

12

that he missed these and that he sometimes fretted at the lack of opportunity to be bold and adventurous.

One of her short-lived uncles, Beech, had earned the tag the Ant Watcher from his obsessive fascination with the way wood-ants carried food to their nests under huge mounds of pine needles. Beech had been watching a little group of seven ants cooperating to move a dead caterpillar when the fox had seen him. The Ant Watcher had not even felt the snap of its jaws.

Marguerite's daughter, Young Burdock, had been tagged the Thoughtful. Like Marguerite herself, she was always trying to puzzle out complex things. Marguerite recalled her own early tag, the Bright One, and wanting to know exactly to what it referred; but even then she had known that it was bad form to question your tag.

Now, with the two youngsters chattering excitedly on the branch outside, she gave up any hope of a doze and nudged her life-mate, Juniper the Steadfast, to wake him.

It had taken him a long time to earn *that* tag. He was two years her senior, and she had never even known his first tag. It had been the Scavenger when she was a dreyling, then the Swimmer after an incident with the invading grey squirrels the year before. Finally, he had earned his present tag by always being reliably at her side through all the dangers and hazards they had experienced together since his first life-mate, Bluebell, had given her life to save others. Bluebell was the only squirrel to have had a tag-change after death; she was awarded the tag Who Gave All to Save Us in place of Who Sold Herself for Peanuts, which had been earned by behaviour they all wanted to forget.

Marguerite wriggled out of the drey, sat on a branch and

groomed herself in the sunshine, licking her fur and combing her tail hairs with her claws. Soon Juniper followed her.

"Perfect day for a Sun-day," he said, looking round at the tops of the pine trees where the rain-soaked needles were steaming away the night's moisture, then down to the pool, which he could glimpse through the tree-trunks below. He sat there, as he did on most fine mornings, combing his whiskers and enjoying the colour of the pool. It was a different colour every day. Sometimes, as now, it would be blue. On other mornings it would start green and change through several shades of turquoise and eau-de-Nil. Even on overcast days it usually ended up that intense sapphire colour that had earned it the Blue tag and which attracted humans to come and see it summer after summer.

Marguerite and her family climbed head first down the trunk of their tree to forage, pausing below branch level to look about and scent for possible danger. Juniper spoke the Kernel:

A watchful squirrel
Survives to breed and father –
More watchful squirrels.

Kernels as important as this one could not be repeated too often. Knowing these gave the youngsters the greatest chance of survival in a world in which a squirrel would be regarded by many animals as nothing more than a welcome meal.

It is so peaceful here, now that the Greys have gone, Marguerite was thinking. So pleasant to live quietly in this beautiful place with her life-mate and their youngsters after

the frenetic action of the previous two years. And yet . . .
No, she didn't really enjoy all that activity, and yet . . . She
had to admit to herself that it was exciting having to plan
for your very survival, using your wits, and your energy and
skills, to keep one leap ahead of your enemies . . .

Chapter 3

Chip woke with a start. It was still dark, but he knew he must be out of the warmth of the dried grass before his parents discovered that he had sinned by indulging himself with comfort. He thought there was a little time yet before his parents would wake, so he wriggled down again into the warm nest. The storm must have blown itself out. There was no wind-sound, though he could feel vibrations through the ground from the sea-swell pounding the rocky shoreline.

He lay there, listening to the breathing of his sleeping parents, trying to identify an unfamiliar feeling that surrounded him. He tried to focus on it, straining his mind and his whiskers to pick up whatever it was. In a way it resembled the warmth of the grass around his body, but it was more subtle than that. It came from the wood above him, from the Man-den, the hut on its little plateau amongst the huge boulders.

There were no men there – he would have scented and heard them moving long before this – but it *was* Man-associated. It was something like the "cared for" feeling he remembered from his mother when she had suckled him back in the spring. Then, in a distant, painful memory, he recalled his grandfather, Old Sarsen, saying, "Don't get squimpish about that youngster. He's not yours. You have only borne him to serve the Sun." And over the next few days that warm, cared-for feeling had been withdrawn.

Now he sensed that the hut was cared for, by humans. Could *things* be cared for? Could squirrels themselves ever be cared for except when they were dreylings? He hugged himself with the excitement of the thought.

A finger of grey light probed under the hut. Chip quietly destroyed his nest in the corner and moved away from the scattered grass to lie down on the cold soil until his parents woke. They lay as they taught him to, with their tails away from their bodies so as not to indulge in the warmth these might unworthily give them. He copied them and shivered.

A herring-gull, perched on the ridge of the hut above, called raucously. Crag and Rusty sat up at the same time and Rusty reached out and shook her son's shoulder where he lay, pretending to be asleep. "Time for prayers, Chip-Son," she told him.

Crag glowered at her.

"Chip, you must wake now," she said, forcing herself to sound hard and uncaring.

The three went out into the chill of the dawn air. If the sun *was* up over the eastern sea, it was hidden by the vast stone bulk of Portland behind them. Crag climbed on to a small rock, gave a quick look round for danger and, seeing none, said the Morning Prayer:

Be not too wrathful,
Oh Great Sun, on those squirrels –
Who sinned in the night.

Chip shifted uncomfortably as Crag went on.

Let us serve your needs
For the whole of this your day
Weak though we may be.

"Let us find sustenance," Crag said, after the long silence that followed, and only then could they start to forage amongst the rocks for food.

On the seaward side of the hut a spring of clear water trickled down through small pools overhung with brambles. Each drank from the stream in turn; first Crag, then Rusty, then Chip.

They found a few roots and a puffball which, though beginning to set spores, was just edible. These, with a few hard-pipped blackberries and some crimson hips, made up their meagre breakfast. Then Crag saw some sloes on a stunted blackthorn bush between two rocks and allowed each of them one of the mouth-drying fruit, before ordering Rusty and Chip to follow him along a Man-track that wound between the boulders.

The light was stronger now and Chip could see many more of the wooden Man-dens between the rocks. Most were brightly coloured and radiated that odd cared-for feeling he had sensed during the night, but a few were dilapidated and forlorn, the wood unpainted and weathered grey, their doors and windows hanging open or broken.

None of the huts appeared to be occupied. Maybe the humans used them only in the summer, Chip thought, as Crag hurried them on. His shoulder brushed against a plant with brown-edged leaves that leaned over the path, and little hooked seeds clung to his fur. He stopped to try to comb them out, but burdocks had evolved the tiny hooks to take their seeds well away from the parent plants, and they were not easy to remove.

Seeing that Chip had stopped, Crag called back over his shoulder, "Keep going. We must avoid meeting humans. They are trouble, and their dogs will chase us."

The sun cleared the top of the cliffs as they hopped along the path which wound in and out, up and down, through the tumbled boulders, and more and more Man-signs were to be seen. Wet paper bags and stinking cigarette-ends littered the sides of the Man-track. Chip found a rusty nail and showed it to Crag, expecting him to collect it as they usually did for the Temple, but was brusquely told, "We'll have to leave it."

His father did, however, pick it up and hide it out of human sight.

Rounding the last of the rocks at the end of the path, they could see ahead of them rows of stone Man-dens ranged behind the great bank of pebbles that curved away into the distance. Crag signalled to them to lie low whilst he climbed up on to a large boulder to plan a route. When he re-joined them, he led them away from the track and down on to the beach.

The smooth round stones here were bigger than the squirrels themselves, and they hopped from one stone to another, keeping on the seaward side of the debris forming the high-tide line.

Chip wanted to stop and look. Huge rollers, a legacy of the previous day's storm, towered in the air before crashing down in a mass of foam and rushing up the beach as though intent on snatching the animals and dragging them down into the depths. Then the waves, losing their momentum, drew back over the stones, which rubbed and tumbled against each other, groaning like a great beast in its death throes, only to be tossed forward yet again. But Crag, with that familiar "nothing will stop me now" look in his eye, urged them on.

After they passed the Man-dens and some brightly painted boats drawn up on the beach, there was nothing on their right-paw side between them and the sky but the top of the pebble bank, whilst to their left the empty sea stretched away to a far horizon. They hurried on, and Portland, well behind them now, appeared smaller each time they glanced back.

Chip was hungry again.

It got harder and harder to make progress along the beach. The pebbles were smaller now, about the size of a squirrel's head, and each rolled underfoot in a way that quickly tired their legs. Rusty called to Crag, "It might be easier if we followed that line of seaweed." She indicated the high-tide mark.

"Things are not meant to be easy," Crag told her.

"If we were not slipping about so, I think we could make better time. Old Sarsen said we were to leave Portland and it is our *duty* to go as quickly as we can. That's all I meant," she added lamely, as Crag glowered at her.

"Very well," he conceded. "But try to keep up with me. Both of you!"

They hopped up the beach and then from one clump of seaweed to the next, clambering over twisted pieces of smooth grey driftwood and splintered spars and old planks tossed up by the sea. Chip wanted to sense and examine all of them, but Crag kept urging them on. The waves to their left continually rushed up the beach, churning the pebbles, grinding them ever smaller.

"Don't hang back," Crag growled over his shoulder when Chip stopped and sniffed at the oil-soaked feathers of a dead guillemot. Chip reached out, however, and touched the sticky black stuff covering the bird before scrambling on after his parents.

Some of the black stuff had stuck to his paw, so he rubbed it on his belly-fur to try to clean it. Looking down, he could see that the stuff was now there as well. He tried to lick it off, but the taste was foul on his tongue.

"Don't lag behind," Crag shouted back to him, and Chip hurried to catch up, leaving a grey mark on every pebble that his paw touched. The smell of the oil was now making him feel ill.

At High Sun Crag called a halt when he found the dried-up body of a dogfish. He thanked the Sun for providing them with unsought sustenance and the three of them gnawed through the rough skin to the stinking, crisp meat within. Chip ate only a little, still feeling queasy, then wandered away from his parents to poke about amongst the strange and fascinating stones and wood.

He was holding up a pebble with a hole right through it when his eye was caught by a glint from a disc of bright metal near his feet. He picked it up. It was as golden as the sun and as round as a pebble one way, but thin and flat the other. He turned it over in his paws. It had been smoothed by rubbing against the pebbles, but he could see that there was a human's head on one side and strange squiggles and shapes on the other. He showed it first to his mother, Rusty, then to Crag, who bit it with his sharp teeth. "Soft and useless metal," he pronounced. "No gift for the Sun!" Throwing the golden coin down the beach, he told them to follow him again.

After another mile of tiring progress Crag led the weary squirrels to the top of the ridge. Beyond them was the lagoon that they had first seen from the cliff-top. It separated the pebble bank from the green fields of the Mainland, though at one place they could see that the lagoon narrowed near a stone Man-den, and the box-things that humans travelled in were passing over the water at that point.

Crag decided that they would go that way and led them down from the ridge. Chip was pleased when they reached an area where the ground was flatter, and the pebbles, bound together with clay, no longer rolled underfoot. Tufty sea-pink, sea campion and other shoreline vegetation was growing between the stones in the hard ground and a huge hare, disturbed by the squirrels, rushed out of its form and lolloped up the beach and on to the loose pebbles, which rattled and clattered behind its enormous back feet.

The air chilled as the sun dropped behind the pebble bank. Chip hoped that they would soon stop so that he could rest at last, with a warm place to sleep, but Crag had other ideas. He kept urging his tired family on until they came to the wide, smooth Man-track which smelt like the stuff on the guillemot's feathers, and where the humans' box-things rushed along. The squirrels crouched, waiting in the dusk, until the roadway was clear, then scurried across it and down through the wiry grass of the bank on the far side. They found themselves in a large hollow amongst the hulking shapes of boats and many new and interesting smells.

Some of the boats were on the ground, others up on trailers ready to be towed away for winter storage. The squirrels prowled round the unfamiliar objects, vainly trying to work out what they were. The scent of dogs was faint on the grass but nauseatingly strong on the wheels of the boat trailers, even though some hours old. Crag set out to find a safe sleeping place as high above the ground as he could.

A rope hung from the bow of a sailing cruiser cradled in its trailer near the road. Crag caught at this as it swung in the wind and climbed up it to the deck. A mast was lashed horizontally on top of the cabin, and from this he called down to Rusty and Chip to follow him. They chased the evasive rope-end and clambered up to join him, whilst he nosed about until he found a gap under the cabin door large enough for them to squeeze through. It was warm inside the cabin and Chip hopped up on to a soft seat, only to be ordered down to the wooden floor.

"Don't indulge yourself, young one," Crag growled.

As darkness fell, the pungent smell of the oil on Chip's fur filled the airless confines of the cabin and they were all bothered by the swish, swish, swish of the cars passing on the road alongside them. In the early hours of the morning these sounds died away, but were soon replaced by the slap,

slap, slap of ropes against the masts of other craft nearby when a night wind rose and eddied about in the hollow where the boats were resting.

Chapter 4

The first glow of dawn was showing in the eastern sky
beyond Portland Harbour when the squirrels in the boat
were wakened by the sound of human voices outside. Crag
hopped up on to one of the cabin seats and peered out
through the round glass into the grey light. The largest
travelling-thing he had ever seen had stopped on the
roadside and men were getting out of it and coming down
the bank, each carrying a box and a long, thin bag. They
passed the squirrels' hiding place and, by moving to
another porthole, Crag could see the men joining sticks
together and settling down at the water's edge to dangle
things that he could not quite see in the rising waters near
the bridge.

Chip lay quietly on the floor savouring the same cared-
for feeling from the fabric of the boat as he had sensed
beneath the hut on the previous night. Crag hopped down
from the seat.

"We must stay in here for a while," he said before he
commenced the Morning Prayer, which was followed by a
longer than usual period for contemplation of their sins.
Chip was glad of the extra rest-time, though he tried not to

let it show, just storing away the memory of his enjoyment of the cared-for feeling, to be purged by apologies to the Sun at the next prayer session.

Crag climbed back on to the seat and watched through the round window.

The sun had climbed high in the sky over Portland when the coach returned to pick up the fishermen, who joked and chaffed one another as they passed the boat on its trailer at the head of the little beach, before swinging themselves up into the vehicle.

As it pulled away, the squirrels, thinking that it was now safe to leave the boat, were about to squeeze under the cabin door when another travelling-box, squarer than most and with a cloth-covered back, came bumping down over the gravel track from the road. They did not move as the Land Rover backed up to the front of the trailer. Crag, watching awkwardly through one of the forward portholes, saw two humans leave the vehicle and come towards the boat. One went out of his sight, but he saw the other bend down and suddenly the angle of the boat's floor changed as the bow was lifted and the trailer was connected to the towing-hook. Crag dug his claws into the fabric of the seat and held tight, but Rusty and Chip were tumbled and thrown into a heap by the unexpected movement. They got up and dusted off their fur, and Chip looked apprehensively at his parents.

Rusty, seeing her son's concern, said, "The Sun must have this planned for us. I am sure that we will be safe." Then, turning to Crag, she asked, "Can we have the Danger Prayer?"

Crag, peering through the porthole, tried to keep his

26

balance while the boat rocked and tilted as the trailer carrying it was towed up the uneven bank and on to the road. He dug his claws into the fabric again and said in a loud voice,

> *We worthless squirrels,*
> *Not understanding your plans*
> *Crave your protection.*

> *It is the Unknown*
> *That we fear. In your good time*
> *Please enlighten us.*

The rocking stopped, and Crag saw the water of the lagoon pass below them as the Land Rover, with its boat-trailer in tow, crossed the bridge to the Mainland, then pulled up a hill with Man-dens on either side. The sensation was totally alien to him. Never in his entire life had he been *inside*, or even *on*, anything that moved in this way. He tried to establish what was reality. About him was the boat, apparently still, apart from a slight rocking motion, but, if he could believe his eyes, the world was moving past *him*.

He called to Rusty, who was crouched on the floor with Chip, "Come up here and look at this. Tell me what *you* see."

She hopped up on to the seat and Chip, risking his father's wrath, also hopped up, and the three of them each stared out through a porthole.

Man-dens and great trees were rushing past their eyes. One huge Man-den had a cliff of its own at the far end, soaring up into the sky. Seeing it, Chip felt a strong urge to be on familiar rock again, high up where he could observe his surroundings and the world was a stable place.

The passing trees created a different and less familiar urge in him, though equally strong. The soft-looking brown stuff that covered their trunks and branches attracted him. His claws itched, and he sensed instinctively that he would feel secure if he could only dig them deep into it.

The youngster waited for the inevitable order from his father to get down on to the floor. He must surely be noticed on the seat at any moment, he thought, but the order didn't come – Crag, with Rusty beside him, was staring out of the window as though mesmerised by the scenes rushing past.

Chip peeped out again. More Man-dens, more trees, green fields like those on the top of Portland, but with hedges and trees around them, then round-topped ridges – all passed in front of him. On one hillside was the gigantic figure of a human sitting on a horse, cut out of the browny-green of the turf and shining white in the September sunshine.

As they travelled on he began to enjoy himself; it was turning out to be a most exciting day. He knew, though, that he would have to repent for all this enjoyment later.

Then, with his brain a whirl of unaccustomed images, he noticed that the movement of the trees past the window was slowing, and he hopped down to the floor, to sit there demurely. Rusty followed him, but Crag stayed on the seat as the trailer was backed into the gaping doors of a barn. Here it was unhitched from the Land Rover and the floor resumed the angle that they recognised from the previous night. The humans went away and the barn doors were closed, leaving them in silence and semi-darkness. Chip suddenly felt frightened, hungry and sick. His punishment must be starting.

Crag's voice, lacking, for the first time that Chip could recall, that tone of total authority, said, "When it has been quiet for a while, we will go out and see why the Sun has tested us this way. But this is the Mainland and we must pray for guidance." He turned to Chip. "Then we must seek a worthy squirrel as your mate."

Chapter 5

___

Blood, a pine marten, was moving about in the darkness of his cage, fretting at the confinement and the stench in the dilapidated stable building near the isolated cottage on Middlebere Heath. He was forced to share this dark space with other animals who bore a resemblance to him in shape, though some were of a much smaller size.

A mature pine marten, or "sweetmart", to give him the Old English name, should be out amongst the trees in the forest, not shut up here, he was thinking.

From the cage below him another wave of noxious scent rose from the pair of "foulmarts", or polecats as they were more commonly called. He retched and tried again to find a way out.

The weasels and stoats were also moving about in their cages, equally uneasy; they had their own dreams of freedom and of a destiny dictated by their wits, instincts and survival ability.

Only the ferrets, born into captivity, were sleeping when the black door of the old stable was quietly opened. The human scent that blew in was not that of their gaoler, and the animals crouched, their hearts beating fast with anticipation. Two hooded humans entered, one, a male, carrying a set of bolt-cutters. The other, a female, stood watching at the door and shining the light from a tiny pencil-torch to guide her companion as he pulled out the pins or cut the padlocks securing the doors on each of the cages. Then, one by one, the cage doors were opened to allow the animals to leave. All, fearing these unknown humans, huddled in the back of their boxes until one of the ferrets, now awake and alert, ventured out on to the cobbled floor, saw an inviting trouser leg and, remember-ing the titbits that his human "master" had given him when they performed their joint party-trick, climbed up the leg inside. The ferret was not unduly put out to find that this human was not wearing the usual two pairs of trousers. He dug his claws in and scrambled up. The leg shook violently.

The man swore.

"Quiet!" hissed the human female.

"There's something climbing my leg. God, it's inside! Here, where's the light?"

"Quiet!"

"There's something in my trousers, I tell you. Oh my God! Shine that damn torch over here."

The man was attempting to take off his trousers whilst standing up, with his shoes still on his feet. The girl was flashing the light in his direction and trying desperately not to laugh.

In the confusion the pine marten, Blood, saw his chance and slipped away, out of the stable and into the fresh air outside. As he did so, the cottage door burst open; a human figure ran out and was momentarily silhouetted against the light behind. Blood saw that the man was holding a stick that was thicker at one end than the other, but knew that he was safe. He ran past the black hen-house, in which the disturbed chickens clucked fretfully, and into the night.

In the cool darkness there was the scent of resin and pine-bark. Blood padded on, heading northwards towards the long ridge of Arne, pausing now and then to sniff and to listen. He climbed the first tree to loom up ahead of him and lay on a branch, savouring his freedom.

When it was light enough, he looked about him. He was hungry and, more than anything else, he wanted *warm* flesh and blood, not the cold rabbits and dead chicken carcasses that had been his fare since his capture so far away in his northern homeland. He moved along the pine branch and leapt effortlessly into the next tree, then went on across the wood, pausing frequently to test the air and watch below him for possible food. An autumn-fat squirrel would be ideal, he thought, but there was not the slightest trace of squirrel-scent in the air or on the branches. He jumped from a pine into an oak tree.

A blackbird was rustling the leaf-litter below the oak and he stalked down the trunk, then pounced, catching the unwary bird whilst its beak and eyes were under the leaves. The pine marten scampered back up the tree, the limp bird in his mouth, enjoying the satisfying salty taste of warm blood. A trail of soft black feathers floated away on the morning air behind him.

Freedom and life for him, terror and death for others. Blood-dread had arrived!

Chapter 6

Across the waters of Poole Harbour, on the Island of Brownsea, enough red squirrels to satisfy even Blood's wildest dreams were planning to celebrate their Harvest. This island, known to the squirrels as Ourland, was an overgrown animal paradise of some five hundred acres of trees, heath and neglected fields, surrounded by a narrow beach.

Since the abdication of the last of the Royal squirrels the indigenous island community and the refugees from the Blue Pool Demesne had been integrating well. The islanders had adopted most of the refugees' customs and traditions, and many of them had accepted Tags awarded by Clover, who combined her Caring vocation with that of Tagger.

The ex-zervantz, now as free as any squirrels anywhere, were learning to live with the concept that they could make choices, and were getting used to the heady feeling of carrying their tails high and not always having to hold them in the submissive position.

Like the ex-Royals, the ex-zervantz still spoke with the 'z' dialect, but all were attending the sessions held to teach

33

Ourland
Brownsea Island

Woodstock Bay

Palm Tree Valley

Lagoon

Ruined Man-dreys

The Pier

Man-track — The Bunker

The Zwamp

Man-dreys

New Council Tree

The Wall

Royal Tree — CHURCH

CASTLE

The Island Screen

Beach Valley

Pottery Point

South Shore

N

Furzey Island

them the ancient Kernels of Truth which were replacing the discredited Royal Law.

Most of them had adopted new names, the males from trees and the females from flowers, but a few of the older ex-zervantz clung to their creepy-crawly names, amongst them Beetle, Bug and Caterpillar. These three old zervantz were the ones who had found it hardest to accept the changes, even though they enjoyed no longer being at the beck and call of each and any of the Royals. *That* way had always been their life, however, and whilst they had grumbled and complained about their treatment then, they now had difficulties making their own decisions and sometimes hankered for the "Old Days".

Much had changed for them, but Bug, Beetle and Caterpillar had maintained their "Zecret in the Zwamp".

Every autumn that they could remember they had slipped away from Royal duties and built a great mound of wet, dead leaves; in this steaming mass they had buried pawfuls of ripe sloes and left them there to ferment. During the following winter just eating one of these ruddled fruits was enough to make them forget all their troubles and cares, at least until the next morning, when they usually wished that they had left the sloes buried in the leaf-pile still.

On this autumn day Oak the Cautious, now Leader of the united Ourlanders, was at the Council Tree in Beech Valley near the centre of the island, talking to Fern the Fussy, his life-mate, and Clover the Tagger.

"We must have a Sun-day soon, to thank the Sun for allowing us to get the Harvest in. I think we've stored more reserves than ever this year," he said.

"I don't recall ever seeing so much food, and it is a beautiful island. The Sun certainly smiled on us when he guided us here," said Clover.

Fern looked to the west. "I wonder how Marguerite and the others have fared this autumn? At least we know that they're safe."

Oak followed her gaze. "I wonder if we will ever see our grand-dreylings. I suppose not. They could never find a way to come here. Remember all the luck we had on our journey here?"

"I like it on Ourland – it's so peaceful and safe, and food is so plentiful – but I *do* miss the Blue Pool. Couldn't we go to them?" said Fern.

Tansy the Wistful had just arrived and overheard the latter part of the conversation. "I'd find a way," she said confidently.

Clover smiled. Tansy had spent so much time looking out to sea after Marguerite and her party had been forced to leave that she had earned her Wistful tag.

"How would you get across the water?" she asked.

"I'd find a way," Tansy said again.

On the other side of the harbour Blood wandered along the shore, frustrated at the sight of the fat ducks who had just flown low over his head and landed in the shallows, and were paddling about out of his reach. Their scent wafted towards him on the easterly breeze, making his mouth water. He was quite ready to swim out to them, but knew that it would be a wasted effort as the ducks would be up and away long before he could reach them.

Then, faint but unmistakable, mixed in with the scent of

the ducks, was *squirrel-scent*. He stood up on his hind legs and tested it. Definitely squirrels – red squirrels. He sniffed again, then moved along the beach until he was clear of the duck-scent. Undoubtedly red squirrels, male *and* female, but a long way off, and over the water. Blood romped along the shore, looking for a way to cross the channel, then, realising that there was no landbridge, he slipped into the sea and swam across to the first of the islands.

There was no squirrel-scent here on Long Island and the breeze had dropped, so he spent the rest of the day quartering the island out of sheer curiosity, and searched along the shore until he found an injured seagull, unable to fly. He killed the weak bird easily, ate until he was full, glanced at the angle of the setting sun and decided that the squirrels would still be wherever they were tomorrow. He slept comfortably in a patch of reeds till dawn.

The morning breeze from the east carried the faint but tantalising scent, but the next land that Blood could see in that direction was a long way off.

He went to the south end of the island and swam across the channel to the Mainland, and waded ashore through the mud and rushes on a projecting point.

Time no longer mattered, discomfort was irrelevant, a swim was nothing; the squirrel-lust was on him. It took three days for him to reach Brownsea (by way of Green Island and Furzey Island), where, as he scrambled ashore, the air was thick with the scent of delicious squirrels. He padded up the bank behind the beach, through a stand of pine trees and on to a level grassy area, ignoring the rabbits which just looked up from their nibbling as he passed, showing no fear. Blood crossed an overgrown meadow and entered a wood, climbing into the trees to avoid the dense rhododendron bushes that covered the ground and moving upwind all the time.

It was in the swamp that he found a squirrel, asleep on the ground close to a pile of steaming leaves. In killing and eating it he both satisfied and inflamed the squirrel-lust burning inside him.

This place, he thought, is a sweetmart's dream. He searched for and found a perfect hiding place in a large, disused Man-cave, around which brambles and ivy grew, covering much of the stonework. After entering the arched entrance where the sun-bleached, wooden door stood ajar, he picked his way over the droppings from the huge and unknown birds he had seen outside, who clearly slept perched on the backs of the mouldering pews. At one end of the great cave he found a hanging rope, and climbed up it into the tower of St Mary's Church, Brownsea, there to sleep and dream of squirrels, and yet more squirrels.

Chapter 7

The Sun-day at the Blue Pool was nearly over. Well into autumn, the daily flood of human Visitors had ceased, and the squirrels had enjoyed a day of feasting, chasing and hiding. There had been a great deal of squirrelation, and now the tired and happy animals were making their way to the Council Tree to hear Dandelion tell one of the stories of Acorn, the first squirrel in the world. Squirrel-mates sat together and unmated youngsters sat with their friends, giggling and jostling for the best positions.

It was here that the Portland squirrels had found them, following the scent and the unfamiliar sounds of enjoyment that had drifted downwind towards the barn that afternoon.

Crag, Rusty and Chip had waited in the boat for an hour before cautiously emerging from their hiding place and dropping over the side on to the barn floor. Wriggling under the huge black wooden doors, they had blinked at the light, then clambered up the stone wall to where they felt safer, on the roof.

From there Chip had looked about him ecstatically. All

around him were trees, trees of every size and shape; their colours ranged from a light green to bright red, and the leaves had the strangest variety of patterns. The Mainland scents had made his head reel; the salty sea-smell of the Portland air was gone, and in its place was an atmosphere of moist leaves, resin and autumn fungus, underlaid by the warm hay-smell from bales stacked at one end of the barn beneath them. His nostrils had been assailed from every side and he had sniffed in pleasure and wonderment. Rusty was doing the same, though Crag was more soberly scenting around and analysing odours.

"There's a group of squirrels upwind," he had said, "probably a mile away. We'll go there and maybe make contact. There might be a worthy mate for you among them."

Chip had tried to hide his excitement, but a little trickle of urine had run down the roof-slates below him.

Crag had looked at him coldly. "Follow me," he had said, and they had followed him back down the barn wall, before crossing the grass and climbing an ash tree.

Chip had never known such a satisfying feeling in his life. Instead of searching the cold rock for a hold, everywhere that he put his paws his claws sank sweetly into the bark and it held him just where he wanted to be.

Crag had allowed them to practise climbing up and down the tree-trunk and running out along the branches.

This must be what my claws were really made for, Chip had thought, as he scratched at the bark and smelt the essence of the tree, moist under his paws.

Then it had been time to leap to the next tree. This was another new and thrilling experience – to leap across space with nothing beneath you and to land in a leafy, twiggy mass, full of paw holds, there to regain balance, before running along a thickening branch to the trunk of that tree.

"Don't get carried away. This isn't a game," Crag had warned him.

Chip had no idea what a game might be, but knew from the tone of his father's voice that the pleasure he had felt must be sinful and therefore hidden, and repented later.

The three had moved from tree to tree, travelling up the wind-line, the scent of strange squirrels getting stronger, until even Chip's unpractised nose could detect it.

They had then come to some pine trees surrounding a large pool, where they had paused, watching the blue of the water fading to green in the gathering dusk. Chip was thinking, sinfully, that he had never seen such a beautiful place in all his life.

They had heard the sound of excited squirrel chatter from the trees on the other side of the water.

"Follow me quietly," Crag had whispered. "Try not to show yourselves."

They had circled the pool and come to a large pine. Here they stopped and listened, concealed behind a screen of pine needles. Many other squirrels were sitting in the next tree, whilst others moved about from group to group.

Chip, quivering from head to foot, felt waves of the cared-for feeling radiating outwards from the assembled squirrels. What seemed to him to be the strangest thing of all was that they were touching each other as they sat. He felt a great urge to leap across and nestle in amongst them, but one look at his father's stern face killed that idea.

41

"Quiet," Crag said, keeping his voice low, and the three sat silently, watching and listening.

"Once upon a time," Dandelion started, in the traditional way of all story-tellers, after the squirrels had settled down to listen, "when the world was very young and there were only two squirrels in it – Acorn and his life-mate, the beautiful Primrose – the Sun looked down and saw that the ground was a mess. No animal or bird ever bothered to hide its droppings, and smelly piles were everywhere.

"In those days it rained only at night: just enough rain to water the plants and the trees and to keep the pools and rivers full, but not the heavy rain needed to wash all the muck away. So the days were always bright and sunny for the creatures to enjoy.

"The Sun let the animals and birds know that they must *bury* their droppings, so that the food they had once eaten could be used again by the plants, but all the creatures were too busy doing other things, and the world was so big it didn't matter. And if all the others buried theirs, it wouldn't matter about their own. All the reasons under the Sun why *others* should do it – but not them.

"Soon it got so that no animal could walk on the ground without treading in horrid things, so the Sun let it be known that if the world was not cleaned up, *something* would happen.

"Each animal and bird looked at the mess and said to itself, I only did a tiny part of that – others did most of it. So each did nothing and, as every creature thought exactly the same, the world stayed in a mess.

"Then one morning, when Acorn and Primrose woke up,

it was raining. They looked out of their drey and the rain was pouring down. This was so unusual that Acorn said the Asking Kernel:

> *Oh Great Loving Sun,*
> *Please explain to us squirrels –*
> *Why is it raining?*

He couldn't add 'in the daytime', which is what he meant, because only five word-sounds are allowed in the last line, but the Sun understood, and made the water at the foot of his tree flash and sparkle so that Acorn could see *his* droppings tainting the pureness, and he was ashamed. It was too wet now to go down and bury them, so he went back into his drey and hid there with Primrose.

"Now, I forgot to tell you that Acorn and Primrose were then living in a sequoia tree on the top of a great rock called Portland, and *that* was the highest tree in the whole world."

Crag turned to Rusty and whispered, "This is all nonsense. Sequoia trees don't grow on Portland!"

Rusty and Chip, however, were listening intently to Dandelion, who continued. "After a few days, when it had never stopped raining, lots of animals waded or swam across from the Mainland to Portland, as they could see it was soon going to be the only part of the world above the water.

"Below where he sat in the sequoia, Acorn could see that some humans were building a boat, big enough to take them and lots of animals as well. By the time it was finished the sea was right up to the top of Portland and washing around the roots of Acorn and Primrose's home-tree. The man was asking all the animals and birds if they would like to come into his boat, and they were all going in and taking their mates with them. This was right at the beginning of the world, before any creatures had had any youngsters, so there were only two of each animal.

"The man called up to Acorn and Primrose and told them to hurry, but Primrose said to Acorn, 'I think that man eats animals. *I'm* staying here.' So the two squirrels stayed in their tree as the boat floated away on the flood.

"It rained and rained and rained, and the water came higher and higher up the tree, until Acorn and Primrose's drey was washed away. The two wet squirrels huddled together against the trunk, higher up, trying to keep dry, and then scratched out a little den in the deep, soft bark to shelter in.

"But the next day the water was up to that level, and they had to make another den-hole even higher. Each day the flood rose and rose, until the only bit of the tree above the water was the very tip-top twig. Acorn and Primrose clung to it, wondering what to do next.

"Acorn said the Needing Kernel:

> *Oh Great Loving Sun*
> *What I need most at this time –*
> *Is for the rain to stop.*

But as this had six word-sounds instead of five, it kept on raining. Then Acorn tried again:

> *Oh Great Loving Sun*
> *What I need most at this time –*
> *Is for no more rain.*

Since he had got the word-sounds right, the Sun drove

44

away the clouds and with them the rain, and soon the water started to go down and down.

"Primrose joined Acorn in saying the Thank You Kernel:

> *Oh Great Loving Sun*
> *We, your grateful squirrels, now –*
> *Thank you sincerely.*

"Then, as the Sun shone to dry the wet squirrels, a great rainbow formed in the sky and, right in the middle of the arch, they could see the man's boat coming back towards them. Finally it grounded on the top of Portland where it was rising out of the water.

"Soon the animals were coming off the boat, two by two. First came two horses, then a cow and a bull, then two dogs, then two foxes, and two cats and all the other animals in pairs, except . . . there was only *one* unicorn, and that was looking sorrowfully and accusingly at the man as it came down the gangplank on to the soggy ground.

"The man shrugged his shoulders and held out his hands palms upwards. Primrose turned to Acorn and said, 'I told you so!'

"Now, you would think that all the creatures would have learned a lesson and buried their droppings after such an event, but they had soon forgotten what had happened, and behaved just as they had done before. So the Sun *still* has to send lots of rain to clean up the world.

"Today, only the cats and humans hide their droppings, and that is why cats hate the rain and humans are always grumbling about the weather."

Dandelion signalled that this was the end of the story and

her audience thanked her. After brushing whiskers with their friends, they set out for their own dreys in the near-darkness, the Sun-day over.

Crag whispered to Rusty and Chip to follow him, and the three slipped unnoticed away through the branches, Crag mumbling, "Blasphemy, blasphemy! It can't be true. *We* know that there are no sequoia trees on Portland. Blasphemy! Heathens, pleasure-seekers, every one of them!" Then, to Chip's disappointment, he added, "We won't find a worthy mate amongst that lot."

Chip was looking over his shoulder, hardly able to believe that there were so many other squirrels in the world and desperately wanting to stay and . . . and . . . Finding no words for "play with", "share with" or even "live with", he settled for wanting to just "be with" these warm and interesting animals that he felt so close to.

"Come on," his father called back gruffly. "There's nothing for you there."

Chapter 8

Blood woke from his dreams in the bell-tower of the disused church, shook himself and came tail first down the bell-rope and into the nave, wrinkling his nose in disgust as the stink of peafowl droppings filled his nostrils. The huge birds were roosting in rows along the back of the pews, and the sunlight, striking through the dusty stained-glass window, lit up the glossy blue of their necks.

Easy meat, thought Blood, but I can take those any time, and he slipped out through the door and down to the swamp to the place where he had found the ruddled squirrel on the previous day. There were no squirrels at the leaf-pile, but he played with the tail and the ragged skin of yesterday's meal, tossing it into the air and catching it, savouring the scent, until, filled again by squirrel-lust and hunger, he climbed a tree and set off on a hunting expedition.

Ex-Kingz-Mate Thizle had been visiting the drey of her son, once Prince Poplar, but who now insisted on being called Just Poplar, and was returning to her own drey through the treetops. She was disappointed yet again that he still showed no sign of being interested in finding a life-mate amongst the incomers' families. She was relieved, though, that he was not so taken by their classless ways that he might choose a female ex-zervant. That would be intolerable. She hoped that she had put a stop to any ideas he might just be having in that direction.

As he neared her drey, between the Zwamp and the Lagoon, she stopped and stared. A brown creature, larger than a squirrel, was climbing up the trunk of her drey-tree. She watched as it pushed its head into the drey and pulled out the Ex-King by the throat. She realised with horror that the creature could only be a pine marten. Terrified, she ran off to warn the other squirrels, finding most of them with Oak the Cautious, finalising the plans for their Harvest Sun-day.

"The King huz been killed and eaten," she gasped breathlessly, forgetting to use the "Ex". "There'z a pine marten on Ourland! A pine marten! Him'z killed and eaten the King!"

They all knew about pine martens, though only from stories and a silly Kernel that they told to unruly youngsters:

> *Pine marten's sharp teeth*
> *Bite off the ears and the tails*
> *Of naughty dreylings*

The idea of a real-live pine marten being on Ourland was horrific. There weren't even dogs and foxes here!

"Are you sure?" asked Chestnut the Doubter.

"Uz zaw it eat the King. Him wuz much bigger than uz iz," she sobbed, "and the zame zort of colour but with white

48

edgez to him'z earz and him can go up a tree az fazt az uz can. What'z uz going to do?"

The squirrels chattered in excitement and fear, looking round as though expecting hordes of bloodlusting pine martens to leap on them, until Oak, exerting his authority, said calmly, "We must hold a Council Meeting to discuss this. In the meantime we will set out watchers to warn us if it is coming this way."

Using the lessons learned the previous year, when they had had to defend themselves from a group of hostile grey squirrels on the Mainland, all those living in outlying dreys were encouraged to come and build nearer the Council Tree. Pickets were set to keep a constant watch.

Having temporarily satisfied his squirrel-lust, and finding that a peafowl would provide a meal for days, Blood stayed in the church, taking a roosting peahen occasionally and seldom venturing out.

The squirrels soon began to believe that the alarm must have been a product of Thizle's imagination, despite the disappearance of Ex-King Willow and the ex-zervant Bug, and relaxed their guard.

A week later the elderly ex-zervantz, Caterpillar and Beetle, drawn by an urge to get thoroughly ruddled again, sloped off unnoticed to the leaf-pile in the Zwamp.

Beetle ate first and was enjoying the drowsy, warm feelings when he saw Caterpillar, who had just dug himself a ruddled sloe from deep amongst the steaming leaves, staring past him. Fear was showing in his stance and in the look in his eyes. Beetle froze. Caterpillar started to move backwards, still with his eyes fixed on something behind

Beetle, whose neck-fur was now rising and his tail-tip swishing uncontrollably to left and right.

Beetle turned fearfully to look over his shoulder, caught a glimpse of sharp white teeth above a white-furred chest; he tried to leap for a tree, but fell in a heap as his limbs seemed to tangle with one another. Then he felt the teeth biting deep into his neck.

Caterpillar dropped the sloe he was holding without even a taste and, turning, abandoned his old ruddling friend to his fate and raced off through the trees to Beech Valley, where he described how Beetle had been killed in such vivid detail that even Chestnut could not doubt him.

There *was* a pine marten loose on their island!

Chapter 9

Next to be taken was a youngster, Hornbeam the Disobedient, who, living up to his tag, had wandered off in search of his favourite fungus and did not come back. His distraught mother pleaded for a search party to go and find him; four squirrels, led by Chestnut, set out cautiously, to return shortly with a limp red tail.

The Council was meeting twice a day trying to come up with ideas for defence, but no useful suggestions were forthcoming until Tansy the Wistful reminded the squirrels of the Woodstock, the magical vine-strangled stick with which her friend Marguerite had accidentally killed an aged Royal the previous year. Marguerite had had it with her when she left Ourland and it must surely be with her now at the Blue Pool.

"If we could get the Woodstock here, we could use it to kill the pine marten and we'd all be safe again," she said.

Her listeners chattered with relief. The Woodstock. Of course, why hadn't they thought of that?

Then reality returned. Some squirrel, or squirrels, would have to get to the Mainland, journey to the Blue Pool, collect the Woodstock – if it *was* in fact there and still worked – learn how to use it and get it back again to Ourland. The whole idea was impossible. They all sat in silence again, tails drooping with disappointment.

"Perhaps we could find another Woodstock on the beach," said Heather Treetops hopefully. Then, realising how unlikely this would be, she added, "Or perhaps we could make one. I sort of remember what it looked like."

Over the next two days, in the protection of watchful pickets, the squirrels looked for suitable fallen branches and pieces of driftwood. Using their teeth, they tried to re-create the twisted spiral they knew as a Woodstock. Some said that the twist ran one way and some said it ran the other, and several "Woodstocks" were made – but none had the smooth lines of the original or seemed to hold any feeling of hidden power.

"I think it was Marguerite's numbers that made it work," said Oak. "Does anyone remember how they looked?"

Her practice scratches on the sand had long since washed away, and the odd pieces of driftwood in which numbers had been cut by her teeth had floated off to other shores.

Clover recalled that Marguerite had cut numbers in the living bark of some birch trees, but these birches were too near the church where the marten's den was thought to be. Another Council Meeting was summoned, but no new ideas were forthcoming.

Tansy looked round at the despondent squirrels and thought of a Kernel taught to her by Old Burdock, the beloved and much respected elderly Tagger who had been such an inspiration to them on their journey to Ourland. Burdock had been Sun-gone since the summer and was buried in the ground below the Council Tree where they were now sitting.

The Kernel said:

If you think you can
Or if you think you cannot
Either way it's true

"I'll go and get the real Woodstock," she told them, and before any could object or raise difficulties, or try to convince her it was impossible, she leapt from the Council Tree and set off through the treetops towards Pottery Point, the nearest place on the island to the Mainland.

Watchful for the pine marten and surprised at her own boldness, Tansy jumped from tree to tree, wondering how she could ever cross the frightening stretch of water she could see ahead.

In a pine tree above the shore she stopped, plagued by doubts. The Sun had sent a door to carry them across to Ourland when they had been pursued by the Greys, and she half expected to see that very door drifting in on the tide. She stared out over the water, but could see nothing. What a fool she had been. Now she would have to go back and admit defeat. No she wouldn't.

Old Burdock had taught them when to use the Needing Kernel, having emphasised that it was for needing and not just for wanting.

Tansy looked up at the Sun and said the first part of the Kernel:

53

Her mind went blank as she struggled to find four more
word-sounds to express her wish to cross the water.

A male sika deer, who had swum over to the island a
moon before to serve the hinds there, stepped out of the
bushes and paused below the tree in which Tansy sat,
exhaustion showing in his eyes and stance.

A weary stag, she thought. Sun-inspired, she said aloud,
"Is a weary stag", and dropped from the tree to cling to his
left antler. The stag shook his head in irritation, gently at
first, then violently, but Tansy held tightly to the hard
horn. The stag waded into the sea and swam towards
Furzey Island, tilting his head backwards and sideways as
he swam, so that the water washed over Tansy, who clung
there, terrified, salt water washing into her eyes, nose and
mouth.

Just as she was thinking that she could hold on no longer,
she felt the stag's feet touch bottom and he waded ashore on
Furzey Island. Refreshed by the cold water and now
seemingly unaware of the tiny sodden animal still clinging
to his antler, he trotted across Furzey, entered the sea again
and swam to the Goathorn Peninsula of the Mainland. As
Tansy altered her grip, her foot touched the hair between
the horns, and the stag tried to dislodge her by brushing his
head against a bush. Tansy leapt into the foliage.

There *is* a way, she thought, if you think you can . . . She
climbed a tree and licked herself dry, gagging at the taste of
salt. Mentally and physically drained by her ordeal, she

searched for and found an old magpies' nest in which to spend the night, alone for the first time in her life and fearful of every sound from the night-life all about her.

At dawn she set off through the plantation, keeping the sun behind her and heading in the direction that she hoped would lead to the Blue Pool, Marguerite and the Woodstock.

Chapter 10

On the night after their visit to the Blue Pool the Portlanders slept in a disused drey on the north side of the pool, well behind the screen of pine trees. The drey had been abandoned by grey squirrels when "Grades" – the Grey Death – had swept through there, wiping the colony out to a squirrel. The lingering scent of the Greys puzzled Crag. It was similar to red squirrel-scent, though subtly different. It was an unusual experience for him to be in a drey anyway, and the scent bothered him.

He had been tempted not to use the drey, which was, he thought, too comfortable for serious Sun-serving squirrels, but the temperature outside was falling fast and the stars were frost-bright above the trees.

"Just this once," he told Rusty and Chip. "Tomorrow we find a more appropriate place. We must get settled before winter really starts or we will starve or freeze to death."

Would he really care? Chip wondered. His father seemed to seek pain and discomfort. He would probably enjoy freezing to death, or starving.

Crag led the way into the moss-lined interior of the drey,

however, followed by Rusty and Chip, who was very conscious of the closeness of their bodies. There was no room to lie away from one another, and he lay awake, rigid and tense, next to his mother, feeling the warmth of her body against his own.

Later, much later, he dozed off, then woke to find his mother's paw around his shoulder and her tail covering him. He nestled against her and slept.

When he awoke at dawn, he found himself alone in the drey. He could hear his parents moving about outside.

"Don't let that youngster sleep on," Crag was saying. "Flush him out for prayers!"

Chip wriggled out into a world made magic by frost. Every twig and leaf was encrusted with crystals of ice, built from the mist that had drifted in over the land during the night and was now dissipating in the sunshine. Each crystal caught the light and sparkled in a tiny rainbow of colour. The young squirrel looked about him in wonder. It was all so beautiful.

"*Your* turn to say the Morning Prayer," said Crag.

Chip had done so several times before, using the standard wording as his father and mother had always done, but today, after the first section,

> *Be not too wrathful*
> *Oh Great Sun, on those squirrels –*
> *Who sinned in the night,*

he felt moved to use his own words:

> *Thank you, oh Great Sun,*
> *For the beauty of your light*
> *In this sparkling world.*

Rusty, thrilled by this unexpected prayer, turned admiringly towards her son, only to cringe as Crag reached out a paw and struck Chip across the head. "Blasphemer!" he hissed, and finished the prayer himself:

> Let us serve your needs
> For the whole of this your day
> Weak though we may be.

Then, glowering at the unhappy youngster, he led his family down to forage on the chill ground. Later they would search for a permanent base to create a New Temple.

It was High Sun when Crag found what he was seeking. In a clearing in the wood a huge gnarled oak stood, twisted by age. Although it was blackened by fire from a lightning strike many years before, lingering autumn-brown leaves on a few branches indicated that it was not yet completely dead. A little way up the tree the hollow of the trunk forked to form two chambers above the large one below.

Crag explored all the hollows, then came down to where Rusty and Chip sat silently waiting on the ground.

"This will be our New Temple," he announced. "There are suitably austere sleeping places for each of us to have their own, and great chambers to store the metal collection."

Chip groaned to himself, his teeth hurting at the very thought of holding rusty things again. He looked appealingly at his mother.

"Is it wise to use a tree that has been struck by lightning? Might it not happen again?" she asked.

"Lightning never strikes twice in the same place," Crag assured her confidently. "Now we start the collection. Honour be to the Sun."

Chapter 11

Slate, a mature female grey squirrel, looked at the remains of the Oval Drey in the giant oak at Woburn Park. A winter and a summer of neglect had made the drey look unkempt and drab. It was hard to picture it as she had last seen it, bustling with activity. That was before the Grey Death had killed its inhabitant, the Great Lord Silver, as well as most of the other Greys in New America.

A few survivors were now clustered round, the males discussing what they should do to set up a centre of government again. Slate could see that they were all at least a year younger than she was and were obviously inexperienced.

"I would suggesst . . ." Slate began, the words hissing past her broken tooth.

As one, the males glowered at her.

"This is a formal meeting," a male – Basalt – said firmly. "Females may only speak when requested to report. You should know that."

"I jusst thought that sinsse so many thingss had changed . . ."

"Females shouldn't think," said Basalt, and turned away.

Slate sat on the branch, angry and frustrated. She had hoped that the one good thing to come out of the Grey Death tragedy might have been an opportunity to right some of the past injustices. Oh well, she thought, there are more ways of opening a nut than waiting for it to grow.

She listened in silence as the males continued. Basalt was dominating the conversation, talking down any opposition to his ideas.

"The Red Ones lived here long before our kind came from our homeland beyond the sunset. The Grey Death did not affect them, whereas it virtually wiped us out. Perhaps the way they live is the right way; here in New America at least."

"They're all squimps," said Chalk, unconsciously using a red word that had crept into their language. "They're all soft and gentle."

"So they may be," retorted Basalt, "but they are also alive. Those we haven't killed, that is. I think we should learn their ways.'

Slate was itching to intervene, but was not going to risk another public rebuff.

"Will we have a Great Lord Silver?" a male asked. "The Reds don't."

"Well, we don't have to do *exactly* what they do," said Basalt. "But we do need a leader to be in charge here and to direct other Greys who may have survived and come back to Base for guidance. The Reds would *choose* one, not fight for the position as we have always done. I propose that I am chosen as Great Lord Silver. All agree? Right. That's settled, then."

The Greys looked at one another in amazement, but Basalt continued quickly, "Who knows anything about the customs of the Reds?"

"They have different names from us," said Chalk. "The males are named after trees and the females after flowers."

"We'll start there, then," said Basalt. "Each squirrel is to choose a new name, but choose trees and flowers from the Old Country."

"I'll be Hickory," said Chalk.

"Sitka for me," said Shale. "I never did like my name anyway. Basalt, you should be Redwood, if you want us to do what a Red would."

This pun, the ultimate form of grey humour, was received with groans. Basalt agreed rather than argue with another squirrel who had just chosen Tamarack, a name he had intended to use himself. He'd got away with appointing himself Great Lord Silver and was not going to push his luck further.

The females had grouped together and were discussing names for themselves. One chose Prairie Rose, another Yucca, and, amid laughter, Tufa turned down a proposal that she be called Skunk Cabbage in favour of Bluegrass.

"What about you?" Yucca asked Slate.

"If we have to go along with thiss nonssensse, I want to be called Ivy," she replied.

"Poison Ivy?"

"Suitss me," said Ivy. "Lotss of true wordss are said ass jokess."

They rejoined the males. Redwood was now issuing orders.

"Hickory, I want you and Sitka to take a mixed party down to the Blue Pool in that part of New America that the Reds call Purbeck. It is the last place that I know of where Reds are definitely still living. Make contact with them and learn their ways. Don't argue, just do what they do. When we know all their habits and customs, we can modify them to suit ourselves."

"What if they fight us?" Sitka asked.

"Reds don't fight, they pray to the Sun. I told you, they are squimps," Hickory replied.

"Don't fight them; don't argue with them. Apologise for our past behaviour so that they are not suspicious. Learn their ways. That's an order." Redwood scowled at the squirrel before him.

"Yes, sir," said Hickory, saluting with his right paw held diagonally across his chest. "Trust me. We'll rest up and leave at first light."

"You'll leave now," said Redwood firmly. "If more Greys come in, I'll send them to join you. Listen and learn."

"Yes, sir," said Hickory, and saluted again.

Hickory had called a halt. He had been urging his group on at quite a pace. They had passed the ancient wood that the Reds had so stupidly called the New Forest, and were on the edge of the heathland that was reported to be the last barrier before the Blue Pool. It was there that the red survivors of the Greys' massacres were believed to be living.

The nights were getting much colder and they had to huddle together for warmth when they rested. Though it was now only mid-afternoon, he could sense that a chilly night was coming.

He looked at the other squirrels. They were in fair condition; dishevelled from their journeying, but in good spirits. Even Poison Ivy, notably older than the rest, was looking fit, if a little tired. She had been most useful in instructing him on the route, even though she had never come this far south or west before. She knew some of the Reds' Kernels of Truth, but she would never tell where she had learned them. How did they go? Five sounds, seven sounds, then five again; or was it six?

Hickory called Ivy over to join him. "How far do you think it is to that pool now?" he asked.

"Over the heather and beyond the treess," she answered enigmatically. "Send out some scoutss. The resst of uss can wait here. We will be safe in thosse piness."

Sitka and three other scouts left and, while they were away, a new group of Greys joined those waiting in the pine trees. Their leader explained that more and more survivors of the Grey Death were arriving at Woburn and many were being sent down to join Hickory's party in Purbeck.

"Redwood calls us all the Second Wave," he said proudly. "The Silver Tide was swept away by the Grey Death, but we are not to give up trying. The Second Wave *will* succeed. Praise to the Great Lord Silver."

What would they call a female Great Lord? Ivy was wondering.

The scouting party returned at nightfall with a report that they had scented Reds, but had not made contact. "Yes, there is a pool set in a hollow in the pine trees. Yes, it is blue. Move over, we're freezing. We're the ones who've been doing all the running round while you just sat about. Who are all you lot?"

"Be quiet and sleep," Hickory growled. "We leave before dawn. We should be with those Reds by sun-up."

Ivy looked forward to meeting them. She had heard that females were treated equally by the natives.

Chapter 12

Marguerite the Tagger woke on that frosty morning after the Blue Pool community's Harvest Celebrations and looked out from her drey. "Juniper," she called, "Oak, Burdock, come and see this", and her life-mate and their two youngsters emerged, looked around, then started to romp through the sparkling treetops, dislodging showers of ice-crystals which filtered down through the branches, catching the sunlight as they fell.

The squirrels' breath made white mist in the cool air as they leapt from tree to tree, their excitement spreading to other dreys until the trees of Steepbank seemed full of happy squirrels, all leaping and sporting in the shimmering treetops.

Then Marguerite noticed the grey squirrels below them. She counted. 1 Z 3 4 5 6 7 — 10 11 1Z 13 14 15 16 17

"Oh, Sunless Pit," she sighed. "I thought we had seen the last of you!"

The Reds' excitement died as others followed her gaze. All the older Reds knew of the strife and trouble caused by the grey colonisers, and how squirrels like these had forced the natives to leave the Blue Pool for sanctuary on Ourland. There the surrounding sea had kept the Silver Tide at bay until the Grey Death swept it away.

One of the grey males hopped forward.

"We come in peace," he called up, keeping his tail in the submissive position. "We would like to talk."

"Stay on the ground," Marguerite called down, and, with Alder the Leader by her side, she dropped to a lower branch.

Alder left the talking to the Tagger, who, though female and younger than he, was a squirrel of "infinite resource and sagacity", as he was fond of describing her to others.

"What do you want of us?" she asked, remembering the territorial demands of the previous colonisers.

Their leader introduced himself. "I am Hickory and this is my second-in-command, Sitka. We are squirrels of the Second Wave and have come to live in peace with you."

Marguerite glanced at Alder. This was unexpected!

The Grey went on, "We have instructions from the new leader at Woburn to learn local customs and to live by those. Our leader has recognised that we were wrong in trying to impose *our* culture in another land.

"On behalf of all squirrels of our kind, I apologise for any sufferings the Silver Tide caused you. We have been punished with the scourge of the Grey Death and we are here to make amends."

"Fine words," Marguerite called down suspiciously. "How do we know that you mean them – and that this isn't a trick?"

"We have composed what you call a Kernel:

> *When in others' lands*
> *Learn all the local customs,*
> *Do as the Red Ones do."*

Marguerite flinched at the extra word-sound in the last line. Not a true Kernel, she thought, but the meaning is good. She glanced again at Alder for authority to continue. He nodded and moved the stump of his tail in what would have been a flick of confirmation, had his tail not been severed after a clash with animals similar to those below them.

"We have suffered badly from squirrels like you, and are not yet ready to trust your intentions. There is vacant land to the north-east. You will know it by a great tree that has been struck by lightning. Spend the winter there, do not encroach, and in the spring, if we have come to trust you, we will meet again and teach you our ways."

The Greys raised and lowered their tails as a sign of acceptance, then meekly trooped away through the pines to find the Lightning Tree in the North-east Wood. The last to leave was Ivy, who was looking over her shoulder at the red female, but she had turned away.

"Well," said Marguerite after they had left, "what do we make of that?"

"I think you did the right thing," Alder told her. "They seemed contrite and well-meaning, but do animals like that really change their natures, just because of – what did they call it? – 'instructions from the new leader at Woburn'? I don't trust them." He reached back and rubbed the stump of his tail ruefully.

It's true, Ivy was thinking, that female was treated as an

equal. There were no fleas on her, though. Not one to be easily bettered in an argument. She might just be useful one day.

A few miles away to the east, between the Blue Pool and the shore of Poole Harbour, Tansy was losing some of her confidence. The Mainland now seemed very big and she was lonely. Having grown up in a community where the Council decided all major issues, she was not used to making many decisions on her own and found herself spending hours dithering whenever there was a choice of routes. She would choose one and start along it, only to change her mind, backtrack and take the other way. She wondered now how she had been so confident on Ourland.

Then, remembering the importance of her mission, she would press doggedly on. She *had* to find Marguerite and the Woodstock to save her family and friends.

Supposing she ran into any grey squirrels? But Marguerite's last message had said that they were all gone. She sniffed at the wind coming from the west. Could that be Greys' scent? It was faint if it was, but it certainly smelt like it. She trembled but pressed on.

Tansy was hungry and tired when she came to a Mandrey, outside which chickens pecked at grains of wheat and maize on the ground. A goose in the next field honked a warning as she approached, snaking her long neck through the wire at the squirrel and hissing ominously, but Tansy could see that the great bird could not get through the fence to harm her. She joined the chickens, enjoying the unfamiliar mealy taste of the dry yellow seeds, then, suddenly sensing the presence of a human dangerously near, turned to leap away.

She was too late to avoid the man's long-handled net.

Chapter 13

Crag dragged a rusted bolt to the Temple in the Lightning Tree. He had found the remains of an old wooden haywain and had set Rusty and Chip to gnaw at the partially rotted timbers in order to free the bolts. He carried them, one by one, up inside the Temple and placed them in nooks and crannies of the hollow branches, along with nails, screws and old cartridge cases that he had sniffed out in the undergrowth.

Coming back down the tree he stopped, peered below and rubbed his eyes. Clustered about the base of the trunk was a group of squirrel-like creatures with silvery-grey fur, looking up at him expectantly.

"Greetings to you, sir," one of them called up "Your friends at the Blue Pool sent us over here, but did not tell us that any other squirrel would meet us. I am named Hickory, and this is my second-in-command, Sitka. And your name, sir?"

"You are squirrels?" Crag asked.

"Why, yes, we thought all of the red kind knew about us by now. Had you not heard?"

"No! Until recently my family lived in isolation and we have only just come to the Mainland. Who are you?"

Crag came down to the ground and stood in front of the Greys.

"We are silver squirrels from over the sea to the west," Hickory told him. "Our ancestors were brought to this country, which we call New America, by humans and we have been setting up colonies here. Unfortunately, *some* silver squirrels got over-zealous and upset you natives. Then we suffered from a plague we called the Grey Death. Now our instructions are to work alongside you all and to learn your ways. So here we are!" He spread his paws wide.

"Did you say that you were sent here by the squirrels over at the pool?" Crag asked.

"Yes. They said we were to spend the winter here, but did not tell us that you would meet us. They were polite to us, but understandably suspicious. Well, here we are, sir." He waited expectantly.

Crag surveyed the Greys. They looked big and powerful, and had strong teeth.

"Follow me," he said, and led them off in the direction of the derelict haywain.

Tansy crouched in the corner of the dark cage. It was daytime, for she could see the winter light under the door, but it was too dark for her to make much sense of her surroundings.

The day before her captor's leather-gloved hand had taken her from the net and thrust her into the empty cage that had last been occupied by the pine marten. It was impregnated with his terrifying scent, but even this was submerged by the rank odours rising from the only other occupants of the cages, a pair of ferrets who snuffled and prowled about or slept noisily somewhere below her.

Tansy was still shaking with fright and her mind was going round in circles. She must get out to find Marguerite and the Woodstock to save the Ourlanders from the pine marten, but before she could do that she must get out to find . . .

The stable door opened and cold air rushed in. A man's dark eyes peered through the wire at her as he bent down to look into the cage.

"Come on, my lovely," he said, the words meaningless to Tansy. "I've brought you some special food."

In his hand was a paper bag containing a variety of Christmas nuts bought from a stall in Wareham market. He opened the cage door slightly and tossed in a handful, then closed it quickly. Tansy hid her head under her paws until he had gone out of the stable, leaving her once again in the cold darkness.

The nuts smelt strange and foreign; she felt for them in the sawdust of her cage floor and was puzzled by the waxy feel of the shells. The hazelnuts she knew, and the walnuts, but the strange three-cornered ones were new to her. She gnawed at the end of one until she could taste the oily kernel inside. She ate only a little of it, then opened a walnut, the flavour immediately bringing back memories of the celebration of the passing of the Longest Night, and the feasting the squirrels enjoyed when they knew the Sun would soon return with the warmth of spring.

Her spirits lifted by the man's gift, she tried every side of the cage for a way out, then crouched in a corner and recited to herself the Kernel of Encouragement:

When all is darkness
Squirrels need not fear for long,
The Sun will come soon

She searched again for a way to escape.

Blood was getting restless. He had finished eating the peahen that he had most recently killed in the church, had played with the feathers, slept for a full day and night and had then wakened with the squirrel-lust on him. He came down the bell-rope, passed the rows of dozing birds on the pew-backs and padded out into a grey winter day. He sprang up on to the gravestone of an earlier, human, inhabitant of the island and peered about, sniffing. The air was clear of squirrel-scent, so he made off towards the leaf-pile in the swamp. All hunters hope to find new quarry where they have successfully killed before.

Only the tails of his two previous victims were there. He sniffed at these until his mouth watered and his mind was filled with nothing but the urge to taste the blood of a squirrel. He ran up the trunk of an aspen tree and started his search.

Blood picked up recent squirrel-signs in Beech Valley. There were newly gnawed cones under the pine trees, fresh scratch-marks on the beech trunks and the tantalising smell was everywhere.

The pickets, though, had seen him coming and quickly spread the word. The females, the youngsters and the older squirrels had hurried off towards Woodstock Bay, whilst the fit males had watched Blood's movements from a safe distance. Soon they put their plan into operation. One, Just

Poplar, showed himself and tempted Blood to follow as he led him from tree to tree up the valley, keeping just far enough ahead of the pine marten to be safe, but near enough to keep Blood bounding through the branches at his fastest rate. Just Poplar knew that neither of them could keep up this pace and this knowledge was part of the Plan.

When he tired, he slipped behind a tree-trunk and the role of "tempter" was taken over by one of the ex-zervantz, Maple, previously called Maggot.

Maple was strong, fit and fresh, and set a merry pace to keep the marten from realising that he had been duped. The Plan was progressing well, the chase curving round and back towards the church. Even the last leap had been judged to perfection: Maple sailed over the gap between two trees that he had estimated was too wide for the heavier marten.

Blood, angry and breathing hard, glared after the departing high-tailed squirrel, gave up the chase, came down the trunk, went into the church and slaughtered a peahen. It was tame stuff, this, the stupid bird putting up little resistance as his teeth bit deeply through the feathers of her neck, the squawk of protest cut off in mid-call.

He ate his fill amongst the drifting specks of down, then climbed wearily up the rope to the bell-tower to sleep the remainder of the day away. Those squirrels would not catch him out with *that* trick again, he vowed to himself.

Ivy did not like the regime that Crag had imposed or the feeble way in which Hickory and Sitka accepted it. They might have instructions to learn the strange customs of the natives, but this metal collecting was a bore. Hickory and

Sitka seemed ready enough to carry out the instructions of the Temple Master, but whenever she had the chance, she would slip away from the work party and go off on her own. Sometimes she would go across to the Blue Pool and watch the Reds there, unobserved, from a distance, just to confirm that the one who called herself Marguerite was treated as an equal by the red males; it was clear that Crag had nothing but contempt for Rusty, his mate. Whenever she watched, she could see that Marguerite was not merely treated as an equal but held in very high regard.

Ivy had found a thin flat piece of grey stone near the haywain which, when she scratched it with another stone, bore a mark. One day, after deserting the working party, she went to where she had hidden this slate and drew the only marks that she could remember on it – **1** for one, **10** for two, **11** for three and **100** for four. This was how the Greys had counted before the Grey Death came, and she realised with a start that she was now probably the only Grey who remembered these marks and this way of counting. The idea troubled her. If she had died, all the knowledge of numbering would have died with her. She knew so much more about so many other things as well. There ought to be a way to record everything she knew, but how?

She wiped the slate clean and did a random line – **01000001**.* She was looking at the shapes, her head tilted to one side, sensing some hidden meaning in these, when she heard a sound behind her and turned to face Marguerite.

* ASCII code for A.

Ivy was surprised to see how small this Red appeared against herself now that they were together on the ground. She did not feel in any way threatened.

"Hello," she said "I'm Ivy."

"I'm Marguerite the Tagger. I came to observe your party and found you on your own. What are you doing?"

Ivy's tail rose. She was flattered to find a senior squirrel interested in her scratching.

"We count thiss way," she said, drawing **1 10 11** and **100** on the piece of slate again. "But I have jusst drawn **01000001** and it seemss to be telling me something."

Marguerite looked hard at the figures. They were similar to the patterns made with twigs and fircones that the first Greys she had met used to make their numbers. Here was a special Grey that she might learn from. Numbers of any kind had always fascinated her.

"Marguerite!"

She looked up, startled at the savagery in Juniper's voice.

He was crouched on a branch above her, quivering with rage.

"Come up here at once. Now!"

Marguerite bristled with anger, yet dared not show disrespect to her life-mate in front of this stranger. She could appreciate Juniper's concern; his first life-mate, Bluebell, had been killed by Greys near that very spot only a year or so earlier.

She leapt for the tree-trunk as the Grey turned away.

Ivy left quickly, abandoning the piece of slate. So much for equality, she was thinking.

*

Hickory and Sitka were discussing Crag in a hollow on the ground near the Temple Tree.

"Do you think that Crag's got all his conkers?" Hickory asked.

"It's hard to tell," Sitka replied. "Apart from the Reds we saw over by the pool, and his mate and son, they're the only ones we've met. We were told that the natives have funny habits."

"I think I preferred the old ways – our parents would just have zapped the lot of them. Start clean, then. None of this Sunless Pit business and sleeping on your own."

"I don't like the sound of the Sunless Pit, so I'm not taking any chances. I'm going to keep my nose clean and my tail dry. Go along with what the old fellow says, for a while at least. Have you seen Ivy? She keeps sneaking away."

Sitka looked around. "We'd better be getting back ourselves, or old Tin Can will be after our tails!"

Chapter 14

Chip's days were fuller than ever before. His father kept him and his mother at full stretch, working alongside the funny grey squirrels, who were so polite to both his parents and himself. Crag had found a pile of assorted scrap metal behind an old Man-cave and had organised the full resources of his new team to carry out the task of moving all the smaller pieces up into the hollow trunk of the Temple Tree.

The Greys were now sleeping there too, every squirrel in a separate corner or bay of the hollows. Crag did the rounds at least once every night to make sure that each squirrel, of whatever colour, was sleeping alone, and not indulging itself with the warmth of a tail for cover.

Once, when it was particularly cold and Crag had just done his rounds, Young Chip, shivering and fearing a rebuff, had crept silently to where his mother was sleeping and had crawled in beside her. Although she must have known he was there, she said nothing and the two lay there through the bitter night, sharing each other's warmth and jointly fearing the Sunless Pit until, at the first glimmer of light, Chip crept away to his own corner, past the Greys that he could see were all religiously observing the "no tail warmth" edict.

At prayers, when Crag came to the "sinned in the night" part, Chip glanced at Rusty, but her head was, like her tail, meekly lowered.

Whenever he had the chance, Chip questioned the Greys about their lives and their beliefs, but they had little to say except that they were now contrite and sorry for what their kind had done to the Reds, and had instructions to learn and to live by the local customs, which would have evolved to suit the conditions in each locality.

On one such occasion Crag had come up behind him when Chip had paused in sorting metal and was talking to Hickory.

"Why do you call this country New America?" he had asked, then had reeled across the scrap-pile as his father had struck him a blow across his head.

Crag snarled, "Don't delay the work with useless questions. We, and that includes you, have a Temple to furbish. Fear the Sunless Pit!"

Chip, his head spinning, had gripped a piece from a broken ploughshare with his teeth and started to pull it backwards through the grass under the trees, in the direction of the Temple Tree.

Crag was thinking about his wonderful Temple. It was far better than the one in the cave on Portland, and the Sun had provided a team of workers to help him fill it with the precious metal. Chip's mating could safely be left until the next year.

By then the Temple would be full. The Sun could clearly

77

see that he, Crag, was a worthy squirrel and would direct them to find a worthy female as a suitable mate for his son. Not one of those Blasphemers over at the pool, with their false stories and immoral ways. He must make sure that Chip was worthy himself by then; he was a bit of a slacker at present.

Wood Anemone the Able and Spindle the Helpful, the ex-zervantz who had left Ourland with Marguerite, had settled well as free squirrels at the Blue Pool. Unlike the other Reds, they had no personal knowledge of how the natives had been treated by the Silver Tide and often spoke between themselves about the Greys.

They did not know of the incident involving Ivy, Marguerite and Juniper, nor about Marguerite's anger with her life-mate. Marguerite had been all for going over to the North-east Wood to apologise to Ivy, but had been dissuaded.

"We agreed to leave them until after the winter. Then we will make formal contact," Juniper had told her, and since it had been a purely family matter, the Council had not been informed.

"Let'z go and zee what the Grey Wonz iz doing," Spindle suggested one afternoon.

"Do yew think uz zhould?" asked Wood Anemone.

"Well, there'z no taboo on it, and uz'z zurprised that Marguerite juzd zent them off like that lazd autumn. If they'z doing anything odd, uz could report back."

Their youngsters were away somewhere having fun of their own as Wood Anemone and Spindle left for the North-east wood. The slight feeling of unease that Spindle

78

felt he put down to his years of being a zervant. Now he was free, he told himself, he could do as he wished, within the Kernel Lore, and there were no Kernels that he knew about not looking at Greys.

They reached the Temple Tree clearing and watched from behind a tree-trunk as the Greys carried various pieces of metal along the paths that converged there. They were wondering what it all meant when a native voice in an unfamiliar accent addressed them from behind. "An inspiring sight, is it not?"

They jumped and turned to face an unknown Red.

"I am Crag, the Temple Master," he said.

"Greetingz, Crag the Temple Mazder," said Spindle, wondering what a Temple was. "Uz iz Zpindle the Helpful and thiz'z uz life-mate, Wood Anemone the Able. Uz'z puzzled by what the Grey furred zquirrelz iz doing."

"They prefer to be called Silvers," Crag told him. "Are you from the Blasphem – the community at the pool?"

"Uz iz. Uz'z the Guardianz of Beachend, in the Blue Pool Demezne," Spindle told him proudly.

"That's a fine place," Crag responded. "Did you have a good Harvest?"

"Yez, zuperb," Wood Anemone told him. "Uz ztored lotz of nutz, enough to zee uz all right through the worzt winter – and the zpring!"

"I'm pleased for you," Crag told them. "Are you Sun-worthy?

"Zun-worthy?" Spindle looked at Wood Anemone and then back at Crag. "If yew meanz, do uz leave the eighth nut az the zun-tithe – yez, uz iz."

"No, I mean, do you worship the Sun?"

79

"Zurely the Zun doezn't need uz to worzhip it," said Spindle. "Uz would have thought it wuz above all that! Yew makez it zound like won of the kingz uz uzed to have on Ourland."

"Oh, no. The Sun needs worship, and metal to be brought to the Temple. And repentance for your sins!"

"What'z zynz?" Wood Anemone asked.

"Things you do to indulge yourselves – unworthy things," Crag told her.

Wood Anemone's face showed her lack of understanding, but she and Spindle waited for instructions. Crag's voice carried that tone of authority that commanded instant obedience and unquestioning acceptance. It was the voice that the Royals had always used. The two ex-zervantz waited in silence for Crag to continue – if he chose to do so.

Crag noted their tail-down attitude.

"In the name of the Sun, I command you to report the position and amounts of all your community's food reserves," he demanded, and unhesitatingly Spindle the Helpful, one-time zervant to the King of Ourland, gave the information.

"There iz many lotz of hazelnutz in the copze near the Dogleg Field. There iz lotz of chezdnutz . . ." He reported as he had done to the Royals on Ourland.

Crag listened intently.

When Spindle had finished, he said, "In the name of the Sun, I forbid you to tell any squirrel what you have seen today, or I, Crag the Temple Master, will ensure that it is the Sunless Pit for you, for your dreylings and for your dreylings' dreylings – for ever!"

"Iz there really a Zunlezz Pit?" Wood Anemone ventured to ask the stern, high-tailed Red.

"Oh, yes – it is an awful place where any blasphemers, and those who disobey a Temple Master, will exist in darkness for ever. Say nothing of our meeting or of what you have seen."

Spindle and Wood Anemone left the North-east Wood, their tails low, feeling that they had done something wrong, but they could not speak of it, even to one another.

Crag watched them go. He was memorising each hiding place. "Many lots of hazelnuts in the copse near the Dogleg Field, lots of chestnuts . . ."

Tansy had finished the nuts that she had been given and was hoping for more. Several times a day she searched for a way of escape, but each attempt was as fruitless as before.

Afraid of getting muscle-weak from inactivity, she would race around the netting of the cage until breathless, then crouch in the darkness, listening to the grumblings of the ferrets in their indecipherable "weasel" language.

She often recited the Kernel of Encouragement to herself, confident in her faith that the Sun would indeed come soon. Then she tried to recall other Kernels of Truth that she had been taught.

Some were routine, just instructions on drey-building, general cleanliness and what food was safe and what was not, but as she remembered each one, with plenty of time to think about it, she realised that most Kernels had much deeper, hidden meanings and that within them they contained a complete philosophy appropriate to the whole

squirrel race. There was one that she especially liked, it
seemed so apt now:

> *"Fear" sniffed at the drey,*
> *"Courage" awoke and looked out —*
> *But "Nothing" was there.*

Tansy was saying this for the seventh time that day,
savouring its message, when the door opened and the man
came in holding the bag of nuts. Instead of staying at the
back of the cage, Tansy came forward boldly and, as the
lonely man opened the cage door and held out a Christmas
walnut, "Courage" hopped on to his sleeve, ran up his arm
and, from his shoulder, leapt for the daylight and freedom.

She scampered across the yard, past the man's
Christmas dinner, which was hanging by its feet from an
elder tree, scarlet blood pouring from its recently cut
throat, and over the wall towards the first tree she could
see. She climbed into a fork and looked back. The man had
come out of the stable and gone across to the goose hanging
from the elder tree. She watched him swing it violently to
and fro, blood splattering across the ground and up the
stone wall, before he went into the house.

Greys held no terrors for her now and, when she was sure
that the man was not coming out to follow her, she headed
directly for where she thought the Blue Pool to be, keeping
to the trees wherever possible, but running openly along
the ground when they were too far apart.

She spent one night in a hollow willow stump and
another in a rabbit hole that was disused and damp.
Finally, on a bitter winter day, with the east wind blowing
her tail over her ears, she crossed the smelly Man-track and

the railway, until only the North-east Wood stood between her and the Blue Pool.

In that cold, dank wood she smelt the oddly mingled scents of both Greys and unknown Reds. Then, along the path, came a first-year Red dragging a tangle of rusting wire.

She called to him and he looked fearfully over his shoulder before answering. He was tired and thin, and did not have the sleek, fat look that a well-fed midwinter squirrel should. Tansy, realising that she herself would not be looking at her best and might have frightened him with her sudden appearance, spoke to him formally.

"Greetings. I am Tansy the Wistful, on my way to the Blue Pool."

"Hello," said the young male, shyly.

Tansy waited for the formal response. When it was not forthcoming, she said, "Are you alone?"

"At the moment, yes. My mother is at the Temple and my father is with the Greys at the metal-pile."

"Is he safe with the Greys?" Tansy asked, and Chip looked puzzled.

"Oh, yes," he assured her. "They are cooperative."

Contrary to custom, Tansy had to ask his name.

"It's Chip," he told her, and she waited for the tag which would give her valuable clues as to the kind of squirrel he was. It did not come.

"Your tag?" She raised an inquisitive eyebrow and her tail indicated "question".

"I don't understand," Chip replied, looking worried.

A snowflake fell from the pink-grey sky and rested lightly on his whiskers. He brushed it away and looked up.

Suddenly the air was full of swirling, drifting flakes and the young male looked at Tansy in puzzlement, as though she were responsible for the phenomenon.

"What is this?" he asked.

"Snow," she replied. "We must seek shelter immediately."

"What about the metal?" Chip asked, indicating the baling wire.

"Leave that," she told him. "Where's the nearest drey?"

"I . . . we . . . we live in the Temple Tree. It's through there." He pointed to the track through the wood, now rapidly disappearing under a white blanket.

"Take me there, quickly, before we freeze," Tansy commanded him.

Chip looked at the tangle of hay-wire, felt the cold of the snow penetrating his fur and, with Tansy close behind, made for the Temple.

Crag, arranging metal in the hollow trunks, looked up as they entered in a flurry of snowflakes.

"Where's your offering?" he asked coldly.

Chip diverted his attention by introducing Tansy.

"Father, this is Tansywistful. I met her on the track. It is freezing cold and 'snow' outside."

"So, you abandoned your duty for a female and because you are a bit chilly. Huh!" Contempt sounded in every word. Crag turned away.

Soon, however, the Temple filled with cold grey squirrels who had returned with Rusty when conditions outside had made it impossible for them to "work their service". Tansy sat in a dark corner behind Chip, watching the Greys eating their meagre rations and rubbing their paws together to warm them. Crag and Rusty ignored her, but Chip fetched her two hazelnuts from the store area. Ivy watched.

As it got completely dark inside the tree, Tansy heard Crag call for silence for the Evening Prayer.

> *Invincible Sun,*
> *Forgive us, your poor squirrels,*
> *For always failing.*
>
> *Tomorrow, we will,*
> *If you will give us the strength,*
> *Try to do better.*

Tansy thought that his voice was colder than the snow outside.

"Do you snug up with the Greys?" she whispered to Chip.

The word was new to him and he savoured it; it had a warm, soft feel. "What is 'snug'?" he whispered back.

"You know, cuddle up in the dark."

"Cuddle up" sounded even nicer. He thought he knew what she meant. "No, we must all sleep apart," he told her.

"Nonsense," she told him, putting her paws around his shivering body and drawing him to her in the darkness. Then she settled down to cuddle him through the night, her tail fluffed and warm over them both.

They were still like that when Crag found them in the first thin light of a bitter winter's day.

"Out, out," he raged. "Sinners have no place in this Temple. The Sun will never, never forgive such behaviour. You, you squirrabel you, corrupting my son! Out, out! It's the Sunless Pit for you both. For ever!"

The confused female and the frightened young male were jostled and hustled out of the relative warmth of the tree into a cold white world outside.

"Follow me," Tansy said, hopping across the frozen crust of the snow which had hardened in the night. "We will go and find my friends."

"What are friends?" Chip asked.

Chapter 15

On the island Blood had scented the snow on the wind. In Scotland, where he had been captured the previous winter, he had often experienced snow and knew that the best thing to do then was to eat well and lie up.

The smell of peafowl drifted up from the nave below him, but he wanted *squirrel*. It had been a few days since he had outwitted the silly creatures when they had tried that same trick again. Did they think he was a stupid fox or something?

He came down the rope eagerly, snatched at the peacock's tailfeathers in passing, just to remind him that he was not to be ignored, and, as the frightened bird screeched in terror, slipped out through the door and up into the trees.

Once again there were no ruddled squirrels at the leaf-pile and he was pleased. Squirrel tasted much better when its blood was really warm from a good chase, and the hunt itself would be exhilarating.

He leapt from tree to tree, sniffing at the air, but even at Beech Valley there was no recent scent. He went along the Man-track up the centre of the island without even a glimpse of a squirrel's tail, and then, as the snow came drifting in on the north-east wind, he gave up the hunt and turned for home and peahen.

After Maple had been outwitted, and eaten in full view of the squirrels of Beech Valley, despair had overcome them. Oak the Cautious, feeling his age in the cold wind blowing in from the sea, had called a Council Meeting, sensing the need to provide stability and purpose in the shattered community.

> *In any crisis*
> *A Leader's first duty is –*
> *To keep hope alive.*

They met in the pines well to the west of Beech Valley, which they now felt was unsafe and dangerous. Watchers were set out and the wary animals discussed ideas to counter the threat posed by the pine marten and enable them to survive.

"It could wipe uz all out," Just Poplar said. "Then there would be no zquirrelz to bury the nutz to make treez to feed future generationz of zquirrelz."

"There wouldn't be any future generations to feed," said Clover the Tagger and Carer in a despairing voice, and the bleakness of a squirrel-empty island overcame them all.

They sat silently, the chill wind tugging at their tails. Then Just Poplar, remembering his Royal days, said, "The Bunker!"

They turned to face him for an explanation.

"Uz don't know if it'z ztill there, but there uzed to be a hollow willow in the deepezd part of the Zwamp with one zmall entranze. It wuz known only to uz Royalz and won or

88

two very truzded zervantz. It wuz where uz Royalz wuz all to go if the zervantz revolted. Uz wuz zhown it only wonz."

"Could you find it again?" asked Oak, eagerly.

"Uz could try, but uz wuz zhown it only wonz."

"Let's go now," said Oak, uncharacteristically, and the meeting broke up without even asking the Sun to bless its deliberations, the squirrels streaming off behind Just Poplar in the direction of the Zwamp.

They searched every mature willow, working their way through the trees above the black pools of water, until Poplar, with an urgent flicking of his tail, signalled success and the others, seeing this, joined him.

It was a perfect hiding place. The old tree leaned out across a pool and high up on its underside was a hole just big enough for a squirrel to enter. But, to get to it, the animals had to climb upside down along the trunk, clinging to the bark, with a drop into the pool below for any that lost a claw-hold.

Just Poplar went in first and flushed out a family of wrens who had regarded it as their winter home. They flew into the ivy covering a nearby alder stump, complaining amongst themselves in their thin voices.

Just Poplar hung his head out of the hole. "Come on in," he called. "Thiz *iz* the Bunker."

It was warm and dry inside, with plenty of room for the entire community. At the back of the hollow they found the old store-pile of nuts that the Royals had prepared for emergency use. Oak tried one; it was stale but edible.

They set a guard at the entrance and relaxed for the first time in a moon. They were even more glad of the protection of the Bunker when the east wind swirled the snowflakes past the entrance hole.

Chapter 16

Chip followed "Tansywistful" across the snowdrifts in the Lightning Tree clearing. The night wind had whipped the snow into fantastic shapes and had hardened and compacted the surface, before dropping to a whisper and fading away with the dawn.

The two squirrels travelled mostly through the treetops but, when they had to come down, they hopped around the great banks and curls of snow which sparkled and twinkled as the light from the rising sun coloured the drifts first pink, then gold.

Tansy showed Chip the marks left by the night animals; the fine footprints of a fox and the yellow spots where it had marked its passage across its territory. She showed him the splayed wing-marks where a heavy bird had taken to the air at the end of a line of backward-pointing arrows, and the golden feather with the dark band that identified it as a pheasant. All across the snow were the marks of two long and two round footprints.

"What made those?" Chip asked her.

"Rabbits," she told him.

"What are rabbits?"

Tansy looked at him in surprise. "Brown-furred creatures with long ears that live in holes in the ground."

"So *that's* what they are called. My father would never say their name. On Portland he said it was a Sun-cursed word and must never be spoken."

"What did he call them, then?" Tansy asked.

"Brown-furred creatures with long ears that live in holes in the ground," he replied, and they both laughed, their breath white in the air.

"Rabbits, rabbits, rabbits. What a funny word," he said.

The two went on together, each comforted by the other's presence, the snow-crust supporting them easily. Chip poked at his ears as they seemed not to be hearing properly; Tansy pointed out that this was the "snow-silence" and all sounds would seem muffled. They came to the top of a bank and looked down on to the pool, not blue that morning but covered in windswept grey ice, and they skirted it, keeping to the treetops.

"I'm expecting Marguerite to have a drey somewhere about here,' Tansy told Chip, and they searched each likely tree. She was right. A snug drey, nestled in a dense mass of pine branches and twigs, showed signs of habitation. Tansy called from outside,

> "*Hello and greetings.*
> *We visit you and bring peace.*
> *Emerge or we leave.*"

She used the ancient Calling Kernel which enabled any squirrel inside to greet or to ignore visitors to the drey, according to that resident's mood.

"Who calls?" a sleepy voice responded.

"Tansy the Wistful," she replied, a slight catch in her voice, "from Ourland, and Chip Who Has No Tag."

"Tansy!" An excited voice came from within the drey and Marguerite pushed herself out and instantly brushed whiskers with her old friend and year-mate.

"Tansy!"

"Marguerite!" They were hugging and whisker-brushing in a display of emotion never before witnessed by the shivering young male beside them.

"I'm sorry," Marguerite said at last, remembering her manners, and she made the formal greeting to him, adding, "Come in out of the cold." Then she said to Tansy, "Meet my youngsters and Juniper. You'll remember him, of course. Come on in, both of you."

Chip followed them into the cosy warmth of the drey and met Juniper the Steadfast, Marguerite's life-mate, and Oak and Burdock, their youngsters. It was crowded inside, each squirrel closely in contact with the others, but with no sense of sinning in the contact. In fact, Chip was over-whelmed by the cared-for feeling; the whole drey was filled with it.

He thawed out in the semi-darkness as he listened to Tansy tell of the reason for her journey.

"Marguerite, have you still got the Woodstock?" she asked as soon as it was decently possible.

"Not the original one, but yes, there is still a Woodstock. We keep it hidden. Why do you ask?"

"There's a pine marten on Ourland killing all the squirrels. I have come to get the Woodstock to kill it."

"How did you cross the sea from Ourland?" Marguerite asked, remembering her journey in the rubber boat and the

92

help the dolphins gave when she and her companions were in trouble amongst the rock towers.

Tansy told Marguerite of the stag, and of being caught and held in the cage. "But I'm here now, thank the Sun. All I've got to do is get the Woodstock back to Ourland and kill the pine marten."

"That's a big, 'all'," said Marguerite, thinking as she said it that she sounded like her father, Oak the Cautious. "Have you thought how you would get it there?"

"No, not really. I had to get *here* first," Tansy replied bleakly, and added, "but I'll find a way."

Marguerite pressed Tansy for details of her own family on the island. Chip could tell that she was astonished to hear of the death of Next-King Sallow and the abdication of King Willow and his other son, Just Poplar.

Then it was Marguerite's turn to tell of her adventures after leaving the island, of the friendly dolphins, and of meeting the refugees at Worbarrow. Then of the destruction of the Greys' Power Square in the Clay-Pan. This brought them to the "Grey" situation, and Tansy asked what Marguerite knew about them now.

"A plague that they called the Grey Death killed all of the ones that were here at that time, except Marble, and he died nobly trying to help us destroy the Power Square. Then, in late autumn, more came, very polite and friendly, but we sent them to the North-east Wood for the winter. They said that they wanted to live with us and learn our customs, but we didn't trust them, and winter was nearly here. If they come back in the spring, we will talk with them then. You didn't meet them when you came through there?"

Tansy told of meeting Chip near the Lightning Tree and of the Greys, and finally about being ejected by Chip's father, Crag, for snugging with Chip. The Reds were aghast at this, so Chip tried to explain the Portlanders' customs. He was hesitant in the company of so many others, and their proximity troubled him a little. Their body contact and ease of speech seemed to him to be wrong in some ways, but right, oh, so beautifully right, in others. Finally he asked the question that was troubling him.

"What is this feeling here? Every squirrel seems to care for every other squirrel."

Marguerite looked at the youngster, pathetic in his concern. She leaned over, brushed whiskers with him and whispered, "We call it Loving."

Chapter 17

Crag was fretting. The sun was shining and he knew that he should be out with his team of Greys getting more and more metal for the Temple. Yet the whole of his world was covered in this Sun-damned snow.

He sent for Hickory and Sitka and instructed them to organise the Greys in rearranging the offerings in the hollows of the tree. Then, dissatisfied, he had them put all the pieces back where they had been before. The Greys grumbled amongst themselves and he had to threaten the Sunless Pit to keep them active and Sun-worthy. Rusty was as silent as usual, but Crag could sense her resentment at the way he had treated Chip and that female who had spent the night with the youngster in the Temple Tree.

What else could he, Crag the Temple Master, have done? Chip might be his son, but building up the offerings in the Temple must always be his main concern, and the Greys seemed easily led and open to any influence. He dared not let standards drop, even for a moment. He was sure that the youngster would be back, suitably contrite and begging to be forgiven, when he found how degenerate other squirrels were. He was sure that he had taught him well.

Training is vital.
As the growing twig is bent –
So shall the tree grow.

Crag moved a rusted gate-latch to a new position, studied it for a minute, then moved it back a nut-width.

Ivy watched Crag moving the metal about. There was something in the intensity of his movements that impressed her. He really did believe in what he was doing. When she found an opportunity, she would ask him what it all meant.

Across the bright snow-covered heath and the cold marshes, beyond the leaden waters of Poole Harbour, in the chill belltower of the disused church, Blood woke and stretched himself, prowled about in the tiny room that was now home to him and decided he would go outside, if only to look around.

He came down the rope into the smelly nave, brightly lit in an unusual way by the reflected sunlight from the snow outside, and assessed his living larder. There were enough of the silly birds to see him through to the spring, even if he couldn't find squirrel again.

The biggest cock bird, known to his harem as Mogul, whose tail swept to the floor, eyed him sleepily.

I'll keep you till last, Blood thought. You're probably tough and stringy anyway. In passing, he pulled out a tail feather with his teeth and, ignoring the squawk of protest, carried it outside, where the sun caught the feather's rainbow eye and even Blood had to admire the iridescent colours.

Moved by an unusual urge, he poked the feather upright

into a snowdrift and pranced around it, making a ring of tracks in the crisp surface, then set off towards the leaf-pile in the swamp, mocked on his way by a pair of magpies, their white undersides appearing dingy against the gleaming brilliance of the snow.

After his first two visits he had never found squirrels at the leaf-pile, but it was worth a try, and he always went that way on his squirrel-hunting expeditions.

The ex-zervant, Caterpillar, in the Bunker, was bored. He had heard all the stories of Acorn, the first squirrel in the world, that any of them there knew. He had listened to endless discussions on new names for the ex-zervantz to replace the creepy-crawly names given to them by the Royals and thought the whole business unnecessary. He had refused the proposal of Catalpa for himself. He had always been Caterpillar and had never even seen a catalpa tree. He doubted very much if such a tree really existed!

And as for a tag – not for him! He would probably end up as Caterpillar the Ruddled, as all the Ourlanders knew of his fondness for the fermented sloes.

A diffused light was filling the hollow of the tree. The pool below was covered in ice and snow and the sunlight was reflected by this up through the round entrance. Caterpillar went and looked out of the hole, the light in the Bunker dimming as his head nearly filled the opening. "I'm going out", he called back over his shoulder.

In the early Bunker days the squirrels, when they needed to drink or to dispose of their meagre droppings, had always gone out in pairs, one to be watchful all the time.

A watchful squirrel
Survives to breed and father –
More watchful squirrels.

Despite the strength of this Kernel, in the absence of any attack or even a sighting of the marten since they had been in the Bunker, some of the squirrels had relaxed and gone out singly, but never for more than a few leaps from the leaning willow trunk. Today most of them were in the semi-dormant state that is not true hibernation, but does reduce the body's calls on the fat-reserves. Oak saw Caterpillar go, but was not concerned; he would be back soon.

Blood bounded along, the midwinter sun just warm on his back, his eyes narrowed against the glare from the snow. The air felt crisp and clean in his nostrils. There was no scent of squirrel as he came to the leaf-pile, dark in the white expanse, where the heat of the decaying leaves had melted the night's covering. He playfully scattered the compost, kicking it backwards from the pile and seeing how far he could spread it; the rotting leaves made brown stains on the white blanket.

As he dug down he found small round fruit, warm from the leaf-heat and smelling like the squirrels he had first found here. He tasted one whilst the magpies chattered and scolded him from a nearby bush. The fruit warmed his tongue, like blood, but as he swallowed, the warmth continued down his throat and exploded inside him. Wow!

He took another bite, and then another. He ate three of the sloes before the trees leaned over sideways and the magpies grew to the size of the eagles he could remember from Scotland. Blood did not care a feather. He ate another of the ruddled fruit.

Caterpillar, his sloe-craving overriding discipline or fear, climbed out from the Bunker entrance and along the underside of the trunk, then dropped to the snow-covered ground. No other squirrel had followed him out. In the muffled silence he stood on a drift and sniffed the air. Nothing, just snow and trees. He looked up at the hole, took a mouthful of snow, cold and crisp, felt it melt on his tongue, then hopped off in the direction of the leaf-pile.

He heard the magpies' warning long before he reached it. It was their "four-footed predator" call, so he climbed an alder trunk and went slowly through the bare branches, from tree to tree, until he could see them fluttering about in a bush near the leaf-pile, on which lay a ruddled pine marten.

Even with his traditional foe so far below him and obviously harmless, he felt the paralysing marten-dread seize him and he had to shake it off consciously. Caterpillar sat there, for the first time able to study their enemy with safety.

The pine marten lay on its back, apparently oblivious to the magpies who were growing bolder and circling closer, their harsh chatter annoying Caterpillar, who now dared to come a long way down the trunk. The magpies saw his movement and, suddenly tiring of their game with no response from the hunter, flew off together through the trees. Caterpillar waited and watched in the silence.

Slowly it dawned on him that the scourge of Ourland, the

terror which had haunted them for so long and which had forced them to live in that Sun-damned Bunker, was lying ruddled and helpless on the leaf-pile below him.

Had he been born a free squirrel, he might have known what to do, but being an ex-zervant, he had been trained from birth not to think for himself, just to do as he was instructed and to report unusual happenings to the Royals.

This was an unusual happening, but there were no Royals now, and if he told Oak the Cautious, their Council Leader, he might insist on punishing him with a denigratory tag for going so far from the Bunker against orders.

So Caterpillar sat there indecisively, and watched the pine marten as the sun's shadow moved round; until, chilled by a cold breeze from the sea, he turned back for the Bunker. Oak was waiting, concerned at his long absence.

"What kept you?" he asked, his voice as cold as the air outside. "Have you been to the leaf-pile?"

Oak manoeuvred himself until he could smell the errant squirrel's breath, but there was no taint of the ruddled sloes.

Caterpillar toyed with a full lie – zervantz were adept at these – then, seeing a slight relaxation in Oak's stance, chose the half-lie.

"Uz wuz bored and ztiff and uz went for a little exerzize," he said.

"To the leaf-pile?" Oak asked, knowing the habits of the ex-zervantz.

"Well, uz did go that way," Caterpillar conceded, then decided to turn the inquisition away from herself and said, "The marten wuz there, him udd been at the zloez."

"Martens don't eat fruit," Oak challenged him.

"Thiz won doez. Thoroughly ruddled, him wuz, lying of hiz back there like a dreyling, gone to thiz world."

"When was this?" snapped Oak.

Caterpillar looked around, trying to judge time from the artificially small amount of light coming in through the entrance hole. "A while pazd," was all he could say.

The other squirrels were alert now and had gathered round, aware of a feeling of excitement. Oak declared a Council Meeting.

"Caterpillar has reported that our enemy is senseless at the leaf-pile. This is an opportunity we must examine. What suggestions are there?"

"Let'z all go and kill it," said Just Poplar at once.

"Hold on," said Oak, his cautious nature asserting itself. "It may be a trap.

> *Squirrels – to survive*
> *Never act impulsively.*
> *Look before you leap."*

To which Just Poplar replied, quoting a Kernel that Old Burdock had taught him,

> *"Fear can paralyze.*
> *Zupprezz it and ACT. He who*
> *Hezitatez iz lozd."*

They looked to the Tagger, Clover, for clarification.

"Those Kernels do seem to contradict one another," she said. "I wish Old Burdock were here; she knew how to resolve these things. I suppose that it depends on the exact circumstances. Now if . . ."

The arguments went back and forth, the light in the Bunker dimming all the time.

Finally, Oak remembered the Leaders' Kernel:

> *Indecision kills.*
> *Act positively and lead.*
> *Action is the Key.*

"We'll go and kill the Marten," he said, then, realising that in a few minutes it would be completely dark outside, added, "in the morning."

Blood awoke. It was warm on the leaf-pile but the magpies were now *inside* his head and chattering incessantly. He stood up, fell over, then stood up more slowly. It was dark. He moved on to the snow and pushed his face into the coolness of a drift. The magpies in his head were not quite so loud now and, as he headed unsteadily for home, they almost, but not quite, stopped pecking at the inside of his skull.

At the door of the church he paused, pushed his face into the snow once more, pulled the peacock feather from the snowdrift and urinated on it, then went into the dark nave. He brushed against Mogul's tail, thought of giving it the usual tug, but his head told him that it could not take the inevitable screech.

He tried to climb the rope to his den in the tower. After the third fall he gave up, crawled under a pew and slept noisily amongst the dry peacock droppings and feather moult.

Chapter 18

———

Tansy had pressed Marguerite to tell her when the Woodstock could be taken to Ourland to deal with the pine marten on the assumption that, with her own parents in danger, Marguerite would drop everything and leave at once.

Marguerite's first reaction had been to do just that, and her busy mind started to organise the venture. Then she realised that she was not a free agent. She was the selected Tagger of this community, responsible for important aspects of their lives. She also had youngsters of her own, rather young for the hazards of winter travelling. It would need more than the efforts of Tansy and herself to take the Woodstock any distance. This, and the unknown future behaviour of Chip's family and the Greys, made the whole project impossible. But then she had been taught that nothing is impossible. The Kernel said:

> *If you think you can*
> *Or if you think you cannot,*
> *Either way it's true.*

So far she had not thought that she could.

"Tansy-Friend," she said, "we *will* find a way to get rid of the pine marten, but there is a lot of planning to be done first. There are many details for me to work out. Rest and sleep while I think about these. Nothing more can be done while this snow lasts. Try to sleep now. Leave it to me."

Juniper had been watching the shadows of the trees at High Sun as they reached out across the snow-covered ice on the Blue Pool. "They're getting shorter," he reported. "The Longest Night is gone. We can have the Midwinter Celebrations any time now."

Chip was exquisitely warm in the drey, constantly and pleasurably aware of the close contact with the other squirrels, especially Tansywistful, who was in a deep sleep next to him. He asked in a whisper, "What happens to the Sun in midwinter?"

Marguerite explained. "Every autumn the Sun, who is tired after shining so hard for us all summer, finds it harder and harder to climb up high in the sky. But, in the middle of the winter, his strength starts to come back, ready for the next year.

"We can tell when this is, because the shadows at High Sun start to get shorter. We celebrate then, because we know that spring and summer are on the way, and that winter will not last for ever." She smiled at the inquisitive youngster, encouraging him to ask another question.

"What's a celebration?"

"That's when all the squirrels get together to thank the Sun and enjoy themselves. We have feasting on our favourite foods, play games and chases and tell stories, usually about Acorn, the first squirrel in the world."

"And Primrose – who wouldn't go in the boat?" Chip asked.

"Yes. Do you know that story?" Marguerite sounded surprised.

Chip remembered that he had heard it when listening secretly with his parents that September night and, guided by an instinctive loyalty, replied, "Yes, I have heard it somewhere", and followed immediately with, "Where do you have these celebration things?"

"It has to be outside, for all of us to get together. That's why the winter one is sometimes late. We have to wait for a warm enough day."

The snow lay for three days, then a warm south-westerly wind came, with rain on its back, and the drifts shrank to dirty ridges before disappearing altogether. In the mild spell that followed the Celebrations were held.

Tansy tried to join in, but her mind was away on Ourland. The funny little squirrel she had brought away from the Cold Ones in the hollow tree stayed near her most of the time, always asking questions. A male of her own year, Tamarisk the Forthright, was also paying her attention and making disparaging remarks about Chip whenever he saw an opportunity.

"Why do you spend so much time with that little sqrunt?" he had asked her whilst Chip was within ear-twitch.

"He *needs* me more than you do – Mouth!" she replied.

"That's a matter of opinion," replied Tamarisk, immediately regretting his remark as Tansy turned her back on him, her tail indicating only too clearly that she had nothing more to say. He sulked away. Tansy's thoughts turned back to the pine marten and what she might have to do to get Marguerite to take some action.

Crag had waited for Chip to return to the Temple Tree, assuring Rusty that it must be the snow that was keeping him from his duties, and that his training and his fear of the Sunless Pit would bring him back. When the snow was gone and the weather had improved, however, Crag left the Greys and Rusty collecting metal, and went alone to the Blue Pool.

The colour startled him as the pool came in sight, azure under the clear winter sky, and he almost allowed himself a moment of pleasurable appreciation, but this was soon mastered and he pressed on with the task in hand: finding his errant son and bringing him back to help collect the sacred metal.

The Greys were now proving to be troublesome and lazy, not working as hard as he wished, and idling if he was not there to supervise. The metal store in the Temple was not growing as fast as he wanted it to. *Every* paw was needed.

One female, Ivy, obviously older than the others, had been asking questions. Why did they collect the metal? How long had they been doing it? Why did they come to this part of the country near other red squirrels but not have anything to do with them? Did red females ever hold equal positions to males?

It was this last question that Crag had found hardest to answer. There had never been females on Portland who had been anything other than producers of young squirrels, and more recently metal collectors, and they had not been good at either of these duties. Even Rusty had only ever managed to produce one dreyling, and he was a disappointment. Rusty was not much use at collecting metal either.

This female at the Blue Pool, though, who called herself Marguerite, appeared to hold a position and have equality. It must be a part of their degenerate ways. He had told Ivy that females were not capable of holding responsible positions, but they could be Sun-worthy and avoid the Sunless Pit if they worked hard at collecting the sacred metal.

Crag didn't meet any squirrels as he passed through the Deepend Guardianship, but on nearing Steepbank he stopped and watched. There were squirrels, red ones like himself, playing and sporting in the branches. That strange feeling, for which he had no name, was spreading out and trying to affect even him. He tensed his muscles to resist it. Were these degenerate ones always misbehaving?

Looking for Chip, he saw him following that squirrabel who had decoyed him from his home and duties, and a disturbing thought struck him. Could they have mated?

They were of different years, but that was no physical barrier. It would be awful if they had. However much one tried not to enjoy THAT, it did create a bond and it would be that much harder to get his son back. Sun forbid that he had mated with a Blasphemer.

Crag thought of the Portland "Bill", decreed by his grandfather, which clearly stated that the mating act was to take place only once each year and was not to be enjoyed. His great-grandfather had also, in that Bill, decreed that there was to be no frivolity, none of the traditional chasing and courting. The act must be done coldly and soberly, as befits true believers and collectors.

He, Crag, had kept to the Bill, but had to admit that it was hard not to enjoy mating, even with a dry old stick like Rusty. Evidently other Portland squirrels hadn't acted correctly and that was why the Sun had punished them with no offspring.

He approached the playful party and was seen by Chip, who moved closer to Tansy, who had reluctantly joined in when she could see that Marguerite would need time to organise a rescue party. Even so, to her the joviality seemed wrong and out of place.

Alder the Leader went along the branch to greet the squirrel stranger who had come to join them on this happy day.

"Greetings, stranger. I am Alder the Leader, selected Senior Squirrel in this our Demesne of the Blue Pool. I welcome you to our Midwinter Celebrations." He waited for the formal reply.

Crag scowled at the squirrels all about him.

"I am Crag, father of that idler," he said, pointing to Chip, who was cowering on a branch beside Tansy, "and I have come to take him back with me."

Alder stared at Crag and was silent in the face of this discourtesy. He had made allowances when the foreign Greys did not know of the correct greetings and customs, but this was a Red like himself, who ought to know the routines!

All the other squirrels looked on in silence until Marguerite said, "Stranger, your attitude puzzles and offends us. We have offered you our hospitality, yet you ignore this and insult your own youngster. If Chip wishes to leave with you, that is his right, now he is of age, but I for one would not blame him if he didn't." She flicked her tail to show contempt for his lack of manners and quoted the Kernel:

> *After Longest Night*
> *Last year's youngsters can decide*
> *Their own destinies.*

Crag ignored her, "Come," he ordered, glowering at Chip, who was still crouching at Tansy's side. She put a paw on his shoulder. He started to obey his father, but, feeling the pressure from Tansy's paw increase, replied, "I choose to stay."

Crag moved forward, then stopped and turned to go. He called back, "It's the Sunless Pit for you, *and* the rest of you. For ever!" His grand exit was spoilt by his missing a paw-hold in his anger and having to drop to a lower branch.

Moving from tree to tree in as dignified a way as he could, back towards the North-east Wood and the Temple Tree, he felt a resurgence of the squirrelation overtake him and, out of sight of the others, he paused irresolutely. There can be no harm in watching what they are up to, he told himself, an old saying of his grandfather's rising to his mind:

> *Know your enemy.*
> *Find out all his weaknesses.*
> *These will be your strengths.*

He circled round to hide downwind of the revellers and observe, but if he had hoped for a true view he was disappointed. The dampening effect of his visit had spoilt the day for most of them, and soon, in an attempt to divert the squirrels' attention, Alder called on his life-mate, Dandelion, to tell an Acorn story. The squirrels gathered around her in the late-afternoon sunshine. Crag moved up quietly to listen, unobserved.

Dandelion looked around, saw that they were all seated and ready and began.

"Once upon a time, on the great rock of Portland, lived Acorn and Primrose. This was a long time after the Flood had come and gone, and hardly any animals lived there because there was not much soil on the rock to grow plants to feed them. The sequoia tree in which they lived was beginning to die as its roots were not able to find enough soil and moisture to feed it.

" 'Let's go and find another place to live,' " Acorn suggested, and his eyes lit up with excitement at the thought, as he always enjoyed an adventure. Primrose was not so ready to leave her home, though she was eager to see more of the new world. Acorn had to explain about the dying tree and how he was sure that there would be many lovely places on the Mainland, which he described as growing with nuts, and sunny, though in fact he had never been there. Even squirrels like Acorn will sometimes describe things in autumn colours when they want to persuade others to do something.

"Now, when my grandfather told me this story I had no real idea of how a squirrel would get from Portland to the Mainland, but Young Chip, who used to live there, has told me all about it. Portland is called an island, but it is not really an island because there is a bank of pebbles, round like birds' eggs, joining it to the Mainland. Acorn and Primrose set off along these pebbles, with Acorn telling Primrose not to look back – there was adventure and excitement ahead.

"As he was telling her this, a great wave came rushing up the beach and swept Acorn out to sea."

"I saw waves like that," said Chip. "They are huge!"

The other squirrels turned to him and Tansy whispered, "You are not supposed to interrupt when a story is being told, Chip-Friend."

"I'm sorry," he said, "but it is just like that. Sorry."

Dandelion smiled at the apologetic youngster. Obviously his family did not tell such stories to one another.

"Where was I? Oh, yes. Acorn had been swept out to sea by the wave and Primrose was left on the beach, heart-broken because she was sure that her beloved Acorn would drown, and she could not swim out to rescue him. However, the Sun knew that if he let Acorn drown, then there could be no more squirrels, as they were still the only ones in the world. So he sent a *second* wave to sweep Primrose out as well. She was terrified, but this wave took her right to Acorn's side where she clung on to him so that he couldn't swim either, and they both started to sink.

"Suddenly, up from underneath them came a big black shape that lifted them out of the water. From near their feet a hole opened and a fountain of water shot up into the sky. Then air hissed down into the hole it had come out of. It was a . . ."

"A whale!" shouted Chip and, as every squirrel turned towards him again, he said, "Sorry, but I saw one once.

They are black and they live in the sea and they are ever so big . . . Sorry."

"I didn't know if they really existed outside stories," admitted Dandelion, "but if Chip has seen one, then they must. Thank you, Chip.

"Now, this whale was very big and whether or not it knew it had two squirrels on its back, Acorn and Primrose couldn't tell. They were afraid that it would sink again and they would be back drowning in the sea. However, this whale started to swim around Portland just as if it did know that it was carrying something very important and knew just where it had to go.

"Acorn and Primrose clung to each other, trying to keep their balance on the smooth skin of the whale as there was nothing else to hold on to. They were afraid that if they dug their claws in, the whale would dive under the water to get them to stop.

"When the whale had swum past the end of Portland, it turned and swam towards some white cliffs, then along the coast for a very long way until it passed a long sandy beach on their left-paw side and through a narrow place where the sea was rushing out. Ahead was an island which Acorn thought was the most beautiful island he had ever seen, with trees reaching out over the water. Under one of these trees the whale stopped, and Acorn and Primrose climbed up an overhanging branch and on to the island. The whale flipped its tail at them, then swam back out to sea.

" 'What is this place called?' " Primrose asked, as she believed that Acorn knew everything.

"He looked around with a knowing look on his face. 'This is Our Land,' " he said.

"And that is how squirrels first came to Ourland and they are still there, as several of you know. Wood Anemone and Spindle were born there." Dandelion looked for the ex-zerventz amongst her audience.

"That'z true," said Spindle, "but it zeemz a long while now zinze."

The listening squirrels flicked their tails as a sign of appreciation to the story-teller and, with some of the young ones yawning and stretching, they went off to their dreys as the sun dipped below the horizon and a chill spread through the winter air.

Crag sat on his hidden branch feeling the cold penetrate his fur. What subversive rot! What rubbish! How could any squirrel believe that? Squirrels being carried on the backs of whales, indeed. Rubbish!

Hunger pangs stabbed at his gut and he dropped to the ground to forage in the dusk. This was one of the places those two naïve squirrels had told him was a store area. He could scent plentiful supplies of buried nuts, hidden by the Blasphemers in the autumn. If my work-team had this food, he thought, they would not have to waste precious metal-carrying time foraging. These Blasphemers and tellers of false stories didn't deserve the Sun's bounty.

He turned and made his way to the Temple. He would have to work extra hard tomorrow to make up for a wasted day, but the Grey team would work better with full stomachs.

Chapter 19

The squirrels in the Bunker had nearly finished the food reserves. Oak had rationed the stale nuts from the first day they had been in the hollow tree and, as all of them were well fed and winter-fat from a plentiful autumn, there had been no real hardship, though Fern the Fussy had constantly complained about the rancid taste of some of the shrivelled old kernels. Oak had had to take her to one side and point out that as the life-mate of the Leader she was expected to set an example to the others.

At first morale had been good; the relief at being in a place away from the constant fear of attack by the pine marten was enough. But when Caterpillar had failed to tell them in time that the marten was vulnerable, and each of the senior squirrels knew that they all shared responsibility for the indecision, many found it easier to blame the individual who had been first at fault. Caterpillar felt himself to be isolated and stayed on his own in a far corner of the hollow.

The ex-Royals – Just Poplar, his mother, Ex-Kingz-Mate Thizle, and his sister, Teazle, as well as his cousins, Voxglove, Cowzlip and Fir – tended to keep together in a group, though Voxglove and Cowzlip were learning all they could from Clover about the craft of being a Carer. Fir would occasionally mix with the incomers, but he did not have much to do with the ex-zervantz.

Amongst the others, liaisons formed and dissolved in the confines of the hollow tree, most ending in harsh words and sulks; the confined space of the Bunker distorted the courting patterns evolved over centuries of open space and tree-life.

Oak guessed that the Longest Night must have passed, and suggested to Fern that they hold some kind of celebration.

Fern was having another bad day; she hated the darkness of the hollow. "With what?" she had replied, witheringly. "Stale hazelnuts and a mouthful of fungus each? Forget it!"

As the days passed, the quarrels increased and Oak knew that some action on his part was needed, but he was unsure what to do and was therefore pleased when another cold spell made all the confined squirrels sink into a semi-dormant state, bringing peace to the Bunker once more.

One morning, as the light in the hollow was beginning to brighten with the rising sun, Just Poplar gently shook Oak's shoulder to waken him.

"I think your Fern is Sun-gone," he said.

Oak turned and looked at his life-mate curled beside him and shook her gently. She didn't stir. Her tail, with the thin grey hairs of age, covered her as a blanket. He hadn't noticed how old she had been looking until then and he felt a twinge of vulnerability as he realised that he too was really quite old now. He shook her again, not believing that she could just have left him in the night, then called Clover to see to her. She confirmed that Fern the Fussy was indeed Sun-gone.

Memories of happier days at the Blue Pool flooded over him. He could picture her sitting on the grooming branch outside their drey there, combing her fur and tail with her claws. Everything had to be just so!

All he could do now was to ensure that she had a worthy burial. Somewhere peaceful where she could nourish a tree, as it said in the Farewell Kernel:

> *Sun, take this squirrel*
> *Into the peace of your earth*
> *To nourish a tree.*

Clover was clearly thinking the same thing. She opened her mouth as though to say the Kernel, closed it again, looked across at the entrance hole and then said, "We've got a problem."

Oak was about to respond by quoting the Kernel which stated that there were no Problems, only Challenges, thought better of it and waited for Clover to explain.

"We *can't* bury Fern," she said. "As soon as we get her through the hole, she'll drop into the swamp."

"We can't keep her in here," Oak replied, and looked at Just Poplar as if he might know how the body could be disposed of in a dignified and fitting way.

The other squirrels had woken and were gathered round Oak with words of comfort and regret. An informal Council Meeting developed and finally it was agreed, with Oak grudgingly conceding, that they would, for the sake of the enclosed community, *have* to drop the body out of the hole into the zwamp.

Fern would not have liked that, Oak thought, remembering how carefully she had groomed herself each day, determined to maintain what she called "proper standards", but he could see no alternative.

Fern's body was dragged to the exit hole and Clover rehearsed the Farewell Kernel in her mind. It was not exactly appropriate, she thought – squirrels like to be buried at the foot of their favourite tree – but times were not normal. She looked at the other squirrels clustered around her in the dim light, then reached out and put her paw on Fern's shoulder. Clover opened her mouth and was about to say the Kernel when Chestnut the Doubter, who had kept silent up to this point, whispered in her ear, "I don't think she'll go through the hole."

Chestnut was right. The body had stiffened in the curled-up sleeping position, and would not straighten. No manoeuvring or shoving could post it to a muddy and undignified end. As the squirrels always buried their Sungone ones at once, they were not to know that if they had waited, their problem would have solved itself. Even in death Fern had managed to maintain "proper standards".

A formal Council Meeting was convened and after an awkward discussion it was decided that, as tradition called for bodies to be buried as soon as possible after death, they had no choice other than to dig a hole in the powdery punkwood at the very furthest corner of the hollow and put Fern in that. Oak and Clover said the Farewell Kernel together as the other squirrels crouched silently around them. Then Oak, suddenly needing to be alone, went out through the exit hole and climbed up the bark of the old willow to the highest branch, where he clung blinking in the bright sunlight.

Chapter 20

Crag sensed a different atmosphere in the Temple Tree when he awoke. There was an ominous grumbling from the Greys and he knew that whilst he had been away they had been plotting against him. Why had Rusty not warned him? Then he recalled that she *had* tried to talk to him the previous night. He had forbidden her to speak as he had been tired, and he had sent her off to her own sleeping space.

Hickory and Sitka were climbing up towards him, followed at a distance by that female, Ivy, or Poison Ivy as he had heard some of the Greys call her. They looked ill at ease.

Crag did not wait for them to speak. "I'm glad that you came up. I have an announcement to make. I am able to increase rations all round and today there will be no work. This is to be a Sin-day to celebrate the passing of the Longest Night."

Hickory glanced at Sitka, then turned back to Crag.

"What's a Sin-day?"

"It's a day when there is no work and we all have extra rations. Go and tell the others. There will be a special meal at dusk. In the meantime you may all rest or forage as you feel inclined. That is all." He dismissed the Greys with a flick of his tail and went outside. He hoped that the local sycamore trees were subject to the same afflictions as the few Portland ones had been.

They were. He sorted through the dead leaves on the ground until he had at least one for every Grey plus one each for himself and Rusty and carried these back to the Temple Tree, watched by Greys sitting about in unaccustomed idleness.

At dusk he called the Greys together and handed each a leaf. Then he gave one to Rusty and held one in his own paw.

"Do exactly as I do," he instructed as he rolled the leaf into a tight tube. He smiled as he did this and the Greys, intrigued by this previously unseen aspect of the Temple Master's character, relaxed, and tried to roll their crisp black-spotted leaf into a similar tight tube. Crag went from squirrel to squirrel, holding his own rolled leaf and directing the others as their tubes sprang open and they rolled them up again. For the first time, laughter was heard in the Temple Tree clearing.

Crag was showing Ivy just how it was done when his own leaf dropped from under his left forelimb and unrolled on the ground. He grabbed it quickly and rolled it tightly, but not before Ivy had seen that this leaf was clear of any of the black mould spots.

Crag moved among the Greys until every squirrel was holding a tightly rolled leaf.

"Now," he said loudly, "we must each eat our own leaf. Stem and all. Like this . . ." He nibbled his way rapidly down the leaf then chewed the brown stem. "There," he said, "nothing to it!"

The Greys, having some unaccustomed fun, followed him and, vying with each other to be the first, crunched on the musty-tasting leaves. Only Ivy, pretending to be having difficulty with her broken tooth, let her leaf unroll and bit at it carefully, unobtrusively dropping the pieces with the black spots on them.

In the night Hickory crawled across to Sitka's sleeping place.

"I feel awful," he whispered. "I know it can't be true, but I feel as if I'm falling through space, spinning round and round like a sycamore seed."

"Me too," said Sitka, and they crouched together, shivering and waiting for daylight.

For them and nearly all the other squirrels in the Temple Tree, daylight did not come that day. Long after they knew it must be light, the helpless, sick animals cowered in apparent darkness, blinking their blind eyes and clinging to the inside of the tree in a vain attempt to stop the spinning, falling feeling.

Ivy, the only unaffected Grey, watched Crag moving silently among them. She noted that Rusty was in the same state as the Greys.

At High-Sun Crag moved into a position where he could be heard by all.

"I am disappointed," he announced. "Not one of you has passed the Sin-test. Each of you must have sinned grievously to be so affected. This is why the test is special. It finds out not only the squirrel who has sinned openly, but those who have sinned in their hearts. All those who are impure will now be experiencing the horror of the Sunless Pit. Falling in darkness for ever. He paused. "But I, Crag the Temple Master, can give you hope. All those who truly repent and vow to serve the Sun in any way I direct will be forgiven and have a second chance. Think on what I have said."

He climbed out of the hollow and up one of the dying upper limbs of the oak. Ivy followed him.

"You misserable crooked worm and tricksster," she said, the words hissing savagely past her broken tooth. "I know that you made them eat poissoned leavess and that iss why they are all sick. Even your own mate. I don't know whether to kill you mysself or tell the otherss what you have done and let them do it."

She looked at Crag in contempt, then spoke again. "There iss, of coursse, one other thing you could do."

Crag looked up at her. She suddenly seemed much bigger than he was.

"You could tell the otherss that I alone have not sinned and becausse of thiss I am to be in charge of all the Greyss."

Crag hesitated.

"Right," said Ivy. "I will denounsse you for the tricksster you are."

"Wait," said Crag. "Tell me just what you want. I am sure that we can work together for the glory of the Sun."

"Ressponssibility," said Ivy, "and a chansse to prove mysself to otherss."

On the third morning after the Celebrations Juniper wriggled out of his drey in a pine overlooking the Blue Pool and started down the trunk to forage for his breakfast. He stopped, head down. The ground below him was covered with grey squirrels, scratching and digging where he and Marguerite had buried their winter reserves. He went carefully on down the tree to investigate, pausing a few feet above the scattered pine needles covering the earth.

"What are you doing?" he asked, the formal greeting seeming inappropriate.

The Greys ignored him. He asked again, and was again ignored as the intruders dug up nut after nut, eating some and preparing others to be carried away.

"What *are* you *doing*?" he asked loudly, for the third time.

None of the busy Greys so much as glanced in his direction. He looked round for support, but no other Red was in sight and he felt the same frustration that he had known when, as a dreyling, his companions had "sent him to the conker tree" for some misdemeanour or other. Juniper went back up the pine trunk to alert Marguerite.

Other Reds were now coming silently through the trees, warily watching the activity below. Soon Alder the leader arrived, leaping across the last gap and landing awkwardly, having no tail to balance himself with. The others looked to him for guidance.

"What's going on?" he asked.

Juniper explained what little he knew.

With Juniper and Marguerite beside him, Alder went down the trunk and asked the Greys why they were digging up all his community's nuts. Alder too was ignored; the Greys just carried on as if the Reds did not exist. Not knowing how to stop them, Alder, after a minute or so, led Juniper and Marguerite back up the tree and they watched the raiders depart, all carrying nuts in their mouths.

An hour later the Greys were back, collecting more of the Reds' precious Harvest, not even leaving the sacrosanct eighth nut as required by the Kernel:

> One out of eight nuts
> Must be left to germinate.
> Here grows our future.

Alder was on the trunk, raging at the Greys, when Marguerite noticed a Red whom she recognised as the father of Chip. He was directing the foraging party. She slipped away through the branches and came down behind him.

"What's going on?" she asked angrily. "Those are our reserves!"

Crag turned to her scornfully. "You deserve to have nothing. You are all blasphemers, story-tellers and pleasure-indulgers – you don't even collect metal! And you've corrupted my son!' he added, venom in his voice. "At least these nuts will feed Sun-fearing squirrels even if they are grey. If you get your lot to repent and help us fill the Temple, I will consider sharing this bounty with you."

"That bounty, as you call it, is *ours*," Marguerite retorted. Then, noticing that Crag was looking over her shoulder, she turned to see that there was a group of Greys close behind her.

"Shall we remove her, Temple Masster?" asked a grey female with a broken tooth.

"She's just leaving," Crag replied, as Marguerite leapt for the tree-trunk. "Carry on collecting the bounty. Don't talk to the Blasphemers."

Marguerite re-joined her family and companions, and

told them what had occurred. When she had finished, Chip slipped away to speak to his father. He found him as Marguerite had, organising the Greys and directing their plundering.

"Father," he said hesitantly, "these are nice squirrels. They are what they call 'friendly', and they *do* respect the Sun, only in a different way from us. Why don't you talk more with them?"

Crag glowered at him. "They really have got you in their paws, haven't they? You always were weak. Well, they won't have you much longer!" He nodded to two Greys who had come up behind Chip, and they seized his forelimbs and dragged him, scratching and chattering in fear and anger, towards the North-east Wood.

Tansy had trailed Chip, or Chipling as she usually called him, when he had gone to speak to his father, and had seen him being taken away by the two Greys. She was annoyed because Marguerite, though always agreeing that they must take the Woodstock to Ourland, appeared to be doing nothing about it. She had vague hopes that Chip might, in some way, be able to help her. Tansy followed them quietly, through the treetops, wondering what it was that one of the Greys had said to the youngster that made him stop calling out. Crag and the laden Greys were coming along the ground below her in a group, hampered by their loads of nuts.

When in sight of the Temple Tree she stopped, hid herself and watched what was happening. She saw Rusty run down the trunk and across the ground, hug her skinny son to her and then, seeing Crag approaching, push Chip away and begin to scold him unconvincingly. "Why did you go away with those Blasphemers?" she asked. "Your father and I were most upset. Come on into the Temple and repent for your sins."

Chip, now alert to such things, had detected a note of warmth in her voice and followed her meekly.

As he went he heard his father issuing instructions to the Greys that "the chit" was to be watched at all times. The broken-toothed female appointed guards.

Inside the Temple Chip could see that there was much more metal than when he had last been here; the main trunk was nearly full and the hollow secondary trunk, which grew away from the main tree like a squirrel's tail from its body, was also being filled. There were many more Greys too; others must have arrived from the north. They were all busy, either bringing in metal or stowing the plundered nuts in the hollows and crevices of upper limbs. Ivy offered him a nut, but he refused it.

Later, when it was dark and Crag had said the familiar words of the Evening Prayer, Chip tried to slip away, but every exit was blocked by an alert grey squirrel.

He sought out his mother's sleeping place and tried to join her, but she pushed him away. He could sense his father's disapproval.

"None of your blasphemous behaviour here. This is a Temple of the Sun," the harsh voice came out of the darkness. Chip went back to his sleeping place and lay there, rigid and cold, thinking of the warmth of his friends' dreys. He yearned to feel Tansywistful's warm body snug against his.

*

Tansy was awake, wondering what her young friend was doing. She knew from her own experience and from Chip's descriptions just how it would be in the Temple Tree. She tried to think of some way of getting him back. In the morning she would have another look at the Temple Tree, if she could avoid Crag and the Greys. As she lay there, thoughts of her family and her friends on Ourland crept up on her and she again felt an agonising guilt that she had not been able to do more to get help to them. There was nothing *she* could do, she told herself, unless Marguerite and the others could be persuaded to assist her. In the meantime that funny youngster needed her.

Eventually she fell asleep, to awake in the darkness, overcome by marten-dread, and she lay shivering until dawn.

Neither Spindle nor Wood Anemone had slept, each sure that their indiscretion had resulted in the raid by the Greys, but neither could speak of it to the other.

Marguerite was trying to find some way of reconciling her desire to help Tansy with her duty as a parent and as Tagger to the Blue Pool community. She had discussed her dilemma with her friend Dandelion, who told her that her life-mate, Alder the Leader, was adamant that Marguerite must put her duty to the community first. He had led them all to the Blue Pool and they needed to stay together as a strong unit, especially as there was now an obvious threat from the unpredictable Greys and the strange Red, Crag. Should she insist on a Council Meeting to discuss it all openly?

The following morning was clear and bright, with frost

crystals sparkling on the pine needles as Tansy slipped quietly through the branches towards the Temple Tree. A party of Greys passed under her, noisily heading for the pool and more "bounty". She crouched on a high branch until they were out of sight, then went on even more cautiously.

Greys were leaving the Temple Tree, each group heading in a different direction. These, she assumed, were metal-hunting parties.

When she reached a pine tree where she could overlook the clearing in which the Temple Tree stood, she could see that some Greys had been left on guard. Seven or eight of the biggest were either patrolling the ground near the tree or were in an upright and alert stance close to the entrances to the hollow. She settled down in a dense clump of pine needles to watch.

As the sun got higher, the patrolling by the Greys slowed down, but she saw the activity intensify when Crag the Temple Master appeared at one of the holes and came down the trunk, followed by even more Greys. They left, heading eastwards, Crag dominating the larger and more powerful grey squirrels. Another party left, heading north, led by the broken-toothed female.

Tansy continued her silent watch.

It was nearly High Sun and several parties of Greys had come and gone when she saw Chip emerge from the highest of the holes in the Temple Tree, with a red female that she knew must be his mother. She watched as the two climbed one of the spiky dead top branches of the stag-headed oak. They clung there, whispering to one another.

Tansy in the pine and the Greys on the ground were

watching them and listening, trying to overhear what was being said, but Chip and Rusty kept their voices low.

"Your father will be furious if he knows that we have been talking like this," Rusty whispered, looking fearfully down at the patrolling squirrels.

"That's just what I mean. We can't live our entire lives in fear of what Crag-Pa will say."

"But if we don't do as he says, it will be the Sunless Pit for us both – for ever."

"Do you really believe there is such a place?" Chip asked. "Tansywistful doesn't. She says it was invented in the old days by the 'Nobles' to make lesser squirrels obey them."

"How would she know?" Rusty asked. "She's only a young squirrel herself." She was about to tell her son about the dreadful night and the day of darkness when he interrupted.

"At the Blue Pool they – we – they – all discuss things, you can say anything you want to and the others will listen to what you say and tell you *their* ideas. It's ever so interesting. Everything is shared."

"What does 'shared' mean?" Rusty asked, keeping a watchful eye for Crag's return, hoping he wouldn't come back for a while.

Chip explained this concept as best he could, then tried to explain "Love".

"All the squirrels 'love' one another. They help each other whenever they can. Even when they disagree about something and quarrel, they soon make it up because they don't like seeing their friends upset." He then had to explain "friends" to a puzzled Rusty.

"But what about sins?" she asked.

"They don't have them. All the things that Crag-Pa calls sins they do all the time, and they don't feel bad about them." He described snugging up and comfort and warmth to his increasingly perturbed mother.

"Don't you think that their way seems more natural?" Chip asked.

"I don't know about this 'natural'. We've *always* done things the way your father told us to." However, she let her mind relax enough to remember the feeling of warmth and rightness she'd had when she'd cuddled her young son when he was a dreyling, so long, long ago.

"What about these untrue stories that they tell, that upset your father so?" she asked, after looking round the clearing again.

"Tansywistful says that stories don't have to be true as long as every squirrel knows them to be 'stories'. They are sometimes just for fun and sometimes they have messages in them which you have to work out." He tried to explain "fun".

"We'd better go down," Rusty said. "Your father will be back soon."

Entering the hollow of the tree by the highest hole, Rusty allowed her paw to rest momentarily on her son's shoulder. He was right, it did feel natural.

Tansy, across the clearing, watched them go in out of her sight, waited a little while longer and then went back to the Blue Pool.

Chapter 21

———

Old Oak was feeling nauseous. There was an overwhelming scent of decay filling the Bunker. Each squirrel knew that it came from the decaying body of Fern, buried in the powdery punkwood at the back of the hollow, but, out of respect for Oak's feelings, none had openly remarked on it. Now, with the temperature rising whenever sunshine heated the hollow tree, it could no longer be ignored. Oak called a Council Meeting.

"My fellow squirrels," he began, "we have been through much hardship and danger together and I have valued your support. Now, though, since my life-mate Fern has gone Sunwards, I am increasingly feeling my age and do not believe that I can give the leadership you all deserve."

He paused and there was a murmur of concern from the others.

"We are virtually out of food, the air in the Bunker is getting sour and soon we will have to leave, despite the danger from the marten outside. I just don't feel up to taking the responsibility of leading you; my brain is tired and I can no longer think as clearly as I used to. I propose to stand down and help you to select a new Council

Leader." He slumped back, exhausted by the strain of this long speech and the relief of having at last given up what had become an impossible burden to him.

The squirrels waited. There were no real precedents for a Leader standing down. Clover the Carer and Tagger fumbled in her mind for a Kernel to help guide them. All she found was:

> *In any crisis*
> *A Leader's first duty is –*
> *To keep hope alive.*

But this did not seem appropriate, though the need to keep hope alive was apparent enough. Could I be Leader? she asked herself, then dismissed the idea. It was hard enough combining the duties of Tagger and Carer. She was training the two ex-princesses Voxglove and Cowzlip to take over the Caring role and they were learning fast, but it would be a long time before she could let them carry on without her help.

She looked around at the assembled squirrels sitting expectantly in the dim light waiting for someone to propose something.

Chestnut the Doubter for Leader? she wondered. If they appointed him, he wouldn't believe it and his attitude was always negative anyway. A Leader must be positive!

His life-mate Heather Treetops? She would like the honour, as she always boasted that her ancestors were noble squirrels, but she had never shown real depth and, though prepared to criticise others, she had few ideas of her own.

What about her own life-mate Larch the Curious? She smiled to herself. Fond as she was of him, he was far too impetuous, and his insatiable curiosity often overtook caution. That wouldn't do in a Leader.

She ran her eye round the circle of squirrels, dismissing the ex-zervantz; they had little concept of action other than doing what they were told.

Ex-prince Fir was sickly, probably as a result of the inbreeding of the Royal family, but Just Poplar looked strong enough. Of course. He was the natural choice!

Without further hesitation Clover said, "I propose Just Poplar to be our new Leader."

Poplar looked uncomfortable and said, "It's lezz than a year zinze uz became King and uz gave that up at wonz, not liking the thingz uz would have to do. Uz don't think that uz'z a zuitable zquirrel to be a Leader."

Each squirrel remembered how Poplar had abdicated and given up all his titles, privileges and duties to become Just Poplar and how relaxed he had seemed after that. But then they thought how helpful and friendly he had been to every squirrel since then and his Royal background still gave him an air of authority. Looking at each other, they seemed to decide, as one, that he *would* make an excellent new Leader and there was a clamour of approval.

"Poplar for Leader, Poplar, Poplar."

One of the ex-zervantz called, "Long live King Poplar", but was glowered into silence by the others.

After listening to the acclaim, Poplar raised his tail. "If it iz the wizh of yew all, then uz acceptz. However, there will be no talk of "King" Poplar. Uz do not care for titles, uz do not even want a tag other than the won uz have been comfortable with. Uz'll only agree if uz can continue to be 'Juzt Poplar'."

A little forest of raised tails indicated unanimous acceptance.

Clover breathed a sigh of relief and Old Oak slumped further as he felt the burden he had carried for so long transfer to younger shoulders.

"Uz muzt make planz," Just Poplar announced, and, as Oak moved out of the Leader's place, he moved across to occupy it.

Peafowl, peafowl, peafowl! Blood was sick of peafowl. There were only eight females left now, plus the big old cock bird with the long tail. I must go and find a squirrel, or at least a rabbit, he thought. He was still puzzled by the mysterious disappearance of the squirrels. Occasionally he caught a whiff of squirrel-scent on the breeze, but never enough for him to track down their hiding place.

He came out of the church into the brightness, blinked and looked about him. Despite the sunshine, he knew that winter was not yet over and that snow and bitter winds could return at any time. Honeysuckle leaves were showing bright green, but no other new vegetation had yet dared to emerge. He climbed a bare-branched oak-tree and scented the air. Ducks and sea-birds in the lagoon; that fishy scent was probably from the cormorants who were drying their outspread wings in the sunshine. No – he wanted mammal-meat today. Even a mouse would be welcome. Two mice, or three, would be better still.

Blood leapt from tree to tree above the swamp, watching the ground but not following any particular route, then, thinking that he was more likely to find live, warm-blooded mammals away from the bog-pools, he turned southwards towards the neglected and overgrown fields. It would have to be rabbit; some would be out in the open today.

He stopped suddenly, just as he was about to leap for the next tree. Squirrel-scent was rising from below to tickle his nostrils and make his mouth water. He clung to the branch testing the air. This was not normal squirrel-scent; this was dead squirrel-scent, long-dead squirrel-scent. He went slowly down the trunk.

Below him was a willow tree that leaned out over a pool of dark water and mud. He dropped on to the sloping trunk. The scent was stronger now and there was a touch of live squirrel in it – not fresh, a few days old at least. He prowled along the trunk, scratching at the bark and sniffing. Where *was* that scent coming from? There were no holes visible and yet the scent was clearly coming from inside. It must be hollow. He went to the foot of the tree and looked up. There was a hole on the underside, above the water and mud. So that was where the squirrels had been hiding for so long! No wonder he hadn't found them.

The stench of dead squirrel was pouring from the hole, turning his stomach and drowning any live squirrel smells that might be about. None could be in the tree now, so where had they gone? Nose down, he began to sniff about in ever widening circles.

Chapter 22

Tansy was doubly worried. Already sick with concern for her family under threat from the pine marten over on Ourland, now her young friend Chipling was being held against his will by Crag and the Greys of the Second Wave.

How could she help him escape? Marguerite, Alder and the other senior squirrels were now totally absorbed in the problem of finding food. All their reserves and even the Sun-tithe nuts had been scented out, dug up and carried away by the Greys. Her friends had little thought to spare for Chip, who at least was unlikely to starve, and, it seemed, even less thought for the Ourlanders under threat from the pine marten.

Tansy slipped away through the treetops to the hiding place from where she could watch the Temple Tree. She could see Chip on one of the dead top-branches talking to his mother again. They sat a little apart from one another, not as close as normal Reds would be when talking within families, but they didn't appear quite as stiff as they had been before.

Several Greys patrolled the ground below, occasionally

glancing up at the two Reds in the high branches. Tansy wondered what Rusty and Chip were saying to each other.

Rusty had given up "trying to talk some sense into her son", as Crag had directed her to do, though she sinfully lied to him each evening that she had tried her best. She looked forward to hearing more and more about life in the Blue Pool community from the youngster. She had heard all the Acorn stories that her son could remember, and he was now teaching her the Kernels that he had learned. Today he had got to the Mating Kernel:

> *Mating is a joy*
> *Sun-given to squirrel folk*
> *To make more squirrels.*

"Tansywistful told me all about it. Fun, and chases through the trees and then joining together with your favourite. Did you do it on Portland?"

"Yes," said Rusty, hesitantly, "sort of. But not quite like you say," she added, recalling the brief, cold act with Crag, once a year in the darkness of the cave. "Yes – sort of."

A thought struck her. "Have you and Tansy – you know – have you and Tansy. . . ?" She could not use the word; it had implications of dreadful sinning and the Sunless Pit.

"Not yet, but I would like to, if she chooses me. But she's not of my year and may prefer another squirrel." He thought a little jealously of Tamarisk the Forthright, and shuddered to think of Tansywistful being pursued joyously through the trees by "the Mouth" whilst he, Chip, who loved her so much, was trapped here, guarded by foreign Greys.

The two of them sat on the dead branch, each silent with their musings, Chip staring vacantly across the clearing.

A red tail flicked momentarily in the tree opposite. Or did it? He focused his eyes and raised his tail slowly. The tail opposite flicked again. Chip quickly looked down, fearful that the Greys might have seen what he had, but the patrolling continued as before. He lowered his tail and raised it. Again an answering flick. It could only be Tansy – his Tansywistful – come to see that he was all right. His heart swelled in his chest and he dug his claws deep into the soft wood of the dead branch.

Tansywistful had come!

Tansy knew that Chip had seen her, but she was powerless to do anything other than watch, and occasionally, when she judged it safe to do so, flick a signal with her tail.

After a while she made the "farewell" signal, waited for the half-concealed acknowledgement, then went back through the treetops to the Blue Pool Demesne, her mind full of impossible rescue ideas.

Rusty and Chip went down and into the hollow of the Temple Tree, their bodies in comforting contact as they squeezed through the hole together.

Just Poplar was not sure if he had done the right thing. True, he had brought the entire group safely from the now uninhabitable Bunker to *this* place, but was this a safe place for them to be? He looked out from the round end of a broken drainpipe and could see Heather and Cowzlip on guard down on the shore, their backs to the sea, watching the trees and bushes on the bank behind him. Once, though he did not know this, a pottery factory had stood on this site and the many broken and badly fired drainpipes and chimney pots had been thrown on to scrap-piles on the foreshore.

In the seventy-five years since the factory had closed and the pipemakers had given up and moved away, the wind had blown sand, soil and leaves in and over the pipe-shards until little remained visible on the surface. Pines and birches had colonised the new ground, growing from tiny seedlings to mature trees with their roots reaching down through and past the broken pipes, many of which were now deep underground.

In this hidden labyrinth the young Prince Poplar, as he had been then, had played hide and seek with his brothers, sisters, cousins and the dreylings of the zervantz until they knew every passageway and dead-end intimately.

In the last two days since he had led his party here he had insisted that every squirrel learn the layout, and know of each exit hole and how to find their way about, even in darkness. At first he had taken them personally through all the passages, then had encouraged games which would last for hours, before he let a few at a time out amongst the bushes and trees of the bank to forage, watched over by alert pickets.

As Just Poplar was about to turn back into the drainpipe, he saw one of these pickets, Heather Treetops, stand to her full height and peer up the bank, her tail moving slowly from left to right and back. It was the "possible danger" signal.

Poplar thought quickly. There were no foraging parties out at present, thank the Sun; the squirrels underground were resting after the last game and only the two guards were outside.

Heather was standing, then crouching, in an attempt to identify something, and the other picket, Cowzlip, was moving closer to her, staring in the same direction. The tails of both were now moving swiftly from side to side. Poplar turned round and called, "Danger", his voice sounding oddly magnified in the smooth glazed pipe. The murmur of voices in the darkness behind him ceased. Then Heather and Cowzlip came bounding across the ground to join him in the tunnel entrance. "It's the marten," Heather said breathlessly. "He's found us."

Blood paused at the top of the bank, savouring the fresh squirrel-scent all about him. He had seen the two on the shore and had watched them disappear underground. He *would* have squirrel today! He padded down the bank, then out on to the edge of the beach, aware that he was being watched. His feet crunched on dry black seaweed and old crab-shells.

He picked a crab-shell up and tossed it in the air. There was no hurry now. He crouched and studied the bank. Holes everywhere, very round and unnatural-looking, but he let his imagination wander. A squirrel in each – just waiting for him to take his pick.

Saliva dribbled from the corner of his mouth as he went up to the first hole and peered inside. He paused there, waiting for his night-vision to come as his pupils enlarged in the dim light. He could hear movement deep in the bank ahead and waves of delicious squirrel-scent wafted out past him. He was sure that he could see the end of a reddy-brown tail and he went into the opening, his claws scratching on the smooth brown glaze of the pipe which sloped slightly uphill away from him. The tail disappeared around a corner and he followed it; the squirrel was always just out of sight, except for tantalising tail-tip glimpses every now and then. Passages that he was sure would contain a squrriel ended abruptly in a mass of roots, or opened on to the beach, and he had to allow his eyes to readjust again after turning back into the dim light of the labyrinth. There were callings and whisperings down every passage and pipe, but he could never see more of any squirrel than that elusive tail-tip.

Blood knew by the scent-changes that his quarry was being switched as one grew tired and another took over, but no matter how hard he tried or how fast he ran, the tempting squirrels were always one corner ahead. After what seemed like hours he was dizzy and tired. Mocking squirrel voices came to his ears from above, below and behind him, and glimpses of red tails flashing in side-passages invited him to turn and chase them, yet never once did he actually get within touching distance of any squirrel.

He was worn out, hungry and, most of all, frustrated. Finally he left the labyrinth at the first open hole he came to and padded off down the beach, glaring back at the open ends of the pipes. It would have to be rabbit today, but tomorrow would be squirrel, definitely squirrel, without any shadow of a doubt – squirrel!

Chapter 23

––––––

"I'm sure that he wants to be back with us," Tansy was telling the Blue Pool Council. "He told me a good deal about what it was like at the Temple Tree before he came to us, and I've seen it myself. Why else would the Greys be keeping guard? They definitely seemed to be there to stop Chipling – Chip – from leaving. I could tell by the way they were watching him. They are *not* honouring the Kernel:

> Squirrels must be free
> To come and go as they please.
> None may be constrained.

She looked round for confirmation.

Marguerite agreed. 'If he is being held unwillingly, then we *must* release him.' Others signalled agreement.

Alder said, "I'll go and talk to that Crag – what does he call himself? – the Temple Master."

It was decided that Alder and Marguerite would go, but that Juniper, Tamarisk and Tansy would follow and stay within calling distance in case there was any trouble. Rowan the Bold, now a respectable father, though still

142

loving action of any kind was, to his disappointment, left in charge of the remaining squirrels and the youngsters.

The party separated into two groups as they approached the Temple Tree, Marguerite and Alder arriving in the clearing just as Crag returned with a party of Greys who were dragging a length of rusty chain between them.

Crag surveyed the Reds coldly. "What are two Blasphemers doing at my Temple?" he asked. "Come to repent for your many sins?"

"We have come to check that your youngster is not being held against his will," Alder replied.

"My son is *my* business," Crag snapped back. "Now, away. I don't want you corrupting these repentant silver-furred servants of the Sun. Away with you both."

The Temple Master turned to direct the grim-faced Greys as they dragged the chain up the trunk to an upper hole. Alder and Marguerite heard it rattle down inside the tree behind them as they re-entered the woodland.

"What happened?" Tansy asked eagerly.

Marguerite told her as they went back to the pool together, discussing what options were now open to them.

"Use the New Woodstock," said Tamarisk. "Curl their whiskers up – they deserve it!"

Tansy had never experienced the full range of the Woodstock's power. Tamarisk explained how different numbers scratched on it after the X had varying effects, from a painful 2, and a whisker-curling 3 or 4, to a killing 6 or 7.

The original Woodstock, he told her, had been

exhausted in destroying the Power Square, but a second one had been found and hidden for possible future need. Perhaps the time had come to use it.

They discussed the points for and against.

"It does give us an advantage," Alder said. "They are bigger and stronger than us, and it was one of their kind who broke my tail." There was a measure of savagery in his voice.

"But it wasn't these actual ones," replied Marguerite, and she quoted the Focus Kernel:

> *The errant squirrel*
> *Should be punished. Do not harm*
> *Its friends, nor its kin.*

"The Greys are all the same," said Tamarisk. "They hate us Reds. Look how they treated Bluebell – they killed her!"

Marguerite glanced at her life-mate, Juniper. Bluebell had been his first life-mate, but she had died while warning other Reds of an imminent Grey attack. Juniper looked as if he would like to take on all Greys himself, with or without a Woodstock.

"We don't know if there is any force left in the New Woodstock," she reminded them.

"We could try it out on Juniper," Tamarisk said mischievously, remembering that it was Juniper who had first experienced the whisker-curling effect of the Woodstock's force.

"Not on your nutpile," said Juniper. "Clover had to bite my whiskers off before my head stopped spinning and it was weeks before I could think clearly or even climb a tree! You're not trying it out on me!"

The mention of nutpiles reminded Marguerite of the acute food shortage which was now following the plundering of their reserves by the Greys. Each time they saw Crag he seemed to have more and more Greys at his command. They must be flooding in from the north and east, part of the Second Wave. Marguerite was regretting her decision to treat them so suspiciously in the autumn and send them to the Lightning Tree area for the winter. But, as she told herself, at that time they hadn't known that Crag and his family were there.

> *Looking behind you*
> *There is never any mist,*
> *The view is superb.*

They had to deal with the situation as it was now. They had little food, a young Red was being held against his will *and* against the ancient Kernel Lore, the land was being overrun by Greys of the Second Wave, all seemingly under the influence of the Temple Master, and on top of all this, Tansy was constantly pressing her to go to the aid of the squirrels on Ourland. So many things to be considered and no clear line of action to be seen.

They had reached the edge of the hollow in which the Blue Pool lay. The surface was calm in the late-winter sunshine and the upside-down reflections of the Beachend trees were green against the blue of the mirrored sky. Even in her agitated state Marguerite felt the surge of joy that always came when she looked at the loveliness of the pool and its setting. The Sun forbid that she would ever have to leave it again. Yet somehow she knew it would come to that.

Chapter 24

It was a night for dreaming.

Crag dreamed of the day when both trunks of the Temple Tree would be filled with metal, safely stowed there to prove to the Sun that he was a *worthy squirrel*. No Sunless Pit for him! The hollows were filling fast; every day more Greys arrived and were instructed by Ivy that this was the local custom and therefore, in accordance with their instructions from the Oval Drey at Woburn, must be followed. She was also adept at describing the Sunless Pit to the newcomers; he could not do better himself.

A few feet from him Rusty, on a ledge in the cold hollow of the Temple Tree, dreamed of loving and cuddling, then awoke shivering with fear, afraid that Crag might somehow know of her sinful dreams.

Chip, in a hollow lower down in the tree, was also dreaming of loving and cuddling, but with no such sense of sinfulness.

The object of his dreams, Tansywistful, in the drey above the pool, was dreaming of a pine marten eating her family one by one, whilst she watched helplessly from a tree surrounded by water.

146

On the island the object of her dream, Blood, had returned from his unsuccessful hunt in the pottery labyrinth to find the church door shut and neither sight nor sound of the peacock and the peahens. There had been a tangle of human-scents around the church, and some of the undergrowth that had been invading the building and its surrounds had been cut back. He had found a dry place under a rhododendron bush nearby, and now slept and dreamed of the peacock. His pride prevented him from dreaming of squirrels that night.

Mogul, the peacock, was at that time crouched uneasily on a beam in an unfamiliar shed, the remainder of his harem of peahens perched alongside him, their heads under their wings. In his restless slumber he was resenting the way he had been shooed out of the stone building that had been their home for so long by a party of humans who had come into the church and started to clean it up after many years of abandonment and neglect.

Mogul's dream was that, when spring came, he would dazzle his hens and all the humans with a display of colour such as none of them had ever seen before. He would especially show off to that man in the brown and green clothes, the man with the picture of the oak-leaves and the acorns on his chest, who was clearly the Cock of the parties of men now busy all across the island.

The object of Mogul's dreams was the National Trust Head Warden, who had recently been appointed when the Trust had taken over Brownsea Island. He was dreaming of – or perhaps it would be more honest to say, lying awake worrying about – all the things that had to be organised and carried out before the official opening ceremony, scheduled for late May.

Apart from the church, the restoration of which was being carried out by a group of volunteers from a mainland parish, there were countless things to be done. Masses of the rhododendrons had to be cleared, buildings would have to be repaired and a power line brought over from the mainland. The diesel generator was just not adequate. So much to do, so little time! Some people just don't realise *how* much; all they kept asking him was "Are the squirrels still there?" Come to think of it, he hadn't seen them for a while. Finally he fell asleep with pictures of squirrels filling his dreams.

Not many of the Ourland squirrels were asleep. Just Poplar, fearful of a return visit from the marten, had employed another trick from his dreyling-hood games. An hour before high-tide he had led the entire party out of the labyrinth on to the shore and they had set off in the dusk, along the beach below the high-water mark. Soon the rising tide would obliterate their tracks and their scent, so it would appear that they had all vanished into the sea! They had left the beach after rounding the point and were now resting uneasily in the darkness near the ruined Man-dreys of Maryland at the extreme western end of Ourland.

Old Oak was asleep. The burden of leadership lifted from him by Just Poplar, Oak seemed to be shrinking in on himself, sleeping often, and little concerned with the events going on around him. Earlier that day he had led the youngsters out of the rear entrance of the labyrinth as the marten had gone in at the front, and had kept them amused whilst the other mature squirrels had confused and demoralised the hunter. Then there had been that long trek over the sand and the pebbles of the beach. His age now excused him from guard duty, so he slept and dreamed of his daughter, Marguerite the Bright One, and his son, Rowan the Bold. What a character *he* was, totally fearless. He would have *enjoyed* today – fooling that marten!

Rowan himself, snug in his drey at the Humanside Guardianship of the Blue Pool, cuddled up to his life-mate, Meadowsweet, tagged Rowan's Love, and their dreyling, Young Bluebell. Rowan was dreaming of the day his sister, Marguerite, had shown him the numbers she had invented for counting things. The odd-shaped figures paraded across the backs of his eyelids – 1 z ʒ 4 5 6 7 — 1o 11 1z   Each had the right number of corners to hide nuts in, as Marguerite had explained, after she had scratched the figures in the clay. 1 had one corner, z had two and so on. Neither of them had dreamed then of the power these numbers would have when scratched on to the smooth surface of the Woodstock.

The Woodstock itself was the object of Marguerite's dreams. She dreamed that she was pointing it at Crag and threatening to curl his whiskers if he did not hand over Young Chip, and stop this business of misleading the gullible Greys.

Juniper stirred next to her, briefly waking Young Oak and Young Burdock who, after wriggling about and nudging one another, dropped off to sleep again, leaving Marguerite awake in the darkness.

She was not sure now if she was dreaming or not. Images tumbled through her mind. At first she felt surrounded by a thick grey mist filled with a hidden menace. Then a shaft of sunlight broke through and in its light she could see the long sweep of a pebble beach as it had once been described to her by Chip. Dandelion had portrayed it again in the Whale story. It was there that the second wave had swept Primrose out to join Acorn in the water before the whale had taken them to safety on Ourland. The Second Wave – that was what the Greys called themselves now.

Did this mean that the Greys were destined to sweep the Reds off the Mainland to Ourland? She tensed, then relaxed to let her subconscious thoughts rise to the surface like cones dropped in a pool. The first picture to come was of the great ruined Man-drey that the squirrels could see in the distance from the tops of the poolside trees on clear days. In her mind a rainbow arched through the sky over the heath, bright against the dark sky beyond. One end appeared to be on the Lightning Tree and the other on the ruined Man-drey.

Before she could interpret this, another picture emerged. She could see a huge slab of stone tilted on its edge and seemingly balanced on other smaller stones beneath. It was surrounded by desolate heathland, but in the distance beyond it was the sea. The rainbow came again, faint and nebulous at first, then glowing brighter and brighter as the sun broke through the grey clouds that massed behind her. Now one end of the rainbow was on the great stone and the other far out to sea. She followed the arch with her imagination and where it ended she could see three black dolphins curving gracefully through the waves. She remembered Malin and Lundy, the dolphins who had helped her when, with Juniper, Spindle and Wood Anemone, she had been carried out to sea in a rubber boat the previous year.

She felt that the two larger dolphins were these same ones and that they were trying to communicate with her. She strained all her senses to try to pick up the silent thought-waves, but the picture faded and she woke feeling sick and empty.

At first light Marguerite slipped out of the warm drey and ran through the mist-wreathed treetops to the drey of Alder and Dandelion. She paused outside and whispered the Calling Kernel:

> *Hello and greetings.*
> *I visit you and bring peace.*
> *Emerge or I leave.*

Dandelion's sleepy voice responded, "Marguerite, come on in. It'll be a bit crowded, but you're always welcome. Do you have news?"

"I must speak quietly to Alder. Is he awake?"

"I'll come out now," Alder called, and emerged, blinking, into the cold air.

Marguerite, as always when she first saw him each day, had to adjust to the fact that he had no tail, and remind herself that this did not mean that he had no brain. In fact, he had proved to be an excellent Leader, though perhaps a little lacking in imagination. She smiled to herself as she remembered what Dandelion had once said to her: that she, Marguerite, had enough imagination for three ordinary squirrels, and some to spare!

They brushed whiskers on the grooming branch, then Marguerite signalled Alder to follow her out of ear-twitch of the drey's other occupants. "I don't want to alarm any squirrel, but last night I had the strangest dream."

Alder looked puzzled, and waited for Marguerite to continue.

"I don't know even if it was a dream; it seemed far stronger than any dream I have ever had before."

"Tell me about it," said Alder gently, seeing how agitated Marguerite was.

She told Alder what she had seen in the night. As she did so, the pictures strengthened in her mind and she became more and more convinced that they were more than just a dream.

Alder asked her to repeat what she had told him to Dandelion, his life-mate.

When Marguerite got to the great rock set in the desolate heathland, Dandelion broke in. "That is an exact description of the Agglestone that my grandfather told me about. It is on the heath between the ruined Man-drey and the sea. He described it to me once. He found it when he was on climbabout as a youngster and slept the night on the top of it. You've had a Sun-scene."

"What's a Sun-scene?" asked Marguerite, the term new to her.

"Do you remember my telling you about the Bard we used to have back at our home near the Barrow of the Wolves? He used to have Sun-scenes. It happened when the Sun wanted to tell us something or warn us of danger. He had a Sun-scene before the Silver Tide came, but we didn't really believe it and that's why Alder lost his tail. You must be gifted like our Bard was.

"We shall have to leave here and head for Ourland.

That's the message for us. Remember the second wave of the Whale story? That ended happily there for Acorn and Primrose."

Marguerite looked at Dandelion. Was she mixing her stories with reality, or were there really Sun-scenes sent to receptive squirrels? It would solve the problem of Tansy wanting her to take the Woodstock to Ourland and yet . . . She looked down on the winter blue of the pool. It would be unlikely that she would ever see that again if they did leave, but they had no food reserves, and who knew what the Greys might do next.

"We must have a Council Meeting," she said. "This morning."

Chapter 25

At the meeting the squirrels discussed Marguerite's Sun-scene and what it would mean for them all. Demoralised after losing their food reserves and ever conscious of the nearness of the Greys and the zealous Crag, there was no resistance to the proposal to move away to the ruined Man-drey, though they all regretted having to leave their beautiful home.

Alder quoted the Acceptance Kernel:

> *If it hurts too much*
> *Thinking of what cannot be,*
> *Put it out of mind.*

"Who knows the best way to get to the ruined Man-drey?" he asked.

"I do," said Rowan. "I went near there when I was on climbabout. There is a great mound in a gap in the hills with towers of stone on top. Humans used to live there, but now they live in smaller Man-dreys on the other side of the mound."

Dandelion said, "That's what they call a castle. Or so my grandfather used to say."

"There's an easy way to go there," said Rowan.

"Through the woods to the east are two metal 'lines' that go right to the Man-dreys by this 'castle' thing. I followed them when I was on climbabout. Easy travel, no swamps or wide streams to cross, but you're on the ground all the time, so you have to be alert."

"I remember crossing those lines last time we had to leave here," Juniper said, "on the way to Ourland. What are they for?" He looked at Dandelion.

"Sun knows. The humans must have made them, but why, I don't know."

Tansy signalled a request to speak. "I know that I have been urging you all to do something about helping to save the Ourland squirrels from the pine marten, and if we are all going, then we surely must take the Woodstock." She paused and the others nodded agreement.

"But before we go, we must also do something about Chipling. He is still being held against his will, contrary to the Freedom Kernel. I propose that we first work out a plan to free him so that he can come with us – if that is his wish."

Tamarisk glowered at her, then turned away as she scowled back.

Alder spoke. "Tansy is right. We cannot leave the youngster like that. Suggestions, please. Then when he is safe, we'll follow those metal lines. We'll need to travel fast, once we've rescued Chip. It'll be like poking a stick in a wasps' nest."

The rescue party approached the tree stealthily so as not to alert the guarding Greys.

The rest of the community had left the Blue Pool, dragging the Woodstock with them, to circle round and cross open country to the south and east until they came to the metal lines. Then they were to follow these towards the castle mound as fast as they could, their speed dependent on the youngsters in the party. Alder was in charge, and they had left before High Sun to gain maximum distance before nightfall.

Marguerite was leading the rescuers; her party consisted of Rowan the Bold, delighted at the prospect of action, Tansy the Wistful and Tamarisk the Forthright. Tamarisk had continued to be unenthusiastic about the need for rescuing Chip at all, but had not spoken against the plan, as Tansy was so obviously in favour.

Now he was rearguard on a highly dangerous mission. At least he might be able to protect Tansy and persuade bossy Marguerite to withdraw if it got too risky!

They climbed the tree which Tansy had been in when she signalled, and saw that Chip and his mother were sitting out on the dead branch, as they did on most days after High Sun. Watching the Greys, Tansy flicked her tail. Chip responded at once. He must have been watching for her, Tamarisk thought jealously.

Tansy was making pointing-signals with her paws, and Chip was sitting up and staring across the clearing. Stupid brat, thought Tamarisk, and was relieved when Chip responded to a signal from Tansy to appear relaxed. Then Rusty sat up and stared until Chip whispered urgently to her. Tamarisk looked down, but the guards were chatting amongst themselves, apparently unaware of anything happening above their heads.

Rusty was the unknown part of their plan. If they were successful, she might come away with Chip, or she might

156

just turn a blind eye as he went off with them. They had all agreed that, as his mother, she was unlikely to do anything to alert the guards or to prevent his escape, but no squirrel could be *sure* when these Portlanders, with their strange customs, were involved.

Marguerite moved quietly through the treetops to the north side of the clearing as they had planned earlier, and dropped a cone to the ground. The Greys, instantly alert, sat up and looked in that direction. Keeping out of sight, Marguerite dropped another cone. The Greys moved forward slowly to investigate, all their attention focused on the north side of the glade.

Tansy flicked an unmistakable "go down and head that way" signal to Chip, holding a paw to her mouth to indicate the need for silence. Tamarisk saw Chip whisper to his mother as though trying to persuade her to come with him, but she shook her head, touched him on the shoulder and watched as he slipped down the far side of the trunk.

Marguerite dropped a larger cone and the Grey guards moved forward, trying to see what was happening. They chattered to one another, all peering in the direction of the sound.

Tamarisk and Tansy moved through the treetops, silently, to circle round and meet Chip.

As they were doing this, Rusty broke off a piece of rotten bark and let it fall from the Temple Tree, causing the nervous Greys to turn and stare up at her. Marguerite dropped another cone and the Greys ran in her direction only to turn again as Rusty called down something that the Reds, now busy withdrawing, could not make out. The Greys too seemed puzzled and sat staring upwards and trying to hear what she was saying, but somehow the words were not clear from the ground. One Grey shouted up to her to speak louder.

Tansy and Tamarisk had, by now, joined a breathless Chip and were heading for the railway line, where they waited and watched from a line-side tree until Marguerite came into sight, skipping along between the rails triumphantly. They all embraced silently. There were no sounds of pursuit.

Congratulating each other on the success of their plan, they hurried along the track, Tamarisk and Chip vying with each other to be nearest Tansy, until they caught up with the party of tired and anxious squirrels where the humans' roadway crossed over their railway on a bridge. Marguerite, checking that Juniper had the Woodstock with him, was intrigued to see how he and Spindle were sliding it along the top of one of the metal rails, each holding an end in their mouths and running, one squirrel on either side of the rail. Apparently this was Spindle's idea – he was good at finding easier ways to do things.

They rested under the bridge and told how they had got Chip away from the Temple Tree. It could only be a matter of time before there was a posse after them, but it was getting dark and there was a hint of snow in the air. The bridge would offer some shelter. Rather than press on and perhaps get caught in the open, they decided to spend the night there and move off in the morning. They all climbed to a ledge out of reach of any possible prowling foxes or dogs, and huddled together, shivering in the draught which blew through the archway.

*

Crag and Ivy had returned to the Temple Tree clearing later than usual. He was pleased with the success of that day's search. Dozens of Greys were following him, each carrying or dragging some metallic object. The hollows of the tree were nearly full, and this surely would convince the Sun that he, Crag, was a truly worthy squirrel. The grey female, Ivy, was proving to be an unexpected ally, urging the tired Greys on with reminders of the horrors of the Sunless Pit.

He could see there was some kind of commotion at the foot of the Temple Tree. Rusty was rolling about on the grass chattering incoherently, surrounded by guards who were trying to understand what she was saying. He shouldered them aside and Rusty fell silent.

"What's going on?" he asked roughly, addressing himself to her as she lay on the ground.

She did not reply, just rolled her eyes wildly.

One of the Greys said, "Temple Master, she has been raving since after High Sun. We did not know what to do."

Crag looked around. "Where is my son?" he asked.

"In the Temple Tree . . ." the Grey replied, his voice faltering as he realised the significance of the question. "That is, unless . . ." He stopped.

"Fetch him down, then," ordered Crag, icily.

The Chief Guard went slowly up one trunk, then the other, searching and calling at each opening, before returning to Crag on the ground, his tail low. He did not need to speak.

Crag scowled at him, looked to where the setting sun was disappearing behind a bank of wintry clouds, and decided that there was enough time for them to go to the Blue Pool.

With their overwhelming numbers, they could and would destroy the Blasphemers for ever. He ordered all the Greys to follow Ivy and himself and they left, ignoring the now motionless body of Rusty at the foot of the Temple Tree.

No sooner were they out of sight than she shook herself, brushed the dust and moss from her fur and scampered from the clearing, following the scent of her son and the two other Reds.

However, before long, being unfamiliar with the business of tracking, she lost the trail and wandered away southwards, hoping to pick it up again later.

Crag, without Marguerite's knowledge of numbers, was unable to estimate how many Greys were following him. The ground was covered in them, all chattering excitedly. More were in the treetops overhead, following him to destroy the Blasphemers and put an end to their sinful ways for ever. He, Crag the Temple Master, was going to do this – a worthy squirrel indeed!

Ivy followed behind, whispering in the ear of any laggards.

They reached the Blue Pool Demesne as the first snowflakes fell from the darkening sky, to find only deserted dreys. Crag ordered a search of the area, then, gnashing his teeth with rage, he turned and led his shivering grey followers back to the Temple Tree.

Chapter 26

Juniper was the first of the huddled squirrels to wake on the ledge under the bridge. He looked down and saw where the snow had blown in and partly covered the lines below him. Through the arch he could see that the ground was blanketed with snow to the depth of two standing squirrels, with the wind stirring it into drifts. Even high on the ledge he could hear the rustle of the wind-hardened grains as they blew along the surface, but there was another sound that he did not know, and it was coming from the lines themselves. They were whining like an animal in pain and the sound was getting louder, now accompanied by metallic groans. He leaned down from the ledge and peered outside. An enormous creature was coming along the lines towards him and was going to enter their hiding place – it must be seeking *them*. In panic he shouted, "Every squirrel, get outside. Run for your lives. Follow me!"

Juniper leapt down from the ledge and ran out into the snow, followed by a gaggle of half-asleep squirrels, stumbling and rolling as they scrambled from the shelter of the bridge into the cold white world. The "monster" had entered the shelter and now followed them out, roaring loudly.

Juniper jumped from the track and dived into a snow-drift, burrowing like a mole in his terror. The others, their hearts beating madly, tunnelled down behind him as the monster, ignoring them, rumbled on towards the little station of Corfe Castle village to engorge its breakfast of human travellers.

Deep in the snowdrift the squirrels lay, panting from their exertion, packed closely together, until, when they realised that the "monster" had gone, they relaxed and wriggled into more comfortable positions.

"What was that?" a youngster asked, but no squirrel could give a satisfactory answer.

The chamber enlarged itself as they jostled about and soon they were in a snow-cave, where each could crouch easily, snug against one another and surprisingly warm; it was certainly better than the draughty bridge-arch. They felt secure and safe deep in the drift and one by one dozed off and slept in the snow-cavern throughout all of that day and the following night, knowing that the snow had concealed their scent-trail.

Only one incident disturbed the calm. Tansy was snugging against the skinny body of Chip when Tamarisk tried to wriggle in between them.

"What do you want?" she hissed, keeping her voice low so as not to disturb the other squirrels.

"Just to be near you," Tamarisk replied, his mouth close to her ear; then he added, "I don't like the way you favour that squimp." Even as he said this he knew that it was a foolish thing to say, but it was too late. He felt her body stiffen and sensed the rejection.

"He's just left his mother to the mercy of the Temple

Master, and we know what *he's* like. If you weren't such a squaker, you would be out there helping her escape!" She elbowed him away and closed her eyes.

Tamarisk crawled up the tunnel and out into the cold whiteness. So that was what she thought of him, was it? He'd show her.

Several times the squirrels in the snow-cave heard the lines whine and groan as the "monster" passed, but as before, it did not attempt to leave its track and seek them out.

On the third morning a westerly wind blew in from the Atlantic, warm from the distant Gulf Stream, and the chamber in which the hungry squirrels huddled started to drip and collapse. Alder led them out into the open and after a little stretching and stamping around they set off again along the lines, the youngsters whimpering for food and being comforted by the older squirrels. Chip was constantly looking over his shoulder as though expecting to see his mother, but the others were more concerned with ensuring that there was not a posse of Greys on their tails. It was comforting to know that their scent would have dissipated into the snow and neither Crag nor the Greys would know in which direction they had gone.

The metal lines were clear of snow and the "monster" had pushed aside any drifts on to the side of the track, so the squirrels easily followed the rails as they curved round towards the ruined Man-drey they could see on the great mound ahead of them. Twice the party left the track and hid when they heard and felt the lines whining and vibrating, but on both occasions the "monster" passed without concerning itself with them.

The second time Rowan sat up and watched it. "It's not a "monster," he told the others. "It's just a lot of the box-things that humans travel about in, all joined together. I could see humans inside it."

After High-Sun they left the lines, went down an embankment, crossed a roadway and stared up at the piles of rocks towering against the sky above them.

"This is the castle," said Dandelion. "I didn't realise it was as big as this."

"Humans must have put all these stones on top of one another," Marguerite said, "though Sun knows why!"

Her youngsters were close to her side. "I'm so hungry," Young Oak told her.

"So am I," whimpered little Burdock. "We haven't eaten for days."

"We must find shelter first, then we will look for food," she told them.

Juniper said, "Where there are humans, I can find food. I used to be tagged the Scavenger once. Did you know that? If anyone can find human food, I can." He was almost proud, then realised that the Scavenger was a lowly tag, one to be ashamed of. How Life changed one's standards when the cones were down!

They all climbed the steep grass-covered mound to the ancient castle walls, dragging the Woodstock up with them, and then explored the rock faces, searching in every nook and cranny, looking for a safe and sheltered hiding place. It was Chip, more at home on the rock than the other squirrels, who found the cave, high up on an outer wall, half hidden by a mass of ivy stems and leaves. It was on the south side, so was protected from cold winds and not too distant from the humans' village, where they hoped to find food in the morning.

For many years jackdaws had used this cave as a nest site, so inside there was a mass of old sticks and sheep's wool that they could use for bedding, even if it did smell musty and unpleasant. It was dark by the time the Woodstock had been carried up the tangled stems to safety in the cave. Twice it had fallen and they had had to climb down to recover it, using the joint efforts of all the mature squirrels. Even so, none of them had noticed that Tamarisk the Forthright had not been with them all day.

Crag's temper had not improved as he led the horde of Greys back to the Temple Tree through the falling snow, and his black mood deepened when he found that Rusty had evidently taken the opportunity to desert him. She had always been unreliable, he thought savagely, much too prone to sentimentality and far too soft towards that youngster. Both of them were unworthy squirrels; he was better off without them! The Greys were harder workers and now he had Ivy on his side the metal collection was growing steadily. The Sun had evidently sent her to help him get the Greys to stock the Temple.

He crouched, shivering, in the cold chamber that was his lonely sleeping place, thoughts tumbling through his brain. If the Sun had sent the Greys to help him, it had probably also arranged for those two unworthy squirrels to be removed. He called down for Ivy.

"When did Rusty last collect metal?" he asked.

"Moons ago," she replied.

Crag cursed. All that time she had lived with him in the

165

sacred place, eating the bounty that the Sun had provided –
and contributing nothing. Nothing! His teeth chattered
with anger and cold. She didn't deserve to live.

Throughout the two days when the snow prevented any
Sun-worthy work being done, Crag crouched in his
chamber, listening to the movements of the Greys in the
hollows below him, but taking no food, even when Ivy
offered some.

After the warm wind caused the drifts around the Temple
Tree to melt away, Crag came out on to an upper branch
and called to the Greys to assemble on the ground below
him. As those in the tree poured from every hole to join
those already on the ground, he looked down, exulting in
the sense of power. The clearing seemed to be alive with
squirrels, all waiting on his word. He signalled to Ivy and
she called for silence. The chattering stopped abruptly.

There was a small cloud between him and the sun,
casting a shadow on the wood, though it was bright enough
on the distant hills, and on the trees not too far away. Crag
waited for it to pass – he wanted to be seen clearly by all
below him – but the cloud seemed in no hurry and the
Greys below started to get restless and whisper amongst
themselves.

Seeing this, Crag spoke, his voice higher pitched than
usual. He coughed and started again, "Fellow squirrels,
although we are of different colours, we have worked
together to the glory of the Sun by collecting sacred metal
and filling this wonderful Temple Tree to prove that I – we
– are truly worthy squirrels and will therefore avoid the
terrors of the Sunless Pit. This Temple Tree is now almost

complete, but" – he paused – "we have been hampered in our efforts by an unworthy female whose name I cannot even bring myself to say. One who has lived off the Sun's bounty, yet hardly ever carried even the smallest offering to this glorious Temple.

"In the name of the Sun and the power I have earned as Temple Master, I declare this female to be a Squarry!"

Crag waited for some strong reaction, but the Greys looked at one another in puzzlement and then up at him, as though waiting for an explanation.

Sitka called up, "Temple Master, this word is strange to us. As you know, our instructions from the Oval Drey are to adapt to, and adopt, your local customs, but we don't know the meaning of 'Squarry'."

"Ignorant fools," Crag said under his breath, then called down, "A Squarry is one who has sinned so dreadfully that it is our right – no, our duty – to see that they go to the Sunless Pit at the earliest chance. A Squarry must be hunted down and killed. This duty takes precedence over all others. Find the Squarry and kill her! No squirrel is to return until they can report her death."

His high-pitched voice reached all the Greys below and was also heard by Tamarisk the Forthright, hiding in the branches of the pine tree across the clearing. He crouched there wondering what to do next. Evidently Rusty was not at the Temple Tree and now the hordes of Greys were going to seek her as a "Squarry".

The word was unknown to him too; it must be a part of the cult these Portland squirrels had brought with them. It was certainly alien to his teachings. One of the Kernels of Truth said:

Squirrels have the right
To explain their own actions,
Fully – in silence.

There was no evidence, from what he had overheard, that Rusty would be given this right of explanation, in silence or otherwise. It seemed that she was to be hunted down and killed without a chance to explain her reasons. Suddenly his mission had taken on a new dimension: not only did he have to rescue Chip's mother to prove himself to Tansy, but he was now the defender of the ancient culture of the Reds.

Ivy was issuing orders as the Greys spread out in all directions to search for the Squarry. Tamarisk stayed put. They were unlikely to look in the tree nearest to the Temple, for they would expect Rusty to be some distance away by now.

The hubbub died down as the last of the Greys left the clearing, and Crag went back into the Temple Tree. Tamarisk contemplated crossing the clearing and tackling the Temple Master. He was younger and could probably win a fight, but this would be contrary to the very Kernel he was acting to defend. He would leave Crag to the Sun. In the meantime he had to find Rusty before the Greys did. Remembering Marguerite's absolute confidence that help would come when most needed, he recited the Kernel,

Have faith in the Sun
His ways are mysterious.
Faith can fell fir trees,

then looked around for some sign that might indicate the way to go. The little cloud that had hidden the sun from Crag had now expanded to fill the sky from horizon to horizon, though a small patch of Sunlight glowed on the side of Screech Hill away across the Great Heath.

Tamarisk felt drawn to the distant brightness, and set off through the treetops in that direction, pausing only long enough to eat some pine seeds, holding the cone in his paws and tearing away the resinous flakes protecting them. He would travel faster if he was not hungry.

Chapter 27

It was Chip who first noticed that Tamarisk was not with them in the cave behind the ivy on the castle wall. The squirrels were preparing to send a foraging party to the human village and Chip was steeling himself for the usual deprecating comments and unkind remarks that Tamarisk whispered to him whenever Tansywistful was not at his side. He looked around the cave in the faint light that filtered in through the leaves and the stems that partly covered the entrance. His antagonist was certainly not there. Perhaps he had gone out before the others? But then, as Chip thought back to when he had last been subjected to Tamarisk's taunts, he realised that he had not seen him since the last night in the snow-cavern. He spoke to Tansy, trying to sound casual. 'Have you seen Tamarisk?'

Tansy looked about, then called loudly, "Has anyone seen Tamarisk the Forthright?"

No squirrel could recall seeing him since the night in the snow, but there were pressing things to be done. The youngsters were whimpering with hunger, and food of some kind must be found. Tamarisk was a grown squirrel, with no family responsibilities; he must be left to his own devices, though some of them felt disappointed that he should have deserted them. However, as the Kernel taught them:

> *Each squirrel is Free*
> *To choose its own route through Life –*
> *Guided by Kernels.*

Tamarisk had evidently chosen his own route, away from Tansy, who must seem unobtainable to him.

Rowan was once more left in charge of the youngsters, the Woodstock at his paw in case of any kind of attack, whilst all the other grown squirrels went to scavenge in the village.

Tamarisk was heading for Screech Hill, where the barn owls hunted, staying behind the searching Greys, whose coverage of the ground grew ever more sparse as the ring of squirrels spreading out from the Temple Tree got larger and larger. Eventually he was able to slip between the searchers unnoticed and, once ahead of them, hurried in the direction of the hill which rose to dominate the countryside, acting as a beacon for him.

Alone, he could travel fast. He was near the base of the hill before the winter dusk drove him to find shelter in a rotten tree, using the abandoned nest-hole of a woodpecker for shelter.

In the morning, encouraged by the dawn Sunshine lighting up the summit, he set off in that direction, strangely confident of finding Rusty somewhere near there.

And so it was. In the highest tree near the hill-top he

found her, trying to get warm in the weak rays of the sun. He went up to her and cuddled her chill form, warming her with his own body, which was glowing from the exertion of his climbing and running through the treetops. When she had thawed a little and her shivering had stopped, Tamarisk said, "I've come to take you to Chip", and was surprised when she said, "I shouldn't have run away. I think it's my duty to go back to Crag. I fear the Sunless Pit. Chip will be safe with your friends." The last word sounded awkward, as though she had never spoken it before.

"Crag has declared you to be something he calls a Squarry," he told her. "All the Greys are out to kill you."

Rusty shrank back in horror. "Me, a Squarry? He wouldn't do that to me!"

"He has," said Tamarisk. "You can't go back."

"I must. Perhaps if I go back, Crag will forgive me and cancel the Edict. Oh dear Sun, me a Squarry. I must go back, it's my only chance."

Tamarisk considered his options. He could abandon Rusty and find the others at the castle. She would then either live or die alone, or be killed by the searching Greys. Or he could try to escort her back through the ring of searchers in the hope that Crag would forgive her, or he could try again to persuade her to come with him to join the exiles and be reunited with her son.

All his efforts were in vain. He explained that the Sunless Pit was only an expression of somewhere awful and did not really exist, but soon he realised that her fear was deep-seated and terrible.

Rusty told him about the Sin-day and the awful night

and day that had followed it. She insisted on returning to Crag.

Tamarisk accompanied her, unable to face Tansy's scorn if she learned that he was too much of a squaker to see Chip's mother safely back to the Temple Tree, if that was her wish.

Together they passed unnoticed through a gap in the ring of Greys, now in groups, searching every patch of woodland and scrub, and through the deserted Demesne of the Blue Pool towards the Temple Tree. A storm was brewing and the silence was oppressive and unearthly. Thunder rumbled in the distance and Rusty looked around apprehensively.

The foraging party to the village had been successful. Most of the Man-dreys had had platforms on the grass areas behind them, laden with food which birds were eating. Jackdaws from the castle took first choice, landing and flying away with large pieces of bread. Then the starlings bustled and jostled each other over what was left. Blue tits and other small birds fed from containers of nut kernels and pecked at the flesh of some kind of huge nut, one half of which hung down from a branch near an opening in the side of one of the Man-dreys.

The squirrels moved in and drove the birds away, having no qualms about taking the food, which humans had clearly put out for other creatures' sustenance. Even if it was not wholly intended for them, they had hungry youngsters waiting up in the castle, and in such circumstances almost anything is "acceptable behaviour".

With hungry youngsters
Actions can be permitted
Otherwise taboo.

The party fed themselves, then returned to the castle cave, each squirrel carrying in its mouth the largest piece of food that it could.

Spindle and Wood Anemone worked harder than the rest, carrying the most awkward pieces and laying these down to assist others before returning for their own loads. Their actions did not seem unusual to the other squirrels, who had often witnessed such unselfish behaviour from the two ex-zervantz. The two, though, were carrying an additional burden that felt like a stone, heavy in their gut; they thought that they were the ones who, through their indiscretion in revealing the whereabouts of the food reserves, had been responsible for the Reds having to leave the pool. Neither could speak of their shame.

Late in the afternoon Chip suggested that he climb to the highest of the stone towers to look out and report. He was secretly rather looking forward to climbing rock again, anticipating the thrill of seeking each tiny hold in the apparently smooth surface and using these to climb up to a place where no other squirrel would dare go.

Alder, hearing the plan, insisted that Chip was not to go alone and Rowan volunteered to go with him if Chip would teach him to climb on rock.

He proved an apt pupil. Utterly fearless, he soon mastered the fundamental concept of three paws holding whilst the other was moved to a new hold, and together the pair climbed the great column of stone that is all that remains of the Queen's Tower of Corfe Castle.

They could hear the distant rumble of thunder that had disturbed Rusty away across the Great Heath. Rowan cautioned his young friend that if a storm came near, they would have to descend swiftly to avoid the danger of a lightning strike in so high a place.

Chip pointed out that the clouds were massing over the Blue Pool area and they would have sufficient time to get down safely if the storm did come in their direction. They searched the vast landscape spread out below them as far as they could see for any sign of grey squirrels, but saw none and were just about to descend when lightning slashed out of the distant cloud to strike somewhere in the wood near the Blue Pool. It struck again and yet again, unaccompanied by the usual rain and, as they watched, a spiral of smoke rose out of the trees where they had seen the flashes strike.

They climbed down in the gathering dusk, neither saying a word to the other yet each sure that the Temple Master would trouble them no more.

Tamarisk and Rusty had reached the Temple Tree as the storm clouds gathered and thunder rumbled over their heads, but Tamarisk had restrained Rusty's desire to go straight to Crag and ask forgiveness. He persuaded her to climb with him up the signalling tree across the glade first.

Rusty had clung to the branch and called, "Temple Master Crag, it is I, Rusty. I have come back to repent for my sins. I fear the Sunless Pit."

Crag's head appeared at the opening near the top of the trunk and he looked about.

Rusty called again, "It is I, Rusty, come to repent." She shook the pine needless to show him where she was and he climbed higher into the dead upper branches of the oak in order to see her better.

"You are a *Squarry*," he replied brusquely. "A Squarry *cannot* repent. You will die – and that will be an example to all squirrels. It will show that the Sun's will must be done. It is the Sunless Pit for you. When the Grey Ones catch you, you will die. Get out of my sight. I cannot bear to look on such an unworthy squirrel."

A shaft of light from the setting Sun shone almost horizontally from under the storm cloud, lighting up the red-brown fur of the Temple Master as he gesticulated wildly.

It was then that the first of the three flashes of lightning struck the tree.

Tamarisk and Rusty, nearly blinded by the intense light, edged backwards along the branch, dropped to the ground and scampered away towards the Blue Pool, followed by the scent of burning wood as the old tree flared orange and red behind them in the dusk. Tamarisk was sure that he could smell seared flesh and singed hair, but said nothing of this to Rusty.

They slept together in Tamarisk's drey near the pool, warm in the mossy lining, as the storm finally broke and rain cascaded down, rattling on the dead leaves. In the dripping dawn they returned to view the Temple Tree, watchful for any Greys. They saw none, but the Temple Tree itself had burned away, leaving nothing but a towering mass of fused metal that could, in the poor light, be mistaken for the form of a gigantic squirrel. They hurried away, the smell of damp wood-ash and scorched metal following them along the track.

Chapter 28

The cave in the ivy, high on the southern wall of the castle, was proving to be a comfortable communal hiding place for the squirrels from the Blue Pool. Each day a foraging party would raid the village bird-tables and return carrying sufficient food for the youngsters and whichever squirrels had been left on guard.

On the first day in the cave Tansy was her usual restless self, asking Marguerite how soon it would be before they could move on, with the Woodstock, towards Ourland. Marguerite pointed out that they needed to feed up first; many of the squirrels were thin and not fit for further winter journeying.

There had been no sign of Greys, and, although Tansy was missing Tamarisk more than she would admit, she was busy with instructing her Chipling in the ways of Mainland squirrels.

Marguerite fulfilled her role as Tagger and teacher, ensuring that all the young ones knew the ancient Kernels of Truth.

Ignorant squirrels
Not knowing all their Kernels
Will act foolishly.

Spindle and Wood Anemone were, unbeknown to each other, watching for a chance to speak to Marguerite. They respected and loved her dearly, but dreaded that a confession would result in a down-tag. Spindle the Helpful imagined being retagged the Indiscreet or perhaps even the Traitor! He could not bear the thought of that disgrace and once again not being able to hold his tail high.

Wood Anemone's imagination did not run to tags, but she feared the scorn of her friend Marguerite and the other squirrels. Yet she could not bear the weight of their secret. On one foraging expedition she spoke to Marguerite when the two were apart from the others.

"Marguerite ma'am," she started, as though she were still a zervant addressing a Royal, then started again as Marguerite shook her head. "Marguerite-Friend," she said, the words like ash in her mouth, "uz muzd tell yew something."

Marguerite heard the tale in silence. This was a stupid thing for them to have done and fully deserved a downtag, and yet . . . If she, Marguerite, had been conditioned by a lifetime as an obedient zervant, would she not have reacted in the same way? Was there any benefit in imposing down-tags on her friends? No – friendship must be left out of this decision. A True Tagger must be impartial.

Would a down-tag act as a warning and an example to others? The circumstances were unlikely to occur again. Did Spindle and Wood Anemone deserve punishment? Not really. The act in question was virtually automatic. One in authority asks; a zervant reports. Marguerite said the Understanding Kernel:

> *If you could know all*
> *Then you could understand all*
> *Then you'd forgive all.*

"You are forgiven, Wood Anemone-Friend. Tell Spindle, and we will never speak or think of this again."

One afternoon, about a week after they had arrived at the castle, the squirrels were sitting in the ivy enjoying the spring sunshine, the snow now a fading memory. The ivy was good to sit in. The curves of the twigs made comfortable couches, the only drawback being the pungent smell, but by now the squirrels had learned to ignore this and often sat there while they built up their strength for the next stage of the journey.

With plentiful food and warmer weather, Marguerite felt that they should now prepare to move on in the direction that Dandelion had indicated would lead them to the Agglestone. She spoke to Alder and he agreed, so she went to tell Tansy, sure that she would be delighted with the news. She found her at the back of the cave, crouched in a corner shivering.

"Tansy-Friend, what's the matter?"

Marguerite was beside her, holding the slim body and feeling the heat of a fever radiating from the young squirrel.

"Dandelion, come quickly," she called over her shoulder, and together the older females settled the younger one in a nest of old sheep's wool and covered her over with more.

"I'll stay with her," said Marguerite. "If she's not better by morning, we'll look for some herbs, but it'll be hard to find anything until they start growing again in the spring."

Dandelion had promised a story that day and they had decided to continue with this despite Tansy's fever. As the youngsters gathered round, Meadowsweet, whose turn it was to be on watch and guard duty, called out, "Squirrels coming."

Rowan scrambled up beside her and looked in the direction she was pointing. Far below, at the foot of the castle mound, a pair of red squirrels were moving forward slowly through the tussocky grass, frequently looking behind them as they did so.

Although the travellers were obviously exhausted, there was something about the way the leading one moved which identified him to Rowan as Tamarisk. The other he did not recognise at first, but as they got nearer, he could see it was Rusty, Chip's mother. Both of them looked tired and travel-worn.

Rowan, Chip and some others went down to greet them and help them up to the cave.

"There are Greys following, not far behind," said Tamarisk. "Rusty is a 'Squarry'."

Only Chip understood the meaning and implication of this and he ran across to his mother and licked her face and paws. She hugged him to her, with no sense of sinning, and told him what had befallen his father.

When she had finished, he said, "I saw the lightning strike, Rusty-Ma. I think I knew then what had happened."

The others had gathered around Tamarisk, who was eagerly chewing on a crust of bread brought up that morning from a bird-table.

"Where's Tansy?" he asked.

Marguerite told him that she had a fever and was sleeping at the back of the cave.

Tamarisk looked concerned, but snatched another bite of the crust. "There are Greys following our trail. They are likely to be here before nightfall. I am sorry we've led them to you, but there was nowhere else for me to take Rusty. We hoped to find you somewhere here. Can I see Tansy?"

Marguerite and Alder posted extra lookouts and the Woodstock was positioned so that it would cover the entrance to the cave.

"We should be safe," Marguerite assured them all. "No squirrel will get past the power-waves and into the cave." She tested the weapon by scratching a Z on the soft wood after the permanent numbers $1\ Z\ 3\ 4\ 5\ 6\ 7\ 10$ and her X which were already cut deeply into the wood. The invisible power that spiralled from the end of the Woodstock was sensed by their whiskers, though not seen by eyes or heard by ears. The ivy leaves around the entrance curled up into tight little tubes.

"They won't pass that force!" Marguerite said.

Rusty and the youngsters, who had never seen the Woodstock in action before, were impressed and comforted.

"Squirrels coming," Rowan called from his lookout point. "Greys, lots of them."

The senior squirrels peered down from the cave entrance and watched a posse of Greys following the scent-trail of Tamarisk and Rusty.

"Do we give them a chance to talk, or do we just use the Woodstock when they reach the cave?" Alder asked, seeking guidance from Marguerite.

"From what Tamarisk and Rusty have told us, they are not going to listen to reason," she replied, "but we'll try to talk to them."

They waited until the Greys had reached the base of the wall and stopped to regain their breath. Their leader was the broken-toothed female they called Ivy.

"What do you want?" Marguerite called down to them.

"We have come to kill the Squarry, Russty. "Iss she with you, Blassphemer?"

"Yes – and here she stays. The Temple Master is dead, so you can abandon your mission." She was bluffing – Rusty had told her that a Squarry Edict could never be lifted – but perhaps the Greys did not know that.

"You lie, Blassphemer," Ivy called back. "Send the Squarry out to uss and you can leave here unharmed."

"I should warn you that we have a weapon whose power would amaze you," Marguerite called down. As she said this, she wondered if these Greys knew how to create the Stone force which their compatriots had used the previous year. If they did, they could trap the Reds in the cave and starve them out.

The Greys ignored what she had said. "We give you until sunrisse to hand over the Squarry," Ivy called up, "then we come for her, and any squirrelss, old or young, maless or femaless, who ressisst will be killed and sent to the Sunlesss Pit."

She did not believe what the Reds had said about Crag being killed. Anyway, it no longer mattered to her. He had served her purpose. No Grey dared disobey her orders. This power was a wonderful thing. She, a mere female, ignored and overlooked for so long, now had only to mention the Sunless Pit and the others scurried to fulfill her commands. If only I had learned how to use the Stone power that the old regime had used to subdue these Reds, she thought, I would have the whole of Squirreldom in my power.

She directed her party to take up positions on ledges on the wall, out of reach of dogs or cats from the village, and they crouched there to wait until sunrise.

In the cave the Reds discussed the chances of their creeping out in the darkness, unobserved.

"We can't, with Tansy ill, and even if we succeeded, they would follow our scent and catch up with us in a less secure place," Marguerite pointed out. "Trust in the Sun," she added, "and the Woodstock.

> *Your prayers alone*
> *Won't do. The Sun will help those*
> *Who will help themselves.*"

A youngster's voice from the back of the cave said, "Can I help myself to a nut? I'm hungry."

The laughter that followed broke the tension and the squirrels settled down to a watchful and uneasy night.

Juniper reported the first movement of Greys in the dim light of dawn and moved back into the cave behind the Woodstock, rehearsing the numbers to release its power. A **1** after the **X** did nothing, whereas a **Z** created a modest force and a **3** was definitely a "whisker twister" at that short range. Numbers higher than that would probably kill. He would start with a 𝟕. There was no point in killing if he could disable the attackers effectively with a lower number.

There was a disturbance in the ivy leaves and he could see a round-eared head silhouetted against the light. He immediately scratched a 𝟕 and felt the force fill the cave entrance. He heard the leaves rustle as a heavy body fell out of control to the ground outside.

A second face appeared and he scratched a 𝟕 again. More rustling and then another thump as a second body fell.

No more faces appeared, and after a while Juniper and Rowan peered cautiously out. There was a cluster of Greys below them, gathered around two others who were pawing at their faces.

Juniper knew from his own experiences that the Woodstock power could curl a squirrel's whiskers into tight spirals and the only way to stop the spinning in one's head was for the curled whiskers to be bitten off. This, though, left the whiskerless animal unable to climb or balance properly. On his own initiative, he sighted the Woodstock at the cluster of Greys and scratched a 𝟕 into the wood.

The cluster broke apart, squirrels tumbling and rolling down the bank, all pawing their faces. The Reds came forward, gathering at the cave entrance to watch the helpless Greys and to congratulate Juniper.

Marguerite drew Alder to the back of the cave to discuss their next action. Tansy appeared to be sleeping at last. They spoke quietly.

"If it wasn't for Tansy, I'd suggest that we left now while

the Greys are in disarray, but she's in no fit state to travel and we can't leave her here."

"Yes you can," said a shaky voice from behind her. "You must get the Woodstock to Ourland. I can follow when I'm well again. I've travelled on my own before, remember."

"We're not leaving here without you. You need our help to get better. A few more days won't make much difference. We know that this is a good defensive position and it's quite likely that the pine marten is dead anyway by now. Try and sleep, Tansy-Friend."

It was more than a few days before Tansy was well enough to move. Her fever raged on, sometimes easing a little, only to return with even more vehemence. They knew that they were being watched by Greys from the hillside opposite, but small parties went out each day searching for different herbs to ease Tansy's fever. Foraging parties visited the village bird-tables daily for food, though for her own safety Rusty always stayed in the cave, sharing the duty of nursing Tansy with Tamarisk and Chip.

The Hawthorn Leaf Moon and the Catkin Moon had both gone before the fever died, leaving Tansy clearheaded but as weak as a new-born dreyling.

The effect of the Woodstock had come as a shock to Ivy and the Greys. Not a single Grey from Purbeck had survived the previous year when the Woodstock had been used in an attempt to destroy their Power Square, so it was completely unknown to them.

When Juniper had used it on the group below the cave, the Greys had all retreated to lower ground. Some had their whiskers curled into tight spirals, others had whiskers that were loosely curled and those who had been close under the castle wall, including Ivy and Hickory, were unaffected. Sitka's whiskers waved like ripples in sand.

"Hickory, Sitka, join me," Ivy commanded. Hickory came at once, though Sitka seemed slower to respond and wandered about before coming to Hickory's side.

"It seemss that the killing of the Squarry iss not going to be ass eassy ass we exspected. The Redss have some weapon that we know nothing of."

Her mind was working fast. She knew that this was a critical time. Her authority rested primarily on her relationship with Crag, who the Reds had told her was dead, and on her false claim to have been sinless, reinforced with her constant reminders of the horrors of the Sunless Pit. Was this enough to prevent them from turning on her, as so often happened to a leader defeated in a battle?

She looked at the other Greys. The majority were in no state to challenge anything. A retreat and regroup was called for now.

"Hickory. The mosst important tassk iss to be yourss. Select two other squirrelss who have not been affected by the Redss' sinful sorcery and watch their every actionss. I will lead the otherss back to the Temple Tree to recover and then we will find a way to kill the Squarry ass we have been directed. If there iss any sign of the enemy leaving, send a messenger to me and follow at a disstansse. Do you undersstand?"

Hickory looked at the other Greys, most of whom were pitifully trying to straighten their whiskers with their claws. He thought briefly of just hopping off to start a new life away from all this peculiar business of metal collecting,

187

Squarry hunting and that coldness, that terrible lonely coldness. Then he remembered the Sin-day. He was not going to risk falling and blindly spinning down, down, down, for ever.

"Yes," he said. "I understand."

Chapter 29

If there was a frustrated pine marten anywhere in the world, it was Blood. After days and days of searching for the squirrels he now knew where they were.

He had found their scent often, but each time, just as he was expecting to surprise them resting, the scent-trail led him down on to the beach and disappeared. He could not believe that the whole party had taken to swimming away each day.

There was a spring warmth in the air when he saw them again. He was prowling behind the island castle near where the last of the peafowl were living when he spotted movement in the treetops. He froze and watched a column of squirrels pass overhead, then climbed a tree and followed silently to discover where they were hiding.

Old Oak always took the last position in the line as they made their daily evasive movements, looping in from the coast as the tide covered their scent-trail on the beach, to find a temporary hiding place, only to move on again at low tide. Twice each day Just Poplar insisted that they did this, and they were all exhausted now, but none more so than Oak. His joints were stiff and he often thought of asking

Clover or one of the ex-princesses for some herbs to help, but he knew that it was age, not illness, that was slowing him up. He reflected on how well the two, Voxglove and Cowzlip, frail as a result of generations of Royal inbreeding, had learned Clover's Caring secrets, leaving her free to develop her role as a Tagger.

Oak was also impressed with the way Clover had grown into that role. Coping with the distress and disruption of their lives caused by the pine marten and her experience of caring for the sick ones had given her a deep insight into squirrel behaviour. All agreed that the tags she allocated were true and fair, and that her advice to the Leader and to the Council was always sound and impartial.

Old Oak was resting, gathering strength to run and catch up with the others, when he saw a movement in a tree in the direction they had come – only a glimpse of brown fur and a flash of white on the chest. At first he thought that some squirrel had fallen behind, unseen by him. Then, with horror, he realised that it was the pine marten – coming his way!

Learning of danger
Leap, scramble, climb, hop or run,
Warn all the others.

He paused. That was the Kernel for this situation. He must warn the others, but he knew that he didn't have a leap or a scramble left in him, let alone a climb, hop or a run. There was only one other action worthy of an ex-Leader. His life was nearly at an end anyway. He rustled the branches to attract the marten's attention and dropped to the ground.

One of the wardens, walking under the trees, looked up

as he heard the sound of the leaves moving, but was not prepared for what happened then, as a squirrel dropped from the branches above and lay still at his feet. He crouched to look at it; its tiny chest was palpitating with fear and its eyes were fixed on something above his head. He looked up again but could see nothing unusual. When he looked down, the squirrel had gone.

Oak caught up with the others where Just Poplar had called a halt once he had found that Oak was not with them.

"The pine marten was following us," the old squirrel said breathlessly. "But a man with the sign of Acorn, the first squirrel, on his chest frightened him away. You should have seen the look on that marten's face – he was terrified of that man!"

Just Poplar, remembering the time before the "Acorn" men came, said, "If he *is* afraid of humans, perhaps we should live amongst them. They have never harmed us."

They all thought about this for a moment.

Clover agreed. "That's right, they never bothered us at the Blue Pool. Yes, let's go and live among the humans. I'm tired of all this hiding."

The weary squirrels climbed over the wall of Brownsea Castle and slept in the shelter of the great sequoia tree there, secure in the belief that the marten would not come so close to where the humans were living and working.

When the late winter finally turned to spring, the Ourlanders were there, marvelling at the activity of the busy humans below, who were clearing the rampant growth of decades of neglect, trying to get everything ready for the scheduled reopening of the island to the public in May.

The squirrels had seen the pine marten in the distance several times and on each occasion they had moved nearer to wherever the humans were active that day, and had watched the marten turn away in fear.

Although by now mating should have been under way and dreys prepared for a new batch of dreylings, no squirrel had felt the urge, even when the sun had warmed them. Their lives were still unsettled, and the constant presence of the marten, though at a distance, was disturbing. How soon would it be before he overcame his fear of Man and attacked?

Ivy reached the Temple Tree clearing at the head of a posse of tired and demoralised Greys. They had taken three days for a journey that could be done in a single day by a fit squirrel, but few were fit. At the end of the first day those who were unaffected bit off the curled whiskers of the others. This did at least stop them wandering around in circles but none of the whiskerless ones could climb and they progressed on the ground, terrified of being found by foxes or dogs.

The Reds had said that the Temple Master was dead. We'll soon know if that is true, Ivy thought, as they came through the last of the trees surrounding the clearing. They stopped and stared.

Where there had once been a great oak tree there was now a gigantic squirrel – made of metal, each piece joined to the next. The squirrel-shaped mass stood on its hind legs, towering above them, its tail high and an accusing look in the eyes formed by two metal discs. Ivy remembered those discs; Crag had been very proud of those. They had been in the centres of larger round things beneath one of those human travelling-boxes and they had shone in the sunshine when Crag and a gang of Greys had levered them off with sticks. Crag had insisted that they were taken to the highest point in the Temple. Now they were partly blackened by fire, but, like Crag's own eyes, they glowered down balefully on the tiny animals below.

"What has happened to Crag?" Sitka asked, his voice wavering.

"Can't you see?" snapped Ivy. "The Sun hass made a metal squirrel out of him to remind uss all that we musst never forget to follow hiss exsample and obey hiss appointed successor – Ivy the Sinlesss. Now search for another hollow tree which even the whisskerlesss oness can get into for safety. Trusst your leader. Hate the Squarry. Go now and look for hollow treess."

Chapter 30

"That must be the Agglestone," Rowan called back over his shoulder.

The other squirrels peered through the heather and bracken in the direction he was pointing. Half a mile away a great rock was propped up at a steep angle, resting on other rocks; it was several times a human's height, but there were no humans near at this time of day. The sun was low in the sky and darkness would not be far away.

With Tansy at last fit to travel and all the other Reds eager and anxious to be out of the confines of the cave, Alder and Marguerite had sent out a scouting party to check on the grey watchers. They knew where the three had their position, in a scrub oak on the bank opposite the castle mound, and the scouts circled round until they could see that all three Greys were there. They reported back.

"We leave before dawn tomorrow," Alder had announced. "We must be clear of the castle mound before it gets light enough for the watchers to see us go. We will head south, though we believe the Agglestone to be to the east. If we are followed or seen, this will help to fool the Greys.

Later we will take the true course. I think Marguerite has a Kernel about that."

> *The unexpected,*
> *Obscure action, confuses*
> *Squirrels' enemies.*

They had left unseen in the pre-dawn darkness and headed south.

Earlier on the day they first sighted the Agglestone they had passed through a strange countryside. Long strips of short grass ended in patches where the grass was even shorter. The squirrels had marvelled at the pigeons' eggs which humans were unsuccessfully trying to smash with sticks; the eggs eventually rolled into holes in the ground, when the humans would lift them out and try smashing them again. It was all most perplexing!

Now Alder looked around for a tree in which to spend the night, where they would be safe from fox-danger, but there were none near enough for them to reach before it got dark. The air was still warm from a day of spring sunshine and the rock ahead looked as though it could offer protection, if not much in the way of shelter.

"Make for the rock," he said. "We'll spend the night there. Don't hurry; forage as you go."

The moon was rising out of the sea when they reached the Agglestone and, as the great silver globe lit the heathland, the tired band of travellers looked up at the dark mass towering above them. Alder and Rowan prowled around the base to find a way up.

There were a number of places where an agile and

unburdened squirrel could climb, but they had the Woodstock with them.

"What about this?" asked Juniper, his paw on the twisted spiral of wood.

"I think we can safely leave it down here," Alder replied. "There's been no sign of Greys since we left the castle mound. Hide it in that holly bush."

He indicated a dense mass of holly a squirrel-leap or more from the base of the rock. The shrubby mass had grown only to the height of three squirrels, most of each spring's new growth having been nibbled off by deer before the prickles had had time to harden.

With Rowan's help, Juniper pushed the Woodstock in under the bush, trying to avoid the spiky leaves, whilst the other squirrels were climbing up the rock with Marguerite in the rear. She had stopped on a ledge and was examining some shapes cut in the face of the stone, presumably by humans. Stark in the moonlight, they were like her numbers but different. One – F – she had seen on the ship that had passed them on the sea the previous year, but the others were new to her. There was a K, a W and many others. What could these be for? she wondered. She pointed them out to Juniper and Rowan, but they were more concerned about climbing up and finding a safe place for the night.

Together they scaled the steep side of the great rock, which stood alone like an island in a sea of heather, and found the others settling down in hollows near the top where tiny plants with fleshy leaves grew in the crevices. The moonlight made the scenery eerie and unreal.

"I'll take First Watch," said Juniper the Steadfast, and

the others did not demur, even if First Watch was favourite as it meant an uninterrupted sleep thereafter. Juniper was, after all, the oldest of the party and, with the hardships of the journey, his age was beginning to show, although he did his best to hide it.

Alder always took Last Watch, the one before dawn, as this too meant that his sleep would normally be uninterrupted. They had all agreed that it was important that the Leader was well rested so that his decisions would not be affected by tiredness. Other watches were allocated by rota.

Rusty settled down beside Chip. She had been practising warm actions on their journey, both towards her son and to the other squirrels. It certainly felt good and made her glow inside. She was learning new Kernels every day. Her favourite was:

> *You will be much loved,*
> *No matter what else you lack,*
> *If you are just kind.*

Rusty savoured the Kernel and tried reversing the lines:

> *If you are just kind,*
> *No matter what else you lack,*
> *You will be much loved.*

It meant the same thing that way, only somehow stronger, rather like seeing a reflection in still water, where the upside-down image was often brighter than the real one. How she loved being with her new friends!

*

A tawny owl was hooting to signal a successful night's hunting as Marguerite shook Alder awake for Last Watch.

She had watched the stars fading from the sky as dawn neared. A Man-light far out over the sea to the east glowed steadily then went out twice in quick succession, then glowed again. It had kept repeating this obscure signal and she had wondered what it was for. Then she turned her mind to the strange Man-carvings on the rock below. What did they mean? Why had men spent time cutting them? What was the significance of the shapes being mostly in twos or threes? She decided to take another look in daylight before she left the rock in the morning.

She had been away from the Blue Pool for so long, the sense of loss at leaving it was diminishing and she was almost enjoying the challenges of the journey, though a deep-seated fear for her parents on Ourland gnawed at her insides. She tried to tell herself that she was doing all she could to get there and that Tansy's illness had unavoidably held them up, but her mind started to go down the "but what if" path. She shook herself. She had taken the action that she had honestly believed to be the best at the time. If events subsequently proved it to be wrong, so be it.

> *Looking behind you*
> *There is never any mist,*
> *The view is superb.*

She smiled as she thought of Tansy, now comfortably asleep between Tamarisk and Chip, who in turn was snugged against his mother, Rusty. Tansy and Tamarisk were together most of the time, Tamarisk much less tense since his rescue of Rusty. He would be due for an up-tag soon, she must put her mind to choosing a suitable one. And Rusty might like her name changed to that of some flower, following the tradition of the Mainlanders.

Chip's dependence on Tansy had lessened during her fever and he spent most of his time with his mother, who was eager to learn all the customs and the traditions of the Mainland squirrel culture. She knew many of the important Kernels. Although initially unsure of herself, which Marguerite put down to a lifetime of dominance by the Temple Master, she was learning that females could and should play active roles in all squirrel affairs. It would soon be time to allocate her a tag as well as a new name.

When Alder had taken over watch, Marguerite snuggled down next to Juniper and closed her eyes, but the strange shapes paraded across her eyelids – FK WS. She tried counting the corners to see if they were numbers. F had three but there was already a number for that. K had three as well and so did W. S had none, like her figure O. Soon she was dozing, warmed by the body heat of her life-mate.

Alder sat on the highest point of the rock, watching the sky lighten in the east. He had come to enjoy seeing the sun rise on these early watches: first the almost imperceptible fading of the blackness, then a hint of grey light as the birds began their dawn chorus. Then any eastern clouds would catch a trace of pink on their lower edges and gradually, so gradually, the light would get stronger and the birdsong louder, until the edge of the sun peeped over the horizon and day had really begun.

This was the time when he had to wake the others, and he was about to do so when, out of the corner of his eye, he saw a movement. He turned but could see nothing out of the ordinary. There were little grey wisps of vapour rising from the ground – it must have been one of those he had seen. Then, just as he was about to turn away, he saw another movement in the same place – a stealthy movement. *Something* was out there, coloured grey, and creeping towards them along the sandy path they had used on the previous evening. It seemed that the Greys had found their scent-trail and followed it! Still unsure, and not wanting to cause unnecessary alarm, he went down and quietly woke Juniper and Rowan.

Alder whispered to them, telling of what he thought he had seen, and the three of them went up to the highest part of the rock. No movement could be seen in the heath scrub and Alder was about to apologise for a false alarm when Rowan saw the heather-tops shaking. Soon it became apparent that there was movement all around the rock.

Alder decided the others should be woken and Juniper quickly went to do this, whispering their fears to each group of squirrels. Rusty's teeth started to chatter and she had to clamp her jaws together. Chip crouched close beside her.

"It's going to be all right, Rusty-Ma," he whispered. "These squirrels will protect us if it *is* the Greys."

The Agglestone would form a good defensive site, Alder was thinking, should it prove necessary. The rock behind them was steep, overhanging in places, and the Woodstock could be used to cover the sloping front face. He looked round for it, then, with horror, remembered that it was on the ground, hidden in the holly bush.

"Dear Sun," he said, quietly, "*don't* let it be Greys."

Then he heard Ivy's voice. His prayer had come too late.

Chapter 31

Hickory had been bored sitting day after day watching the castle mound for signs of the Reds leaving. Each day he saw parties going down to the humans' village and returning later and, although unable to count very well, he knew that it was not all of them, and he never caught a glimpse of Rusty the Squarry.

In idle moments he thought of just moving on westwards and leaving that crazy Ivy behind. He regularly sent his fellow watchers back to report, and from them he knew that Crag was dead or, as the more simple of them believed, had been changed into a giant metal squirrel. Ivy was behind all that, he was sure. But if he did go westwards, he would be on his own and might never meet other squirrels for the rest of his life. Then there was the business of the Sunless Pit . . . No, he would stay for a time and see what happened.

Jackdaws were carrying sticks into the cave. He looked again. It was true. They would not be doing that if the Reds were still there. He felt sick. They must all have slipped away in the night.

Hickory shook his fellow watchers and cursed them for

not being alert and the three set off down the hillside, crossed the stream by a fallen tree and went cautiously up to the foot of the wall below the cave. Had the jackdaws not been flying in and out, he would have suspected a trap and feared the whisker-curling power that the Reds had. But, convinced that they had gone, he climbed up to find the cave empty of squirrels.

He sent one of the watchers to tell Ivy that the Reds had at last moved on, and with the other Grey close behind him, followed a fading scent-trail southwards.

Ivy, at the head of a posse of Greys, had caught up with him four days later, following the marks, symbols and scents he had left to guide her. Now they were looking across the heath at a huge stone outlined against the dawn sky.

Earlier, Hickory had seen the Reds dragging the twisted stick along and had guessed that it was the source of the whisker-curling power they commanded. He had suggested that they stop at a distance from the rock and find out where this stick was.

"Go down and challenge them, sinful one," Ivy had instructed him. "Then we can tell if the power workss outsside a cave."

This is a different Ivy, Hickory thought. She's got much more confident of herself while I've been watching the cave. Now she's expecting me to sacrifice my whiskers for her!

"It is obvious that the power works only on sinful squirrels," he replied. "As you are free of sin, you can go safely and see if they have the power stick with them."

Ivy looked disconcerted for a moment, then, realising that her whole basis of authority had been openly challenged, replied, "Cowardly one, if you are afraid to show yoursself, then I musst do thiss tassk mysself."

She gave him a scornful look, signalled to the other Greys to hold their positions and hopped down the path, her heart beating fast, knowing that she had gambled everything on this one act. She stopped and studied the sloping stone face in the growing light. She could see many red squirrels, but could not see the twisted stick that Hickory had described to her. Neither could she see any place on the rock where it might be hidden.

Risking all, Ivy stood to her full height and called up.

"Send down Russty, the Squarry, and we will leave you in peasse, Blassphemerss though you be."

Alder said nothing, but signalled to the senior squirrels to take up defensive positions, the males at the lower edge of the sloping face of the rock and the females where they could repel any Greys who might try to clamber up the rock to their rear. The yearlings, toughened now by the hazards of the journey, were to form a reserve in the middle and be ready to fill any gaps in the defence.

"Send down Russty, the Squarry," Ivy commanded again.

"She stays with us," Alder replied.

> *"Squirrels in trouble,*
> *Always stand by each other*
> *None suffers alone."*

"Then you will all die together," Ivy replied. "The Temple Masster hass taught uss that *nothing* musst stop uss fulfilling the Squarry Edict."

"The Temple Master is dead," Alder called down.

"That may be so," Ivy replied, "but hiss Edict standss. Now, send down the squarry!"

Alder felt a body press against his as he stood, looking over the edge of the rock, wondering what to do next. It was Rusty.

"I'll go down," she told him. "My life is not worth all of yours."

Rusty felt a paw on her shoulder and looked around. Marguerite had anticipated her intentions and had joined her where she crouched next to Alder. She told Rusty,

> "Evil will triumph
> If good squirrels don't resist –
> Even do nothing."

"That's true," said Alder. "We stand or fall together. Now, both of you, back to your positions."

Marguerite went up to the highest point. From here she could see all around. By leaning out over the edge she could see Greys on the ground, studying the rock for ways to climb.

She counted them, then turned to look in the other direction and tried to count the squirrels there. These had now come out of the heather and were milling around on the bare sand where the vegetation had been worn away by the hard feet of human Visitors, as though they knew the Woodstock could not be used on them. Some more Greys could be hidden from her sight beneath the overhang of the stone's lower edge. The Reds were well outnumbered and they had left the Woodstock down in the holly bush. She blamed herself for not insisting that they had carried it up the night before; she had been too interested in those shapes cut in the rock. Those would not save them, but the Woodstock might have.

Looking behind you
There is . . .

Too late for that now.

They did have the advantage of height, though. If it came to a fight, it could go either way. Trust in the Sun!

"Death to the Squarry. Death and the Sunlesss Pit for all thosse who protect her," called Ivy.

"Death and the Sunless Pit," chanted the other Greys, and the attack commenced.

The Reds held strong positions at the edges of the rock and were able to bite and scratch at grey paws and faces as the attackers tried to come over the rock-edge, but with their extra numbers and greater size and strength, the Greys were soon driving the Reds back up the slope. Juniper, at the lowest point, though slashing and biting in all directions, was unable to hold back the pressure from below.

On the upper edge the females were having more success. Every time a grey climber reached the top of the rock two red females would bite its paws and the Grey would drop backwards, yowling with pain and twisting in the air to land upright; it would then have to retire and lick the wounds on its crippled forepaws, unable to take any further active part in the fight. Another would take its place, however, and there was never a moment's respite for the defenders.

Marguerite was praying as she fought, facing the Sun.

Please help us, great Sun
To defend our beliefs – so
Evil may not win.

Across the heath near Wych Farm a geologist pressed the button that exploded one of his test charges buried in the ground, the echoes from the rock formation far below confirming the existence, and indicating the extent, of a vast reservoir of oil. Oil formed by vegetation which had grown in the Sunshine of a primitive earth, long before squirrels or indeed any other mammal had evolved.

He checked his instruments and moved across to connect the batteries to the second charge.

As Marguerite said the last line of the Kernel, the great ironstone rock, glowing red in the light of the early sunshine, trembled under their feet, and the squirrels, red and grey, clung on apprehensively.

"The Sun is with us," called Marguerite, and the Greys retreated down the rock, dropped to the ground and clustered together at the base.

"The Sun iss with *uss*," Ivy shouted, the words hissing past her broken tooth. "It iss shaking the rock to disslodge the Blassphemerss. Follow me, the Sun iss with USS!"

The Greys rallied and their attack recommenced.

The Reds were now hesitant in defence, but Marguerite called loudly from the top of the rock, "The Sun is with US. It shook the rock to discourage the attackers!"

Beneath their feet the great slab of stone trembled again, and each side, believing that the sign was favourable to them, fought more resolutely.

As the sun rose higher, the greater numbers and strength of the Greys were telling and they were pressing the Reds back towards the top of the rock. Juniper disappeared under a ball of grey bodies which rolled backwards and fell to the ground, limbs flailing in all directions.

The red defence faltered, and the Greys pressed home their advantage. The whole of the lower half of the sloping rock was a seething mass of grey pressing upwards against a thin line of Reds. Alder turned to signal for the reserve of yearlings to engage the enemy, only to find that they were already in action, fighting in pairs. Somehow they had broken off flakes of rock and one of each pair was leaning over the edge hammering at the Greys whilst the other held on to its back feet.

In the thickest part of the action Tamarisk was fighting side by side with Rowan.

"I wish we had the Woodstock up here," he said, between slashes at a grey male who was trying to outflank him. "That'd knock a few off the rock!"

Rowan leapt back to avoid a savage bite from another Grey, and replied, "Could we get it? It's worth a try, we're losing here. Nothing venture . . ."

"Follow me," called Tamarisk, and, with Rowan at his side, ran between the startled females, judged the distance, realising as he did so that he had never made such a jump before, and leapt from the rock to land in the holly bush.

As Rowan jumped a grey head appeared over the edge of the rock in front of him and a grey paw reached up and caught his leg as he flew over. The Red and the Grey fell, fighting, to the ground below.

Tamarisk, in the holly, wriggled his way down through

the spiky leaves which pricked his skin painfully. A needle-sharp spine pierced his left eye and, though he felt the stab of pain, he fumbled around amongst the stems in the shadow of the dark green leaves until he felt the smooth twisted shape of the Woodstock.

The Greys on that side of the rock, intent on trying to avoid the teeth and claws of the defending females, ignored the "deserter" who had appeared to abandon his companions and was probably fleeing for his life somewhere behind them. They could hunt him down later.

Tamarisk, half blinded by the blood pouring from his left eye, pushed the Woodstock some way out of the bush and directed it at the Greys at the back of the rock. He was about to scratch a *3* when he saw a flash of red fur amongst the mass of grey. He held back, wondering what to do.

Rowan's head came up out of the mêlée. He called to Tamarisk, "Use the Woodstock – now!" and the head went down again.

Tamarisk brushed away the blood from his face, aimed it into the writhing mass and scratched a *3* just as the great rock shook for the third time. Then he directed the power of the Woodstock on to those Greys clinging to the sunlit side. They felt agonising pains around their mouths and nostrils and, with their heads spinning and their claws no longer able to hold on to the crevices, they fell backwards, to land in moaning heaps on the ground. Here they lay, pawing at their faces and trying to straighten the tight curls now seemingly burned into their previously straight whiskers.

Engrossed in their own distress, the Greys ignored Tamarisk as he attemped to drag the Woodstock round to the other side of the great stone.

A grinning Rowan was suddenly beside him, helping. "I turned my back, got my head down and hid my whiskers," he said breathlessly, in answer to Tamarisk's unspoken query.

"I'm glad you're here. My eyesight's funny – I can't judge distance."

Rowan sighted the Woodstock and scratched a bold ⟨

The grey reserve on the ground, watching the fight above and ready to clamber up to join in if called on, didn't notice the two Reds with the peculiar stick until too late. The spiralling force struck them and they fell back, pawing at their faces. The Reds above, now assisted by the females, who no longer had to defend the rear, pushed down the rock, driving more Greys into the range of the Woodstock.

Soon only a few, including Hickory, were still able to fight. There was no sign of Ivy. Alder called a halt and the two sides each withdrew a squirrel length and paused, facing each other, panting for breath, but with the Reds' tails conspicuously high.

Marguerite came forward and, having got a nod of assent from Alder and unable to see Ivy, addressed Hickory.

"The Temple Master is dead. The Temple itself has been destroyed by the Lightning Force and now, with the help of the Sun, your party is defeated and your compatriots will have to suffer a whiskerless life for at least a moon. Will you accept that this squirrel, Rusty, is no longer to be what the Temple Master called a Squarry?"

Hickory lowered his tail as a sign of submission, but said nothing.

"Where is the female you call Ivy?" Marguerite asked.

Hickory shrugged his shoulders, but another Grey called

up, "She is here, Red One."

Ivy's body was dragged out from under the rock, Juniper's teeth through her throat.

Rowan went across to Juniper and put his paw on the bloodstained chest of the old squirrel, then did the same to Ivy.

"They are both Sun-gone," he announced.

"Deal with your injured," Marguerite said to Hickory. "We will talk more later."

She climbed to the top of the rock to be alone.

Chapter 32

————

Marguerite looked down on the Greys at the base of the rock. The few without injuries or curled whiskers were helping the others. She felt sorry for them and in a way responsible. They had come to her asking to be taught native ways and because she had sent them away, they had fallen under the influence of the fanatical Temple Master. Because of this, her life-mate, Juniper the Steadfast, was Sun-gone along with several Greys, and many more squirrels were hurt. The Reds had been forced to leave the Blue Pool and were now in the middle of a heath with no trees near to give Juniper a proper burial *and* they still had to get to Ourland and tackle the pine marten.

Turning her head, she could see Ourland over the water beyond the heath. If only she could see if the pine marten was still there, but it was much too far away.

To her right was the sweep of a sandy beach and over the sea beyond that she could just see white cliffs. Further to her right were the rock columns where the dolphins had come to her rescue the year before. She thought of them, Malin and Lundy, and wondered if they were, even now, out in that vast expanse of sea.

She looked down at the Greys again. They had come to the Blue Pool to learn native customs. She knew from the intensity of her Sun-scene that her destiny had to be on Ourland, but she asked herself briefly if she should not go back with the Greys and teach them the Kernels of Truth and how to live at peace with nature and one's surroundings. It also seemed important that the cold creed taught them by the Portlanders should be permanently replaced with one of Love under a friendly Sun.

She felt drawn to the idea of staying. She wanted time to work out the meanings of the humans' carvings on the rock. Her life-mate was Sun-gone, her youngsters were strong and healthy and could get along without her. But . . . a Tagger's first duty was to her community . . . and she did so want to know what had happened on Ourland since she had left. She sensed that Old Burdock had gone to a worthy rest, but hoped that Oak and Fern, her parents, had not been taken by the pine marten.

She couldn't stay; she was the only one who really understood the power of the Woodstock, and that would be needed there to destroy the marten. No – *she* couldn't stay!

Rowan, whose injuries from the fight were relatively light, was having similar thoughts about the Greys. He was discussing them with Meadowsweet, his beloved life-mate.

"Some squirrels ought to stay and teach these Greys all the Kernels," he was saying. "If they are going to be the new Guardians, some of us must teach them the proper way to do it. Would you stay with me if I offer?"

"Rowan, my love, where you go, I go. Where you stay, I stay. Young Bluebell too."

"If we are going to keep our kind alive on the Mainland,

we will need more than one family to stay. Should I ask the ex-zervantz?"

Spindle and Wood Anemone, although realising that they might never see Ourland again, readily agreed to stay on with their two youngsters, if the Council approved. Wood Anemone especially was glad that she would not have to make a sea-journey again.

The matter was discussed and settled at a Council Meeting held on the rock after High Sun. Hickory and two others of the "whiskered" Greys had been invited to attend as part of their retraining. They appeared to welcome the offer of help from Rowan.

The body of Juniper was buried near the holly bush, as the next best thing to a tree. The Reds, with the Greys behind them, gathered round to say the Farewell Kernel to a valiant fighter and a squirrel who had learned his wisdom through severe hardship.

> *Sun, take this squirrel*
> *Into the peace of your earth*
> *To nourish a tree.*

The bodies of the dead Greys were buried on the side of the holly bush and, with Hickory's permission, the Farewell Kernel was said for them as well.

Then, whilst the sun was still quite high, Rowan and his party led the low-tailed Greys away across the heath in the direction of the Blue Pool, planning to reach the safety of a tree before darkness overtook them. They moved slowly, the injured Greys hobbling as best they could and the few whiskered ones among them guiding the others.

An emotional farewell had taken place in the unspoken

knowledge that it was unlikely that they would ever meet again, and the remaining Reds climbed to the top of the Agglestone to flick the "farewell" signals with their tails until the departing squirrels were out of sight over the ridge.

Marguerite half expected Tansy to ask if they could move on, with the Woodstock, at once, but Tansy was more concerned with Tamarisk. She was at his side all the time helping him move about. The sight in his left eye had faded and was now lost completely. It was obvious to Alder and Marguerite that at least the rest of that day and a night of recuperation would be needed before they would be able to travel.

While they rested, Marguerite turned her attention to the Man-carvings on the rock, but there seemed to be no pattern to them.

The intensity of her concentration kept thoughts of the loss of Juniper and the departure of her brother and his family from her mind. She was no nearer understanding the meaning of the shapes cut in the rock when she realised that it was too dark to see them. She had not eaten, but was too weary to care, so she climbed up and joined the others high on the rock.

"I think we can do without keeping a watch tonight," said Alder, hardly able to stop his tail-stump from dragging, as he crawled painfully to the shallow scoop in the rock where most of the others were already asleep.

Marguerite agreed. No squirrel could have stayed awake in any case. They were all too exhausted and would have to accept whatever risks the night might bring.

The moon was high in the sky and the stars sparkling and twinkling above her when Marguerite woke feeling refreshed. She looked for the pattern of the Great Squirrel and followed the line of its paws to find the "Star that is always in the North". That was the direction in which Ourland lay, she was thinking, and she climbed to the top of the rock to see if she could see it in the moonlight.

Her attention was drawn to the Man-light across the sea. It glowed, then died, glowed briefly again, died again, then glowed steadily. Then the signal was repeated. Was it trying to tell her something? She stared out across the sea, concentrating hard.

Her whiskers were tingling in a way she had only experienced once before, when she had found that she could communicate with dolphins without actually speaking. She moved her head from side to side until the tingles were equal. Into her mind came gentle voices, like the soughing of the wind in distant pines, and she focused on these until the voices became clear.

"Can you hear us? Is that the small creature we were able to help last year? We sense that you have been part of a great triumph. Truth and fairness have beaten evil and bigotry. If it is you, we join you in hope."

Marguerite concentrated her thoughts and stared into the night towards the flashing light.

"Yes, it is I. Greetings to you both."

"We are three now. We, Malin and Lundy, have been Sun-blessed and have a youngster. We call him Finisterre. Your voice is faint. Are you far inland?"

"I am on a great rock in the middle of a heath, a day or so's travel from the sea."

"You are leaving the Mainland." It was a statement, not a question.

"Yes, I am needed on the island in the great pool."

"Your destiny is there."

This too was a statement, and Marguerite recalled Lundy telling her that dolphins could sometimes "look forward". She had been right in deciding not to return to the Blue Pool.

"The day after tomorrow we will come into the sandy bay. If you need help, speak to us again then. Farewell."

The voices faded and an owl called tremulously from across the heath. Marguerite felt a curious mixture of loneliness and hope.

Chapter 33

The squirrels had got to the sea.

Marguerite had told Alder of her contact with the dolphins and he had decided to have a meeting on the rock to discuss the next course of action. The most direct route to Ourland was north across the heath, but then they would have to find some way to cross the water themselves. If, however, they headed eastwards, they would reach the sea in the direction from which Marguerite had heard the dolphins' voices, and they had promised help. But in that direction were many Man-dreys, with the possibility of meeting dogs. Finally it was decided to head north of east until they reached what appeared, at that distance, to be a tree-covered knoll with a deserted part of the coast beyond it. They hoped that the dolphins would find them there.

It had been hard work for the depleted party, several of whom were injured, to drag the Woodstock across the heath and it had taken them all of that day.

They had slept in pine trees on the knoll on which there was a large Man-drey, but with no scent of the dreaded dogs, and from the pines they watched humans coming and going in their travelling-boxes, their actions as incomprehensible as always. For spring, the foraging there had been good, and even better when the humans had noticed the squirrels and had put out a variety of foods for them behind the Man-drey.

In the early morning Marguerite had asked Alder to summon a special Council Meeting for a tagging ceremony. This had been held in the highest of the pinetops, a warm breeze blowing in from the sea and rustling the needles gently.

"It is sad when a Tagger has to allocate down-tags," Marguerite had said, her face stern, then, as the squirrels had looked at one another in dismay, she had smiled and added, "but a joy when up-tags are to be given."

There had been an audible murmur of relief.

"Firstly, I propose to up-tag Tamarisk the Forthright. After his brave action turned the tide in the Battle of the Rock, he has earned the tag Great Leap. He will now be known as Tamarisk Great Leap. All in favour?"

There had been nods of approval and tail-flicking all around. Tamarisk's one good eye had glowed with pride.

"Tansy the Wistful," Marguerite had continued, "has shown great courage and fortitude in coming to us to seek assistance for our comrades on Ourland. My proposal for her is Tansy Stout Heart."

There had been more approving nods and tail-flicks.

"Finally, Rusty and Chipling, our friends from Portland, who until now have had no tags. For Rusty I propose Rusty the Kind, and for Chipling, as he wants us all to call him, the tag Who Seeks Love."

Chipling had looked a bit disappointed, but had to agree that, with Tansy now preoccupied with Tamarisk, it was a true tag and he had vowed to himself that he would earn a better one soon.

The plentiful food and the pleasure of the tagging ceremony had put the squirrels in high spirits as they crossed the roadway when it was clear of traffic and struggled through the sand dunes, dragging the Woodstock with them.

They paused at the top of the last dune, the marram grass high above their heads, and listened to it rustling as the salt-laden breeze, blowing in from the sea, bent the tops of the grass landwards.

Apart from some seagulls pecking amongst the wisps of seaweed at the high-tide mark, the beach was deserted in the morning sunshine. The squirrels crouched in the shelter of a clump of the coarse grass and waited. Several of them, tired from the struggle over the dunes, slept fitfully, sand blowing into their ears and nostrils.

As the sun got higher, some humans walked up the beach from the south and took off their coverings, replacing them with smaller pieces before sitting on the sand. A few, mostly young ones, ran into the water, shrieked and ran back up the beach.

Near High Sun, when the heat of spring warmed the squirrels comfortably, they watched several of the humans venture into the water and swim around aimlessly before coming out and sitting or lying on the sand again.

There were no swimmers when Marguerite felt her whiskers tingle with the dolphin vibration. She stood up and looked out to sea. Two large dolphins and one small one curved up out of the water and slid back down into it with hardly a splash.

One of the humans had also seen the dolphins and, calling to the others, ran down to the water's edge, pointing and gesticulating. The humans stood up and looked the way the man was pointing. The dolphins appeared to ignore them.

All the squirrels were alert now, standing and staring out to sea. The three black backs curved through the waves.

"Are you there?" a voice in Marguerite's head asked, and she knew it was Malin "speaking".

"Yes, except for my life-mate, Juniper, who nourishes a holly bush, and some who have chosen to remain, we are here."

"Stay in the sand-grasses until it is dark, then we will bring a boat to take you to your island in the Great Harbour."

"Do dolphins have boats?" Marguerite asked.

"Not of our own," came back the reply. "We'll use a boat of the humans."

"Will they let you?"

"They won't know it is us. If they miss it, they'll think it is other humans; they are always taking one another's things. We will bite through the rope and when we have finished with it, we will push it ashore at high tide where they can find it. Without hands like theirs we can't re-tie, but we will leave the boat where it will be safe."

"Is it 'right' to do that?" asked Marguerite, remembering the Kernel:

If not in your care,
You must ask the Guardian –
Before you use things.

"In principle, no. But humans no longer hear when we 'speak' to them. And considering what *they* are doing, we have no qualms about using a boat now and then," replied Malin, with an unexpected tinge of bitterness in his "voice". "The way they treat the Sea!"

"How is that?" asked Marguerite, thinking of the humans she could see, clustered at the water's edge.

"They pollute it, that's how," came back the reply.

As Marguerite watched, the three glistening bodies curved up out of the blue of the water again. She marvelled at how that simple action, which a minute before indicated peace and contentment, now expressed anger and resentment.

"This beach, the one they call Studland, is one of the few that are really clean now. But at many places along the coast they pour their dung into our Sea."

Malin continued, sadness replacing the anger in his voice, "Only a few days ago we swam up the Channel past the Man-dwellings in that place the humans call the English Riviera. They are very proud of that place and their dwellings are all along the coast and up the hillsides."

Lundy's thoughts washed over Malin's. "The squirrels are not concerned with this. They have problems of their own that we are here to help with."

Malin ignored her. It was obvious from the strength of his thoughts that this was a major concern of his.

"We took a short cut between Thatcher Rock and the

Mainland near there, and human dung was streaming out of the end of a tube on the seabed, tainting the water for miles."

"I thought humans buried their dung like cats do," said Marguerite, remembering the Flood story.

"They may have once, but now they just pour it into the Sea. I wonder how they would like it if thousands of dolphins sprayed *their* dung into the air over the land!"

Marguerite thought of the squirrel saying:

> *People puzzle us*
> *With their strange actions – but then*
> *They're only human.*

A moment of appreciative thought carried across the waves, followed by, "I wish it was as simple as that, but there are disturbing metallic tastes in the Sea now, especially around the estuary of the Great River and up the coast to the north of it. It made young Finisterre quite sick when we took him up there. Sometimes it is hard to find clean water near the coast at all!"

Marguerite did not know how to reply, there was so much sadness and concern in the dolphin's thought-voice.

Then she heard Lundy again. "I am sorry to bother you with our problems. Malin gets washed away sometimes; pollution is a real peril to us and we feel so helpless, unable to do anything about it.

"We will leave now and come back when the moon sails the sky. We will have a boat for you then. Listen for us."

Out in the bay the three black shapes curved out of the water and vanished again below the surface. The humans waited for a while then drifted up the beach and settled down on their towels to enjoy the sun and the breeze on their bodies.

It was now uncomfortably hot on the dunes and, though shaded a little by the marram grass, the squirrels lay panting in the heat. They could hear the waves on the beach and the cries of seagulls and excited young humans at play, but were not disturbed.

As the sun dropped in the sky, the humans re-covered themselves, gathered up their things and wandered away along the shore. When they were out of sight, Dandelion, remembering her days on the beach at Worbarrow the year before, led the squirrels down to the shoreline and showed them which seaweeds were edible, and they raced the seagulls to any scraps of food left by the humans.

The sea had been going away from them, but started to return as darkness fell. The squirrels sitting in groups on the sand felt vulnerable, but completely confident that the dolphins would return, bringing with them a "boat", though the yearlings had no real idea what such a thing was.

Chip, at his mother's side, was watching Tansy washing and cleaning Tamarisk's blind eye with her tongue. Tansy Stout Heart was still kind to him, but her main concern was with Great Leap, though Tamarisk was more subdued than he had ever been, and gave more thought to his words before he spoke.

Rusty, after knowing for a lifetime that a Squarry Edict was "until death", could not really believe that she was free and safe amongst these wonderful, warm-hearted squirrels, and kept glancing towards the heath, fearing the return of the Greys to impose the Edict.

Alder was restless. He had never been in a "boat", and he was apprehensive. He had grown to trust Marguerite's judgement and had no qualms about the integrity of "her" dolphins. But he was about to commit his whole party to some new experience out of his control and at the end of it they would be landing on an island strange to him. Then they might have to tackle a pine marten, the ancestral enemy of all squirrels!

This whole venture was absurd, though he seemed to have no choice but to go along with it. He would have to trust in the Sun and not show his fear.

> *When the cones are down,*
> *Even if you doubt yourself,*
> *Hide all your concerns.*

Dandelion wondered if she should tell a story to pass the time, and was about to call the youngsters together to hear one when the edge of a huge yellow moon rose above the horizon, casting weird shadows on the dunes and the beach. The squirrels, with the fear of attack by Greys behind them and the island with the pine marten still somewhere in the future, seemed strangely moved to be in the open, under this odd light. Before long some of the yearlings were scurrying up and down the beach, turning sharply in flurries of fine sand and leaping over pieces of flotsam.

Squirrelation took over, all caution thrown to the night wind, and the beach became alive with leaping, running and scampering squirrels of all ages, until Marguerite, who had briefly forgotten the loss of Juniper, called, "The dolphins are coming."

The excitement changed to anticipation as the outline of an unmanned rowboat appeared and was driven on to the sand by a push from one of the dolphins swimming behind it.

The squirrels clustered around the severed mooring rope hanging from the bow, nudging each other, until Marguerite, who had clearly taken charge, said, "Up the rope, one by one", and the squirrels climbed as swiftly as they could, and disappeared over the gunwale.

Marguerite gave one last look around the beach to see that no squirrel had been forgotten and followed the others up the rope.

Chapter 34

Flapping and splashing in the shallows, the dolphins turned the boat in the rising water and towed it out to where Finisterre, their calf, was waiting, poking his head above the waves as he swam back and forth anxiously watching for the return of his parents.

As they reached Finisterre, a current caught the boat and moved it southwards, parallel to the shore. The dolphins sensed Marguerite's concern that it was going in the wrong direction and Malin spoke.

"We use the currents. It would be possible to push the boat all the way to your island, but we can guide it from current to current and get there effortlessly and just as quickly. Trust us."

The three dolphins swam alongside. Marguerite wondered if they would leap, as she had seen them do from the beach. No sooner had the thought formed in her head than the three black bodies, gleaming in the moonlight, curved up and out of the water, to the astonishment and joy of the squirrels standing on the rowboat's seats. The presence of the dolphins seemed to have banished the squirrels' instinctive fear of water and all were enjoying themselves, giving little thought to the hazard to be faced when they reached the island.

The dolphins cavorted and leapt all around the boat as it drifted along, until finally, when they knew it would not frighten the squirrels, they leapt in unison right over the boat. Drops of salt water rained down from their tails on to the animals below, causing the youngsters to shriek with delight.

Then, as a current caught the boat and bore it inexorably towards the narrow mouth of Poole Harbour, Marguerite asked, "Won't the humans see us?"

"They are mostly asleep at this time," came the reply from Malin, "but they are usually so concerned with their own immediate affairs that they notice little else. Did they see you on the beach?"

"No," replied Marguerite, "but we kept ourselves hidden in the grasses on the sand and watched out for them. Why did some of the humans go into the water? They just swam about and came out again."

"It's an ancestral memory that prompts them to do that. Do you recall last year that we told you how dolphins once lived on the land and then went back to the sea again. Well, humans nearly did the same. It is in our History Training.

"Far, far back in time, when humans stopped being creatures of the trees, they lived on the ground in dry places for aeons and then, when these got too dry, they lived on the coasts of the country they now call Africa. They spent most of their time in the shallow water where they were more comfortable walking upright, and it was then that they lost most of their body hairs, keeping only enough on their heads for the Man-cubs to cling to when their parents swam. It was at that time that scent became unimportant to them and they had to learn to be clever with their voices so that they could communicate with each other whilst they were swimming."

Marguerite was trying to keep up with the mass of new images passing through her brain. It was tiring, but she was determined to learn all that she could from these wonderful and helpful creatures who had befriended her and her companions.

"Do humans remember that time?" she asked.

"I don't believe so; they don't teach Long History as we do. But when the sun starts to get warm each year, they follow old urges and make for the Sea. They still love to swim for the pleasure and the feeling of being in the water. I sometimes wonder what would have happened if they had carried on evolving that way until they became totally creatures of the Sea as we dolphins did. They still shed tears, you know!"

"What are tears?"

"Nature gave us sea mammals a special place in our eyes where we can get excess salt out of our systems. Humans still have these, but they only use them when they are distressed. They should use them all the time, knowing how they are treating our Sea!"

"Malin, leave that," said Lundy, severely.

"Humans are strange creatures," Marguerite agreed, "though harmless to squirrels as far as our memory goes. But we don't trust them fully; so much of what they do seems inexplicable. We have a squirrel saying:

If you could know all
Then you could understand all
Then you'd forgive all.''

"For 'Innocents', you squirrels certainly think a lot!"

The other squirrels were unaware that any conversation was taking place, as Marguerite had learned that it was only necessary to think her questions, and did not have to speak them out loud. Most of the others were dozing on the floorboards by now, though Rusty and Chip were watching the Man-lights at the harbour entrance getting nearer, as the current bore the boat that way.

"What do you call an 'Innocent'?" Marguerite asked.

"We call all 'small-brained' creatures 'Innocents', as they just have to survive and breed and do not concern themselves with moral issues. I sometimes envy them.''

Marguerite felt slightly offended at being called "small brained", but then realised that physically it must be true.

"We meant no offence," Malin assured her. "It can be a burden to be involved with greater issues than which fish you fancy eating today, or if your mating approach will be reciprocated.

"Most 'Large-brained' sea mammals carry this burden. Sometimes we try to communicate with the 'Great-brains', the whales. Their intelligence is *awesome*. You should hear them sing their philosophies!"

Malin was silent as Marguerite tried to understand the concept of "singing" and could only get a pattern of rising and falling voices in her head. She felt her "small-brain" limitations.

Lundy's voice flowed in. "We cannot understand why

humans kill the whales. Perhaps it is some kind of jealousy. The whales know things about the meaning of Life which even *we* can't get our minds around!"

"Perhaps they eat them," Marguerite ventured, remembering the unicorn in Dandelion's story of the Flood.

"Oh, no, it can't be that," replied Malin. "Humans are 'Large-brains' like us. They couldn't be *that* short-sighted and stupid."

The conversation ceased as the dolphins steered the boat into the centre of the channel between the points of land that formed the entrance to Poole Harbour. As the narrows passed behind them, Lundy said, "We will take you to the other end of the island. The humans have made a structure there which will help you all get out of the boat easily. Then we must hurry to get the boat back to its place before dawn."

The moon had set and grey light was creeping into the sky as the boat was pushed in against the pier at the western end of the island.

Marguerite sensed the dolphins' concern about returning the boat, and urged the sleepy squirrels to scramble out on to the pier. Her head was aching after a night of such intense concentration and she climbed out last, almost falling into the water as the dolphins, in their haste, started to push the boat away.

She remembered to thank them, urging her tired brain to project her thoughts: "Thank you, and farewell."

"Farewell, your Sun be with you," came back three simultaneous replies as the boat moved away out of sight around the point and past Woodstock Bay.

230

Marguerite recalled that that was where she had found the first Woodstock on the beach. Who had the New Woodstock? She looked around, then realised with horror that they had left it in the marram grass behind Studland Beach.

Chapter 35

Marguerite hurried along the pier after Alder, and drew him to one side.

"We have left the Woodstock in the dunes at Studland," she told him. "It's my fault. I was carried away by the dolphins and the boat and . . . I'm sorry, I should have remembered it."

"You've many things on your mind, Marguerite-Friend. *I* won't blame you for it. I should have thought of it myself, but I got caught up in the squirrelation. And then the boat came."

He rested his paw briefly on her shoulder. "We will have to get along without it. But first we must get everyone hidden in case that marten is about. Trust in the Sun."

They slept most of the day in some rhododendron bushes where they felt that any enemy approaching on the ground would betray itself by the rustling of leaves, and the dense foliage would keep them from being seen from the trees above. The breeze was from the south-east, so their scent would be blown out over the sea. Even so, they were restless and unhappy.

Tansy was eager to be off, to look for her parents, and

was torn between her concern for them and for Tamarisk, whose eye was still painful. She was also worried that there was no squirrel-scent at that end of the island at all. Were all the Ourland squirrels dead?

In the late afternoon and evening Alder allowed them to forage, a few at a time, and then insisted that they pass another night in the rhododendrons. Marguerite spent most of her foraging time unsuccessfuly searching for another Woodstock, feeling guilty that her forgetfulness had left them without its power when they needed it so much.

At dawn they moved off together above the old Man-track along the centre of the island, keeping to the trees and listening and watching out for any marten-danger. They saw rabbits and a sika doe with her fawn, and the heronry was raucous with the calls of the young birds, but there was no scent of squirrels or marten. At High Sun they rested in the great pines near the middle of the island where the exiles had first met the Royals nearly two years before.

Blood was angry and frustrated. There was food all about him: nestling birds, eggs for the taking, young rabbits just waiting to be eaten, peafowl at the snap of his jaws. He wanted squirrel, he needed squirrel, he deserved squirrel – but they were too close to the humans for him to dare to attack there. Thoughts of the time when he was caged flooded over him. He couldn't risk that again, even for squirrel.

There were only a few peahens left now, and the cock bird, Mogul. In the spring sunshine Blood watched them on the Man-track below where he lay on a branch high in a tree behind the church. The peacock was behaving differently. He usually dragged that stupid tail of his around behind him, trying to keep it out of the mud, but today he had somehow made it stand up behind him and he was strutting about so proudly, showing it off to the hens.

Not much to be *that* proud of, Blood thought, seeing it from behind. Then, as the male bird turned and the Sun caught the front of the tail-fan, he was dazzled and even Blood had to admit that it was special.

Arc after arc of gleaming iridescent eyes patterned the most beautiful long, bluey-green feathers and caught the Sunlight as the bird strutted back and forth in front of the admiring hens. The blue of his neck and the little bobbly crest flashed and glimmered, but Blood was no longer an admirer. In his frustration he was a despoiler.

He leapt down from the tree and, caring nothing that men might be near, ran openly across the grass towards the huge birds. The peacock's tail-fan collapsed in an instant and the birds scattered. Blood followed the peacock. Mogul ran faster and faster, then, realising that he was losing the race, launched himself heavily into the air with a screech of anger, and flew down the track to land on the branch of an oak, seemingly out of reach.

Blood followed on the ground, climbed the tree-trunk and ran out along the branch. The peacock, still breathless, shrieked, launched himself into the air again and headed for the Man-tree with the thin vines reaching out to the next "tree". He landed awkwardly on one of the power lines, trying hard to keep his balance as the wire swung to and fro.

Blood was not to be outdone. He dropped from the oak, ran to the foot of the Man-tree, wrinkled his nose at the scent of creosote, dug his claws into the barkless wood and climbed. Two thin leafless vines stretched out to the next Man-tree on either side, on one of which sat Mogul, watching the marten with his head on one side, ready to fly off again.

Blood knew that he would have to move fast. Reaching past a shiny white thing, he grasped the thin vine with a forepaw whilst holding on to the trunk with his feet. There was a flash inside his head brighter than the light on the peacock's neck, and he was falling, falling, falling through a pit where the sun never shone. Falling, falling, falling. Then a thud and – nothing.

Mogul screeched in triumph, lost his balance, fell backwards and fluttered to the ground.

By the time he had walked back to the group of staring hens he had recovered his composure. As they gathered around, he raised his tail as though nothing had happened. Blood was forgotten in the primeval mating display.

Later, a man with one of Acorn's badges on his jumper buried the pine marten's body in a place in the meadow where the peahens had scratched away the turf, and it was in the dry soil above Blood's grave that the peachicks played and dusted themselves through the long hot summer that followed.

Chapter 36

Oak and Just Poplar had been together in the sequoia tree when Blood had first chased the peacock. Oak's eyes were not strong now, so Just Poplar had described what was happening, his voice mounting in excitement.

When Blood fell, lifeless, from the power lines, Just Poplar was overcome with relief. At first he could not believe that their enemy was truly Sun-gone. It was not until he saw a human pick up the limp body and carry it away that he really allowed himself to believe what he had seen, and he ran off to tell the news to the other Ourlanders foraging in the castle grounds. Oak limped stiffly along behind him.

"The marten is Zun-gone, the marten is Zun-gone!" Just Poplar called and the other squirrels looked up, then gathered round to hear how it had all happened.

"Him wuz chazing the great bird who flew on to won of the vinez of the new Man-treez, and the marten climbed the trunk. The Zun zent a little lightning flazh to ztrike the marten and protect the great bird. Uz zaw the flazh, but there wuz no thunder. Let uz thank the zun."

The squirrels were unable to believe this. Could it all

have happened so quickly? They stood looking at the breathless Poplar, hope wrestling with disbelief.

"You're quite sure of all this?" Chestnut asked doubtfully.

Oak had reached them and confirmed Just Poplar's story.

"I saw the human pick up the body. They wouldn't do that with a live pine marten!"

Clover the Tagger moved forward, a Kernel forming in her head:

> *We thank you, oh Sun,*
> *For freeing Ourland from the*
> *Fear of the marten.*

Then wild squirrelation took over. With the sudden removal of the one thing in the whole of Ourland that they feared, their relief exploded. Squirrels raced up and down the trees, leapt across pathways and capered wildly, to the delight of the humans who were streaming ashore from a fleet of boats for the official reopening of the island by the National Trust, and for the rededication of the church, on that sunny day in May.

The humans on the ground, and the squirrels in the trees, swept inland towards the little island church, whose tower, for so long the home of the scourge of Ourland, showed above the treetops.

Mogul, the peacock, strutted and displayed as if he knew that he alone was responsible for *all* the celebration.

It was a far more sombre party of squirrels who were progressing through the island treetops from the west.

Going slowly for the sake of the injured squirrels and the

one-eyed Tamarisk, Marguerite and Tansy were aware that, if the Ourlanders were safe, and had survived the attacks of the marten, there ought to be squirrel-scent in the trees. But they had reached the centre of the island without finding any.

They moved cautiously on eastwards.

The jubilant Ourland squirrels watched the humans as they entered the stone building until there was no room for any more. Other humans clustered outside in the sunshine. The males were wearing dark coverings and sweating in the heat, the sun hot on their bare heads, whilst the females were in bright coverings of many colours, and each had a different-shaped cover on her head.

The squirrels peered down in amazement. They had never seen such a gathering of humans, or seen them in such a happy mood.

Oak whispered to Just Poplar, "It looks as if the humans are celebrating a Sun-day."

It was then the singing started, never before heard by these Ourland squirrels. Waves of human voices, in unison, were rising and falling in rhythmic patterns like the sea on the beach, or the wind in the pinetops. Each squirrel sat and listened in rapture.

As suddenly as it had begun, the singing stopped and a single human voice was heard, the words meaningless to the squirrels.

Oak looked around. His fading sight had caught a movement in the trees to the west and for one awful moment he thought the marten was alive and stalking them. Then, realising that this could not be true, he pointed the movement out to Just Poplar, who peered in that direction.

"It's squirrels!" he called out, nearly falling from the branch. "I can see Marguerite and Tansy and Tamarisk and . . ."

His voice choked with emotion. Then the whole band of Ourland squirrels raced through the treetops to greet their friends.

Such hugging and whisker-brushing, such joy and sadness, so many stories to be exchanged and the death of the pine marten to be rejoiced over that, when the human singing began again behind them, they hardly heard it. Marguerite, sitting with her father, Oak, was hearing how her mother, Fern the Fussy, had died in the Bunker, when she felt herself moved by the rising and falling sounds and wondered if the singing of the great whales sounded like the singing of the humans in the church beyond the trees.

When the boats had taken most of the humans back to the Mainland, Marguerite, Tansy and Tamarisk explored the area around the church. They marvelled at how it had been cleaned up and how the overgrowth that they remembered had been cut away and burned.

Marguerite discovered that the humans had just planted a tree near the church. She examined its shape and the way the young branches stood out from the stem and even tasted the bark carefully, but could not indentify it.

If the humans are planting trees, perhaps they are beginning to use their "large brains" again, she thought, then raced across the grass to join the others who were returning to Beech Valley to celebrate their all being together again and to start rebuilding their dreys.

Chapter 37

In the summer that followed there were so many things for the squirrels to do. There were Guardianships to be allocated and established, and life-mates to be chosen by the yearlings. Soon the trees were alive with courting rituals and mating chases. Tails were high all over Ourland.

There was speculation as to whether Just Poplar would propose a life-mating between himself and Marguerite. It seemed to many to be a natural outcome, but she was withdrawn and preoccupied. Perhaps she was missing the comfort of Juniper's presence or was concerned about Rowan, Meadowsweet and the ex-zervantz with their huge task of educating the Second Wave of Greys on the Mainland.

Then at the Longest Day Celebrations Just Poplar surprised them all by announcing that Rusty the Kind, or Rush as she now preferred to be called, had consented to be his life-mate, and she joined him in the Council Leader's drey in the tree above the pond in Beech Valley. Chipling was delighted.

Tansy Stout Heart and Tamarisk Great Leap became

life-mates as expected, and took a Guardianship near the church. Tansy loved to watch the humans and listen to their singing whenever they celebrated a Sun-day, which seemed to be once every week. Her journey to the Mainland might not have been successful in bringing the Woodstock back, but it had resulted in her finding a truly appreciative life-mate and she knew that soon she would have a family of dreylings to tell her story to.

Chipling, though fully grown, attached himself to Marguerite and became her willing pupil. He did not appear to be interested in any of the yearling females now that Tansy was unobtainable.

Marguerite was pleased to have a listener. It was Clover, the established Tagger of Ourland, who taught Kernels, Traditions and Manners to the youngsters, and yet Marguerite was an elected Tagger as well. The squirrels of Alder's party were pressing for her to act as the official Tagger – at least for them.

Sensing that a dispute might develop which could spoil the new peace of Ourland, Marguerite and Clover, calling on the wisdom of an ancient Kernel, decided to get the squirrels to resolve it by Tail Pairing.

> *Big disagreements*
> *Are only settled safely*
> *By a Tail Pairing.*

Marguerite, who knew from the traditions how a Tail Pairing worked, thought that she had an easier way to arrive at a result. Instead of matching a "yes" squirrel with a "no" squirrel and seeing which side those left over represented, she proposed a Tail Poll as she and Chip could both count above eight.

She was concerned to see how much the issue of who was to be Tagger divided the squirrels.

The two ex-princesses, now jointly tagged the Carers were vociferous in their support for their teacher, Clover. Voxglove, knowing that Alder would back Marguerite, put it around that he should not have a vote as he had no tail to signal his preference.

Clover and Marguerite joined forces to quash that suggestion. "It is the brain which votes; the tail is only used as a signal," Clover told Voxglove sternly. "Alder has other ways of making his intentions clear."

Chipling, being the only other squirrel besides Marguerite who knew numbers above eight, was very proud to be appointed to count the votes.

Excited squirrels gathered in the Council Tree on Poll-day. Just Poplar took charge. Fortunately there had been no conflict between him and Alder for the Leader's position; Alder was a recent incomer and had no desire to take on the responsibility. Mentally exhausted from the trauma of leading his party to safety through the early part of the year, he was glad to be able to live a quiet life on this lovely island with Dandelion.

"Squirrels who wish Clover to be Tagger, move to the south-side branches and raise your tails," Just Poplar directed. "Those who wish Marguerite to be Tagger, move to the north-side branches and do the same." Just Poplar moved to the south.

Chipling, very positively on the north side, started the count, mumbling the words to himself. Marguerite had already counted quietly to herself and knew that they were evenly divided. It was going to have to be settled by a drawing of twigs!

Chipling finished his count and a thought crossed his mind. He could ensure that Marguerite would be elected and no one but Marguerite would know. He glanced at her. She read his thoughts and shook her head.

He was about to declare "Equal Acorns" when old Oak slumped across the branch where Burdock had passed to the Sun a year before and, losing his grip, fell to the ground below.

The squirrels scrambled down to find that the fine old squirrel, Oak the Cautious, was truly Sun-gone. Later that day they buried him beneath the Council Tree near his friend Burdock.

Sun, take this squirrel
Into the peace of your earth
To nourish a tree.

The count was never declared. Marguerite, sad at losing her beloved father and recognising defeat without his vote, "climbed down" and wandered the island seeking a role for herself. Clover, seeing her thus, offered to share the Tagger's position.

"Thank you, Clover-Friend, but it wouldn't work. A True Tagger must accept total responsibilty for the tags she gives. It can't be shared. I feel the Sun has another task in mind for me."

The two friends brushed whiskers and hugged one another.

*

Chipling, tired after helping with the collection, burying and storing of the Autumn Harvest, found Marguerite one evening on the beach as the tide was going out. She was making patterns in the sand with her claws.

"Look at this," she said, pointing to where she had scratched a symbol A in the sand.

"What is it?" he asked.

"It's an A. A is for Acorn!"

BOOK THREE

THE GOLDEN FLIGHT

Characters

RED SQUIRRELS OF OURLAND

Marguerite the Seeker
Burdock and *Oak*, her daughter and son
Just Poplar the Leader; his life-mate *Rush* the Kind
Her son, *Chip* Who Seeks Love
Dandelion the Story-teller; her life-mate *Alder*
Larch the Curious; his life-mate *Clover* the Tagger
Their son *Elm* and daughter *Trefoil*
Chestnut the Doubter; his life-mate *Heather* Treetops
Tamarisk Greatleap; his life-mate *Tansy* Stoutheart

Ex-Kingz-Mate *Thizle*
The ex-princesses, *Cowzlip* and *Voxglove* the Carers
Their brother, ex-prince *Fir*

Walnut (Old Wally) a long-dead squirrel who made
prophecies
Caterpillar an ex-zervant
Sycamore, a young red squirrel

RED SQUIRRELS ON THE MAINLAND

Rowan the Bold; his life-mate *Meadowsweet* Rowan's Love
Their daughter *Bluebell*
Spindle the Helpful; his life-mate *Wood Anemone* the Able (was *Woodlouse*)
Their twin daughters *Rosebay* and *Willowherb*

GREY SQUIRRELS ON THE MAINLAND

Hickory
Sitka
Sumac; his life-mate *Tumbleweed*

THE THREE GREY LORDS

Lord *Malachite*
Lord *Obsidian*
Lord *Silica*

The Great Lord Silvers – *Redwood* and *Monterey*
Monterey's namesake, a young grey squirrel
Many Colonisers under training

OTHERS

The Dolphins, *Malin* and *Lundy*
Their son *Finisterre*
Acorn and *Primrose*, the mythical first squirrels in the world
Swans from Abbotsbury Swannery

Chapter 1

———

March 1964 roared in upon Dorset.

The great sweep of the Chesil Bank in Dorset was taking the full force of the south-westerly gale as a deep depression drove in from the Atlantic. For over twenty miles pebbles snarled and ground as the heavy seas rushed in, each wave tumbling over the previous one in its haste. The churning action rounded the stones and moved them ever eastwards, sorting the pebbles by size as they trundled along. To the west the shingle was pea-sized, whereas at the aptly named Deadman's Bay at the Portland end of the beach it ranged in size from that of a potato to that of a giant swede.

By nightfall the waves were breaking over the crest of the Bank and rushing down the far side, tearing out the mats of sea-campion that grew on the landward slope above the more sheltered waters of the Fleet Lagoon.

The usually smooth surface of the Fleet was choppy and debris-laden as gusts of wind carried plastic bottles, fishing-net corks, small pieces of driftwood and dead seaweed from the top of the Chesil Bank and tossed them all into the lagoon behind.

Where Mute swans had nested on the mainland side of

the Fleet for over six hundred years, a flock now huddled on their nest sites, heads tucked under their wings to keep dust and flying reeds from their eyes.

There was no rain, but even at that distance, the air was misted with a fine salt spray which formed little pools on the swans' feathers and trickled in tiny rivulets to the ground.

The most seaward pair of the Dragon's Teeth, a double line of concrete tank-stops that had straddled the beach since the fear of invasion in 1939, were undermined by the waves and drawn down into the depths by the suction of the undertow. The deep rolling action of the waves disturbed the wrecks that lay off that treacherous coast, and pieces of jagged iron from landing craft and tramp steamers, together with waterlogged timbers from emigrant ships and Armada galleons were thrown up the beach and dragged down again, artefacts and treasures spilling across the seabed.

Further along the coast, the massive bulk of Portland stood firm against this storm as it had for ten thousand years and a thousand similar storms, protecting the deep waters of Weymouth Bay to the east.

Even so, the cliffs from White Nothe to Saint Alban's Head were being pounded and eroded by the giant waves gnawing at their feet, bringing down cascades of chalky rock. Only at Lulworth Cove, where the narrow entrance excluded all but an occasional wave, was there calmer water. Here a few waves rolled in and exhausted themselves in the enclosed bay; the swoosh as each ran gently up the beach being drowned by the howling of the gale overhead.

The wind tore at the cliffs surrounding the cove, probing into every nook and cranny as though seeking out seabirds to toss through the air, but these birds, sensing an impending storm, had already flown inland.

Frustrated, the wind raced over the land, shaking and felling great oak trees and working loose the tiles and thatch on the cottages of the humans.

At the Tanglewood Knoll on the Great Heath, the wind found no new trees to topple. Another such storm some fifteen years before had felled all those that were not well-rooted or were past their prime. The tangled trunks and branches on the ground below the standing pines gave the wood its name and protected it from the forays of gun-bearing humans.

In one of these pines, three elderly grey squirrels huddled together in a drey, feeling the wind rock the tree and expecting any minute that the drey itself would be blown out of the fork, and the twigs and mossy lining scattered over the wood. They feared that they too might be flung to the ground but each tried to hide his fears from the others.

Further to the east near the Blue Pool, now a wind-whipped mass of foam and bubbles, seven red squirrels had just had their drey torn to pieces around them. Shaken and breathless they were hurrying along the ground to seek shelter in a hollow tree, known to them as the Warren Ash. The wind fluffed up their tails and fur, and the stronger gusts bowled them over on the shifting, rustling mass of pine needles forming the forest floor.

Even further to the east, the wind picked up speed as it crossed the frothing waters of Poole Harbour to throw itself at the screen of trees that encircled the island of Brownsea;

3

trees that surrounded and protected the meadows and the woodlands at the island's centre. One violent gust caught a giant pine growing just behind the southern shore and snapped its trunk some six feet above the ground, the top bounding and rolling across the trackway behind, to lodge in the mass of romping rhododendron bushes.

This final act of vandalism seemed to satisfy the wind. As darkness fell, the force slackened and the stars, pricking through the blackness above the island, looked down on a ravaged landscape.

A moon later, in the mild spring sunshine Marguerite, a mature red squirrel, sat on top of The Wall. Not a wall – The Wall.

This brick-built structure was in the centre of Ourland, a beautiful island of woodland, meadows and heath set in the now placid waters of Poole Harbour. The Wall had once formed the back of a range of glass-houses which had provided grapes, peaches and other exotic fruit to the inhabitants of the Castle at the island's eastern end. After many years of neglect, all that remained of the hot houses and the vegetable garden was The Wall.

It was about twice the height of a man and ran parallel to a track which had recently been cleared of undergrowth.

Marguerite had climbed the weathered brickwork, her claws finding holds in the crumbling mortar between the bricks. In these crevices moss grew, and from the top of The Wall, gossamer spiders' webs reached out to nearby bushes.

She sat listening to the young squirrels playing at the other end of The Wall. From where she was she could not

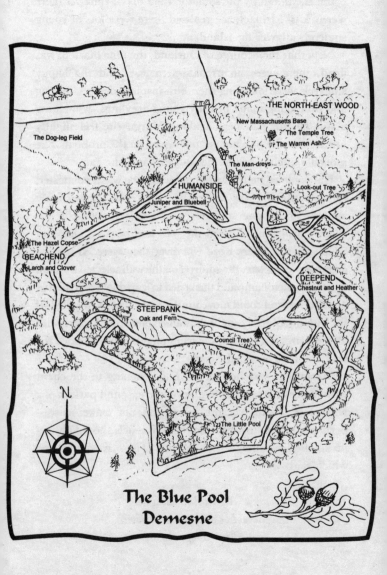

THE NORTH-EAST WOOD

New Massachusetts Base

The Temple Tree

The Warren Ash

The Dog-leg Field

The Man-dreys

HUMANSIDE

Look-out Tree

Juniper and Bluebell

The Hazel Copse

BEACHEND
Larch and Clover

DEEPEND
Chestnut and Heather

STEEPBANK
Oak and Fern

Council Tree

N

The Little Pool

The Blue Pool
Demesne

count them, but by the sound of their playful chatter there were "lots". In fact, she realised there were lots of young squirrels all over the island.

Now that the Scourge of Ourland, the pine marten, was dead, there were no predators to fear, and the happy squirrels were following their Sun-inspired desires, mating and producing many healthy young dreylings. Something about all this had been making Marguerite feel slightly uneasy but she had not yet put a paw on the problem. She moved along the top of the wall to watch the game.

Having lived on the Mainland when she was a youngster, this island game was new to her. The rules seemed fairly simple. The young squirrels would scurry about on the ground while one climbed the wall and began a chant, at which all the others froze wherever they were. When the chant was complete, the squirrel on the wall selected a victim by calling their name and then tried to leap down onto him or her. No squirrel could move until a name had been called. If the leaping squirrel caught the named one, it could nip it with its teeth, but if it missed, the triumphant victim climbed the wall and took over as Leaper.

Marguerite watched for a while, listening to the chant with interest. It had the five, seven, five, sound pattern of a Kernel of Truth, yet the words did not make sense – perhaps she was mis-hearing them. Kernels should always make their meaning clear at once. There was even one which said:

A Kernel's message
Should be wrapped in gossamer
Clever wraps obscure.

6

She moved closer, but her presence disturbed the youngsters, who held her in some awe. The game stopped, leaving the young squirrels sitting about uncomfortably.

"I'm sorry," Marguerite called down. "I didn't want to spoil your fun, I was just trying to hear what you were saying. How does that chant go?"

The current "Leaper", who she recognised as Dandelion's youngest daughter, turned to her and replied,

> *I honour birch-bark,*
> *The Island Screen. Flies stinging –*
> *A piece of the sun.*

"What does it mean?" Marguerite asked, intrigued.

"I don't know," the youngster replied. "It's what we always say – does it have to mean anything? It's just a game."

Another dreyling, Elm, Larch's son, called up from the ground, "When you get caught and nipped, it's like a fly's sting."

"Uz father wuz ztung by a wazp onze," another youngster volunteered, his accent showing that his father must be one of the original islanders. "Nazdy, him zaid it wuz. Him taught uz to ztay away from yellow thingz that flyz."

No other comments were offered and Marguerite thanked them politely and as she went back along The Wall, she heard the game restart.

> *I honour birch-bark . . .*

7

What could it mean, she wondered.

She had recently abandoned her attempts to make sense of humans' name shapes. **A** for Acorn was fine, and she had always used **X** as her special mark, so **X** must be for Marguerite; but after this she could get no further. Here was a new challenge!

> *I honour birch-bark*
> *The Island Screen. Flies stinging –*
> *A piece of the sun.*

She repeated it several times to herself. The Island Screen was the name that the squirrels called the ring of trees which surrounded the open areas and the woodland, protecting them from the gales and the storms, but the Screen was mostly pine with only a few birches. Why should *their* bark be especially mentioned?

She climbed down The Wall, and wandered aimlessly towards the meadows to the south. Much overgrown from many years of neglect, the meadows were host to a variety of fungi in the autumn and a few grew right through from spring. Even now there were rings of small buff-coloured mushroom-shapes pushing up through the rank grass. Marguerite had often wondered why this kind grew in rings and why some squirrels called other kinds, toad's stools. Although Chestnut the Doubter wouldn't call them that. *He'd* never seen a toad sitting on one.

She nibbled cautiously at the edge of a small one, it was not unpleasant though the cap was quite tough. It would probably store well for winter food, she thought. One had to be very careful with tasting, especially fungi, she knew that some could be deadly poisonous and should be avoided.

Curiosity
Drives discovery. Beware –
Daring fools may die.

Another Kernel of Truth. Her mind went back to the chant. If the *chant* was a Kernel, she was thinking, it should not be obscure – *Clever wraps obscure*. One could equally say *Clumsy wraps obscure*. Kernels should be clear and easy to understand!

Nearing the Zwamp, she decided to call on Ex-Kingz-Mate, Thizle, who had lived there alone since the deposed King had been killed and eaten by the pine marten. She knew many of the old island customs.

Thizle was pleased to see her and welcomed her in the island dialect, "Greetingz to yew, Marguerite-Friend. What newz do yew have fur uz? Uz do mizz the Pozt zquirrelz."

Marguerite could just recall the smart Royal Post Squirrels who used to sit on their posts at Dawn, High-sun and Dusk waiting for messages to be given to them. These they would relay faithfully and accurately to other squirrels all over the island. How proud they had been and how accurately they had reported; but with the abolition of the Monarchy, the Post Squirrels' role had also disappeared.

Marguerite sat with the old squirrel in the sunshine outside her drey and told her of the many things that were happening on the island. How, with so many squirrels, it was no longer possible for all of them to put their views at

Council so attendance was falling. There was talk of having to have two or even more Councils covering different parts of the island.

"Uz can't zay uz'z happy about that," the old Ex-Kingz-Mate told Marguerite. "Yew can get each lot quarrelling with the otherz, and Zun-knowz where yew endz up then.

"Uz do mizz the Old Dayz – uz loved the ceremoneez. There wuz Vinding the Verzd Veather – the Monarch'z Moon Muzhroomz – Greeting the Geeze – uz loved all of thoze."

Marguerite smiled at her, then asked about the Birch-bark Kernel.

"That'z one of old Wally'z prophezeez," she was told. "Wally uzed to live near The Wall, before uz wuz born. Wally'z real name wuz Walnut, and many zquirrelz thought he wuz not quite right in the head. He wuz alwayz coming out with zum prophezy or other. Rubbizh, mozt of it."

"Do you know what the Birch-bark one means?" Marguerite asked again.

Thizle recited it.

> Hie honourz birch-bark
> The i'land'z zcreen. Fliez ztinging –
> The pieze of the zun.

Marguerite noted that Thizle had said *Hie* instead of *I* or *Uz*, and had used *The piece* instead of *A piece.*

"Isn't it *A piece?*" she asked.

"It used to be *The* pieze but uz mate, King Willow, Zun rezd hiz bonez, changed it. He zaid that a fly'z zting iz hot like a pieze of the zun, zo it zhould be *A pieze*. It made more zenze, he zaid."

Marguerite still could not make of sense of it and so changed the subject. "Do you think this fine weather will last?" she asked.

Chapter 2

———

Chip took the sloe that Caterpillar handed him. It was warm from the heat generated inside the leaf pile, and it smelled over-ripe and rotten.

"Try it, it won't hurt yew," Caterpillar told him.

Chip hesitated. He knew that Marguerite would not approve, and that eating the ruddled sloes was only permitted to the three ex-zervantz who had successfully pleaded to the Council that they would be ill if they did not have one regularly.

"Are yew frit?" asked Caterpillar.

"Of course not," said Chip, looking about him before biting into the wrinkled black skin. The taste was not unpleasant and he swallowed the mouthful, feeling a warm sensation as it passed down into his stomach. He took another bite.

Caterpillar was already eating his third when Chip's legs tangled with each other and he fell forwards onto the moist warm leaves.

Word passed round the island as quickly as the scent of gorse on a summer's day. Chip, Marguerite's protégé, had been found ruddled at the leaf pile and had been summoned to appear before the Council. It would have to be a down-tag for him. Every squirrel knew the rule about the ruddled sloes. Would Marguerite stand by him?

The Island Council met in the tree above the pond in Beech Valley to hear the case against Chip. Though recently few squirrels had been attending meetings, so many squirrels were present that day that some had to sit in the next tree, straining their ears to hear the proceedings above the gentle rustle of the wind in the beech-leaves.

Clover the Tagger was in charge. Chip, his head thumping, sat, tail low, on the branch near her. Marguerite was at his side.

"Chip Who Seeks Love," Clover began sternly, quoting the tag Chip had earned the previous year. "It has been reported that you have been eating ruddled sloes, although you know this to be forbidden. Is this true?"

Chip looked at Marguerite, who nodded her head. "Yes," he replied, his tail drooping even lower.

"Why did you do this, when you knew it to be wrong?" Clover asked.

Chip looked around at the mass of squirrels but could not see Caterpillar. "Just did," he replied sullenly.

Clover waited, but Chip rubbed his paws together nervously and said nothing more.

"Does any squirrel have anything to say before I consider a new tag for Chip?" Clover asked.

Marguerite stepped forward and quoted the Understanding Kernel:

13

If you could know all
Then you could understand all
Then you'd forgive all.

Clover looked at her old friend and recalled how the year before they had stood against one another for the position of "Tagger of Ourland" and knew that Marguerite was doing her best for Chip. However if *he* would not explain his actions, there was no other choice but to down-tag him.

Clover waited, looking expectantly at Chip. He sat very still until she ordered him to leave the Council whilst they discussed his action. He moved to a tree out of ear-twitch.

There was little discussion. The offence was clear, the offender had admitted it, and had been given the opportunity to tell his story. As it said in the Kernel:

Squirrels have the right
To explain their own actions,
Fully – in silence.

Called back, he was given the tag "the Ruddled", and, feeling ashamed of himself, Chip the Ruddled left in disgrace, his tail trailing.

As for Caterpillar, he seemed to have important business that kept him on the far side of the island for several weeks!

Across the waters of the harbour, on the Mainland, Lord Malachite woke in his bachelor drey in one of the Scots pines on Tanglewood Knoll. He looked over to the next tree where Lord Silica had a similar establishment, and then

14

across the sunlit glade to where Lord Obsidian lived, also on his own.

What are we doing here? he thought, not for the first time. Two, maybe even three, winters have passed since we set up that Power Square to protect us from the plague of the Grey Death. We'll all die here forgotten in this foreign wood unless we get out there and do something.

The thought disturbed him and he recalled his ambition.

As with all the male grey squirrels in New America, he had cherished the idea of becoming the Great Lord Silver. Like his two companions, he had earned the first rank of Lord through his ruthless treatment of the native Reds. Then the Grey Death came, forcing the three of them to flee and hide here on this knoll in the Great Heath. Humans never came into this wood, the storm-felled tree trunks on the knoll having made an effective barrier.

"Lord Silica," he called across to the next tree, "are you awake?"

"I am now, damn you," a voice growled from the next drey. "What is it?"

Taken aback by the gruffness of the response, Lord Malachite did not answer, but came fully out into the sunshine and sat on the branch listening to the soft "Coo – coo, coo-coo" of a wood pigeon on the other side of the wood.

"What is it you want?" Lord Silica had emerged from his drey and was looking across at Lord Malachite.

"I was just wondering if we were going to pass the rest of our lives here, that's all. I'm bored and was wondering if the Grey Death has gone yet?"

A rustling of pine needles betrayed the approach of Lord Obsidian. "What are you two plotting?" he asked.

Ourland
Brownsea Island

Woodstock Bay

Palm Tree Valley

Lagoon

Ruined Man-dreys

The Pier

Man-track

The Bunker

The Zwamp

New Council Tree

Man-dreys

The Wall

Beech Valley

Royal Tree

CHURCH

CASTLE

The Island Screen

Pottery Point

South Shore

N

Furzey Island

"Not plotting anything. Just wondering if it was safe to go and see if the Grey Death has gone."

Malachite noted that Obsidian was looking older. So was Silica. Paunchy, too; the living here on the knoll was easy, with plenty of nuts and pine cones for just the three of them.

"If we ever mean to leave, we'd better make it soon," he said. "Why don't we go as far as that Blue Pool place; see if any squirrels survived there. If they did, they probably can't pass the plague on to us after all this time."

"We'll go tomorrow," said Silica, "or maybe the day after." He yawned and went back into his drey.

Malachite was half watching an ichneumon fly probing through the pine bark with the long spike under her tail, seeking wood-boring grubs in which to lay her eggs. The other half of his mind, preoccupied with his ambition, ranged across New America to the Oval Drey at Woburn where the leader of all the Silver Squirrels lived and ruled by edict. One day I will be the Great Lord Silver, he was thinking. One day!

Near the Blue Pool, in the woodland that the Greys called New Massachusetts, but was known to the native Reds by the more prosaic name of the North-east Wood, a middle-aged red squirrel known as Rowan the Bold was preparing the last teaching session for the batch of Greys that had formed his Early Spring class. These had arrived soon after the storm had blown itself out and, finding most of the old dreys had been torn down, eagerly began building new dreys to replace them. Rowan had noted with interest that they built to a new design, more basic than the traditional "family" ones. Their new dreys had room only for a single squirrel, though two Reds, being smaller, might just have been able to share. The Greys had a new name for them too – dreytels.

Rowan was joined by his life-mate Meadowsweet, their daughter Bluebell, and the ex-zervantz Spindle and Wood Anemone together with their twin daughters, Rosebay and Willowherb.

After greeting one another, Rowan asked Spindle if he had seen Hickory and Sitka.

"Them'z probably zeeing that the coloniztz have left the dreytelz tidy; them'll be along here zoon." Spindle replied, his accent giving away his island origin.

Hickory and Sitka had been the leaders of the Greys who had been misled by the Temple Master the year before. After losing the battle at the Agglestone Rock, they had stayed here with Rowan and his party, helping to teach new batches of colonists the ways of the natives, as directed by their leader, the current Great Lord Silver, from his base at Woburn.

The Early Spring class had learned well and were now moving on to colonise lands to the far west, though one pair, Sumac and Tumbleweed, had decided to make their home on Screech Hill across the Great Heath to the south-west.

The session that Rowan had prepared for this last teaching day was mostly revision of the more important Kernels of Truth and, by High-sun he could sense that the Greys were all eager to leave and put some of these teachings into practice. He dismissed the class and the Reds brushed whiskers with their ex-pupils and watched the new colonists troop excitedly off across the Dogleg Field, heading westwards.

"Do you know when the next batch is due in?" Rowan asked Hickory.

"I would think that they'll be here with the first showing of the New Moon," he replied.

Chapter 3

Sumac, with his mate Tumbleweed, had been among the new graduates when they had crossed the Dogleg Field and the humans' roadway. On the far side of that they had waved farewell to their class-mates. The mass of Greys had headed west, seeking lands to colonise.

Some of the ideas these friendly Reds had introduced him to were very different to the traditional concepts of the Greys. Guardianship, for instance; being responsible for an area instead of owning and defending it against all comers. Then there was this idea of Life-mating. He looked at Tumbleweed as she sat watching the others going out of sight. Did he really want to spend his whole life with her, rather than "play the wood" as Grey males had traditionally done? Did she share his views on all the things they had been taught?

Sumac had decided that they would not travel with the others but would see if he could find a vacant territory to look after on Screech Hill which he could see forming a hump on the skyline to the south-west. Supposing that any Greys he encountered were not friendly or still practised the old ways?

"Wait here," he told Tumbleweed, "I need to go back and ask Rowan something. I won't be long." He checked that there were none of the humans' travelling boxes coming along the roadway from either direction, and then scurried across.

The horses that lived in the Dogleg Field were down at the far end of the field and did not see him as he hopped across it, avoiding the piles of dung that littered the cropped grass, sun, rain and beetles breaking each down to return the borrowed nourishment to the soil below. Soon he was with Rowan.

"Hello, Sumac-Friend," Rowan greeted his star pupil. "I thought you had left."

"I had, but there is something that I needed to ask you."

Rowan raised an eyebrow and waited.

"It's about the Sun. I've listened to all you taught us and everything makes sense to me, but most of the other Greys were not so convinced. How can I tell whether or not any Grey I meet is a true believer?"

"As you are obviously a Sun-squirrel, I will let you into a secret." Rowan replied. "What does *this* mean to you?"

He scratched ⊲✕ in the dirt where they were sitting.

"It looks like a fish to me," said Sumac.

"Right," said Rowan. "That's what it is. Marguerite, my sister, learned the shape from some dolphins – you remember I told you about them. We Sun-squirrels use it to let others know what we are."

"But what has a fish got to do with being a Sun-squirrel?"

"Nothing, that's why we use it. If we used a symbol like this, ☀, it would be easy to guess its meaning. So, if you are not sure of a squirrel's beliefs just idly make the fish mark and any Sun-squirrel will recognise it and identify himself."

"Thank you my friend."

The red and the grey squirrels brushed whiskers.

"The Sun be with you."

"And with you."

Sumac was about to hurry back to Tumbleweed when he remembered a Kernel that Meadowsweet had taught him.

> *Squirrels do not live*
> *By nuts alone. Take time off*
> *To seek out beauty.*

He changed his direction and set off to circle the Blue Pool for one last time, relishing the bright azure colour of its still waters where it lay deep among the green of the pines and the banks of purple rhododendron flowers, flamboyant against their glossy dark leaves.

Tumbleweed was waiting impatiently. "Where in the Sunless-pit have you been?" she snapped.

Sumac decided that it was not the right time for him to explain about ❮❯ symbols and Sun-squirrels.

Larch the Curious looked at the tree that had lost its top in the Great Storm. The splintered trunk was silhouetted against the dawn sky and he thought it looked like a giant squirrel; two spikes of torn wood fibres forming its tufted ears.

He ran up the scaly bark and bit at some of the exposed wood, then came down for another look. It was even more like a squirrel now, only the nose was wrong. He went up again and gnawed at that area. By the time the sun was well up, his teeth and jaws were aching from his efforts and he climbed an unbroken tree to rest. It was too early in the year for the boatloads of human visitors to arrive, but he always enjoyed this daytime snooze in the high branches. He wished that his life-mate Clover would join him, but knew that she was off somewhere with the two ex-princesses, Cowzlip and Voxglove.

Clover had told him that she had been planning a special kind of drey with them. Cowzlip and Voxglove had taken over her role as Carer and had suggested that they ought to have another drey near their own for sick squirrels to use. A further drey was to hold a selection of healing herbs.

This was all very well, thought Larch, but with Clover doing her best as Tagger for the increasing population of the island *and* this involvement with the Carers, she had little time to spend with him.

Larch admitted to himself that he was bored. Making that broken tree look like a squirrel had been fun; it had certainly made the time pass more quickly.

He was waking from a lazy afternoon's dozing when his son and daughter joined him.

"Greetings, Larch-Pa," they said together and he greeted them in return.

"Come and look at this," he said, leading them to where they could see the shape of a squirrel's head against the sky.

"That's great, Larch-Pa," Elm said, glancing at his sister and trying to keep a straight face, "but its forepaws are wrong."

23

"I haven't done anything to those," Larch said.

"It looks as if it's holding a Woodstock," said Trefoil. "With a bit of careful shaping it would scare off any pine marten."

Larch looked round apprehensively. It was only the year before that the pine marten which had terrorised the island squirrels had been killed. Sun, save us from any more, he thought.

Trefoil and Elm were already up the broken tree biting at the flaking bark and trimming off some of the dead twigs and small branches which were sticking out.

"A bit more off that one," Larch called up to Elm.

Chapter 4

Marguerite was concerned about Chip. Since he had come to Ourland he had outgrown a lot of the shyness which had, without doubt been caused by his fear of his father, the dreadful Crag. The young squirrel, for whom she had a special affection, had proved to be very clever, but since he had been down-tagged, little had been seen of him. She asked other squirrels if they knew where Chip was and one told her that he was twisting rushes together down near the Zwamp. It was here that she found him, engrossed with something that he had made and, so as not to frighten him, she called, "Chip, it's me," as she approached.

The young squirrel looked up, apparently pleased to see her, and held out the thing he had made. "Look at this," he said proudly.

Marguerite reached out and took the square of woven rushes from his paws. Across the hollow of the square were single pithy stems of reedmace and on each were threaded several rings of cherry bark. Marguerite had often seen hollow reddish-brown tubes of bark on the ground beneath wild cherry trees where the tough outer coverings of fallen twigs and small branches had been slower to rot than the softer wood inside. Chip had evidently bitten one of these tubes into rings. She counted eight rings on each rush stem.

"What is it?" she asked him.

"I haven't given it a name yet, I just call it a bark-rush thing. Do you like it?"

"Well, it's very neat and well made, but what's it for?"

She tipped it sideways and all the rings slid to one end.

Chip reached out and took it back. "It's for counting on," he said, his tail rising with pride. "Look."

His paws moved the rings back and forth along the rush stems so fast that Marguerite could hardly follow the action.

"There you are," he said, "that's a hundred." He shuffled the rings back and forth again. "And that's a thousand."

Chip passed the bark-rush thing to Marguerite. "You try," he invited.

By High-sun she was using it to count nearly as fast as he was, and each was trying out new ideas.

"Supposing we have a pair of squirrels," Chip said, "who have four dreylings each year for four years, we would have that many squirrels." He held the Bark-rush out to Marguerite.

"No we wouldn't," she told him, "each of those would be breeding, so we would have that many!" The rings flew backwards and forwards under her busy paws.

"Wow," said Chip. "That's a lot of squirrels!"

"Of course it's not true," Marguerite told him. "Foxes and other predators take many of us, that's a fact of squirrel life. Others will go off and live elsewhere and some may not have four dreylings every year. Even so, that's an oak-sized figure. Has any other squirrel seen this?"

"Not yet," he told her, "only you and I can count above eight, so it wouldn't mean much to them."

Marguerite went away, unable to get the picture of all those "calculated" squirrels out of her head. Chip was shuffling the rings again.

Marguerite wandered through the valley, past the broad-leaved palm trees, the last relics of some human's attempt to create a sub-tropical garden on the island, and up to the pines on the cliffs beyond. Here she lay out on a resin-scented branch enjoying the cool breeze coming in from the sea.

It was late afternoon and, just as she was thinking of going down to forage, her whiskers started twitching with the feeling that she now knew signalled that dolphins were near. She sat up and looked out over the harbour.

She could see three black heads and backs curving up out of the water and sliding down again, effortlessly keeping away from the few human boats that were sailing in on the tide. Then the thought-voices that she loved filled her head.

She heard Malin first. "Are you there, squirrel-friend?"

Marguerite thought back, "Yes, I am here," and the three heads immediately turned towards where she sat high above the beach.

Lundy's thought-waves reached her. "We are on our way up-channel to a school at the Goodwins and decided to swim into the harbour to see if all was well with you."

The dolphins and the squirrel exchanged pleasantries, then Lundy said, "We have been for a sea-change, down to the Island of Madeira. We could see blue trees on the land there, and I thought of you and how you would love to see them."

"Was it the leaves or flowers that made them blue?" Marguerite asked, intrigued.

"I think it was flowers, but they were too far away for us to be sure. The local dolphins call them Jacaranda trees."

Marguerite played with the name. She was so used now to communicating mentally that she could even sense the sounds of the thoughts. This blue tree had an exotic and exciting sound to it. Jacaranda, Jac-ar-an-da, Jacaranda.

"Did you meet many other dolphins?" she asked.

"Not as many as we have on earlier visits," Lundy replied sadly. "Humans are using a new kind of net which catches a lot of dolphins as well as fish. The nets are made of such thin lines that we can't detect them. It is easy to get entangled and then we drown."

Malin's voice flowed, swamping Lundy's. "Stop being a teredo. Our friend doesn't want to know all *our* problems."

Marguerite did not know how to respond, so asked, "What are you going to learn about at your school?"

"Actually we are to be the teachers on this session. You may recall that our patrol area is either side of the Rock of Portland. On the far side is a curved pebble beach that forms what we call the West Bay. Humans go there to catch fish with lines thrown out into the water. It was there that Malin discovered that when he goes near a line that is tautly stretched from a human's thin-stick out to the sea-bed, he can understand what *that* human is thinking."

"Is that a right thing to do?" asked Marguerite.

"We were not sure at first," Malin replied. "It did seem like an intrusion and while we are near their lines they don't catch any fish. But when we did listen we learned things which may help us understand them better; and *that* must be a good thing. I know that *you* often have difficulty in interpreting their actions."

"That's true."

> *People puzzle us*
> *With their strange actions. But then*
> *They're only human.*

"We often feel like that. So, on balance, we felt it was not wrong to listen."

"Have you learned anything important?" Marguerite asked.

"Much of interest, and we will tell you some of it when we return. Time is short for us now, and dolphins must never be late. I think we have told you our little reminder on this."

> *Punctuality*
> *Is vital. Others' time wasted,*
> *Is stolen by you*
> *And can never be returned.*
> *Lost minutes sink for ever.*

"Shall we swim in and tell you about the humans on our way back?"

"Yes please, if you would," said Marguerite; any new ideas thrilled her. She wished the dolphins farewell, then watched their black heads seem to get smaller as they swam for the harbour entrance and the open sea.

A sense of loneliness enveloped her as her sea-friends disappeared around North Haven Point.

Marguerite fed alone, then slept in one of the palm trees in the valley. The coarse fibres around the base of the leaves made a snug nest, but the unusual sound of the wind rustling the great flat leaves bothered her, and she slept badly. She dreamed of watching her friends, both squirrels and dolphins, drowning in nets. Waking from that dream, she drifted into another where the island was so densely populated with squirrels that several families had to share each tree.

She awoke shivering, even though the sun was above the horizon and the dawn air was pleasantly warm. She came down the trunk of the palm to forage, instinctively stopping well above the ground to look out for predators, before remembering that here on Ourland there were none. Realisation hit her like a peregine falcon striking a pigeon.

As there were no predators on this island her second dream was likely to become a reality. Squirrels would multiply with no natural checks, and there was nowhere for the extra ones to go. Even if they could find a way to get back to the mainland, that was effectively grey squirrel country now, so was not an option. She went down to the Zwamp to find Chip.

He was rethreading a bark-ring to replace one that had broken, and, after the formal greeting, she asked him to re-do the calculations that they had done the previous day.

If each pair of squirrels . . .

They did many calcuations before resting at High-sun, and by then Chip was sharing Marguerite's concern. After her rest she went to find the Council Leader, Just Poplar.

He was at the Council Tree in Beech Valley with his life-mate, Rush the Kind. Rush had borne three dreylings that spring, two males and a female, half-brothers and a half-sister to Chip her first son. The youngsters were off with the others, probably playing the Wall-game.

After greeting and brushing whiskers with her friends, Marguerite tried to express her concern.

"Chip and I have been working out how many squirrels there will be if we all breed at the rate we are now. With no predators, the island will soon be overrun."

Just Poplar did not share her worries.

"Zumthing ztopz it happening," he told her. "In the old dayz uz Royalz wuz alwayz trying to have lotz of dreylingz but they moztly died and the zervantz never had too many. There alwayz zeemed to be about the right number of *them*. Don't yew worry now."

Rush offered Marguerite a piece of her favourite dried fungus and changed the subject.

"Lots of squirrels have stopped coming to Council Meetings," Rush said. "They all seem to be doing other things. We – Just Poplar and I – we don't know all the odd things that are going on."

"That'z true," Just Poplar added, "Uz'z zuppozed to be Leader and uz doezn't know if uz zhould encourage it or zupprezz it."

"What zort, sort of things?" Marguerite asked.

"Well, uz'z heard that Larch and hiz family are biting a tree into a zquirrel zhape over by Pottery Point, and that Chezdnud and Heather have got their clan growing Woodztockz. But Uz don't know how true it all iz."

"You sound like Chestnut the Doubter himself. He never believes anything unless he has seen it – at least twice."

They all smiled.

Marguerite bade them farewell and went through the trees to where Chestnut and Heather had their home near the ruined Man-dreys of Maryland. She found three generations of their family in a hazel copse digging up honeysuckle seedlings and replanting them at the foot of small hazel saplings.

"What are you doing?" she asked, though she could see for herself.

"Hello Marguerite," said Heather Treetops. "Chestnut doesn't believe that we and our family are safe here and so we are making sure we have plenty of Woodstocks to defend us all if Greys come here, or if a pine marten gets to the island again."

Marguerite looked at the young honeysuckles. Some were already reaching up and twisting round the hazel stems. She knew that in a year or two, a silent battle would commence between the encircling bine and the host sapling.

If the hazel grew fastest it would break the creeper, but the honeysuckle bine could strangle the sapling if it was the stronger. In either case the Life Force would be trapped while this was happening, forming the twisted whorl the squirrels knew as a Woodstock. It had been Marguerite who had learned how to release this trapped force with devastating effect, as many a Mainland Grey could tell.

She thanked Chestnut and Heather for showing her their plantation and headed for Pottery Point.

When the island's screen of protective trees loomed up ahead of her she remembered Wally's prophecy.

I honour birch-bark
The Island's screen. Flies stinging
The piece of the sun

Or should it be *A* piece? Either way it still seemed to be a nonsense.

Marguerite found Larch the Curious working with his sons, daughters and their youngsters biting at the wood of a broken tree and she stood and looked in amazement at what they had created.

The pine that had been broken off in the Great Storm had been chiselled by many teeth into the shape of a giant squirrel, staring out over the sea towards the Mainland. The face of the great animal scowled threateningly and it held a carved Woodstock diagonally across its chest.

Larch saw her, came over and brushed whiskers. She waited for him to explain.

"We got bored," he said, slightly embarrassed. "There is such a lot of food here, we don't have to spend much time foraging and we don't have to watch for predators, so we thought we'd make something. At least this should frighten any invaders away."

"Sun rule that no more come," Marguerite replied. "But this, this is . . ." she struggled for a word, "magnificent."

Larch stood proudly, his back to his creation.

"Where's Clover the Tagger?" Marguerite asked, looking round for Larch's life-mate.

"She's busy somewhere else. She doesn't really approve of all this," he added, waving a paw at the huge stump outlined against the setting sun. She thinks it's all a waste of time, but what is time anyway if you have plenty of it?

"A bite more off there," he called up to one of the busy youngsters, as Marguerite turned back along the shore towards the eastern end of the island.

Chapter 5

———

Marguerite spent several days in the South Shore area eating and sleeping alone. Twice she returned to the screen of trees above Pottery Point and from a distance watched the shaping of the giant squirrel progressing, but did not make contact with the chisellers. Her mind was busy with a web of ideas, trying to untangle thoughts that were hopelessly intertwined.

Early on the fifth morning, as the sun lifted over the eastern horizon and the tide surged in from Poole Bay, she knew, by the tingle in her whiskers, that the dolphins had come again. She went down to the low bank at the water's edge and projected her thoughts across the rippled surface of the harbour.

"I am here, my friends, I am here."

Three heads lifted above the wavelets in the quiet dawn-light and the two larger ones surged in towards her, while the smaller dolphin moved slowly up and down the waterway farther out.

Malin and Lundy rested in the shallows a few feet from Marguerite. She had never seen a dolphin at rest before and they looked huge, much bigger than a human.

"Hello, squirrel-friend," they said together, followed a moment later by a shyer greeting from Finisterre as he swam in.

"We promised to tell you what we learned from the fishing-men and we don't have to be back on patrol until tomorrow," Malin told her. "We decided to come early before any humans were about."

Lundy sent her thoughts up to Marguerite, "We told you that we often patrol just off the Chesil Bank and there are nearly always fishing-men on that beach trying to catch cod and conger eels. When we learned how to pick up their thoughts from the taut-lines, we were surprised to find that most are not even thinking about fish at all. Some come there just to get away from unhappy situations with their mates and others to relax and let their minds go blank. One was hiding his face behind a flimsy sheet of what they call paper all day, and his mind seemed full of nothing but enormous mammary glands. Then he stared out to sea, as if expecting a dugong to swim by."

Marguerite wondered briefly what a dugong was, but suppressed the thought. She was having a little difficulty in understanding, but wanted to know more.

"Why can't you just *know* what they are thinking, like you do with me?" she asked.

"You have an open mind," Lundy replied. "Humans try to keep their thoughts in a shell as though each was hiding some terrible secret. Only when they are alone on the beach do they relax and then their taut-lines convey their thoughts down into the sea like a trickle of water down a pipe."

"What else do they think about?" Marguerite asked.

36

Malin's thoughts washed in, "One was excited about things he was studying called 'computers'. You may know that humans in this part of the world do something called work which most don't like, for five days out of every seven and then they have two days for doing other things they do like, such as fishing. Then they do five more days of work."

"What is a computer?" Marguerite asked.

"It was hard to read that. I could only get a picture of a box, but it used numbers inside to find out all manner of things. That human was convinced that within a few years the computers would be doing much of the work the humans have to do now, and then they would share out what was left and each would be able to spend only four days doing work and have *three* days for fishing."

Overhead Marguerite heard the W-wow, W-wow sound of a swan's wing-beats and looked up as the great bird flew over. Finisterre's thoughts reached her. "I wish I could fly," he was thinking.

Malin said, "There will be humans about soon. We must go now."

"Are you going back out to sea?" Marguerite asked. "I've a friend I would like you to meet. Like me, he is interested in numbers."

"We plan to show Finisterre around Poole Harbour today – we could come back at dusk."

"I would like that," Marguerite said, and the dolphins wriggled backwards into deeper water and swam away up the harbour on the rising tide.

It was to be a long day for Marguerite. First she sought out Chip and tried to explain all that she had heard from the dolphins. She had told him before how she could communicate with them without actually speaking. Now she reminded him.

"I seem to be the only squirrel who can do it," she said.

"Not so," said Chip. "You remember when we were in that boat last year? I knew all that the dolphins were saying to you, but I couldn't hear what *you* were saying to them. Your mouth was shut all the time."

"You never told me this before," said Marguerite.

"I was always a bit scared of you then. You know – Tagger and all that." He smiled at her. "Now I know that you are just an ordinary squirrel like the rest of us . . . Ordinary, but special," he added.

Marguerite smiled back. "I often wish I could be *ordinary* – it's just that extra-ordinary things seem to keep happening to me."

Chip hung the latest version of the Bark-rush on a twig and sat back to listen to Marguerite's tale.

She told him, not only about the human's computer-box but about Chestnut and Heather's plantation of Woodstocks and the tree being made into a huge squirrel shape. "Sun knows what's going on in other parts of Ourland. We never get together as we used to, there are just too many of us. And since there's no danger now, it doesn't seem so important."

Chip looked grave. "I've done some more calculations," he told her. "In a few years time there will be more squirrels on this island than it can possibly support. I've tried to see what would happen if we increased the Sun's tithe and, even if we left half of the buried nuts to grow, there wouldn't be enough room on the island for all those trees. We're

38

going to have to slow down our breeding rate, or find a way to get the extra squirrels to the Mainland."

"As far as we know, the Mainland is all Grey territory now. I don't know how they would react to us coming back," Marguerite said. "I often wonder how my brother Rowan and his party are doing. Only a squirrel as bold as he is would have dared to stay on and try to teach them *our* ideals. I worry about him a lot."

"He's got Meadowsweet, Spindle and Wood Anemone and all their youngsters with him; he's probably all right," Chip comforted her, but he knew from his own experiences that the Greys were unpredictable. Their morals and actions seemed to depend on who the Great Lord Silver was at their Woburn Base, and what that Great Lord believed was right, or expedient, at the time.

Marguerite's thoughts had moved on. "If we're going to get over to the South Shore in time to meet the dolphins, we'd better leave," she said.

Chip hid the Bark-rush and together they raced through the treetops in the gathering dusk, enjoying the activity and forgetting their worries in the pleasure of judging and executing graceful leaps between the trees.

The dolphins were waiting just off the beach.

"I'm sorry we're late," Marguerite panted, speaking the words out loud so that Chip could hear them as well as the dolphins. "I know that time is important to you. I remember you saying, *Lost minutes sink for ever*."

"We have only just come ourselves," Lundy told her. "We waited until we could be sure that there were no humans about. They make such a fuss if they see us too close. Is that the friend you told us about?"

"Yes, like me he can understand your thoughts. I told him what you told me this morning. We both wish to hear more."

Marguerite and Chip settled in a tree near the shore. From there they could just see the shapes of the three dolphins in the water as the evening light faded and the tide started to ebb.

"We will have to move out farther as the tide falls," Lundy told them, "but darkness makes no difference to our conversation. Was there something you especially wanted us to tell you?"

"It's about that human's computer. Does it have rings of bark that move backwards and forwards on rush stems?"

"Not as far as we could tell. But the human only pictured the box that covered it. There might have been fish swimming backwards and forwards inside it for all we could tell."

Chip looked disappointed. "Do you think it will do what the humans want it to do?" he asked.

Malin appeared to be discussing something intimately with Lundy, shutting the squirrels out of their thoughts. Then he came back to them. "I once told you that dolphins can sometimes Look Forward but we don't often do it. I looked forward ⋖/2 years to see if the human's predictions were correct."

Marguerite interrupted, "I'm sorry, but how long is ⋖/2?"

"It is I who must apologize, I forgot that you count differently to us. ⋖ is our symbol for what the humans would call sixty, so it would be one half of that. Thirty years to them."

Marguerite was about to interrupt again to point out that squirrels counted in eights, not tens as humans did, but suppressed the thought. She was far more interested in the dolphins' ability to Look Forward. Was this what Wally had been able to do?

"Was the man right about only four days of work and three days for fishing?"

"Sadly, no. He was right about computers taking over much of the work but the humans had *not* shared out what was left. Most were still working for five days out of seven and others were able to fish on all seven days. Our fishing-man was one of these, but he was not happy about it. Odd creatures, humans."

"I'm hungry." Finisterre's thoughts reached the squirrels. Marguerite smiled. All young males must be the same.

"Thank you, my friends," she said. "This has all been most interesting. I think your youngster wants to forage. Farewell and thank you again."

The dolphins turned in the darkness and swam for the open sea. Marguerite was glad that Chip was with her and the two of them climbed higher in the tree and settled down in a fork to discuss what they had learned, before drifting off to sleep, each enjoying the warm comfort of the other's body next to theirs.

Chapter 6

Marguerite had been glad of Chip's warmth. The night had been cold for sleeping alone in the open, and the sun was hidden behind low clouds when they woke and foraged together in a chill breeze from the sea.

They moved through the screen of trees, finding morsels of food here and there and, by the time they reached the old meadow they were comfortably full. Only occasionally did they sit up and look round, an unnecessary but still instinctive action, as they knew there were no predators to harm them. At the edge of the meadow they stopped.

"Look at all those rabbits," said Chip. "There must be a thousand."

The whole of the greensward was covered with hopping and nibbling animals. Some were sitting up, scratching at their long ears with their back feet. Others were brushing their whiskers back with their forepaws and a few were biting at the bark of young trees on the edge of the Screen.

Marguerite was angry. Grass was for rabbits – trees were the squirrel's charge. What the rabbits were doing would kill the saplings.

She ran at the ones nearest to her, chattering her anger

but, as soon as she turned away, they started nibbling the bark again.

"Come on," said Chip, "they're not taking any notice," and he led her away across the meadow, the lean rabbits opening a way to let them pass.

"No wonder they are eating bark; look – the grass has been eaten down to its roots."

All over the field there were scuff-marks and bare patches of earth, showing where even the roots themselves had been dug up.

On the far side of the meadow they rested in the bracken below a pine tree. Marguerite was calmer now and said the Understanding Kernel.

> *If you could know all*
> *Then you could understand all*
> *Then you'd forgive all.*

"Those poor creatures are starving!"

Later, with the help of Chip's Bark-rush, they calculated the breeding rate of rabbits on a predator-free island.

"If each pair of rabbits has a litter of eight, three times a year and each of these young ones has . . ."

The result was just what they had seen for themselves that morning in the meadow.

They tried the squirrel calculation again.

"If each pair of squirrels has . . ."

The result at six generations was not as bad as at six generations of rabbits, but it was clearly far more than the island could ever support. Marguerite imagined squirrels as lean and as hungry as the rabbits, and looked at Chip in horror. "We must do something," she said.

Something was already being done as far as the rabbits were concerned. A newly-dead corpse of a mainland rabbit had been surreptitiously laid in an island rabbit-hole by a human, and the fleas were leaving the cooling body to seek a living host. The fleas were themselves hosts to a virus, known to humans as myxomatosis.

A few days later Marguerite was telling Ex-Kingz-Mate Thizle of her concern about the likelihood of there soon being too many squirrels on the island.

"Why didn't the squirrels overpopulate the island before we came?" she asked the dignified old Ex-Royal.

"The King dizcouraged it."

"Discouraged what?" Marguerite asked, "Mating?"

"Oh no. Him encouraged that zure-enuff; said it was good for zquirrelz. Him wuz fond of that himzelf. No, what him dizcouraged wux zervantz having too many dreylingz."

"But if they mated, surely there were dreylings later?"

"Zumhow not, uz forgetz why now." Thizle shifted uncomfortably.

Marguerite felt that the old squirrel was holding something back and said, "I'm afraid that if there are too many squirrels a plague will come, like it has with the rabbits. Have you seen them?"

"Yez, poor beasties, hopping round blind until they are Zun-gone. A relief for them then. No zquirrel huz caught it, huz they?"

44

"Nothing has been reported. But all squirrels have been warned to keep away from the rabbits, even if they seem well. The humans are collecting all the bodies they can find and burying them."

Thizle changed the subject. Marguerite had noticed on previous visits how the old squirrel could not concentrate on one thing for very long.

"Yew rememberz that Kernel yew azked uz about? Old Wally's prophezy."

Marguerite nodded. A pigeon flew into their tree, perched unsteadily on a brach too thin for it, was about to hop to another, then, seeing the squirrels so close, flew off again with a loud clapping of its wings.

Old Thizle's thoughts seemed to have flown away with it.

"What wuz uz talking about? Oh yez, Wally'z Kernel. Well, uz'z been thinking about that. Maybe the I'land'z Zcreen should be the I'land'z Queen."

"What's a Queen?" Marguerite asked.

"Her'z a vemale King. If the eldezd Royal youngzter is a vemale, her becomz Queen when the King is Zun-gone."

Marguerite recited the Kernel using the new words.

> *I honour birch-bark*
> *The Island's Queen. Flies stinging*
> *The piece of the sun.*

"Like that, it sounds as though the Queen was called Birch-bark. Is that possible?"

"No, my dear," the old squirrel said affectionately. "Vemales uz alwayz named after flowerz and the malez after treez like yew lot duz. Birch-bark izn't a flower."

Her eyelids were drooping and she was glancing towards the entrance of her drey. Marguerite tried to turn the conversation back to the subject that concerned her but Thizle was asleep. She left quietly.

Near the Zwamp Chip was working on the Bark-rush.

"What are you calculating this time?" she asked.

"Bumblebees," he said.

"Bumblebees?"

"Yes." He pointed at what looked like a mouse's hole in the bank beside him. A female bumblebee, with brown and buff bands across its body, buzzed past their heads and landed heavily at the edge of the hole, pads of pollen bright gold on her legs.

The bee paused for a moment, then crawled into the hole.

"I've done some calculations," he said. "I've taken the size of its wings and the probable weight of its body and the fastest rate at which it can possibly beat its wings. See."

Chip slid the bark-rings back and forth along the rush stems, Marguerite straining to keep up with the calculations.

"Can it beat them that fast?" she asked.

"Just possible, I should think," said Chip. "Certainly no faster. But look what the result is!"

"What?" asked Marguerite.

"It can't fly," said Chip. "It's quite impossible."

"But we've just seen it fly," said Marguerite.

"I know, but I've done the calculations many times and I always get the same answer – it can't fly."

"I'll believe you," said Marguerite, "but don't tell the

46

Bumblebee. While it doesn't know it can't, it'll keep on flying."

If you think you can
Or if you think you cannot
Either way it's true.

Chapter 7

It was well into summer and the days were hot and lazy. In the Tanglewood the elderly grey squirrels who still called themselves the Three Lords were lying out on the highest branches hoping for a caressing breeze.

"You two keep saying that you will come with me to see what the world is doing since the plague, but you never do," Lord Malachite grumbled.

"Go on your own then," said Lord Silica, "I'm comfortable here."

"What about you?" Malachite asked Lord Obsidian.

"Go to – sleep," was the only reply he received.

Malachite stretched and shut his eyes. Visions of the ambition of his youth filled his mind. He was the Great Lord Silver, seated outside the Oval Drey at Woburn Headquarters surrounded by a retinue of adoring acolytes and females ready to serve him and fulfil his every wish. Tomorrow, *he* was going to leave the Tanglewood whether or not the others came with him.

The cooing of the pigeons announced the dawn. Lord Malachite waited impatiently until his compatriots came out of their dreys to forage.

"We are leaving today," Malachite announced, hoping that the sound of authority in his voice would suppress any thought of resistance, and was relieved and a little surprised when Silica and Obsidian appeared to conform though they insisted on eating first.

After some discussion and bickering about the exact direction, they headed almost due east, backtracking on the route they had used years ago, after setting up the Power Square.

Malachite was sure that they had only taken one day when they had fled from the Clay-Pan to the Tanglewood but, as dusk fell, they were still some way from their objective, and had to stop and spend a night in a hedgerow tree before moving on soon after daybreak.

They crossed the roadway near to the Blue Pool and wriggled through the hedge into the Dogleg Field. There was no sign of humans, though two horses were grazing there, one white and black in large irregular patches, the other the colour of a ripe chestnut in autumn. As the squirrels slipped through the grass, the horses approached, head down, sniffing and snorting at the little animals they usually only saw in the trees on the other side of the field.

The Three Lords hurried on, to stop, breathless, when they reached the safety of that wood.

"Stupid great creatures," said Lord Silica when they had recovered somewhat. "Come on. The Clay-Pan is this way."

Standing on the edge of the shallow depression where they had once directed the laying out of the stones, they could

49

see the shattered trunk and the decaying branches of the fir which had destroyed the alignment of the stones and hence the power of the great Square.

Lizards basked on the gleaming white cakes of clay. Malachite stalked one which was sleeping in the sunshine. He slashed out at it, pinning its tail to the ground. The lizard ran off, leaving the end of its tail writhing under the squirrel's paw. Malachite flicked it away.

"All that work for nothing," said Obsidian, forgetting that it was ordinary Greys who had actually built the Square, while the Three Lords themselves had stood on the bank supervising.

"No squirrels round here now," Silica observed, sniffing the air.

"Let's try the Blue Pool itself."

They passed the Little Pool, over which gaudy dragon-flies hawked for gnats and other insects, then cautiously approached the Blue Pool. Soon they could look down onto the water, sparkling and sapphire-coloured under the late morning sun.

Human visitors were walking on the sandy paths below them, and although there was the scent of grey squirrels in the trees, surprisingly, there was also the scent of Reds as well.

"Can you smell natives – Reds?" Silica asked.

"I think I can, but they shouldn't be here, especially if Greys are in occupation," Malachite replied.

The three circled the Pool, passing behind the Man-dreys, and eventually saw a group of squirrels, including both Reds and Greys, in a tree on the edge of the North-east Wood. They watched for a while, then moved forward.

Rowan the Bold looked to where Hickory was pointing.

"Welcome," he called. "Come and join us."

The elderly greys came forward and he greeted them formally. "I am Rowan the Bold." He turned to a Red female beside him. "This is my life-mate Meadowsweet Rowan's Love, and these," he indicated two other Red assistants, "are Wood Anemone the Able and Spindle the Helpful. This is Hickory, one of your own kind, and all of these – these are Greys learning our ways, here at Blue Pool Base, as directed by your Great Lord Silver."

The Three Lords glanced at one another, then Malachite stepped forward.

"I am Lord Malachite, this is Lord Silica and this is Lord Obsidian. We greet you in the name of the Great Lord Silver." Malachite held his right paw diagonally across his chest and Silica and Obsidian did the same.

Rowan could feel Meadowsweet trembling on the branch beside him. "Are you the Three Lords who ordered my father's group to head for the sea when you found us on that barrow?" she asked, trying to keep her voice steady.

"It could have been, we met a lot of your kind then. Did your father have no tail?"

"Yes," Meadowsweet replied. "One of your kind broke it."

Silica stepped forward. "If we told you to go to the sea, what are you doing here?" he asked fiercely.

Meadowsweet did not answer, but moved behind Rowan, who asked, "If you are those same Three Lords, how did you escape the Power Square? Marble told us that he saw you overcome by the power-waves at the Clay-Pan."

"Is Marble Threepaws here?" Silica asked, looking round. "I thought the Grey Death would have got him."

"He died helping us destroy your Power Square," Rowan replied. "How did you escape?"

"We were caught by the waves and thrown down the bank," Obsidian told him, "but we crawled into a rabbit hole and found a way out through a bolt-hole to the Heath. We've been resting since then. What is going on here?"

Hickory came forward and explained.

"Sirs, the new Great Lord Silver directed all of our kind to learn the ways of the native Reds and live like they do, but when we got to this place there was a misunderstanding, and we fought with Rowan and his companions. They used a weapon called a Woodstock and beat us. Since then we have been learning native ways and teaching these to all the colonising Greys passing through."

"You let natives teach you!" exploded Malachite. "Natives!"

Rowan looked offended, then, realising that these three had been in isolation and were out of touch, he relaxed. They did not look fit enough to be a danger.

The Greys whose class was being disrupted, giggled and nudged one another as they saw this overweight and aged grey squirrel making a fool of himself. All that the Reds had taught them so far was very sensible and in tune with how things were, here in New America. The Kernels of Truth they had learned held subtle messages to guide behaviour, and Rowan and his companions were able and patient teachers. No doubt this fat stranger and his paunchy friends would soon be sent away.

"Would the three of you like to join our class?" Rowan

asked. "We are discussing Leadership. This morning we learned the Kernel:

> *In any crisis*
> *A Leader's first duty, is –*
> *To keep hope alive.*

"Did you know that one?" he asked Silica.

"Of course I did, we all do," Silica mumbled. "Get on with it."

Meadowsweet moved forward. "Today I am going to tell you a story that makes an important point about leadership. It is one my great grandfather used to tell in the old days at Wolvesbarrow before. . ." she paused, "before things changed."

The three settled on the branch, the sun hot on their backs.

Chapter 8

Meadowsweet started her story. The Three Lords appeared to be dozing and she thought that Silica was snoring, but it might just be that he was having difficulty breathing. She had seen this problem with elderly squirrels before.

"Once upon a time," she started, using the time-honoured wording, "at a place called Gaudier, where the leaves were a brighter colour than anywhere else in the world, the old leader was Sun-gone and no other squirrel had been selected to succeed him. In Gaudier they had a Kernel that said:

> *Whichever squirrel*
> *Solves the challenge of the Knot,*
> *Will be the leader.*

"The Knot had been made many years before by their Bard and Sage, who was also Sun-gone. Before he died he had tied stringy cherry bark into a great tangled knot, and left it out to weather.

"By the time it came to choose a leader no squirrel could undo that knot no matter how hard they tried.

"Then a bright young squirrel called Zander came along and asked what they were doing. No one has ever explained to me why a squirrel was named after a fish rather than a tree, but that's not the point.

"Young Zander took one look at the Knot and *bit* it through and so they made him their leader. He was very successful, because it is important in a leader to see different ways of solving challenges and not just to do what everyone else is doing. Zander's daring exploits earned him a new tag and ever since he has been remembered as Zander the Great.

"Are there any questions on that story?" Meadowsweet asked, looking expectantly at the assembled Greys.

"Surely what he did was against the rules?" a Grey asked.

"Not really," Meadowsweet replied. "The Kernel just said *Solve the challenge of the Knot*, it didn't say *Untie the Knot*. The others just assumed that is what they had to do and, as we learned yesterday, it is dangerous to 'assume'. Who can remember that Kernel?"

Several Greys raised their paws and Meadowsweet chose one near the back to answer.

Squirrels who don't check,
May "assume" a fox's mouth
To be a safe den.

"Correct," said Meadowsweet and the Grey looked pleased with himself.

55

"Rubbish," Silica mumbled, only half awake. "Rules are meant to be broken – do whatever you can get away with. Might is right – so fight."

Meadowsweet glanced at Rowan.

"I think we have learned enough for today. We'll meet here again tomorrow after dawn-foraging. You are welcome to join us if you wish," he said to the Three Lords.

"We'll see, we'll see," Malachite replied. "Where do we sleep if we should decide to stay?"

"There are dreytels in the wood over there," she said, the ugly word harsh on her tongue. Greys seemed to prefer these characterless one-squirrel structures to the traditional, comfortable, communal dreys whilst they were studying here, or when they stopped off in passing.

The Reds, as they always had, still used a drey for each of their families on Steepbank near the Blue Pool.

The next morning, to Meadowsweet's surprise, the Three Lords did come back to the class, taking their places quietly among the other Greys.

She asked for a volunteer to retell the story of Zander the Great and the Gaudian knot and she was flattered when Lord Malachite recited almost word for word what she had said the day before.

She thanked him, and Rowan was about to move on to the Action Kernel when there was a disturbance in the tree-tops and Sitka, Hickory's assistant, leapt into their tree.

"There's a *new* Great Lord Silver at Woburn," he announced breathlessly. "A batch of colonists have just arrived and told me all about it. A Grey from a place called Seven Oaks arrived at the Oval Drey at dawn with a band of supporters, and challenged the Great Lord Silver to fight for his position. The challenger didn't even wait for a reply; just pitched straight in and had Redwood's tail off before he was fully awake, but they say he's quite an old squirrel himself and may not last for long."

There was a murmur of excitement from the class. Each knew that a change of occupant at the Oval Drey meant a change of policy. At least Redwood's had been benign. What changes would this new leader bring?

"What's the name of the new Great Lord?" Hickory asked Sitka.

"Monterey," said Sitka. "By all accounts his views are very different to Redwood's. Some are saying that he doesn't believe in the *Learn from the Natives* policy. It might be back to the *Take and Hold* philosophy again."

Rowan moved closer to Meadowsweet and put a paw on her shoulder.

"The class is dismissed for the day," he announced and, looking frequently over his shoulder, he led Meadowsweet away to find their daughter, Bluebell, and the ex-zervantz and their two daughters, Rosebay and Willowherb. They found them replacing the moss used for the linings of their dreys in the tree they all shared on Steepbank, next to the Blue Pool.

"We have a new challenge," Rowan said and went on to tell what he had just heard, and explain its significance.

"I think we would be wise to slip away and try and get back to Ourland somehow. Before we're missed. You can't trust these Greys when there's instability at their Headquarters."

"That doesn't sound like my Rowan the Bold," said

Meadowsweet. "I've never known you to 'slip away', as you put it. Are we just going to abandon all the good work we've put in here. If we've done a worthwhile job the Greys won't harm us; we've taught them most of the Kernels."

Rowan looked ashamed. "Sorry," he said, "I panicked – not like me – sorry."

"What *should* we do then?" asked Spindle, hoping for firm leadership from his hero, Rowan.

"I'll go and talk to these new colonists – find out all I can."

"I'll come with you," said Spindle.

Rowan turned to Meadowsweet. "Go down to the Little Pool, all of you. Stay out of sight. We'll be back by High-sun."

High-sun passed and Rowan and Spindle did not return. The females waited through the long afternoon, their concern growing as the shadows of the trees grew longer.

Chapter 9

"I think we should pray," said Meadowsweet as the sun dipped below the horizon and there was still no sign of Rowan and Spindle.

The five squirrels bowed their heads and followed Meadowsweet as she said:

> *Oh great loving Sun*
> *We are in need of guidance*
> *Please enlighten us.*

They sat as though expecting something to happen immediately.

"We will have to wait until morning," Meadowsweet said brightly. "We musn't worry. Several of the Greys are friends and Rowan is good at overcoming challenges."

She had herself taught Leadership Kernels to the Greys, but had never imagined herself in this situation.

> *When the cones are down*
> *Even if you doubt yourself*
> *Hide all your concerns.*

The squirrels crouched together on a branch. It was a warm and slightly moist night, typical of early August. Each dozed a little but they were uneasy, listening hopefully for the sound of Rowan and Spindle's return, but also fearing the approach of danger in the darkness.

"What's that?" whispered Bluebell.

"I didn't hear anything," Meadowsweet replied.

"No. Over there – what is it?"

Meadowsweet sensed the direction her daughter was facing and peered into the darkness. On the far side of the Little Pool something was glowing greeny-white in the darkness.

All of them were alert and apprehensive now, and each could see the mysterious light. They watched it, all the while whispering to each other, but it did not move nor seem to threaten them in any way. As long as it stayed on the ground on the far side of the pool they knew it was safest to stay where they were until daybreak.

Dawn came with a light mist obscuring the sun and Meadowsweet was thinking of a break-fast meal when she heard a rustling of pine needles in the next tree.

"Rowan?" she called tentatively.

"No, it's me – Hickory." A grey face with rounded ears peered out of the foliage.

"Where are Rowan and Spindle?" Meadowsweet asked, the other females all sitting up in a row on the branch beside her.

Hickory leapt across to their tree and looked behind him before speaking.

"They're being held while it is decided what to do with them. I don't think they're in danger at present. They are under guard in the Warren Ash."

Meadowsweet knew the Warren Ash tree. It was the over-mature ash tree in the North-east Wood, so named because it grew out of a sandy bank riddled with rabbit-holes, which, since the Rabbit Plague, were now deserted and empty. There was a squirrel-sized hole in the trunk of the ash tree which the Reds had used as a weather-proof storage chamber in the past and as a refuge in the Great Storm of that spring.

Greys had enlarged the hole to allow their bigger bodies to squeeze through when they had pillaged all the Reds' reserves in the days of Crag the Temple Master. The large cavity inside was floored with powdered punkwood which filled the trunk to a couple of tail-lengths below the entrance.

"I must go now, or I'll be missed," Hickory said. "If I learn anything more I'll try to get away and tell you. Trust in the Sun."

So Hickory has become a Sun-squrriel like us, Meadowsweet thought. I can believe what he says.

"Thank you," she called after him. "The Sun be with you." Then turning to her companions she said, "Who's coming with us to see what was making the light we saw in the night?"

They all circled the Little Pool, keeping together in the treetops until they were above the place where they agreed they had seen the mysterious glow.

"There's nothing here but a rotten log."

Wood Anemone had climbed down to investigate. She poked at the soft fibres, damp from the mist. They smelt mouldy and particles came away on her paw. She rubbed it against her belly fur and then tried to brush off the crumbs of wood that stuck there.

"Come on up," Meadowsweet called to her, "we'll go and see if we can contact Rowan and Spindle. Move quietly now."

"Kill them both," said Lord Malachite. "Natives are just a nuisance. The only good native is a dead one!"

"There can't be many Reds left now," said Lord Silica. "It'd be a pity to kill them all. Perhaps we could make a reserve for them to live in. Our youngsters could go and look at them and know what New America was like before we came."

"They'd only breed and then we'd have the same problem again."

"We don't know yet what the new Great Lord Silver's attitude to natives is," Lord Obsidian said. "I think we should keep them under guard until we know that. We'd better capture the females." He turned to Sitka. "How many of those are there?"

Sitka hesitated for a moment, then replied, "Five. There's Rowan's mate, Meadowsweet, and their daughter, Bluebell; and Spindle's mate, Wood Anemone, and their two daughters, Rosebay and Willowherb. Those two are identical – I can never tell which is which."

"All natives look the same to me," said Malachite. "Useless creatures the lot of them."

"That's not true," said Hickory, whose absence and return had been unobserved. "You can't make broad-leaved statements like that. The ones I know are honourable and decent. They should be judged by their standards, not ours."

"So you're a native-lover are you?" sneered Malachite.

"I'm just trying to be fair, but I agree with Lord Obsidian. We should keep the red males secure while we learn what Woburn's views are. The females are not likely to go far away while we are holding their males."

Malachite was thinking of how exciting it would be when he was the Great Lord Silver, with the whole of Grey-Squirreldom in New America waiting on his pleasure and responding to his every whim. Young Grey males were taught that the position was attainable by any one of them.

"Anyone know where the females are?" Lord Obsidian asked.

The Greys shook their heads, except Hickory who was scratching and biting at some irritation on his back, his face buried in his fur.

The females, moving cautiously in a single file led by Meadowsweet, were nearing the Warren Ash. They made a pretty sight as they moved through the treetops. A weak sun was just breaking through the mist, lighting up their glossy fur. Each squirrel was well groomed and tidy, though none were as fanatical as Rowan's mother, Fern the Fussy, had been. Their tails were clear of tangles and their claws neat and clean. There was just a suspicion of the ear tufts that made the Reds so distinctive in winter.

"If you see any Greys – freeze," Meadowsweet whispered.

When they were in view of the Warren Ash they stopped and watched. Two Greys who they did not recognise were on guard, one on either side of the hole which showed up clearly where squirrel's teeth had over many years, worked to keep the bark from growing and closing it.

Meadowsweet quoted the Reconnaissance Kernel:

In a strange country,
Be careful. Time spent looking
Is seldom wasted.

They crouched and observed, unnoticed by the guards.
Soon two other Greys came and relieved these. Both of
the new guards stayed near the entrance hole.

"Does anyone know if there are any other openings in the
tree?" Meadowsweet asked hopefully.

"There izn't any otherz," Wood Anemone whispered
back. "Uz knowz that tree well. Uz uzed to keep uz nutz
there wuntz."

Meadowsweet was looking at the many big holes in the
ground around the base of the tree, remembering when she
and her parents had lived in rabbit holes three summers
before. "Follow me," she said, "quietly."

They approached the warren from the side away from
the guards and slipped unseen into the first entrance they
came to. It seemed very dark inside, then as their eyes
became accustomed to the dim light they were able to look
around. Meadowsweet was especially interested in the
roots which showed through the roofs of the tunnels.

"Most hollow trees are hollow right to the ground," she
told her companions. "If this one is, then we may be able to
dig up through the soil from below."

"Thiz wun izn't," said Wood Anemone. "It'z vull of
punkwood."

"Yes, but that's soft, we can dig through that easily."

Then looking at Wood Anemone, she said, "What's that on your belly?"

They all looked. Her belly fur and right paw were glowing in the darkness.

"It muzd be zum of that rotten wood uz all zaw lazd night. Uz muzd have got zum on uz fur." She brushed it violently.

"Wait," Meadowsweet told her. "The Sun has heard our prayer. We asked to be enlightened, it looks as if you have been. Come with me, all of you."

An hour later they were back, travelling on the ground, avoiding the human visitors near the pool and each bringing as much of the damp rotten wood as they could carry. Inside the warren they made a heap which glowed brightly, giving off enough light to show their faces clearly.

"We may take some time to complete the rescue," Meadowsweet said. "Wood Anemone, will you take Rosebay and Willowherb and collect all the food you can carry and bring it in here. Watch out for Greys. Bluebell and I will try and see if we can follow the roots back to the tree.

Each squirrel is free
To choose its own root through Life
Guided by Kernels.

It gives a whole new meaning to that."

Meadowsweet heard the others chuckling and saw Rosebay nudge Willowherb. Two jokes in as many hours;

she had never been known to tell even one. The twins followed their mother out into the open, still smiling.

Bluebell took a large piece of rotten wood and held the glowing mass up near the tunnel roof. She could clearly see the roots and tried to judge which was the thicker end. Mother and daughter followed the twisting tunnels, stopping frequently to study the root shapes.

"Meadowsweet-Ma," Bluebell said suddenly, "how will we find our way back?"

Meadowsweet stepped to one side and Bluebell could see her smiling over the bundle of rotten wood she was holding. Back down the passage that they had just followed, a line of glowing dots shone in the darkness. Meadowsweet broke off another piece and dropped it on the floor of the tunnel.

"I think the roots are getting smaller again," Bluebell said. "We must have passed under the tree."

They circled round in various tunnels until they were sure that they were at the most likely place. Meadowsweet reached up and scratched at the roof. A shower of dry soil and powdered wood enveloped her.

"This is it," she said. "We'll leave a marker here and get the others."

They laid out the shape of one of Marguerite's Xs on the ground with the last of the wood they had carried with them, and followed the glowing fragments back to the entrance. The other three had already returned with food which they shared out and ate. Each squirrel then took a piece of shining wood and followed the markers to where the X indicated the centre of the tree trunk above them. Meadowsweet reached up and scrabbled some of the punkwood down into the tunnel. The fine dry dust enveloped them and they coughed as it filled their throats and lungs. It was dry and bitter on their tongues.

Taking it in turns, they pulled more and more of the powdery punkwood down into the tunnel, the others pushing and carrying it away into side passages.

"If the rabbits ever come back, they won't be very pleased," Bluebell said.

"Never mind the rabbits, it's Rowan and Spindle who are important today – keep digging," Meadowsweet told her.

The squirrels were covered in fine dust and particles of the incandescent wood. They all glowed as they dug upwards, the glowing particles giving off just enough light to see by.

Meadowsweet looked up to where she imagined the Sun to be and breathed a heartfelt "Thank you", totally unaware that the sun was on the other side of the world and it was now completely dark outside.

Above them Rowan shook Spindle awake.

"I'm going to see if the guards are still there," he whispered.

"Yes, be careful," Spindle responded, needlessly.

Rowan had looked out once during the day, only to have his face savagely slashed by a grey paw.

He climbed up from the soft punkwood floor and reached a tentative paw out of the hole. It touched fur, and teeth nipped it hard. Rowan withdrew his paw, trying not to cry out. He dropped back down to the bottom of the hollow and licked away the blood. It was salty on his tongue and he felt thirsty.

Spindle was scratching in the darkness.

"Do yew think uz could tunnel out? Uz don't remember a hole lower down in thiz tree but anything iz better than zitting here doing nothing."

"There isn't another hole. I know this tree well," Rowan replied, then regretted saying it. Here was an ex-zervant showing initiative and he, Rowan the so-called Bold, was pouring cold water on the idea.

"You're right," he said, "anything's better than just sitting here. There may be a hole we don't know about." He started to dig.

At first it was easy. Under the top layer of finely powdered wood was a layer of empty hazel-nut shells and a few dry leaves which crackled as they moved them.

"Quiet," hissed Rowan. "We don't want to alert the guards."

As the hole they were making got deeper, their challenge was how to dispose of the debris. They piled it around the sides of the chamber but soon the debris started to trickle down on them and they had to lift it out again. Eventually a pile of fine powder poured down onto Spindle and buried him. He wriggled up, coughing and spluttering. Then all the stacked punkwood slid down into the hole and filled it. Rowan and Spindle climbed up to the inside of the entrance hole and hung there precariously hoping to find clearer air.

"What are you two doing?" a gruff voice called from outside.

Below them, the females were making better progress, gravity being on their side. There were frequent cascades of powdered wood, mixed with the scales and dried remains of insects and the occasional leaf or nut-shell. The glow from the particles of rotten wood on their fur allowed them to see what they were doing and avoid the worst of the dust-falls. Even so they were tiring and the rate at which they were moving the rubbish away was slowing noticeably.

Then with a whoosh of sound, a huge mass of punk-wood fell, covering those working below, and pitching a bewildered Rowan and Spindle down onto the wriggling bodies of the five females who were struggling to free themselves.

A rush of cool air passed them, drawn up the tree as if it were a chimney. A stream of fine powder poured out of the hole past the guards.

"What's going on in there?" a voice from outside called huskily and the squirrels below tried not to cough.

"Which way is out?" Rowan asked the glowing figure of his life-mate as they embraced.

Hearing no sound from within the tree for at least a minute, one of the guards cautiously pushed his head into the hole, even darker inside than the night around him. He withdrew it rapidly, his eyes full of dust. The other guard, who had gone round the tree to see if he could find out what had made that odd whooshing noise, rubbed his eyes as he saw what appeared to be a line of glowing squirrel-shapes materialise from nowhere in the darkness below him, then scurry towards the pine trees. He watched them fade away between the trunks before returning to his companion.

"Did you see anything?" he was asked.

"No," he replied, his voice high and a little shaky. "Nothing at all."

An owl hooted derisively and the squirrel shivered.

Chapter 10

———

"Do any of you have anything to say before we consider a tag change?"

Clover the Tagger looked at the three youngsters on the branch before her, then at the assembled squirrels of the Council. There were many gaps. Apologies had been sent by squirrels busy on various projects. Larch had sent a message saying he was at a critical stage on his carving. The ex-princesses, Voxglove and Cowzlip the Carers, had responded by saying that they were building a special drey where sick squirrels could be treated and that ex-prince Fir was helping them that day by testing different plants for healing properties.

Heather Treetops had just sent word to say that she and Chestnut were "unavailable", but there was a sprinkling of ex-zervantz, though again no Caterpillar. Marguerite was there with Chip, as were Just Poplar and Alder, but very few of that year's new generation were present, although they were entitled and even encouraged to attend.

The three youngsters had been found, ruddled and helpless, at the leaf pile and when sober, had been summoned to appear before the Council.

One of the offenders, Sycamore, sat up, tail high.

"Yes," he said. "There's nothing for us to do on this Sun-damned island. We just get bored. It was all right for you lot, you could go on climbabout when you lived on the Mainland. We can't. And it must have been exciting when that pine marten was here. Nothing like that happens here now. It's all so dull. That's all."

Clover looked at Marguerite then back at the youngsters.

"Does anyone else have anything to say?"

The other young squirrels shook their heads, so she sent the three out of ear-twitch and looked around at those who had attended, most clearly taken aback by the lack of respect shown.

"Do we have any choice but to tag them 'Ruddled'?" she asked.

"Perhaps Sycamore should be 'the Ruddled and Disrespectful'," Marguerite suggested.

"Where have you been?" Clover replied sharply. "Most of them are like that, I really don't know what to do. It'll just have to be 'the Ruddled' and we must hope they will grow out of it."

The three were called back and told that each would have to bear the low-tag "the Ruddled". They turned to leave, led by Sycamore, their tails high.

"Wait," said Clover the Tagger. "You have been downtagged, lower your tails. You are in disgrace."

"What about him then?" asked Sycamore, pointing to Chip. "He's supposed to be Chip the Ruddled, but he goes around with Miss Hoity-Toity, his tail as high as ever."

Without waiting for an answer, Sycamore dropped to the ground and sauntered off.

Marguerite looked around to see who Miss Hoity-Toity was, then realised with horror that Sycamore had been referring to her. Was that what they called her behind her back? She looked at Just Poplar; he was engrossed in conversation with Alder, and Clover was on her way to join them. Chip had slipped away unnoticed. Feeling angry and left out, she went quietly down the tree trunk alone.

Another group of dreylings were playing at The Wall as she passed, and she realised with a shock that Sycamore the Ruddled had been among those she had watched here, earlier in the year. These playing the game now were youngsters from Second Litters. Were these dear little ones, going to grow up loutish, like the three at the Council Meeting? Would *they* think of her as Miss Hoity-Toity? She heard the chant coming from behind her.

> *I honour birch-bark*
> *The island screen. Flies stinging . . .*

The Island's Queen . . . She corrected mentally then turned to seek the Ex-Kingz-Mate. Marguerite was sure that the old Royal knew something that she might be persuaded to tell.

Ex-Kingz-Mate Thizle was not on her branch in the sunshine when she arrived at her drey so Marguerite said the Calling Kernel:

> *Hello and greetings*
> *I visit you and bring peace.*
> *Emerge or I leave.*

73

She waited, ready to go if there was no response.

"Marguerite," called a feeble voice from within the drey. "Come yew in, please. Uz'z glad to zee yew."

Marguerite wriggled in through the entrance and found the old squirrel inside, very feeble and weak.

"Thank the Zun yew came," Thizle said, struggling to pronounce the words. "Uz'll be Zun-gone zoon and ther'z zumthing uz muzd tell yew."

Marguerite propped her up and tried to make her comfortable. "Yes," she said, "I'm listening. What is it?"

"Woodlowz knows . . ." The old squirrel stopped and Marguerite repeated her words.

"Woodlouse knows . . ."

"How the muzhroomz of the moon . . ."

Marguerite repeated this, "How the mushrooms of the moon . . ."

There was a long pause, Thizle breathing with difficulty. Marguerite waited.

"Controlz the breeding." The words were very faint and indistinct.

"Controls the bleeding?" Marguerite queried.

"No, no! Controlz . . ."

Thizle's head fell back against Marguerite's shoulder and the old Ex-Kingz-Mate drew a last rattling breath and slumped down on the mossy lining of her drey.

Marguerite put a paw on Thizle's thin chest. It was still.

She laid the body out straight and went to tell the others and to get help to carry the body down to the ground for burial. The loss of her friend and confidante left her feeling as though a piece had been painfully bitten out of her own chest.

"Woodlouse knows how the mushrooms of the moon controls the bleeding." Marguerite repeated the message again and again as she went. Was that what Thizle had said? It was almost as confusing as Wally's prophecy about honouring birch-bark.

Woodlouse was the original name the Royals had given to her friend Wood Anemone, one of their zervants who was now on the Mainland with Rowan. What did *she* know about the Moon Mushrooms, whatever these were? And how did they control bleeding? Why had old Thizle suddenly thought it important to tell her about them as she was dying?

Marguerite had reached the Council Tree.

"Clover. Old Thizle is Sun-gone. I've just come from her drey."

Thizle was buried at the foot of her drey-tree and most of the island squirrels were present. One of the ex-zervants had brought along a small feather from a peacock's tail, with a gleaming eye in the fan, similar to the feather once carried so proudly by Thizle in the days when she was Kingz-Mate.

Thizle's son, Just Poplar, took the feather and laid it alongside the body of his mother before saying the Farewell Kernel:

> *Sun, take this squirrel*
> *Into the peace of your earth*
> *To nourish a tree.*

Chapter 11

Hickory was waiting at the Little Pool when the Reds arrived back, tired and dirty, in the early dawn.

He listened to the story of the escape and looked at Meadowsweet with a new respect. To think what that old fool Malachite had said about natives!

"What do you plan to do now?" he asked Rowan.

"We'll need to get cleaned up first," he said, seeing his life-mate looking ruefully at her claws, torn and broken from the night's digging, "then decide on action."

> *Indecision kills.*
> *Act positively and lead.*
> *Action is the Key.*

"We can't stay here," Rowan went on, "but it'll be the third time in four years that you Greys have driven me out. It's getting to be routine. Do any of the others know you're here?"

"No, I thought of telling Sitka but I'm not sure if I can trust him. I think he's got ambitions to be the Great Lord

Silver and he might believe it would go against him if he was known to have assisted natives."

"Don't you have that ambition?" asked Rowan.

"Not now. I used to once, but I've learned a lot from your teachings and there are more important things to me now." He glanced across at Bluebell who was licking her paws and cleaning her fur.

"What about the others?" Rowan asked.

"All the colonists will be plotting to be Great Lord Silver now; even those three old fools from the Tanglewood fancy their chances. You should hear them bickering over who would win if they were to fight one another. It's pathetic." He paused. "Can I come with you?" he asked.

"Let me get cleaned up, then I'll ask the others. I can't decide that on my own."

The guards stayed on the Warren Ash-tree, near the hole, long after it was light, hoping to hear sounds from the inside to confirm that their prisoners were still secure. They were puzzled by the updraught that was blowing particles of dust out into the open air, each mote dancing in the sunshine as it was caught by a gentle breeze that eddied round the tree.

Eventually, the bravest one put his head inside, then pulled it out and turned to his companion. "Oh Great Lord Silver," he groaned, "are we in trouble!"

At Blue Pool Base the Greys heard the guards tell of how they had looked in the hollow of the Warren Ash after hearing no sounds from inside during the night, only to find that the prisoners had tunnelled their way out. Malachite conferred with Silica and Obsidian then ordered an immediate tail-chop for the senior guard and a tail-halving for the other. Sentence was carried out gleefully by one of the more recently arrived Greys. Sitka watched in horror. Was this to be the new order of things?

He had waited for an hour, expecting Hickory to reappear. He did not know where his friend was, but he assured the three Lords "that he will be back soon".

"Slack sort of base this," grumbled Malachite. "Never like this in my day."

An hour later Lord Obsidian led a party of colonists to search for the Red males and the missing Grey Leader. They returned to report that a scent trail, and speckles of wood dust particles, led away from the Warren Ash towards the Deepend of the Blue Pool where there were also traces of Hickory's scent.

"The traitor," snarled Malachite. He glowered at Sitka. "I'm taking full command of this precinct. Watch your tail if you know what's good for you," he declared.

Rowan knew they would be pursued soon and he must lead his party to safety, but he must first resolve the question of Hickory coming with them. Hickory was an alien, one of the colonisers who had taken over his land and harassed and persecuted the native Reds. The Greys' whole philosophy had been based on different principles and ideals. The native concept of the guardianship of an area of country was as difficult for a Grey to grasp as "ownership" was to a Red. True he had been teaching native ways to several groups of Greys during the last year, but apart from Hickory and Sitka all the others had moved on west and south, hopefully taking these "native" ideas with them.

The new batch he was teaching had only just started their training and he could not rely on them for support. Sitka might be reliable, but he had never been as enthusiastic nor as friendly as Hickory. Then there were the so-called Three Lords. They were probably harmless enough, far too old and unfit to be a danger.

Rowan remembered that:

> *A delayed Action –*
> *Stultifies. Find the root cause,*
> *Grub it out and Act.*

There was no difficulty in identifying the root cause here; it was that Hickory was a Grey. Could he trust him as one of their party?

Rowan joined the others.

"Hickory," he said, "would you wait over there. I must consult with my companions."

"Of course," said Hickory, "I understand."

When he was safely out of ear-twitch, Rowan spoke. "We can't stay here, so until the situation becomes clearer, we must go into hiding. We will go to the Eyeland in the pool across the Great Heath. Hickory wants to come with us, even though he doesn't know where we are going. Who has views on this?"

He looked at Spindle who spread his paws wide and said, "I've no objections. He's always treated me well. I trust him."

Wood Anemone nodded her assent, as did Rosebay and Willowherb, their heads moving in unison.

Rowan turned to Meadowsweet. "What do you think, Meadowsweet-mate?" he asked.

"I think you should really ask Bluebell," she replied and Rowan looked at her quizzically. Was something going on here that he did not know about? He turned to his daughter.

"Bluebell?"

"Hickory has asked me to be his life-mate," she blurted out. "I've been meaning to talk to you about it, but the time has never been right. I do love him, Rowan-Pa."

A host of queries poured through Rowan's brain, but there was no time to consider them now. One thing was clear though; they all seemed to think that Hickory could be trusted to be on their side in any confrontation.

"We'll have to discuss that later," he said. "I take it then that we are unanimous; Hickory comes with us."

Rowan signalled to Hickory, who came bounding over.

"You can come with us. There are other matters to discuss, but they can wait. Now we will make for a safe place and see what develops. Follow me, all of you."

He headed off towards the Hazel Copse and the Dogleg Field.

The sun was high and the air was warm when they reached the trees whose lower branches spread out over the field. The horses were standing close together, resting in the shade. They were facing in opposite directions, each flicking its tail to keep the flies off the other's head.

"If we go straight across the field and we are followed, our scent will give us away, we'd better lay some false trails."

They were discussing who was to go in which direction and where they were to meet, when Meadowsweet called to Rowan.

"Do you remember Tansy telling us how she came across the harbour on a deer's antler?" she asked. He nodded.

"Well, humans keep horses so that they can travel about the country sitting on their backs. Why can't squirrels ride on horses?"

Rowan looked at the horses below. What would they do if squirrels dropped onto them unexpectedly? But it was a splendidly original idea – worthy of Zander the Great.

"We'll try it," he said. "We won't leave any scent trails that way. That'll fool those Sun-damned Greys." Then, seeing Hickory wince, he added, "Sorry – present company excepted."

The horses had long tails, and manes of coarse hair on the top of their necks and tassels of hair hanging between their eyes.

"Aim for the neck of the chestnut-coloured one. Drop and cling on when I say 'Go'. I expect them to run off when we do that. Then, when I say 'Jump', leap off and follow me."

They all climbed down through the branches until they were just above the horses. They paused there, listening to the gentle snorting noises that the horses made as they communed with one another. Rowan signalled to the squirrels to line up on a branch just above the chestnut.

"Go," he said. "Go now!" and they dropped, each scrabbling for a hold, the unfamiliar smell of horse strong in their nostrils.

The dozing animal reared unexpectedly and Rosebay

and Willowherb, who had not yet got their claws into the security of the mane, slid down the horse's back, unable to grip the short hairs of its summer coat. As they tumbled over its rump, they grasped at the tail and hung on as the frightened animal raced across the field, followed by its puzzled companion, the piebald mare.

Rosebay and Willowherb were swung from side to side as the tail was switched violently in an attempt to dislodge them. When the hedge loomed up in front of it, the chestnut turned, rearing and plunging, its frightened whinnying showing its distress.

"Jump," called Rowan, "Jump now!" and one grey and five red squirrels leapt from the horse's neck for the safety of the hedgerow. Rosebay and Willowherb dropped from its tail and dodging the flying hooves of the black and white mare as it raced by, they scampered for the hedge to join the others.

"That'll break our scent trail," Rowan said, exhilaration in his voice as they stood together, composing themselves after their ride, "Meadowsweet-mate, that was a brilliant idea!"

Chapter 12

Lord Malachite was watching Obsidian and Silica to see
how *they* would react to his assumption of command. It was
a daring move on his part, he was thinking, appropriate to a
born leader. Often the best way – act positively and other
lesser squirrels will follow meekly. The more confident you
sound the less likely they are to challenge.

Now the lesser squirrels seemed bemused, waiting for his
next move. He must keep the initiative; reinforce his
position.

Where was Sitka? He was the other one to watch. If that
traitor Hickory was off with those native Reds, Sitka might
go too. They had both had many moons of that poisonous,
corrupting Red influence. Ah, there he was, ready to obey.
That was better.

"Right, this is the situation. A group of natives has
infiltrated their way into this precinct under the guise of
teaching us Silver Squirrels their nasty native ways. We
will not tolerate this indignity. The two males we held in
the Warren Ash tricked their guards – who have been dealt
with in an appropriate way – and escaped. No doubt they
have joined their pretty little females. Worst of all, Hickory,

rot his name, appears to have joined them. Probably fancies a bit of red-tail. We will hunt them down and dispose of the problem once and for all. Never trust a native with their sneaky, underpaw ways. Follow me."

He led off towards the Little Pool, followed by a posse of Greys, with Sitka behind them and Obsidian and Silica bringing up the rear and grumbling at the effort.

Malachite halted the column before they reached the Deepend area. He was breathing hard.

"We will pause here," he said. "We must not alert the enemy by rushing out and letting them get away."

"Lord Obsidian," Malachite called across. "Take a party and circle round to the east? Lord Silica – do the same to the west? Sitka will go right round and cut off their retreat. When you are in position I will advance from here. Don't let any escape. Kill on capture. Death to all Reds – and all traitors." He scowled a warning at Sitka.

Sitka, with a dozen Greys at his heels, ran from tree to tree to get behind his teachers and erstwhile friends as if to cut off any way of escape. He was surprised that Hickory had abandoned both his own kind and any hope of challenging for the position of Great Lord Silver. Hickory had, at one time, been as keen on this as any Grey male. But what a fool this Malachite was. Still, it was best to go along with him for the time being, he didn't want to lose his tail and there may be a way to help the Reds without compromising his own position.

When Sitka's posse was beyond the Little Pool they picked up the clear scent of Reds, with Hickory's among them, leading away towards the Hazel Copse. The enemy had gone. The trap, if one could call it that, was empty.

Sitka contemplated following the trail at once but decided it would be wiser not to risk the anger of their new self-appointed chief. He turned up-trail and reached the Little Pool as a disappointed Malachite arrived from the other direction.

Sitka reported what he had found.

"Right," said Malachite, "just what I expected. They've sneaked away. That's good news. Now we can have a proper hunt – I always enjoyed those. An exhilarating chase across country, overtake the quarry, surround them, outnumber them, then the kill. Great sport! The quarry probably enjoys it too. Good fun all round. Who said natives are all bad? Follow me."

The Grey force followed Malachite along the scent trail, and through the Hazel Copse to the trees on the edge of the Dogleg Field where the trail came to a dead end. They sniffed around, some going down to the ground where the horse droppings obliterated any more delicate scents, but even when searchers had ventured out into the field beyond the trees there was nothing to indicate which way the quarry had gone.

"Crafty little tree-rats," Malachite declared. "They must have back-tracked. We will rest for a while, then fan out and search either side of the trail. Someone wake me after High-sun."

Rowan kept looking over his shoulder, fearful that their trick with the horses might not have worked and that they would soon hear the sounds of pursuit. He urged his party on, though they were making good time, all being strong and fit, with no very young or old squirrels to slow their progress. He would not be happy until they were safe on his Eyeland in the pool that was named after him – Rowan's Pool. They could hide up there and, if they were found and attacked, they would have the advantage of being able to defend the Eyeland from firm ground while attackers would be wading ashore. All he needed now was a Woodstock.

He scanned every clump of hazel and goat-willow as they followed humans' pathways and old overgrown tramways across the Great Heath. He chose a route to the south of the direct line to his pool; he would overshoot and work back towards it with as many false trails as they could lay. These would help to confuse any possible pursuers.

There were a lot of bushes on which honeysuckle was growing, but nowhere could he see the tight strangling spirals that forced the host plant to grow the bulging twists of wood that trapped the Life-Force and gave the Woodstocks their power. Most bines trailed loosely through the branches or, if they did twist, were too slack to affect the host. Twice he thought they were lucky but, on climbing up, he found that the honeysuckle had won the battle and strangled the life out of the hazel. The Woodstock that had once formed was now just a hollow of dead bark filled with fragments of rotten wood.

In another place they found a rotted Woodstock lying on the ground. The success of the woodbine in killing its host had resulted in both the woodbine and Woodstock collapsing to the ground in a tangled heap.

The squirrels checked briefly when the fresh scent of a fox drifted across their path, inducing Fox-dread.

"Off the ground," Rowan ordered, and they scurried up

the nearest tree, a stunted pine, Hickory staying just behind Bluebell. They were safe here, but they could not stay indefinitely. Rowan asked for two volunteers to join him in a scouting party to establish if the fox was far enough away for them to pass. He hoped they would not have to lose time by back-tracking.

The entire party volunteered and he selected the twins, Rosebay and Willowherb to come with him; it was time these two came more to the fore. They tended to stay behind the others, always whispering to one another. Rowan explained his plan.

They would drop to the ground, then work upwind following the scent. He would lead. The others were to keep him in view but stay well behind so that if he was ambushed they could report back. If this did happen, they were *not* to attempt a rescue; their job would be to inform the others.

At ground level the scent was quite strong and the scouting party moved up the scent-line, with Rowan a long squirrel-leap ahead. He climbed onto a stump and stood up to his full height, his nostrils twitching. The fox was close; probably in that clump of bracken just across the grassy track. He stared at it, every muscle tense and quivering, separating stem from frond with his eyes. The dark mass was heather, he was sure of that. Above it was a brown shape that *might* be an early tinge of autumn colour.

Rowan leapt sideways as the fox sprang. By the time it recovered its balance he was running along the track, leading the fox away from where his companions were waiting in the stunted pine.

Rowan ran, passing several single trees that would have offered him immediate safety, until he came to a clump with a thicket beyond. He leapt for the nearest pine trunk, hearing the snap of the frustrated fox's jaws below him.

He climbed leisurely up to one of the higher branches and watched it prowl about below, then pause, prick up its ears and, after listening for a moment, slip noiselessly away into the furze. Rowan listened too; human voices were just audible. He lay on the branch, the smell of warm resin strong in his nostrils, as two humans, with sticks in their hands and bright blue loads on their backs, passed underneath, heading towards the place where he had left his party.

He ran down the tree trunk to the ground and followed close behind the humans until he was near the tree where the other squirrels were hiding.

Rosebay and Willowherb had reported back, breathlessly.

"Uz zaw a vox jump out at Rowan, him jumped zidewayz."

"Rowan jumped zidewayz when the vox jumped at him."

"The vox mizzed him and him ran away."

"Him ran away when the vox mizzed him."

"The vox wuz chazing him."

"Him wuz being chazed by the vox."

"Slowly, slowly," said Meadowsweet as the sisters told the story, Willowherb as always echoing Rosebay. "He'll be all right. Rowan will have some trick to play on it. Was it a fox or a vixen?"

"Him wuz zleek and vat."

"Vat and zleek him wuz."

"Probably a fox then. Vixens are thin and scraggy at this

time of year. Feeding the cubs wears them down. The scent was almost certainly from a male. You'll remember it now?"

"Yez," the sisters nodded together.

Spindle and Hickory were sitting up, alert. "Humans coming," Spindle said. "Keep out of sight."

Rowan called up when the walkers had passed under the tree.

"Come down quickly and follow me. The fox won't come near the humans, and *they* never watch their tails."

"They don't have tails to watch," said Meadowsweet, brushing whiskers briefly with Rowan.

Chapter 13

On this same fine summer morning, two squirrels were talking together in one of the Ourland trees, much as their mother Marguerite and her brother Rowan had done years before at the Blue Pool. These yearlings were Marguerite and Juniper's son and daughter, Oak and Burdock. Oak was named after his grandfather and Burdock after her great grandmother, both of whom were long Sun-gone and buried together, nourishing the Council Tree in Beech Valley. Their father, Juniper, had died heroically on the Mainland in the battle against the Greys at the Agglestone Rock the year before.

Neither Oak nor Burdock had chosen mates this year, much to Marguerite's disappointment, though each had a drey near to her own.

"If we'd stayed on the Mainland," said Oak the Wary, "we'd both have been on climbabout by now. I've been round Ourland so many times I know every tree and bush. I'm bored – think of something for us to do."

"I must admit that, with food everywhere, and nothing trying to kill us, life is just too Sun-damned easy," Burdock the Thoughtful replied. "We should be grateful to the Sun, but yes – I'm bored too." She was silent for a moment then said, "I know. Let's be News-squirrels!"

"What are News-squirrels?"

"Squirrels who tell the others what is going on. No one hears anything much now. Any news that does get told is by old Post-squirrels with no imagination."

"Surely News-squirrels shouldn't have imagination. They should just report what they see, accurately," Oak said.

"Boring, boring, boring," said Burdock. "News should be exciting, fun, entertaining – like Dandelion's stories."

"But news often isn't exciting," protested Oak, warily.

"It could be if it's told right," replied Burdock. "Come on. Let's be News-squirrels."

"Don't we need permission or something?"

"I don't think so. We'll soon find out if we just do it. Let's find something happening."

They called at the drey of Tansy Stoutheart and the one-eyed Tamarisk Greatleap. They were foraging together with their three dreylings. Greetings were exchanged but it was obvious that nothing newsworthy was going on here. These two, who had lived such dramatic lives on the Mainland, were now happily domesticated.

"We're News-squirrels," said Burdock, "seeking a story. What's new?"

"Nothing much," said Tamarisk, after a moment's hesitation, remembering how, when he was young, he had been prone to blurting out whatever came into his head. As Tamarisk the Tactless he had hurt many feelings and given away secrets which it would have been better to have left unsaid. "What sort of things do you want to know?"

"Anything unusual."

"Chip the Ruddled has got something odd down in the Zwamp," Tamarisk said, looking at Tansy with his one good eye. He knew that Chip still carried a catkin for her and wasn't sure if she didn't do the same for him. "There might be a story there for you."

Chip, absorbed in his Bark-rush, did not see Oak and Burdock until they were close to him.

"It's a good job we're not predators," said Oak.

"Yes," said Chip crossly. "Were you looking for someone?"

"You," said Burdock. "Tamarisk said you had something odd here. We're News-squirrels," she added.

Chip was trying to hide the Bark-rush behind his back. There was a big difference in Marguerite seeing it and these two prying about. They might be her son and daughter and of his age, but they had never been close, despite journeying together the previous year.

"Come on," said Oak to Burdock. "He doesn't want us to see it, whatever it is."

"Not so fast," Burdock replied. "I'm sure that Chip would rather tell all about it, than have us guess and tell wrong things to other squirrels. Wouldn't you Chip?"

"Well," said Chip, hesitantly, "I call it a Bark-rush. You can count on it and work things out."

"Like what?"

"Like how many squirrels there will be on the island if everybody keeps on having dreylings at the rate they are."

"Neither of us have got any," said Oak defensively.

"Hush," said Burdock. "Chip is going to tell us about his bark-rush thing. Why do you call it that?"

"Because it is made from bark and rushes," Chip replied.

"But that's a silly name – how does it work?"

Chip slid the rings back and forth but neither Oak nor Burdock could see what made Chip so proud of it.

"That'll have to be our story," said Burdock. "Chip the Ruddled invents a Bark-rush."

"Do you have to use my tag?" asked Chip.

"Not if you tell us everything," Burdock replied. "Now what were you going to tell us about all those dreylings?"

Marguerite heard the story second or even third paw.

"Chip's Bark-rush invention is going to make all the squirrels have lots of dreylings and soon the island will sink under the weight of them all."

"Chip said that?" Marguerite asked her informer.

"Well, something like that. The News-squirrel – your daughter, Burdock – told my friend only this afternoon and she told me. What should we do?"

"Leave it to me," said Marguerite.

She found Oak and Burdock at their dreys and asked about the "story". Oak told her what Chip had told them about the Bark-rush.

"Did he say that the island would sink under the weight of all the squirrels?"

Oak was silent and Burdock said, "Well, not exactly, but that made a good story."

"That's downright irresponsible," said Marguerite. "You two, of all squirrels, ought to know better."

"Why us?" asked Burdock.

"You're my family."

"So what – does that make us different?" Burdock snapped back.

Oak put a restraining paw on his sister's shoulder but she shook it off.

"I'm fed up with always being your daughter and other squirrels expecting us to behave better than *they* have to. We – I at least – am a News-squirrel and I shall say whatever I like about whoever I want to."

She ran along a branch and leapt into the next tree.

Oak called after her but Burdock snarled over her shoulder, "You can go and get lost for all I care!"

Marguerite sighed and looked upset.

Oak went to her and said, "Marguerite-Ma, I'm sorry that Burdock spoke to you that way, but it's true. It is hard being your family and trying to live up to what you, and other squirrels expect of us. Especially now."

"Why especially now?"

"Things are not right here on Ourland – I'm sure you can see that. There's no danger to keep us alert and wary, as squirrels should be. No excitement. There's masses of food everywhere; our Mainland ideas are not fully accepted by the island squirrels, and the old Royal ways and disciplines you've told us about, don't apply any more. Squirrels just don't know where they are."

Marguerite looked at her son proudly. He had summed up exactly what she had been feeling. She let him carry on.

"By all accounts, Just Poplar made a good leader when

you were not here on Ourland. He always tries to be fair and live up to his 'Just' tag, but he feels over-awed by you."

"*Me?*" said Marguerite incredulously. "*Me?*"

"Yes, you, Marguerite-Ma. Every squirrel can see that you are far cleverer than he is. He's afraid that you will disagree with his decisions."

"I would never dream of interfering." Marguerite felt herself to be on the defensive. "I never would."

"I know that, but it makes him uneasy and indecisive. Remember he is used to one strong squirrel being in charge. A King in fact."

"That's all over and done with," said Marguerite. "It was Just Poplar himself who gave up being King."

"I know, but there are a few squirrels – more than a few – who would like *you* to be Queen."

"Me? Queen of Ourland? Out of the question. I thought they all called me Miss Hoity-Toity."

"Only a few of the younger ones. Don't take any notice of them – they speak from under their tails."

"What do *you* think?" Marguerite sat back, tail low, awaiting her son's verdict.

Oak thought for a moment, then replied, "It's difficult for me. If you were Queen then I would be Next-King and I'm not sure if I want that. There is no doubt that you are the cleverest squirrel on the island, bar none."

Marguerite's tail rose a little.

"Squirrels say Chip is clever, and he is, but he hasn't got your experience, nor wisdom, nor your ability to find the truth buried beneath the facts."

Marguerite's tail rose higher.

"I think you would make a good Queen, or Leader, call it

95

what you will, and I think all the squirrels would accept you, though some of the ex-zervantz might not be too keen on the idea of being zervantz again."

"They needn't be. Just because there was a Queen, or a King, there needn't be zervantz!"

"True, but it would take some time to convince them. Nothing should be done hastily," said Oak the Wary. "Now, what *is* the truth in what Chip told Burdock and me about Ourland being overrun with squirrels?"

Chapter 14

Lord Malachite was woken from a dream in which he was taking his place in the Oval drey as the new Great Lord Silver. The trees around were full of respectful Silver squirrels chanting his praises as he climbed to his rightful position. Then some minion was shaking his shoulder.

"Wake up sir, it's past High-sun."

"How dare you," he snapped.

"I'm sorry, sir. You said to wake you."

Malachite scratched at an invisible flea. "Yes, so I did, so I did. Anything to report."

"No, sir. We've been waiting for you."

"Quite right, quite right. We must find where the quarry backtracked. Everybody search. Leave no trees unsniffed."

Miles away across the Great Heath, the human walkers had reached the road passing to the west of Rowan's Pool and turned along it towards Screech Hill. In the hedges on either side of the road were many trees and bushes with honeysuckle growing up them; the sweet scent of the yellow trumpet-shaped flowers drowning the tarry smell from the hot surface of the road.

The squirrels watched the humans walk away out of their sight, confident that the fox was no longer a threat, but listening for the hum of the travelling boxes that humans used on these roadways. Whenever the road was clear, they again searched for a suitable Woodstock, hiding in the hedges when vehicles came by.

It was Wood Anemone who found one, a bulky twist on a hazel sapling, with the honeysuckle bine almost buried in the wood that had grown out and around it. Rowan sensed its power; running his paws over the bark, his whiskers vibrating with the hidden force trapped in the fibres.

"This is a strong one," he said, then started to gnaw at the stem above the twisted bulge.

In a short time he had cut the sapling through above and below the twist, and had bitten away the bitter bine itself, letting the Woodstock fall into the hedge. From there they dragged it out onto the grass verge and across the road towards Rowan's Pool.

"Uz wouldn't like to have to take thiz wun var," said Spindle, remembering the long journey of the previous year. "What diztanze iz yewr pool from here?"

"Not far, just through those chestnut and pine trees."

Even so, it was twilight when they dragged the Woodstock through the trees and reached the bank that surrounded the pool. They looked down on the Eyeland that they hoped would offer safety for them all once they had swum across to it.

A tree had been blown down, probably in the Great Storm, and was lying in the water – making a bridge from the Mainland!

Rowan said something under his breath but perhaps a

little too loudly. Meadowsweet looked at him, her eyes wide. "Rowan!" she said.

Rosebay and Willowherb giggled and nudged one another. Hickory looked surprised and glanced at Bluebell.

"Stay here at the top of the bank and keep alert," Rowan said. "Spindle and I will go and investigate."

The two males crossed the water using the fallen tree, and dropped from it onto the tufty grass and lichen that covered the ground. There was no scent of danger there, nor in the three trees. The Eyeland seemed to Spindle to be much smaller than when he had seen it two years before, It was little more than a squirrel leap from one side to the other.

"What now?" he asked.

"This'll have to do for tonight," Rowan replied. "In the morning we'll find a safer place. At least here we can only be attacked from one direction. Let's get the Woodstock over here."

The twisted stick was rolled down the bank and carefully dragged across the tree trunk to the Eyeland as the moon rose in the east, throwing an eerie light on the busy squirrels. Rowan was trying to remember the shapes that Marguerite had cut on earlier weapons and wished now that he had taken more notice when she had tried to teach him numbers.

There was a **1** then a **Z**. After that was a **4**, or was it a **3**?

"Who remembers the numbers that go on a Woodstock?" he asked, turning expectantly to Meadowsweet, who spread her paws.

"Sorry, Rowan-mate," she said.

"Uz doez," said Wood Anemone. "Uz doezn't know what they iz called, but uz knowz the zhapz well 'nuff. Uz uzed to polizh the old Woodztock when Marguerite wuz not there. Uz liked to zee it all clean and tidy-like."

Rowan set Rosebay and Willowherb to guard the bridge and sent Bluebell up the tallest tree to listen for any sounds of approaching danger. The others all worked at stripping off the bark and biting the magic numbers deep into the hazel wood – 1 2 3 4 5 6 7 10 X.

Hickory watched in fascination, taking his turn in the cutting and asking questions about the shapes of the numbers.

There was some argument about the X. Rowan said it was Marguerite's special mark and was therefore not needed, but the others, especially Wood Anemone, felt it was important. "It worked vor uz with that X there; it may not work without it," she argued, and so the X was cut, leaving space for the numbers which activated the force and controlled its power and range.

Bats circled between the trees and flittered away down the length of the pool, snatching at moths and other night flying insects, their shrill cries sharp in the still air. A night-jar churred from a branch across the water reminding Rowan of the year he had lived on the Eyeland alone.

Whilst they had been dragging the Woodstock to the pool a young Grey was once more waking Malachite.

"Lord Malachite, sir. We've found the trail. It's on the other side of the field. It crosses the roadway and goes onto the Great Heath."

Malachite looked at the angle of the sun. Was it really

that late? He must have been dozing again. The quarry would have a good start. Too late to follow now. They would set out at first light and allow a full day for the hunt. In the meantime he had some other business that must be seen to.

"Everybody back to base," he ordered. "Get a good night's rest. Where are the Lords Silica and Obsidian?"

"They retired early, sir. They went back to their dreytels."

In the North-east Wood, Silica and Obsidian were discussing Malachite's behaviour.

"He's fallen off his stump!" said Silica. "Can't he see that things have changed. I'm surprised that the other Silvers follow him so readily."

"I think they're thrown, with Hickory leaving like that. Fancy a Silver running off after Red-tail, assuming that's what's behind it."

"Dangerous to assume. What was it that Red female told us?"

> *Squirrels who don't check*
> *May assume a fox's mouth*
> *To be a safe den.*

"Don't start quoting their Kernels at me," Lord Obsidian growled. "You'll be wanting *me* to behave like a little native next."

They were silent for a while, each busy with their thoughts. Finally Silica spoke.

"Do you think we've been out of action too long?" he

asked. "The whole world seems to be upside-down now. I'm tempted to slip back to the Tanglewood and live the quiet life. Be lonely on my own, though. Would you come with me?"

Then, before he had an answer, he added, "Obsidian-Friend, as the Red ones put it."

"Sun-dammit I will – as the Red ones would put it. Let's slip away before the hordes come back – Silica-Friend."

"What about Malachite?"

"Him! He's obsessed with the idea of becoming Great Lord Silver. When he's got over that and finds us gone, no doubt he'll follow us. Come on, I've had enough of this."

Lord Malachite returned to New Massachusetts with Sitka, explaining to him why he had put off following the fugitives until the next day. "We'll all be fresh then, have a good day's hunting. Run those natives down by High-sun I'm sure. And the traitor! You can have the honour of killing him. I'll remember that when I'm in high places. You'll need to show which side you're on since you've been mixed up in this native business for so long. See you at first light. What was your name again?"

The moon was high when Malachite slipped out of his dreytel and went silently through the branches towards Silica's. It was good that Obsidian's dreytel was some distance beyond that. This was worthy of Zander the Great: original thinking, the element of surprise, ruthless-ness – good leadership qualities those. If he could get Silica and Obsidian while they were asleep, he could kill them before they knew what was happening. Bite the throat and hold on – it should only take a minute or two to get those rivals out of contention. But he would have to do it without waking the other Silvers.

At Silica's dreytel he paused and listened. There was no sound of breathing. A thought flashed across his mind. What if Silica had planned the same thing? Maybe Silica had already killed Obsidian and was now on his way to kill him. No – he would have seen or heard him.

Malachite went and listened outside Obsidian's dreytel. Silence again.

He thought up some pretext about changing the start time for the hunt, and shook the twigs of the sleeping place, then put his head inside. It too was empty.

Perhaps they were out together, looking for him! He imagined sharp teeth biting into his neck; looked around fearfully in the spooky moonlight, then sought an unused dreytel, well away from his own, and spent a restless night there, only dozing off when the moon had set.

"Lord Malachite, sir. It's dawn, sir. We had a job to find you, sir. It's all right, sir. It's only me, sir. Are you all right, sir?"

Malachite looked bleary-eyed at the youngster, one of the new arrivals.

"Yes, yes. Of course I am. What was your name again?"

As dawn lightened the sky over the little island in the pool, the Woodstock was as complete as Rowan and Spindle could make it. They relieved the guards on the bridge and sent all the others up the trees to sleep. Wood Anemone gave the gleaming twisted wood one last rub with a piece of soft moss.

"Watch that I don't fall asleep, Spindle-Friend," Rowan said.

"Yew'd better do the zame for uz," the ex-zervant replied.

Rowan watched as a heron flapped slowly over the pool before starting a long glide down to the shallow water at the far end; the trueness of its flight indicating that there was no apparent danger from that direction.

Chapter 15

———

Hickory had come with Bluebell at mid morning to relieve Rowan and Spindle at the bridge.

"Call me if you see anything suspicious. I'll sleep near the Woodstock in case we need to use it," Rowan told them.

Though desperately tired, sleep did not come easily. From where he lay in a tussock of grass he could see Hickory and Bluebell sitting on the peeling bark of the bridge, saying things he could not hear. It was clear from the way they sat so close together how they felt about one another. How had he missed this before?

What would happen if they mated, as they clearly planned to do? Remembering Bluebell's namesake and the Greys of the Silver Tide, he knew that a mating must be physically possible. But would the Sun bless the union with dreylings and, if it did, what would they be like? Would they be grey or red, or a patchy mixture, like the horse in the Dogleg Field? Whatever colour they were, they would be his grandchildren and he would love them.

Rowan finally dropped off to sleep, dreaming of being a grandfather and playing under a peaceful sun with a tumbling mass of piebald dreylings.

Malachite asked the assembled Greys if anyone had seen the other two Lords. None had, neither that day nor the previous evening. He selected two young males and briefed them privately.

"I've got a special and secret mission for you," he said in a conspiratorial voice. "I have chosen you out of all the others to follow Lord Silica and Lord Obsidian and report back to me exactly what they are doing. Don't let them see you, and tell no one but me what you find out." He put a claw to his lips. "No one but me. Understand?"

The youngsters nodded, proud to have been selected, though they were disappointed to be missing the hunt.

"Wait until we have gone, then follow your noses. I will expect a report tonight. If we are not here – follow our trail."

He turned back to address the others, surprised and pleased to see how many had turned out for the chase. Not only were most of those who had been at Rowan's current training present, but yet another new batch of colonists had just arrived and they were eager to join in.

The squirrels crossed the Dogleg Field in a grey mass and flowed over the road in the early light. Scouts had been sent ahead to find the scent and they guided the hunters through the furze, heather and fern of the Great Heath.

By High-sun the scouts had reported that the quarry were trapped on an island in a pool, with a tree-trunk bridge leading to it.

"I don't think they have seen us," Malachite was told by the scout leader. "Most of them are asleep, but the traitor, Hickory, and a Red female are on guard."

"Rot his tail," said Malachite to Sitka. "How do you fancy single combat on the bridge. That should be good sport."

Sitka looked apprehensive. "He was my friend," he said.

"Not now, surely – he's a proven traitor. You kill him, then we'll deal with the natives."

"Let's see exactly what the situation is first," said Sitka. "The Red ones taught us a saying."

In a strange country,
Be careful. Time spent looking
Is seldom wasted.

"Humph," said Malachite, but sent out parties of squirrels to surround the pool, in case the quarry tried to escape by swimming, then approached the edge of the bank where they could all look down onto the island.

Hickory was sitting on the bridge with Bluebell at his side, both facing the mainland. He felt her body stiffen.

"Don't look at once," she whispered, "but I am sure there are squirrels up there on the bank, watching us."

"Red or Silver?" Hickery whispered back.

"Grey," she said.

"Go as casually as you can and wake your father. Tell him what you've seen. I'll stay here."

Bluebell stretched and went slowly back along the fallen trunk and relieved herself behind a clump of rushes, conscious as she did so, that, though out of sight of her party, she was in full view of "lots" of enemy Greys.

Then she went over to where her father lay at the foot of

one of the pines and said, "Rowan-Pa. Wake up, the Greys are here. Slowly now, they don't know we have seen them."

"Climb the tree and tell the others," he said calmly. "I'll cover the bridge with the Woodstock."

"My Hickory is down there, call him back if you have to use it, don't curl *his* whiskers,'" Bluebell told her father, then slowly climbed the tree, as though she was going up to sleep there.

Hickory was watching the top of the bank. Bluebell had been right, there were lots of Silvers there. He turned his head – there were more to be seen on the opposite bank, all just sitting and watching. The fur on the back of his neck rose slowly and his tail started to swish from side to side, betraying his fear.

He saw a Silver come down the bank towards him, tail low, in the "Parley" position. It was Sitka.

Hickory sat still as he approached.

"Hickory-Friend," Sitka said quietly. "That old fool Malachite wants me to challenge you to single combat. What should I do?"

"Look fierce," said Hickory, "and talk."

Sitka raised his tail, arched his back, stamped his feet on the bridge and churred the Challenge. Hickory did the same.

"Hickory, come back here," Rowan called, "clear of the bridge."

Hickory signalled an unmistakable "leave me alone" with his tail, while still facing Sitka.

"What do you want to do?" he hissed at Sitka.

"Find a mate, live in peace and bring up a family under the Sun – that Great Lord Silver business is a sham. I can see that now," Sitka hissed back.

"You won't do that with Malachite in charge. His head is full of punkwood. Come and join us."

"I can't do that, you're outnumbered many times. You'll all be zapped by nightfall."

"We've got a Woodstock," hissed Hickory. "I don't think old Punkhead knows what that is. Come and join us."

"Get on with it, damn you both," Malachite's voice came from the bank behind Sitka. "Or are you rabbits?"

They ignored the insult and went on with the charade.

"Are you a Sun-squirrel?" Hickory asked.

"Yes."

"You never told me."

"You never asked. Are you?"

"Yes."

"You never told me."

"You never asked."

A small pine cone splashed in the water beside them as a gruff voice called down, "Get on with it."

"I'll go and ask Malachite to give you all safe passage," Sitka said, while going through the motions of stamping and arching his back again.

Hickory made the same movements, advancing towards Sitka who moved backwards.

"Not a chance, the old fool is using this, and you, as a step towards the Oval Drey. He fancies himself as Great Lord Silver."

Hickory moved backwards to allow Sitka to make a forward feint.

"I've got to give it a try. We Sun-squirrels have to do what we think is right."

Hickory stood to his full height, saluted with his right

paw diagonally across his chest. Sitka, facing him, did the same then they embraced briefly as a shower of cones flew around them, bouncing off the bridge and dropping into the water.

Sitka turned and, tail high, went up the bank to where Lord Malachite sat glowering down at him. Sitka lowered his tail, remembering the Request Kernel he had been taught by Rowan, though forgetting for the moment that Malachite would not know this.

> *A submissive stance*
> *And a request, presumes help –*
> *Give it if you can.*

"Lord Malachite. These are good squirrels, all friends of mine, please let them pass safely."

"They are natives and traitors, as you are showing yourself to be. A cowardly one at that. Your body will hang in a tree as an example to others. Zap him!" he ordered and a group of Greys leapt on to Sitka, biting and scratching.

The Reds on the island, and Hickory on the bridge, watched, unable to see clearly what was happening in the mêlée at the top of the bank. Then they saw a limp grey body being hauled up a pine trunk and dragged out along a branch where it was suspended, with its neck jammed in a fork. The tail moved slowly in a slight breeze.

Hickory saluted again.

"Come back here, Hickory-Friend," Rowan called, and the Grey turned and slowly climbed the gentle slope of the island to where the Reds were clustered around the Woodstock. Bluebell moved over to crouch beside him.

"They will attack soon," said Rowan, "but we are ready for them."

Chapter 16

———

Malachite looked down at the island and was about to order "Attack". He had decided to stay up on the bank and direct from there, rather than get involved himself. "Only fair to give these youngsters a chance to prove themselves," he was telling himself. "Wouldn't do to get injured myself when I am about to make the journey to Woburn and challenge the Great Lord Silver. Must keep myself fit for that."

There was something about the way the natives on the island were clustered together. Not in terror or in panic as he would have expected, but confidently, as though they knew something he didn't. Were there reinforcements on the way? Instinctively, he glanced over his shoulder, then realised that there were no other natives in the area. It couldn't be that.

The nearby Silvers were all looking to him for leadership, waiting for the order to pour across the bridge and dispose of the quarry. He looked again at the natives. There was something on the ground in front of them. He rubbed his eyes; just lately he found he could not see distant things as clearly as he used to.

"What's that in front of them?" he barked at a youngster near him.

"It's a stick, sir. A sort of knobbly one."

"What's it for?"

"I don't know, sir. It might be some kind of totem, these natives do have some funny customs."

"There's a prime territory for any squirrel who can bring it to me – spread the word. What's your name?"

"Monterey, sir, same as the new Great Lord Silver, sir."

"Well, Monterey, how do you fancy living up to that name. Go and get that knobbly stick. If you bring it to me you get a choice of territories. Off you go now – go on."

Monterey braced himself, rushed down the bank and leapt onto the bridge. He saw one of the natives scratch at the knobbly stick and then felt as if he had been hit by an invisible whirlwind. His head swam, lights flashed in his eyes and, losing his balance he fell from the bridge into the water. The shock cleared his head a little and he struggled for the bank, splashing clumsily. The squirrels who helped him ashore saw that his whiskers were coiled into tight little curls. He begged them to bite them off before he could report back to Malachite.

"It works," Rowan said, "we must have got those numbers right." He looked at the sun.

"About four hours to sunset, I wonder if they will try again?"

Lord Malachite, who had never seen a Woodstock in action before, was interrogating Monterey.

"A wave hit you? I didn't see any wave, you've lost your

brains as well as your whiskers. Everybody on this side get ready for a mass charge. Ready now. CHARGE."

Malachite watched a flood of squirrels pour down the bank towards the bridge. As the first reached the fallen trunk it rolled sideways, clawing at its face, as did the next and the next. The other squirrels turned and scrambled up the bank leaving the three behind.

Malachite watched in astonishment. This was more than a totem that the Reds had. It was an amazingly powerful weapon. It was as well that he had been wise enough to stay up on the bank. Wouldn't do for his battle group to lose their Commander.

"Bring up the injured," he ordered.

The Reds watched a small party of Greys come cautiously down the bank, their tails low, and help the three with the curled whiskers climb back up.

"What now?" Hickory asked.

"Wait and watch," said Rowan.

Unknown Danger near
Lie high, wait, watch and look out.
Trust in the Sun's light.

"The danger's not unknown," said Hickory.

"Kernels don't always fit exactly, but the message is clear. Keep alert – Trust in the Sun."

Meadowsweet asked if she should organise the building of dreys in the trees.

Rowan looked up at the three trunks, then across at the mainland.

"It goes contrary to squirrel nature, but I think we should make a ground-drey. There's no fox-danger here at present and if we are on the ground and all together, we can react faster to anything the Greys do."

With one watching the bridge and another scanning the bank across the water behind them, the other Reds collected fallen twigs, biting off and dropping more dead ones from the trees. With these they built a hollow mound, large enough to take them all. The females used their skills with grass and moss to make a warm lining.

Dusk was falling and there was no sign of another attack. Rowan sat outside the ground-drey, thinking, his paw on the Woodstock. Across the narrow strip of water he could see Sitka's body hanging, the tail moving eerily whenever the evening breeze eddied among the trees. Another Sun-squirrel gone. At least he had died standing up for what he believed in.

Rowan remembered how Sitka and Hickory had helped with the classes for the colonists passing through, allocating them to those skimpy dreytels. Then organising the new-comers so that they all absorbed the messages of the Kernels and were at least partly Sun-worthy before they moved on to take up Territories. He could not, even now, get used to the idea of squirrels owning things, especially woods.

What had happened to all those Greys he had taught? They had left after each course was complete, vowing friendship with their teachers and with each other, brushing whiskers and embracing, and arranging reunions that Rowan had ruefully thought were unlikely ever to take place once the harshness of survival in a hostile world overtook those who had just graduated.

Why were these Greys now persecuting them? Then he realised that they were only fresh-squirrels, newly arrived, and at most had only a few lessons. How easily they had accepted the Three Lords. Those old fools would not have been able to influence a more experienced class.

Rowan's stomach rumbled and he looked around for food.

There were some fallen cones lying under the trees; there might be a seed or two in those. He looked up at the pines. There were clusters of cones silhouetted against the sky but they would not feed eight squirrels for long. Nothing much on the ground, no fungus; some lichen, but that had little food value, and some tufts of grass which might have done if they were rabbits but was not much use to squirrels. Food was going to be a problem if they had to stay here for long.

He called the others out of the drey and explained the food situation, watching the bank and the bridge as he did so.

"It is unlikely that the Greys will attack again until dawn, they don't care for the darkness any more than we do. But we must stay on guard. You will all be hungry and we don't know how long we must stay here. Eat what you can find tonight, share it out equally and we will think what to do for more in the morning."

Rowan was feeling very tired. He tried to hide a yawn, then said, "Spindle, will you allocate guard duties? One hour periods – two squirrels at a time. Take over now. I am exhausted and must sleep."

He went into the ground-drey, curled up and slept until dawn. Spindle had deliberately omitted him from the roster.

Spindle and Hickory were on duty at midnight, listening to the night sounds and watching for movement. The moon had set and the stars were bright above them. Spindle pointed out the North Star.

'Zee those zeven ztarz there. Uz callz thoze the Great Zquirrel. Thoze are hiz two front pawz. Follow a line up from thoze and that next ztar iz the Ztar that iz alwayz in the North."

There was a rustling on the bank across the water. Hickory crept down to the bridge to investigate, tense and ready to scamper back if danger was too close. A cone arched through the sky and landed in the water beside him. They *were* being watched. He retreated up the bank as a shower of tiny specks of light shot across the sky and were gone before either squirrel could focus on them.

"Thoze iz zhooting ztarz," Spindle told Hickory.

A little later they woke Bluebell and the twins, taking care not to disturb Rowan. They briefed the females and stayed with them until they were sure that their eyes had adjusted to the darkness and they were fully alert.

"Wake us all if anything seems to be happening," Hickory said. "It's Wood Anemone and Meadowsweet's turn next – wake them in an hour." He brushed whiskers with Bluebell, and Spindle did the same with his daughters. "Yew keep alert, now. Don't let them zurprize yew."

Spindle and Hickory wriggled into the ground-drey and slept.

Chapter 17

Wakened by the light filtering through the sides of the ground-drey, Rowan poked his head out, looked round at the dew-laden grass and drew a deep breath. The smell was familiar to him; the year he had once spent living on this Eyeland, as he had called it then, was still strong in his memory. That was before the tree fell, bridging the water. In those days he had swum back and forth to the Mainland.

Now, he could see Hickory's back down near the bridge and when he turned round he saw Spindle gathering pine needles and throwing them onto the top of the drey. He went and faced him.

"Why didn't you call me – I've missed my guard duties."

"Yew wuz all burned out, Rowan-Friend. Yew will be able to lead uz better now yew iz rezded."

"Thank you, Spindle-Friend, but I should *always* take my proper turn," he said.

The day wore on with no sign of aggression from the Greys. At first the Reds could see them moving about on the top of the bank and in the trees on the Mainland. They waited apprehensively for another attack until Bluebell said,

"Rowan-Pa, I know there are no Kernels to guide us in war, because we have always been peace-loving squirrels, but if there were, I am sure that they would tell us to take the initiative. I hate sitting here waiting for something to happen. There is the one that says:

> *Your prayers alone*
> *Will not do. The Sun will help*
> *Those who help themselves.*

"I know we've all been praying, but surely there is something we can do?"

Rowan nodded, thought for a moment then crept backwards to where the Woodstock lay on the grass. He turned it slowly towards a Grey who was peering at them through the branches opposite, and scratched a 4 on the smooth wood. The Grey dropped to the ground stunned, then, rubbing his whiskers, climbed slowly up the bank to disappear over the top.

The next Grey to show his face met with the same fate. Three more suffered in the same way before they realised that the Red's weapon had a long reach.

Malachite saw the first Grey fall and kept behind his tree-trunk out of sight of the island. The victim was sent for and came, reeling and stumbling, to the foot of the tree to explain what had happened and how he felt.

"Bite off his whiskers," Malachite commanded. "Light duties for three days."

When the third Grey came before him with tightly curled whiskers, Lord Malachite was angry.

"Can't you see what happens when they point that totem thing at you. Keep your heads down, all of you. They've got no food over there; we'll starve them out. Damned unsporting lot, rot their tails. Watch through the grass or from behind leaves, don't let them see you. Back to your positions – now!"

The two youngsters found Malachite behind his tree when they came to report on the Lords Obsidian and Silica.

"They are in a wood on a knoll which is covered in fallen trees," he was told, and he soon established that the two Lords were back in their old dreys in the Tanglewood.

"You have done well," he told the messengers. "Now keep your heads down and find food. Tell no one else." He put a claw to his lips and winked.

Rowan was quite sorry when there were no more heads to discharge the Woodstock at, but knew that he ought to conserve it. The power it held was not infinite and there was no way of knowing how near it was to exhaustion.

The early evening sun shone gently and the Reds sat in a cluster, each facing a different way, watching the bridge and the banks of the pool across the water. No movement was to be seen anywhere.

"Huz them gone away?" Rosebay asked, echoed by Willowherb, "Gone away, huz them?"

"I don't think so," Meadowsweet said. "We can't be sure, better to wait. It may be a trap. My mother would tell a story at times like this. Anyone want to hear about Acorn and the swan's feathers?"

Squirrels never say no to a story but Rowan cautioned them to stay alert while they listened.

Meadowsweet began. "Once upon a time, there were only two squirrels in the world, Acorn and his lovely life-mate Primrose.

"On the day I am going to tell you about, Primrose was relining their drey with new, sweet-smelling moss, and Acorn was walking by a river, thinking. He was thinking how beautiful everything was and what lucky squirrels they were to have such a wonderful world to live in. There were so many things to see and find out.

"He had seen how the seeds grew when the spring sunshine warmed the ground, and he had seen how the autumn sunshine ripened all the fruit and the nuts so that they could be stored ready for eating in the winter.

"Thinking of the winter days, when cold winds blew and snow covered the ground, he began to believe that he could have arranged things better if he had been the Sun. Why have winters at all? Life would be much easier if there were only springs, summers and autumns. In fact, why have summers? It was often too hot in summer to be comfortable.

This is a brilliant idea, he thought.

"He was about to rush back and tell Primrose, when he remembered that she would probably find some good reason for there to be summers and winters. She often spoilt his best ideas by being practical. This was far too good an idea to be spoilt by practicalities. He walked on, enjoying his plans for a year with only springs and autumns. He was not seeing all the good things around him now – he was thinking of a way to tell the Sun that it had got it all wrong.

"Now, as often happens when you think hard enough, and want a thing enough, something will turn up to help you towards getting it.

"This happened to Acorn. There on the river bank were feathers. These had been moulted by the First Swan in the World when the summer heat had told it to shed its old feathers and grow new strong, clean ones for the next year. The swan had taken most of the soft, downy ones to line its nest and keep its eggs warm, but on the bank were the stiff white quills from its wings.

" 'If I could fly like a swan,' Acorn said to himself, 'I would fly up to the Sun and tell it what a mistake it had made creating winters and summers, when all we squirrels need are springs and autumns.'

"Acorn picked up the two longest feathers and held them out, waving them up and down, pretending to be a swan. He would go and tell the Sun. He would. He would. He closed his eyes and flapped as hard as he could.

"When he opened his eyes again, the ground was far below him and he could see the river winding backwards and forwards, looking like a snake does from high on a tree.

"He was so surprised that he forgot to keep his paws, which were holding the feathers, moving up and down and he was falling towards the river. He started to flap the feathers again even faster than before.

"The Sun had been watching all this, smiling warmly to see that one of its little creatures was beginning to think for himself, but had not yet come to rely on the wisdom that it had given to the females.

"The sun decided to teach Acorn a gentle lesson. By now he was flying out over the sea so the Sun decided to drop

Acorn into the water and let him swim to the shore because, as you all know, squirrels, excepting my Rowan, don't like swimming. He loves it and used to swim a lot when he lived all alone on this Eyeland two years ago."

Meadowsweet smiled at her life-mate who was watching the far bank.

"Where was I? Oh yes. The Sun had decided to drop Acorn into the sea as a lesson. The Sun never acts directly in these things, it needs to seem impartial and uncaring, but if you look very closely at things you will see that in some way it influences and directs everything we do. It will arrange things to achieve what it wants. So the Sun made a swallow swoop close beneath Acorn, brushing under his forearm with its wing-tip as it flew by chasing flies. Acorn was so ticklish that he let go of one of the feathers and started to fall. The feather floated away out of his reach, twisting and spinning like a sycamore seed.

"Acorn clung onto the other feather as he fell. He could see that he was going to splash into the sea and would have to swim all the way to the shore – and he did not like the thought of that!

"Now, males often think quickly in emergencies like this, and he did still have *one* feather. He reached up and caught the tip with his free paw and found that he was not falling quite as fast. Then he found that, by twisting the feather, he could go in any direction he liked. He swung round to glide towards the land, intending to come down without even getting his feet wet.

"The Sun was watching this clever little squirrel outwit it, and thought that would never do. So it made an updraught where the wind blew against the cliff; we used to watch the butterflies tossing about in this when we lived near the sea.

"The Sun let Acorn float up again on the rising air, but he soon learned how to twist the feather to take advantage of the updraught and began to glide in towards the soft cliff-top grass. He was starting to think that he had again outwitted the Sun. Clever Acorn, he was thinking.

"The Sun though, was playing with him, and as Acorn had chosen a good place to land and was steering towards it, the Sun reached down a gigantic paw and scooped out a hollow just ahead of him. The hollow was right on the edge of the sea and water rushed in through the gap, foaming and bubbling and soaking Acorn who had to swim ashore – just as the Sun had planned all along.

"When Dandelion told me this story, she said the hollow cove is still there, full of the sea."

"What happened to the scoop of land, Meadowsweet-Ma?" asked Bluebell.

"The Sun looked at it and thought, Where could I have another hill? and seeing that the Great Heath was perhaps just a little too big, dropped it on the south side of that.

"If you climb the tree behind you and look that way you can see it. It's where the barn owls live – Screech Hill."

On Screech Hill itself, Sumac was worried. Word had just reached him on the colonists' woodbine, that a party of Reds were being hunted to the death, over near the Blue Pool.

The only Reds he knew of there were the Teachers – Rowan, Meadowsweet, Spindle and Wood Anemone, with their youngsters. Surely no one was hunting *them*? They were doing a tremendous and worthy job, teaching all the Silvers how to live successfully and peacefully in New America. They were wonderful squirrels and had taught him to be a Sun-squirrel, though it was not something one spoke about too openly. One day, when there was a Sun-squirrel in the Oval Drey perhaps, but not now.

If it *was* his friends and teachers who were being hunted, he ought to be doing something to help them. He told his life-mate Tumbleweed, that he had to be away for a few days and slipped off towards the Blue Pool without further explanation. She still harboured some of the old prejudices, even though she had been taught in the same class as he had. She was not yet ready to become a Sun-squirrel.

Skirting round the edge of the Tanglewood he caught the scent of Obsidian and Silica and crept up on them cautiously, then seeing their apparent age and condition, called to them.

"Do you know anything about some natives being chased?" he asked.

"Who are you?" Silica called back.

"A friend of the Teachers. Is it them?"

"Yes," said Obsidian, but before he could say more, Sumac was off in a flash of grey fur, heading for the Blue Pool.

He ran as fast as he could across the Great Heath and through the woods to New Massachusetts, hardly pausing for breath even when he reached the pool itself. Human visitors looked up as the frantic grey squirrel passed overhead on its way to the North-east Wood.

Here everything was eerily silent. The dreytels were unoccupied and the whole wood empty of any squirrel activity. Sumac snuffled around among the confusing scents, then followed the strongest towards the Dogleg Field.

Chapter 18

———

Marguerite knew that things were now seriously wrong on Ourland. Instead of peace and prosperity bringing pleasure and happiness to the island, the virtually un-limited leisure time was undermining, if not destroying, the whole culture of the squirrels.

She had retired to one of the palm trees in the sheltered valley to think. Few humans came here and very few squirrels. Not that she disliked humans, they had never threatened her, but she just could not understand them.

They still celebrated their Sun-days every seventh day which seemed rather too often to her. The squirrels' Sun-days were the Longest Day and the Longest Night, the Coming of Spring and the Harvest Safely In. However, the humans did seem to have special Sun-days for the last three of these, as Marguerite, who loved to listen to the humans singing in the island church, had noticed extra activity at those times.

The squirrels' Longest Day celebrations had not gone well that summer. There had been plenty of youngsters romping and playing, but very few of the older generation came along to organise the fun and chases, or to tell stories.

Dandelion had told one of Marguerite's favourite tales about the squirrel who was beaten and then saved by humans, but the youngsters had been inattentive and fidgety.

Marguerite recalled how *she* had always listened in silence when she had been young but this year . . .

Dandelion had started as always, "Once upon a time . . ."

". . . A squirrel went down from Bloxworth to Wolvesbarrow. Some boys, as humans call their young males, set upon this squirrel and threw stones at him. They chased him with sticks, beating and hitting him until he saw the sky go black and blood ran from his nose. Then the boys kicked the poor thing into the grass on the side of a roadway and ran off, laughing.

"All day the squirrel lay there, bothered by flies and afraid that a fox or dog might come and kill and eat him, but he was too stiff and sore and sick to move.

"Several times squirrels passed in the trees overhead and saw the injured one lying below. The first squirrel was in a hurry and pretended not to see him.

"The second one did not want to get involved. It was none of her business, and, anyway, it was the injured squirrel's own fault if he had got himself into trouble.

"The third came down the tree and went a little closer to look. When he saw that the squirrel was a stranger he passed by on the other side.

"Then a human came, saw the creature lying in the grass and took pity on him. He took it to a clean white place where he lived with other sick animals. Here other humans nursed him back to health and then released him where he had been found.

"That injured squirrel was my dear grandfather, and he often told this story as a warning that you must not expect all of one kind to behave in the same way – especially humans.

"My grandfather could never understand how humans could care so much for their pet dogs and cats and for sick creatures, then go out and kill free animals and birds just to have fun."

Dandelion had looked around expecting to see the nods and tail-flicks of appreciation that usually followed her story-telling and was upset when Sycamore said, "You're always going on at us with your silly stories. I'm off." He turned his tail on Dandelion and leapt for a tree trunk, displaying insolence in his every movement. Other youngsters had followed him.

What could be done, Marguerite wondered. Every generation thinks the older ones are stick-on-the-grounds. She could remember having such thoughts herself, but her year-mates wouldn't have dared behave like that. Perhaps it had been better here when there was a king to impose some authority – perhaps an island needed that. Maybe the Mainland ways would not work here where life was so easy and without any threat of danger. Maybe . . .

She decided to seek out Chip. It was unlikely that his Bark-rush would have the answers, but Chip himself had a good brain and always seemed glad to talk with her.

At the Zwamp she found him crossly searching through the undergrowth.

"What are you looking for?" she asked.

"Someone's broken up my Bark-rush and thrown all the rings away," he said gruffly. "I've only found about seven. Can you help me look, please."

"Did a human do that?" she asked.

"No, it was squirrels, young ones. Their scent was all around here. Sycamore's and his hoppos I think. Sundamn him!"

"Chip," said Marguerite sternly. "You know I don't like that kind of language."

She helped him find the rest of the bark-rings and left him threading them on new rush-stems. She had found a number of sloe stones in the bushes and suspected that they had come from the leaf-pile where sloes were left each autumn by Caterpillar to ruddle in the heat. She went to the pile to see if there were any more there.

Lying next to the steaming leaves was Caterpillar himself, groaning and trying to rub his back with his paws.

Ruddled, she thought, ruddled old fool, and was about to pass him on the other side of the pile, when she remembered Dandelion's story and went over to him.

"Are you all right?" she asked.

"Uz've got thiz awful pain in uz back. Can yew vetch Voxglove or Cowzlip to zee me." He groaned again and a dribble of urine dropped onto a dead leaf. It was bright red.

"I'll get them at once," she told him and hurried off to the drey set aside for sick squirrels. Voxglove was there and Marguerite told her about Caterpillar.

"Painz in the back and blood in hiz piddle – that'z zervantz' zicknezz. Too many ruddled zloez!"

They hurried back together but were too late. Caterpillar was Sun-gone, but they were in time to drive away a magpie that was about to peck out his eyes.

While Voxglove went to fetch other squirrels to help bury the ex-zervant's body, Marguerite stayed near in case the magpie returned. Next to the leafpile was the blackthorn bush that was already laden with the dark green berries that would soon turn a dusky black as they ripened. She thought hard and could think of no other such bush on the island, though they were plentiful on the Mainland.

A daring idea came into her head. It was contrary to all that she had ever learned, especially the Kernel which old Burdock, her grandmother, had taught her.

> *Squirrels protect trees,*
> *They have enough enemies,*
> *Treat them as your friends.*

She looked round guiltily then, sure that she was not being observed, hopped over to the blackthorn and bit away a ring of bark all round the base. I may be killing a tree, she told herself, but I am saving many squirrels.

The exposed wood gleamed accusingly white so she rubbed soil into the raw wood until it was hardly noticeable, then brushed the dirt from her paws.

With the squirrels who had come to bury Caterpillar was Marguerite's daughter, Burdock the News-squirrel. She greeted her mother coolly then went and prodded Caterpillar's body. "How long has he been dead?" she asked.

Later when they were scratching leaves over his grave and saying the Farewell Kernel, Marguerite noticed Burdock looking closely at the base of the blackthorn bush.

The news was swiftly carried around the island.

DYING SQUIRREL KILLS THE TREE HE LOVED

Caterpillar, known for his fondness for ruddled
sloes, took a last final revenge on the tree that led
to his death . . .

In the concern over Caterpillar, Chip's annoyance at the
damage to his gadget seemed minor, but there was another
case of wilful damage reported the next day. All the little
Woodstocks, so lovingly trained around the hazel saplings
by Chestnut and Heather, were uprooted and left to die.
Sycamore was blamed and called before the council.

He sat there sullenly, his body radiating contempt.

"It has been reported," Clover the Tagger said, "that
you have wilfully destroyed trees despite knowing the
Kernel:

> *Squirrels protect treees,*
> *They have enough enemies,*
> *Treat them as your friends.*

"What have you to say for yourself?"

Marguerite felt very uncomfortable. Was what
Sycamore had allegedly done been so very different from
what she had done herself only the day before? At least she
had a motive. Perhaps Sycamore did too. Should she be
trying to find out? With no further thought she spoke out.

"I would like to suggest that this meeting is suspended
while Sycamore and I talk about his reasons in private. I
know it is against custom but please trust me. I am sure I
can help."

Clover said, "It *is* against custom, but so many things
that are happening now are against our customs. I value

Marguerite's judgement. Unless any squirrel is against, we will wait for Marguerite's report. Sycamore the Ruddled, you will do exactly what Marguerite tells you and answer all her questions. We meet again here in seven days." Marguerite signalled to Sycamore to follow her and the two left together.

"I want to know why you do all these things," she told him. "But don't answer now, I want you to think carefully before you tell me. I want the real reason, not whatever comes into your head – that's too easy. First though, we will go and apologise to Chip and see if he needs help remaking his Bark-rush."

Chip was not happy to see Marguerite with Sycamore. A tinge of jealousy stabbed him and he ignored the proffered apologies, turning away and scratching at a flea bite so vigorously that a trace of blood showed on his fur.

"Chip!" Marguerite said sternly. "Behave yourself. I look to you to set an example."

Chip looked contrite and mumbled his apology. Marguerite was staring at the blood on his fur, her mind obviously far away.

"Not bleeding – breeding!" she said out loud. "Woodlouse knows how the mushrooms of the moon control breeding. *That's* what Thizle was trying to tell me."

Then her face fell. Her dear friend Woodlouse (now called Wood Anemone), who appeared to hold the future of the Ourland squirrels in her paws, was out of reach. She had stayed on the Mainland to help with the teaching of the Greys.

Marguerite knew she must find a way to get a message to her.

Chapter 19

The stern-faced scoutmaster called his boy scouts together and instructed them to sit on the grass. He was not looking forward to what he had to say.

It was a pity. The camp had gone well so far. The boys had made bridges, rafts and bivouac shelters. They had all worked well together and played exciting wide-games and learned about stalking and concealment. Now this had happened to spoil it.

His knees were burning. Unaccustomed to short trousers, the last two sunny days had left their bright red mark. He wondered briefly if what he was going to have to announce was unfair but then decided crossly that the little blighters must be taught a lesson.

"I do feel that one or more of you have let the side down," he said. "This troop was selected from all the scouts in Dorset to camp here on Brownsea Island on the very place where Baden-Powell held the first ever scout camp nearly sixty years ago. That was a real privilege for our troop. Now someone has chopped a tree about so that it looks like a squirrel. I had to promise the wardens that all axe-work would be strictly supervised. I want the person who is responsible to own up."

He waited but no one spoke.

"Come on," he said. "Someone must have done it."

"Perhaps it was a squirrel done it," a young scout ventured.

The other scouts laughed nervously and the scoutmaster glowered.

"If no one owns up by lunch-time none of you will go to help launch the hot-air balloon this afternoon. Dismiss."

The scoutmaster went angrily back to his tent to rub calamine lotion on to his sunburnt knees. If none of the little blighters owned up he would have to miss seeing the flight himself.

Away from his hoppos, and with no access to the ruddled sloes, Sycamore was really pleasant company. After his apology to Chip he seemed eager to learn numbers from Marguerite and find out what the Bark-rush could be used for. She told him of her concern about the possibility of the island becoming overpopulated by squirrels and she reminded him of the dreadful plague that had virtually wiped out the rabbits earlier in the year. Then Chip, at first reluctantly, taught him how to calculate using the bark rings. Marguerite sat apart from them, trying to think of a way to get a message to Wood Anemone.

Later on that hot afternoon, the three of them were together, resting in one of the trees that formed the Island Screen. Chip seemed unhappy that Marguerite planned to spend so much time alone with Sycamore and when she had suggested they go to look at the Mainland from the South Shore trees, he had tagged along.

"What in the Sunless Pit is *that*?" Sycamore asked, when

a roar as of some great animal came from the direction of the meadow between them and the church.

Moments later the sound came again and the three squirrels hurried through the trees to where they could look out over the open grassy area. They could see a few humans gathered round a hump, the colour of a buttercup flower, which billowed and rippled in the breeze. Nearby a peacock and his harem of peahens scratched and pecked at the ground as though nothing unusual was happening.

"What's that thing?" Sycamore asked again in a hushed voice.

"I don't know, I've seen nothing like it before," Marguerite replied, climbing higher for a better view.

There was a longer roar and the glossy yellow hump, seeming to have a life of its own, rose above the heads of the humans and tossed about in the breeze. An unfamiliar and disturbing burning smell blew directly towards the squirrels in the pine. The humans were now clustered below the yellow thing, which had become a round ball, and were holding something beneath it that the squirrels could not see.

"It's the Suns-child," whispered Marguerite, "come again!"

"What's the Suns-child?" Sycamore asked, hoping for a better answer this time.

"Twice in the past, the Sun has sent its child when we squirrels have been in trouble. Now it's here again, only it's grown much bigger. Look at the size of it!"

The balloon towered above the humans who were debating amongst themselves as to whether or not it was safe to fly with the wind rising and blowing so strongly from east to west. The pilot was annoyed that the boy scouts had not turned up as promised to help with holding the basket, even though a boy had come at the last minute with an apologetic message.

Finally, having decided that it was *not* safe, the pilot tried to release the hot air but the ripcord seemed to have jammed. With the other helpers hanging grimly on to the basket, he climbed onto the woven wicker edge and reached upwards for the cord.

He was doing this when a sudden swirl of wind spun across the meadow, lifting the dried soil from the peacocks' dusting places, and blowing it into the eyes of those around the balloon. Each, believing that others were holding it down, let go to wipe their eyes. The balloon suddenly lifted. The pilot, also temporarily blinded, let go and fell backwards off the basket, knocking two of the helpers to the ground.

The balloon jerked violently away, rose higher and floated off in a westerly direction towards the trees, trailing a rope.

"Grab that rope someone. Grab hold of that rope," the pilot shouted, getting to his feet and running after the balloon which was now nearly above the trees. Others joined the chase.

The squirrels heard the incomprehensible shouting and saw the humans running after the tail-end of the rope, now far out of their reach. It trailed through the branches towards them.

Marguerite sensed that the Suns-child should be restrained and called to Chip and Sycamore, "Help me catch that rope, we must help the Suns-child," and snatched at the trailing line as it slithered past them.

In a moment, the three squirrels, all clutching the rope, had been torn from the treetop and were being lifted bodily high into the air. "Hang on for your lives," Marguerite shouted.

It was suddenly calm and, looking down, Marguerite could see the island falling away behind them. Below was the blue water of Poole Harbour, dotted with the white spots of boat sails. There was no sensation of dizziness as there had been when she had once climbed the chalk cliff to the Barrow of the Flowers. Somehow the ground was remote and distant, not a part of the world they now found themselves in.

"Climb up after me," she called down to Chip and Sycamore and the three climbed easily, their claws gripping firmly into the fibres of the rope until they reached the basket and scrambled over the padded edge. They explored the box of woven willow stems, which contained only a few loose items of human's coverings and two round red metal things as big as tree stumps.

Marguerite was puzzled by the silence. Apart from the occasional creaking of the willow box, there was no sound at all. Down in the trees the wind had been singing its gentle song, so familiar to the squirrels that they hardly noticed it. There pine needles had rubbed against one another, leaves shook and rustled and the movement of air past the twigs and branches always had a special sound of its own.

Suddenly she realised what had made the change – they were floating and drifting on the very wind itself!

How many times had she watched the white-winged gulls flying effortlessly on the breezes over the sea and envied them? Now she and her companions were doing the same. Her tail rose with pleasure as they climbed to the edge of the basket and sat there, claws gripping the soft padding.

"We are flying on the wind," she shouted and Sycamore grinned across at Chip. This was *much* more fun than the stupid things he had been doing lately.

There was land below them now and the Suns-child seemed to be slowly getting nearer the ground as they drifted along.

"There's the Blue Pool," Marguerite said excitedly, as she recognised her old home demesne, the pool itself glowing sapphire in the green trees, below and to the south of them. The Sun had sent its child once again to help her and now it was carrying her to Wood Anemone. She prepared herself for the Suns-child to come down out of the sky but it floated on.

Perplexed, Marguerite recited the Kernel:

> *Trust in the Sun.*
> *His ways are mysterious.*
> *Faith can fell fir trees.*

"That must be Rowans's Pool down there." She pointed out another small pool now passing beneath them, shaped like a crouching animal with an island where its eye would have been. And still the Suns-child floated on.

> *Have faith in the Sun*
> *His ways are mysterious . . .*

Rowan looked up and saw the yellow balloon above the three trees of his Eyeland.

"The Suns-child has come again to save us," he called, and the besieged squirrels followed his pointing claw, then saw his face fall as the great yellow ball, its fabric now billowing lazily in the wind, drifted westwards apparently without seeing them.

The balloon floated on, the wind veering slightly and blowing more from the north-east. Below them, Marguerite could hear the gun-fire from the Lulworth ranges and see the flashes as the humans played with the thunder and lightning force. The Suns-child was now much nearer the ground and heading for a ridge of hills, beyond which she caught glimpses of the sea.

As it dropped even more the basket bumped along the ground on the top of the ridge, and their movement slowed briefly. Before the squirrels, tumbled in the bottom of the basket, could compose themselves and jump clear, it lifted again and floated feebly out towards the sea. Then, as if giving up, the Suns-child collapsed with its flaccid skin draping the mellow stone walls of a ruined barn.

"That was fun," said Sycamore, crawling from the basket and brushing himself down, followed by Marguerite and Chip who did the same. "Where do we go from here?"

The sun was setting, painting the sky in dramatic shades of gold and red, all reflected in the waters of the circular cove to their right. A great mass of rock far out to sea in the south-west was dark against the glow. Chip pointed to it. "That's the Isle of Portland. That's where I was born," he told Sycamore.

Rowan had watched the Suns-child disappear and suddenly felt very tired. He looked at the bright western sky and the setting sun.

> *In times of great stress*
> *Rest is a sound investment –*
> *Restoring one's strength.*

"Organise the night watch again, Spindle-Friend," he said, "but count me in this night."

He went into the ground-drey, curled up and closed his eyes.

On Ourland, a Council Meeting had been called and was better attended than most.

Just Poplar called for order.

"Doez any zquirrel know what huz happened to Marguerite, Chip and Zycamore? They zeem to have left Ourland with the round yellow thing the humanz brought here. The thing that looked like the Zun and floated in the zky?"

Chapter 20

The humans arrived at the ruined barn as it was getting dark, folded the Suns-child and carried it, with its basket, away into the night. The three squirrels hid in holes in the decaying stonework until the humans had gone, then climbed up to the highest point and looked around.

Somehow we've got to get back to the Blue Pool, Marguerite was thinking. But if the Sun had meant us to go there, why has the Suns-child brought us to the coast?

She turned towards Portland far across the bay and watched as it seemed to sink into the water as the light faded from the sky. Stars appeared, twinkling and sparkling above her head and she sensed a sadness trapped in the stone walls below her. Chip seemed to feel it too and he urged her to leave.

"Wait," she said. "Hush." She had felt tingling at the base of her whiskers which usually indicated that the dolphins were trying to contact her. She cleared her mind to listen.

It was Lundy's lone voice she heard, and by turning her head, she could locate its direction – far out in the sea to the south.

There was an urgency and concern in it that was new to her. Marguerite had only ever known calmness in the dolphins' voices – except when Malin spoke about pollution. Lundy's voice was far from calm now.

"Squirrel-friend, where are you? I am on my way to your island to find you, but I sense that you are not there, but are somewhere nearer."

Marguerite projected her thoughts seaward. "I am here with two friends. We are near a place where the sea is in a circle with land almost all round it. Do you know this place?"

"That must be the Cove of Lulworth. I'll come at once. Can you get down to the water's edge? I need your help – desperately!"

Marguerite roused her companions, who were dozing near her, and in the light of a moon that was now casting a silver sheen over the seascape, she told them what she had just heard.

"The dolphins need us. Lundy is coming to meet us soon. We must go down to the edge of the water in that round hollow."

Treading warily and alert for night-danger they went along a stony Man-track and through a wire fence, then under dark bushes the foliage of which was permanently bent landwards by winds from the sea. Slippery paths and steps took them down to the shore.

The water in the bay was calm and lapped quietly on the shingle beach. Smells of damp and rotting seaweed filled their noses as they waited, looking towards the gap in the cliffs with the open sea beyond. Soon a black shape, a dorsal fin clearly visible in the moonlight, rose from the water some distance from the shore, and they heard the sound of air being blown through the nostril on top of a dolphin's head.

"We are here, Lundy-Friend," Marguerite called.

"I am pleased that you were so near. My prayer must have been heard."

"The Suns-child brought us," Marguerite replied. "You prayed for us to come?"

"It's Finisterre. He's tangled in a human's fish-net on the other side of the Bank of Chesils. He is safe at the moment lying on the pebbles, but there is a storm coming and the net is stopping him from swimming."

Marguerite looked up at the night sky and remembered the sunset.

A red sky at night
Heralds a delightful day –
Dawn to dusk sunshine.

"Are you sure about a storm?" she asked.

"Yes, the red sky was deceiving. The wind is shifting to the west and then the south-west and a storm is coming. We have learned a lot about the weather in the last ✶⤐ ⤐ ⤐ years. Believe me!"

"I do," said Marguerite. "How can we help?" Wood Anemone and the troubles on Ourland were forgotten.

"I must find a way to get you to Finisterre before the storm reaches him. Can your teeth cut away the Man-cords of the net."

✶⤐ ⤐ ⤐ = 60 x 60 x 60 = 216,000 years.

144

"We will do all we can," Marguerite replied, "Can you get a boat?"

"There won't be time for that – can you hold on to some wood if I carry it in my mouth?"

"We will do our best. Have you brought some wood?"

"No, can you find some on the shore? Please hurry."

Marguerite quickly explained the situation to Sycamore who had only heard one side of the conversation and the three squirrels scurried along the high-tide mark, searching for a suitable piece of driftwood. Lundy, in the water, kept pace with them, her agitation sweeping in waves towards the land.

At first there was a total absence of wood, the glowing embers of a human's fire explaining this. They briefly watched the tiny flames, some blue from the salt in the wood and others a soft green around a copper nail. Marguerite hustled them on until, farther along, Sycamore found the handle of a broken oar, half-buried in the slimy ribbons of kelpweed. They struggled to free it, tiny crabs scuttling for cover as they did so, then rolled it down the beach to the water's edge.

"What now?" Marguerite called out to Lundy.

"Are you *all* coming?"

Marguerite looked at the others.

"Yes," said Chip simply, and once Sycamore had been told he said, "Wouldn't miss this for all the nuts on Ourland."

The squirrels grasped the wood, Chip and Marguerite at one end, Sycamore at the other.

"Hold tightly to the wood – I'm coming in."

There was a rush of water as the dolphin surged towards

the beach and the squirrels felt the oar handle being picked up and held high, as the great black body thrashed in the shallows and turned about. Then, with another heave and a violent beating of her tail, Lundy was in deep water again, holding the oar handle crossways in her mouth. All three squirrels were soaked and, as the dolphin swam rapidly towards the opening from the bay into the open sea, a cold night wind blowing from the south-west quickly chilled them.

Lundy was right about the wind changing, thought Marguerite, digging her claws deeper through the layers of peeling varnish and into the soft wood below.

"Thank you all. Hold on tightly." Lundy let her thoughts envelop the squirrels, then she closed her mind to interrogation and tuned in to the minds of each squirrel in turn.

The young one is enjoying this; it's nothing more than a great adventure to him. The other male is here because Marguerite is here, he would follow her anywhere. He loves her – I wonder if she knows?

Marguerite, my friend, I seem to know you so well. You have never even thought of Chip as a suitor. You really *do* want to help me and you have such complete trust in your Sun that you *now* believe you have been sent to do that. This is a strange friendship – but one I value highly.

Lundy reopened her mind as she swam steadily on; Marguerite was asking how far they had to go.

"I came round the end of the Isle of Portland, through the tearing waters of the Race, but we won't go back that way. We are swimming the Bay of Weymouth and then we'll cross the Harbour of Portland to the Lagoon of Fleet, between the Bank of Chesils and the Mainland. Malin and Finisterre are on the seaward side of the pebble bank, with other dolphins helping, but none have teeth to cut like yours can. We should be there soon after dawn – if my strength holds."

Marguerite sensed that swimming with her head out of water was tiring Lundy. She would normally swim submerged, only coming up to breathe.

Occasionally the dolphin changed course slightly to take advantage of the different currents that she seemed to know intimately. She was holding the oar-handle steady and firm, and by the time they passed between the great rocks forming the breakwater that protected the ships in the Harbour of Portland, the squirrels' fur had dried in the wind.

"The tide is against us," Lundy told Marguerite, and the squirrel sensed the extra energy the dolphin was having to expend to swim against the mass of water rushing out through the narrow gap.

The moon was turning pale and the dawn showed grey behind them. Huge metal cylinders leaned with the flow, the seaweed and barnacles on the undersides and the anchor chains of the giant buoys smelling dank and salty on the morning air. Lundy swam doggedly on against the current.

At the Ferry-bridge they passed under the metal girders, past the round black bridge supports where the whole weight of water trapped in the lagoon was trying to follow the moon's pull and rush out into the Harbour before the earth rotated enough for it to be drawn back to fill the lagoon once again.

Marguerite knew that Lundy's strength was failing. "You must rest," she told her.

> *In times of great stress*
> *Rest is a sound investment –*
> *Restoring one's strength.*

"I can't," she replied. "The storm is too close. My son will be battered to death on the beach."

Unexpectedly Chip who, with Sycamore had been concentrating on holding tight to the oar-handle said,

> *When quite exhausted*
> *Keep on going while you must,*
> *Never, ever quit.*

"I won't," Lundy responded, and Marguerite asked Chip where he had learned this Kernel. She was sure that she had not heard it before.

"I don't know," he told her, "it just came into my head. They often do."

Marguerite turned her attention back to Lundy. "Can you make it?" she asked.

"I will. We dolphins have a saying—"

> *If you think you can,*
> *Or if you think you cannot*
> *Either way it's true.*
> *Sun and Sea will support you –*
> *Buoy your determination.*

Lundy swam doggedly on.

"We have a saying like that too," Marguerite said and then was silent, to let the dolphin concentrate on her swimming.

They had passed the boatworks and the caravan park on their right side and a gaggle of fishermen's huts on the pebbles to their left, and Lundy was now forcing herself to swim against the tidal flow at the narrows where the buildings of the Army Bridging Camp loomed against the sky.

The black heads of cormorants bobbed up around them then disappeared as the birds dived, only to reappear with small flatfish in their beaks which they swallowed awkwardly, their thoats bulging as the fish went down. Others, fully gorged, sat on the concrete ramp their wings spread to catch a drying wind.

The flow eased as the lagoon widened but Marguerite could sense Lundy's strength ebbing. "Come on, my friend – If you think you can . . . I know you can, I know you can. Carry us to your Finisterre."

She felt the exhausted dolphin find new reserves and surge forward again. "You can, you can, YOU CAN," Marguerite urged her as more dolphin voices within her head were joining her own.

"Lundy," one was saying. "Keep going, we are here with Finisterre. Keep going. You have the squirrel with you?"

"Better than that," Lundy responded, her tiredness apparent in every wave of her voice. "I have *three* squirrels."

"Keep going. Bring them to us. Keep going. Lundy, keep swimming."

Chapter 21

As dawn broke, the dolphin swam into shallow water on the Chesil Bank side of the Fleet Lagoon. On the pebbled shore were several large white birds. The squirrels recognised them as swans, even though they had never been near any of them whenever they had flown in and landed on the lagoon at Ourland.

Lundy's head drooped and the oar-handle floated out of her mouth, rolling over in the water with the weight of the squirrels.

Marguerite let go of the wood and called to the others, "Swim to the beach."

Chip and Sycamore followed her through the brackish water and crawled onto the pebbles. Cold and bedraggled, they shook themselves and blinked the water from their eyes, only to find a pair of swans, their necks bent low, hissing fiercely at them. Before this hostile reception they had no choice but to retreat back into the cold water.

"LEAVE – THESE CREATURES – ALONE."

It was Lundy's voice, speaking slowly and with great authority. The swans raised their necks, waved their heads from side to side and walked away as though the squirrels no longer existed.

"Please, my friends, go over the bank to help my son. I must rest here. Come back to me when you are successful. Go now, please!" Lundy pleaded.

Wet from their swim ashore, tired from lack of sleep and stiff from many hours clinging to the oar, the three squirrels scrambled over the shingles to the top of the bank.

Though the sky was clear, the wind, now blowing strongly from the south-west, was forcing huge waves to roll in from the bay and crash onto the shingle. The wind tore and tugged at their ears and tails and buffeted their chill damp bodies. On the beach, being thrown about by the waves, they could see the young dolphin, its flippers entangled in a mass of fine white threads. Just seaward of it, a semi-circle of dolphins who were trying to shelter it were themselves frequently getting tossed up onto the beach. They would then roll back with the undertow and swim out to try and stem the force of waves once more.

Marguerite stood on her hind-legs to assess the situation before acting. The dolphins, seeing her tiny body silhouetted against the skyline, sent waves of welcome through the air to envelop her and her companions. She recognised Malin's voice as he greeted her.

"What should we do?" She focused her thoughts on him.

"Can you reach Finisterre and bite away the net?" There was a desperate pleading in his thought-voice. "Are your teeth strong enough?"

"We will try," Marguerite replied aloud. "If you think you can . . ."

Her voice was lost in the roar of an even bigger wave

rushing up the beach towards her. She turned to Chip and Sycamore.

"Follow me," she said, and scurried down the pebbles.

The three reached the water's edge just as a wave was withdrawing. They followed the retreating line of foam as far as the young dolphin who was eyeing them thankfully.

Each squirrel grabbed at the tangle of fine nylon threads, and held on tightly, biting vigorously until the next wave came crashing in and smothered them in salt water and sea-foam. They hung on, holding their breaths as the wave spent its energy and rolled back, then started biting again, severing the thin hard filaments one by one. Blood seeped through the tangled mass where these had cut into the dolphin's smooth black skin.

"I'll go to the other side," Sycamore shouted above the roar as yet another wave rushed in to submerge them. As he clambered over Finisterre's slippery back, the wave tore him free and the undertow dragged him down the wet pebbles and sucked his squirming body into deep water. The next wave towered up.

I'm going to drown, he thought as his lungs filled with salt water and he struggled frantically towards the surface. Then he felt himself caught in a gentle mouth and he was lifted clear of the wave while he coughed and coughed and coughed.

A voice enveloped him, "Can you carry on, or do you need to rest?"

"Carry on," he responded and Malin surfed in on the next wave to deposit Sycamore once again on Finisterre's left side. On the stranded dolphin's other side, Marguerite and Chip were still biting and gnawing, their teeth and jaws aching with their efforts. Malin lay on the shingle at Finisterre's tail ready to catch at any squirrel who might lose its grip, his huge bulk helping to break the rush of each wave.

The tangle of nylon was beginning to come free and more blood was flowing from the dolphin's wounds as they tugged and pulled at the severed filaments. Suddenly the whole mass came loose and was drawn down the beach by a retreating wave, the three squirrels rolling with it as they clung on.

Malin caught the ball of nylon filaments in his mouth and surged up the beach on the next wave to drop it just above the highest point reached by the waves. He turned and pushed Finisterre into deeper water as other dolphins swam forward to help support the youngster with their bodies.

The next wave to reach the squirrels was a chorus of "Thank you" from the dolphins in the sea. The squirrels dragged their tired and aching bodies a little further up the beach.

As they lay there, Marguerite picked up instructions being given by Lundy on the other side of the bank.

"THREE SWANS —

GOTO THE FAR SIDE OF THE RIDGE —

FIND THE THREE SMALL ANIMALS —

PICK THEM UP — CAREFULLY —

BRING THEM TO THE SHORE HERE —

AWAIT INSTRUCTIONS —

ACTION NOW —"

A few minutes later three white heads with orange beaks and black masks, appeared on the skyline.

Chip did not see them. Tired as he was, something else had attracted his attention. Immediately under his right paw was one of the bright yellow discs of soft metal that he had once found near the Portland end of the beach and which his father had discarded as useless. It gleamed in the sunshine and he turned it over. There was a Man-head on the one side and indecipherable squiggles on the other. He wanted to keep it more than anything he had ever wanted before. As he drew it to his body, he felt the skin on the back of his neck gripped firmly and he was lifted into the air, still clutching the golden disc.

Dangling there wriggling helplessly, he saw that Marguerite and Sycamore were being treated in the same way and the three swans carried the squirrels over the beach and down to the shore on the sheltered side. The storm-clouds, that had been massing on the horizon, covered the sun and cold rain came driving in towards the land.

"SWANS —

THESE ANIMALS ARE AS PRECIOUS AS UNHATCHED EGGS —

ONE SWAN — SHELTER THEM —

TWO SWANS — FETCH GRAIN-FOOD FROM THE MEN ACROSS THE WATER OF THE FLEET —

ACTION NOW —"

Lundy was still lying in the shallow water issuing instructions to the swans, who reacted to her programming exactly. One scratched a hollow in the tide-wrack and each lowered their squirrel into it as the rain came slashing down the beach. One swan spread its wings and settled over the three weak animals, warming them with the heat of its body. The other two swans waded into the water and swam through the storm towards the Mainland.

After the initial feeling of being smothered, the squirrels found that they could breathe easily, air moving freely through the feathers. Underneath the swan it was dry and snug, and as they sheltered their fur dried and their teeth stopped chattering. One by one they fell asleep.

The storm had passed when Marguerite awoke and peered out at the clean-washed world from under the swan's wing. There was a small pile of wheat-grains near her and she woke Chip and Sycamore to share a meal. The swan seemed content to stay where she was.

In the evening sunlight Marguerite could see Lundy's fin sticking up out of the water and projected her thoughts in that direction.

"Lundy-Friend, are you all right?"

The fin moved and Lundy's head appeared above the water; Marguerite could just see her usual grin.

"Yes, I'm stronger now. I've never been so tired. Malin tells me you saved Finisterre. We can never thank you enough."

"Is Finisterre safe? I was concerned about his injuries."

"We believe so. He is young and fit and the sea water helps the healing if it is not polluted. It is clean here at present. He should be himself again soon."

"What will you do now?" Marguerite asked.

"I am resting here tonight. You must do the same. Stay under the swan; you will be safe and warm there. Then we must find the best way to take you back to your island. After that I will rejoin Malin and Finisterre."

"Will that be difficult?"

"Oh, no. Think how easily I can contact you when I put my mind to it. What is your friend holding?"

Marguerite saw that Chip was hugging a disc of bright metal. She described it to Lundy.

"A golden coin. We know where there are many of those on the seabed. Humans rate them highly. They are pretty but not worth fighting over."

"Humans fight for those?"

"Fight *and* kill one another."

Marguerite took another look at the coin.

People puzzle us
With their strange actions – but then
They're only Human.

When the moon rose that night, a hungry fox padded along the walk-way through the rushes and onto the pebbles of the beach. He had found no Man-scraps and had failed to catch even a mouse. He scented the air, no food-smell there, so he followed the shore of the Fleet Lagoon hoping to find a dead bird or a fish on the tide-line.

He passed the Dragon's Teeth. To the fox these huge weathered concrete blocks had always been there; seemingly as old as the medieval chapel on the hill opposite.

The fox saw the three sleeping swans and walked towards them cautiously, puzzled by an apparent scent of squirrel mixed with the familiar swan-scent. He did not approach too closely – all local foxes had tried to tackle a swan once, but only once. He turned up the beach to follow a faint blood-smell that was teasing his nostrils.

On the pebbles over the ridge he found the ball of nylon that had nearly caused the death of Finisterre and had now been blown up the bank by the force of the gale. He crept towards it, nose twitching. The blood he could smell was inside it. He licked the nylon, then tried to push his nose further into the tangled mass. A thread caught behind a tooth; the other side of the loop under his lower jaw. He tried to push the loop off and his right paw caught in another. His left paw could not free it either, and then that too was tangled. Soon a back paw was also trapped and, growling and struggling, the fox rolled down towards the breaking waves which were rushing up the beach as if they had a hunger greater even than his own.

His one free paw reached forward in a last effort to disentangle himself and as it did so a Seventh Wave towered higher than the rest, crashed onto the pebbles, roared up towards the helpless fox and dragged him down into the deep water off-shore.

That night the scavenging conger eels learned a new taste, though by dawn one of their number was himself trapped by the fine filaments. Later, crabs dined on the body of that conger eel. When the net was finally thrown up the beach again, a human burned it in a pile of driftwood, along with the empty carapaces of a dozen crabs and, the body of a herring gull that had been tempted by the crab meat.

Unaware of the drama being played out so close to her, Marguerite, warm under the swan, dreamed of their flight in the balloon. A new and exciting idea was filling her head when she woke.

Chapter 22

"Lundy, are you awake?"

Marguerite projected her thought towards the black fin, visible in the dawn-still waters of the Fleet. The rumble of the waves on the far side of the Chesil Bank could just be heard, but the wind had died away during the night.

"I am here, we don't sleep in the same way as land animals."

"How do you get the swans to do what you want them to do?" Marguerite asked.

"Birds have simple brains. Mostly they act as their instincts direct and do not reason as we do. If you can reach their brains with clear instructions they follow those instead of their instincts. You heard me do it yesterday."

"Is that a right thing to do; to dominate another creature for your own benefit?" Marguerite asked.

"Not if it will harm that creature and the need is trifling. What I did yesterday saved you from cold-death and did not harm the swans. They are only passing time now until their next nesting season."

"Could *I* dominate them?" Marguerite asked.

"*If you think you can* . . . Try repeating what I say, slowly

158

and positively. I will submerge my thoughts so that it is yours that reach them. Swans – "

"SWANS –" repeated Marguerite and the three swans nearby raised their heads.

"Fetch me a pebble – Action now – "

"FETCH ME A PEBBLE –

ACTION NOW – "

Each swan picked up a pebble, brought it to Marguerite, laid it at her feet and stepped back to wait for more instructions.

Chip and Sycamore, who had only heard part of the "conversation", watched in amazement, Chip still clutching the golden coin.

"Do you think the swans would carry us through the air, flying to Ourland or the Blue Pool?" Marguerite asked.

"For an Innocent, you do have imaginative ideas," Lundy replied.

Marguerite knew that "Innocent" was the dolphin word for smaller-brained animals, and was not offended as she knew that literally it must be true.

"Each swan could easily carry one of you," Lundy went on. "But it's probably never been done before. Would you risk it?"

"At one time, *everything* we do had never been done before," said Marguerite, thinking of all the stories of Acorn, the first squirrel in the world. "But I think I will practise instructing the swans first.

THREE SWANS –

SWIM ACROSS THE FLEET –

SWIM BACK TO ME –

ACTION NOW – "

Within an hour, Marguerite was confident of success and was briefing her companions on her plans.

"We will each climb onto a swan's back and grip the feathers tightly. Hold as many feathers as you can with each paw but do not hurt the swans. I will give them instructions to take us to the Blue Pool where I have to talk to Wood Anemone. Then we will fly on to Ourland. After that I will give the swans directions to return. Chip, I think you will have to leave your metal disk here."

Chip looked crestfallen. "I *would* like to take it. I think I could hold it under my body. If it slips out and falls I don't have it any more – but then I don't if I leave it here."

"Very well," Marguerite told him, sensing how important it must be to him. "But don't risk falling yourself trying to catch it. It's not like falling from a tree – we've all done that. We will be a lot higher – like we were in the Sunschild."

Lundy had her head out of the water, watching with great interest as Marguerite instructed the swans.

"THREE SWANS –

SOON YOU WILL EACH PICK UP ONE OF US SQUIRRELS –

YOU WILL PLACE YOUR SQUIRREL ON YOUR BACK AND WAIT WHILE IT TAKES A FIRM HOLD – IT WILL NOT HURT YOU –

YOU WILL WADE INTO DEEP WATER AND THEN YOU WILL FLY EASTWARDS ABOVE THE BEACH TO THE BRIDGE –

FROM THERE YOU WILL FLY ACROSS THE SEA TO THE COVE OF LULWORTH

WHERE THE SEA IS HELD IN A RING OF CLIFFS –

FROM THERE YOU WILL FLY US TO A POOL WHERE
THE WATER IS BRIGHT BLUE —

Do you know this place?"

The three heads bowed "Yes".

"YOU WILL LAND ON THE WATER THERE —

YOU WILL TAKE US TO THE SHORE —

YOU WILL THEN RECEIVE MORE INSTRUCTIONS —

By tonight you will be back here. Thank you for your
cooperation.

ACTION NOW — "

Lundy watched the swans pick up a squirrel each, as
they had done the day before, lift it round onto their backs
and, shortly afterwards wade out into the calm water.

Marguerite's farewells blended with her own as, one
behind the other, the swans ran across the water, their feet
making less and less commotion as the great white wings
swept the air away below them. Then there was no sound
but the W-wow, W-wow, of the wing-beats. Two of the
swans dropped back slightly to take advantage of the easier
flying in the turbulence created by the leader's flight, and
the V formation climbed higher and disappeared into the
distance.

Lundy swam leisurely down the lagoon towards
Portland Harbour, the open sea and reunion with her
family.

Chapter 23

The wings of the three swans beat steadily. The formation had reached the height chosen by the leader and they flew above the beach until they passed over the Ferry-bridge, then turned slightly to fly across Portland Harbour.

At first Marguerite had clung tightly to the swan's back, her head buried in the feathers. As she gained confidence, she lifted her head and, moving one paw-hold at a time, edged forward until she could look down past the side of the bird's neck. Far below she could see the curve of the pebble beach reaching out to the great rock of Portland, the waves seeming to wriggle along the shore like a grass snake swimming after frogs. How different it all looked from up here compared with the roaring and crashing they had suffered the day before.

The wings beat rhythmically, W-wow, W-wow, W-wow.

Below her the humans' travelling boxes were crossing the bridge and then the swans were over the grey ships at anchor in the harbour. Flying seemed so effortless compared with the strain Lundy had suffered carrying them the day before.

Was that really only the day before?

She recognised the harbour breakwaters and, raising her head, she could see the white cliffs on the far side of Weymouth Bay. The great wings rose and fell, rose and fell, the air hissing through the pinion feathers, W-wow, W-wow, W-wow.

She turned to look at Chip and Sycamore. They grinned at her past their swans' heads.

With the distinctive shape of Lulworth Cove below them, she felt the change of direction that would take them across the land to the Blue Pool. Her instructions were being followed exactly and it would not be long before she was with Wood Anemone, learning the secret of the mushrooms of the moon. It would be good to see her friend again.

Rowan and Bluebell were aiming the Woodstock at the top of the bank across the pool from the Eyeland. Bluebell had caught a glimpse of grey fur and had pointed out the position to her father. He had calculated that a **Ƃ** would be required to curl whiskers and incapacitate any Grey at that distance. He rehearsed the movement and stood alert, the Woodstock sighted on the top of the bank, Bluebell standing behind him.

"Now," she shouted as a grey head showed, and Rowan scratched a **Ƃ** on the bare wood. The head dropped back behind the bank at the very moment that the shape of three flying swans appeared over the horizon in the same direction.

The invisible, spiralling force, though weak at that extreme range, seriously affected the birds. Their wing beats faltered, they lost formation and, fluttering and flapping out of control, they tumbled through the air then, seeming to recover somewhat, spread their wings and turned to make a long glide towards the open water of the pool.

Marguerite was enjoying the flight when the Woodstock's power-wave stuck. Reacting as quickly as she would when a gust of wind struck a branch on which she was sitting, she grasped the feathers tightly and hung on as the swans fell out of the sky. She fought to dominate their thoughts.

"SWANS —

FLY —

FLY —

ACTION NOW —

FLY —

ACTION NOW —

SPREAD YOUR WINGS —

HOLD THEM FIRM —

MAKE FOR THAT WATER BELOW —

ACTION NOW —

ACTION NOW —

LAND ON THE WATER —

ACTION NOW — "

The swans lowered their webbed feet, twisted their wings to resist the air and slid across the surface of the pool, then stopped, shaking their heads and hissing angrily.

"SWANS —

YOU ARE SAFE NOW —

RELAX —

ACTION NOW — "

In the silence that followed, the swans paddled gently

along the pool, dipping their heads under the water as if to clear their brains, then lifting them and shaking off droplets of water.

"What happened?" Chip called across to Marguerite. "My whiskers are hurting."

"So are mine," she said. "I feel like someone has used a Woodstock on me."

"Marguerite, Marguerite."

Marguerite was sure that she could hear her brother's voice calling her – but it was just not possible. Whatever force had brought the swans down out of the sky had clearly addled her brain.

"Marguerite. We're here. Here on the Eyeland."

"SWANS –

TAKE US TO THE ISLAND –

THAT WAY –

ACTION NOW – "

The great white birds, each with a squirrel sitting upright on its back, paddled along the pool, past the pink and white water lilies and waddled ashore onto the island near the pool's end. As they did so, Chip, clutching the golden coin, lost his balance and the coin fell into the orangy-brown water near the Eyeland shore.

"Marguerite!"

"Rowan! Meadowsweet! Bluebell!"

Marguerite had an overwhelming feeling that this had all happened before, then realised that it had, in that summer when they had journeyed from the coast to win back the Blue Pool Demesne from the Silver Tide.

Now though, she also recognised the feeling of being in a battle-zone. She brushed whiskers briefly with her brother and his life-mate and her handsome young niece, saw the Woodstock on the ground at Rowan's side then said, "What's going on here?"

"We are surrounded by Greys, led by one of the Three Lords. There has been a change of leader at Woburn and we were trying to escape to join you on Ourland. Were you really *flying* on these swans?"

"Yes. I'll explain later. How many Greys are there?"

"Lots," said Rowan, and Marguerite regretted never having found the time to teach her brother to count above eight.

"Lots, or Lots and Lots?"

"Lots and Lots!" Rowan replied and Marguerite noted the tiredness in his voice.

He led her up the mound to the top of the Eyeland, Bluebell and Meadowsweet dragging the Woodstock between them. A tree trunk lay across the water from the Mainland, forming a bridge. It had not been there when she had last seen the Eyeland.

Clustered near the bridge were the two ex-zervantz and their daughters, all looking bright-eyed if rather tired and thin.

Most surprising of all, there was a Grey on that side of the bridge, amongst the Reds.

"Wood Anemone-Friend, Spindle-Friend," she called and they turned to look up at her.

"Marguerite-Ma'am," said Wood Anemone.

"Marguerite-Friend, please."

"Marguerite-Friend. Where have you come from? Did you drop out of the sky?"

"Something like that. Look out behind you!" she shouted.

A phalanx of grey bodies was moving purposefully down towards the far end of the bridge.

"Heads down," shouted Meadowsweet to the squirrels below, and as they turned their backs on her, she swung the Woodstock towards the Greys and scratched a 3 on the bare wood.

Some of the attackers turned and scrambled back up and over the bank while others rolled down onto the level ground at the far end of the bridge, pawing at their whiskers, before wriggling back up the slope and out of sight. The Reds watched them go.

Rowan said, "We get a charge like that several times a day – they're not giving up easily. I don't know where they're all coming from. The trouble is we don't know how much power is left in the Woodstock – there can't be much now."

Marguerite glanced at the Grey, it seemed foolish to be giving away their weakness in front of one of the enemy.

Rowan saw her look. "Don't worry about Hickory, he's a Sun-squirrel. He's with us."

Marguerite looked across the water. There were no Greys in sight now and she went down to the bridge-end with Chip and Sycamore to make the formal introductions and greetings. She brushed whiskers with them all, even Hickory. Though she remembered him as one of the enemy leaders at the Battle of the Agglestone, he was obviously trusted and respected here.

Chapter 24

Rowan's and Marguerite's groups exchanged news while watching the banks for signs of another attack. Chip was at the water's edge peering down at the place where they had come ashore but was unable to see anything as the swans' feet had stirred up the clay making the water a milky white. The swans themselves were now feeding quietly in the water, reaching down with their long necks and searching the pool bottom for tasty morsels.

Marguerite's mind was already formulating an escape plan. She stood up and looked along the pool.

"SWANS —"

The swans raised their heads.

"CAN YOU FLY WITH TWO SQUIRRELS EACH?"

The swans raised their heads in unison.

"CAN YOU FLY WITH THREE SQUIRRELS EACH?"

The swans appeared to consult each other, then shook their heads violently.

"THANK YOU — STAY CLOSE."

She counted their combined party and did some calculations, wishing that she had Chip's Bark-rush to help. She called Chip over and explained the problem. He counted on his claws.

"With three swans, six squirrels can go at a time, so if six go on the first flight and one squirrel comes back, we then have five, and with the one who came back, that'll make up six for the second flight – two for each swan. No problem."

It was decided that Marguerite was to take the other five females on the first flight and return for the five males on the second.

Lord Malachite had seen the swans land on the water and had overcome his fear of the Woodstock sufficiently to peep from behind his tree.

He was amazed to see the three swans wade ashore, each pick up a squirrel and lift it onto its back, then do the same with a second squirrel. He was even more amazed when the swans waded into the water, swam out a little way, flapped their wings and ran along the surface before taking off heavily and flying away to the north-east. He was furious; half his enemy had escaped!

Marguerite guided the swans to land on the lagoon at Ourland in a place away from where they might be seen by humans. The squirrels hurried away, led by Wood Anemone who was the only one to have lived on that island before. Marguerite instructed the swans to return to Rowan's Pool.

"SWANS –

ONE SWAN PICK ME UP –

THREE SWANS FLY BACK TO WHERE YOU HAVE
COME FROM —

ACTION NOW — "

The swans ran across the water and took off, Marguerite
on the back of the leading swan. This is getting to be almost
a routine, she was thinking. What a wonderful way of
travelling this flying business is.

She turned her head to watch the unladen swans behind
her. There was only one other there! Away to her left, and
now well on its way towards the swannery at Abbotsbury,
was the other swan.

"THIRD SWAN —

REJOIN THE OTHERS —

ACTION NOW —

REJOIN THE OTHERS —

ACTION NOW — "

Marguerite projected her thoughts in the direction of the
single swan, now just a speck in the distance but there was
no sign that they were being received.

"TWO SWANS —

STAY TOGETHER —

FLY DOWN TO THE POOL BELOW —

ACTION NOW — "

Rowan seeing only two swans return, rushed down to the
water's edge, fearing the worst.

"Are the females all right? Meadowsweet, Bluebell . . ."

Marguerite reassured him, explained what had happened, then turned —

"TWO SWANS —

Chip was counting on his claws again.

"There are six of us and two swans, which can each carry two squirrels. So four can go but one must come back, so there must be two flights, with only three squirrels on the last flight."

Rowan tried to insist that *he* stay for the final flight but it was eventually settled by drawing twigs. Spindle and Hickory drew the short ones. They would stay, with the Woodstock to protect them.

Rowan and Marguerite were lifted onto one swan and Sycamore and Chip onto the other. Chip had hoped that he could recover his golden coin and had searched for it surreptitiously, while waiting for the swans to return, but without success.

"TWO SWANS — "

Malachite watched the birds fly off. He was not good at counting but knew there could only be two squirrels left on the island – three at the most. If they got away, so would his chance of ever becoming the Great Lord Silver. He would be the laughing stock of New America. He ordered one more charge . . .

Spindle and Hickory were sitting on the highest point of the Eyeland, Spindle keeping the Woodstock sighted on the bridge and Hickory watching the opposite bank.

When the grey attackers poured down towards the bridge, Spindle waited until the first were actually on the fallen trunk before scratching a 3 after the X on the Woodstock.

The force spiralled out and several Greys fell into the water. Spindle scratched another 3 and the mass hesitated, then turned and scrambled awkwardly up the bank. Spindle tried a 4 as they went over the top but there was no noticeable effect on the enemy and no familiar tingle in his own whiskers. The Woodstock'z power huz all gone, he thought.

The last of the wet Greys had hauled themselves ashore and climbed out of sight when a streak of blue and gold flashed past Spindle's head. A compact little bird with a long straight beak perched on the stump of a broken branch projecting from the fallen tree and peered down into the water below.

"Turn thiz way, very zlowly," Spindle said.

Hickory took one look along the opposite shoreline and did as Spindle had instructed. He saw the brilliantly coloured bird.

"What is it?" he asked in a whisper.

"Him'z a kingzfizher bird. Yew hardly ever zeez wun of them. Uz'z lucky today."

Hickory smiled to himself. He had grown fond of the ex-zervant, with his patient, helpful manner, always ready to accept whatever Life threw at him. Here were the two of them, on a tiny island, outnumbered many times over by squirrels with a totally different outlook, who were determined to kill them both, and he was saying they were lucky to see a bird!

Now he was even quoting one of their Kernels:

Zquirrelz do not live
By nutz alone. Take time off
To zeek out beauty.

Hickory looked at the bird again. The blue plumage of its back and tail was brighter than the sky above, brighter even than the reflected blue of the water below. The feathers on its underside glowed more red than gold, more gold than chestnuts. He did not even know a name for that colour.

The bird tilted off the broken branch and dived into the water, to rise a moment later with a dragonfly larva in its beak which it smashed against the tree and swallowed head first.

With a flicker of its wings it sped along the pool, a gold and blue streak above the pink and white of the lilies.

"My Wood Anemone do call kingzfizherz the birdz of happinezz," Spindle said.

Hickory's tail arched into a "question", sensed by Spindle though he was still watching the bridge.

"Her zayz that it iz no good expecting to be happy *all* the time, Life'z not like that. Now and then yew will get a glimpze of happinezz – like now and then yew will zee a kingzfizher bird. Enjoy it when yew can, her zayz."

"Kingsfishers or happiness?" Hickory asked.

"Both, yew zilly zquirrel," Spindle said, amusement and affection in his voice.

"Uz *iz* lucky then, izn't uz, Zpindle-Friend," said Hickory imitating the Ourland accent as the Greys again poured down the bank for another attack.

Hickory was alongside Spindle. "Use the Woodstock,

use the Woodstock," he shouted as the Greys streamed across the tree trunk.

"Him'z Zun-gone," said Spindle kicking the twisted stick down the bank and into the water as he leapt for a tree. Hickory leapt for another, ran up it and across a branch into Spindle's tree.

"Up to the top," he said. "Follow me."

Greys were climbing all three trees, trying to get above the two fugitives but the tree Spindle had chosen was the tallest and the two stopped just below the highest cluster of needles and turned to face downwards, one squirrel on each side of the slender trunk. The top swayed with the movements of the many Greys climbing towards them.

Lord Malachite, having learned that the Totem Stick was dead, had come out of hiding and was standing on the bridge urging others on.

"Prime territories for those who kill," he shouted. "Kill the traitor. Kill the Brown Job. Kill, kill, kill!"

"This is it, Spindle-Friend," said Hickory, twisting his tail around the trunk where it met Spindle's. The tails hooked together as a ring of savage Greys climbed ever nearer. The Red and the Grey, their tails tightly intertwined in a symbolic twist of friendship, hung by their back feet and slashed desperately at the attackers.

Grey after grey fell back, faces torn and bleeding from the claws and teeth of the squirrels above them until Malachite called a halt and the attackers withdrew down the trunk to gather round the old Lord as he gave them new instructions.

Hickory and Spindle, tails still linked, strained unsuccessfully to hear what was being said.

Soon the change of plan became apparent. Four Greys climbed the tree together, stopped just out of reach of the bloodstained claws above them and started to gnaw simultaneously through the thin trunk. Chunks of bark and splinters of wood fell among the massed Greys waiting on the Eyeland below. The scent of fresh resin drifted up to Spindle and Hickory.

"Uz do love that zmell," said Spindle.

"Take a good sniff then," replied Hickory. "It'll probably be our last. The Sun be with you."

"And with yew," said Spindle as the tree's top lurched sideways and fell into the grey mass below.

Marguerite flew back from Ourland to Rowan's Pool for the final pick-up, taking care that her instructions to the swans could not be misunderstood. As they glided in and landed on the water she knew that something terrible had happened. The swans paddled towards the Eyeland which seemed silent and deserted. Then she saw the two bodies, one red and one grey, hanging from the highest tree, their necks jammed into forks, their tails swinging in the evening breeze. High in a tree on the deserted bank of the Mainland she glimpsed a grey movement. It was another tail, that of Sitka.

Floating torpidly in the water near her was the abandoned Woodstock. Sun forbid that the Greys learn the secret of its power, she thought, and was about to direct her swan towards it, when the twisted stick, as if it was now too tired to float, tilted slowly into an upright position then sank in the deepest part of the pool. It seemed to the exhausted squirrel as if it was being drawn down by an invisible, underwater paw. Sunlight glinted on the tiny ripples created as it disappeared.

"SWANS – " she said wearily.

"SWANS –

FLY ME BACK TO THE BIG ISLAND –

ACTION NOW – "

The swans turned and once more ran down the surface of the pool, taking off and circling to gain height. Marguerite, looking down past her swan's neck, saw the mass of Greys on the ground below, heading towards the Blue Pool. Even from high above, a sense of jubilation was apparent in their movement and her anger rose.

"SWANS –

FLY LOW OVER THOSE GREY CREATURES –

ACTION NOW –

FLY STRAIGHT . . . STEADY . . .

EMPTY YOUR BOWELS –

ACTION . . . ACTION . . . ACTION . . . NOW!

FLY ME TO THE BIG ISLAND –

ACTION NOW – "

Chapter 25

Lord Malachite looked up when he heard the W-wow, W-wow, W-wow of the swans' wings overhead and watched the two white birds circle round in a wide arc, then fly in straight towards him. He was staring at the leading bird, trying to see if there was one of those hated natives clinging to its back, when a shower of stinking green dung splattered him from head to foot.

"Lord Malachite – Lord Malashite – more likely," a voice called from behind him, and he turned furiously but was unable to see which of the grinning squirrels had spoken.

"Silence!" he shouted, trying to wipe the slime from his face. "Back to your duties, all of you."

He stayed behind as the other Greys passed him, wrinkling their noses pointedly. Then he sought out one of the small pools that had formed in the remains of the many worked-out clay-pits scattered over the Great Heath. He found a pool with a fallen post reaching out into the shallow water and went along it to the end, stopped and splashed himself, washing the swan-dung from his fur and tail. When he had finished, he peered at his reflection in the water. Was that him? That old, fat squirrel staring back at him.

He sat up and looked around. The pond surface was still, except for tiny disturbances where whirly-gig beetles swam in frantic circles. Round his head damsel-flies with blue or brown bodies flitted. A pigeon coo-ed its familiar call from a pine and he suddenly felt homesick for the Tanglewood.

But no. He braced himself; there were troops dependent on him at the New Massachusetts Base, his place was there with them. He hurried off in that direction.

When he arrived, the Greys were milling about aimlessly. He climbed onto a stump and called for order. No squirrel heeded him. He called again.

"Shut it, Malashite," a Grey called. "We're all leaving. Something about this place stinks!"

The speaker flicked his tail insolently and headed off westwards, followed immediately by the others.

Lord Malachite sat on the stump until they were all gone, then hopped off in the direction of the Tanglewood, curiously light-hearted.

Burdock, the Ourland News-squirrel, was planning a field day. Even before dusk fell, she had extracted all the details of the Eyeland rescue from her mother and was preparing to spread the news across the island at first light.

TEACHING SQUIRRELS SNATCHED FROM CERTAIN DEATH

In a rescue unique in the history of squirreldom, Marguerite saves her brother and others from the raging hordes of Greys and returns with them high on a bird's back . . .

Marguerite woke to the sound of her daughter's voice and listened sadly to young Burdock telling a dramatised account of the events of the last few days, then she turned away to seek out Wood Anemone and comfort her for the loss of her life-mate, Spindle. She would probably be building a new drey in the same tree where she had had her home when she was a zervant on the island years before.

As Marguerite hopped along, Burdock's words repeated themselves in her head – high on a bird's back – high on a bird's back. The words seemed familiar, but she was sure that she could not have heard them before. No one had ever been *high on a bird's back* or even considered the possibility. She must be wrong, yet the words would not go away.

She was concentrating so hard that she nearly ran into a party of humans who had just arrived on the island by boat, hoping to see the famous red squirrels. Marguerite fled up the nearest tree, a mature birch, to their "Oo's" and "Ah's" and hid behind the trunk, catching her breath. Her claws bit deep into the silvery-white bark as she clung there. Birch-bark.

I honour birch-bark, she said to herself. *High on a bird's back – that* was the pattern of words.

Forgetting the humans, she tried Old Wally's prophecy again.

> *High on a bird's back*
> *The Island Screen. Flies stinging –*
> *The piece of the sun.*

Or it could be:

> *High on a bird's back*
> *The island's Queen. Flies stinging . . .*

If *Queen* was right then it could be:

> *High on a bird's back*
> *The island's Queen flies . . .*

But then it would be:

> *. . . Stinging . . .*
> *The piece of the sun.*

Not a lot of sense in that, although the first part felt right. Forget it; there aren't any Queens on the island now anyway, though Wally couldn't have known that when he composed his prophecy. So ran Marguerite's thoughts as the humans walked on and she resumed her search for Wood Anemone.

She found her with her twins, building a good sized drey in a pine tree, helped by Chip. She greeted them and Wood Anemone paused in her work to talk. Marguerite said how sorry she was that Spindle had been killed by the Greys, but Wood Anemone seemed to have accepted the fact easily.

"Him would have been pleezed to go like that. Him liked to help otherz, it wuz hiz whole life really. Him'z left uz two good daughterz."

She indicated the twins who were with Chip collecting moss for lining the drey. They too did not seem unhappy.

Wood Anemone continued, "Uz only regret iz that hiz body iz hanging from a tree, inztead of being cozy under the ground nourizhing won, like iz proper. But there uz iz . . ."

Chip watched until he saw the conversation cease, then hopped over.

"Quite an adventure we had . . ." then stopped, his head on one side.

"Yes," Marguerite replied, "if only we hadn't lost Spindle and Hickory, it would all have been wonderful. The flying was most exciting."

Marguerite turned to Wood Anemone, "Did you ever hear Old Wally's prophecy that starts *I honour birch-bark*?" she asked.

"Oh yez."

> *Hie honour birch-bark,*
> *The i'land'z Queen fliez, bringing*
> *The pieze of the zun.'*

"Did you say *bringing*, or *stinging*?" Marguerite asked.

"Zum zay ztinging but uz iz zure it uzed to be bringing."

"It didn't start *High on a bird's back* did it?" Marguerite asked.

"It might have done, wonze. Theze thingz changez over time, Marguerite-Friend."

> *High on a bird's back*
> *The Island's Queen flies, bringing*
> *The piece of the sun.*

"That would make some kind of sense if we knew who *the Queen* was, and what is meant by a piece of the sun," Marguerite said.

Chip was sure that *he* knew. He had heard a little about queens from Just Poplar and how beautiful they had been. The Queen in that prophecy must be his beloved

Marguerite, and the piece of the sun was that golden disc that he had so stupidly dropped in the water at Rowan's Pool. But he said nothing. He must find a way to get the gold and fulfil the prophecy. Then he would ask his Queen to be his life-mate.

"If I could get over the water I'd go back and bury Spindle," he said unexpectedly.

"Zo would uz," said Rosebay who had just joined them.

"Uz would too," said Willowherb.

As they were saying this, Sumac, on the Eyeland, was engaged in just this melancholy task.

The previous day, following the trail from the Blue Pool towards Rowan's Pool, he had heard the sounds of a group of excited Greys coming towards him and had hidden to hear what they had to say. ". . . totem stick was nasty . . . lots of curled whiskers . . . some very sick still . . . serve the Reds right . . . good native is a dead one . . . hanging there . . . covered in it he was, head to tail . . . silly old fool . . ."

Sumac heard enough to know that he was too late to be of any help. When the posse had passed, he had come out of hiding and run after them.

"Sorry to have missed the action. Only just arrived. What happened?" he asked breathlessly.

When he had heard the full story, including Malachite's humiliation, he slipped away and followed the well-beaten trail to the Eyeland Pool. It was all just as he had been told, the body of his friend Spindle was hanging from one of the island trees alongside that of Hickory, while Sitka's corpse dangled grotesquely from a tree above his own head.

Sumac climbed and dislodged Sitka's body, which fell to

the ground amid a buzzing of disturbed flies. He dragged it across the tree-trunk bridge onto the island and buried it at the foot of one of the trees, then did the same with the other two, one beneath each tree.

Judging by the accounts of the rabble he had just met, these were three fellow Sun-squirrels, two of them Silvers, who had died defending their beliefs even though it meant being branded as traitors by their fellows.

Moved by a feeling he had never before experienced, he gnawed away a small area of the pine-bark just above the ground and cut a fish symbol into the trunk of each tree.

The setting Sun lit up the bright patches of exposed wood and a tiny tear of resin oozed from the bitten bark above Spindle's grave. Sumac turned, crossed the bridge and headed back over the Great Heath towards the bulk of Screech Hill. Tumbleweed would be wondering why he had been away so long.

Chapter 26

Bluebell approached her aunt shyly. She had learned to respect Marguerite on the journey the previous year which had culminated in the battle of the Agglestone. Since Marguerite had flown in on the swan's back to rescue them, her aunt had been elevated to an almost Sun-like status in her eyes.

Marguerite looked at her niece, Rowan's daughter, waiting for her to speak, and remembering the first Bluebell who had given her life to warn the Reds of an impending attack by the Greys of the Silver Tide.

"Yes, my dear?" she said to break the ice.

"I wanted to thank you for coming and saving us, well – most of us, anyway. Did my father or mother tell you about Hickory and me?"

Marguerite shook her head.

"Well, he was a Sun-squirrel like us, even if he was a Silver, and I loved him. I can't bear to think of him hanging in a tree to be eaten by maggots. Is there any way we can go back and bury him?" she asked.

Marguerite felt a surge of love towards her kin-squirrel. Bluebell was ready to risk her own life just to bury a dead

Grey who she had cared for. This was the second time in two days that squirrels had wanted to return to the Mainland that she had thought they had left for ever.

"Leave it with me, my dear, I'll think about it and see if we can do anything."

She went to look for Chip but found her son, Oak, first.

"Is it true what Burdock is saying about you and the swans?" he asked.

"Mostly, but Burdock does like to add bits here and there to make a more dramatic story. She says more squirrels listen to her if she does that."

"What's it like flying? Nothing exciting seems to happen here on Ourland."

Marguerite outlined her adventures; the balloon flight, crossing the sea on a broken oar held by a dolphin, the rescue of Finisterre and the flight home on the swan's back, not forgetting the lifting of Rowan's party from the Eyeland.

"Wow! All that in two days. Nothing ever happens here, I wish I could go to the Mainland."

Sycamore joined them.

"Oak-Friend," he said, all his previous sullenness gone. "You should have been with us – did we have some fun?"

"I wish I had been," Oak replied.

"Marguerite."

She turned to see Rowan, with Meadowsweet beside him.

Meadowsweet spoke first. "Our Bluebell says that you are going to get her back to the Eyeland to bury Hickory. Is this true?"

"She asked me if it was possible and I said I would think about it. Rosebay and Willowherb want to go back as well; even Chip says he would. Now I've got Sycamore getting Oak wanting to go. I'd have thought that they would want to stay here, where it's peaceful."

"They're all young," said Rowan. "They need adventure, something to make their blood flow, give them a tingle."

"I'd have thought, except perhaps for Oak, they would have had enough. I have."

"Yes, but you're older. All youngsters need adventures and challenges; they get bored and troublesome otherwise."

"Should we let them go back, if that's what they want?"

"If it was me, you'd have a job to stop me," said Rowan. "If they do go back to bury Spindle, Hickory and Sitka, I'd be pleased. I don't like the idea of them all hanging there. And the youngsters might be able to find out what the Greys are up to."

"But how? Remember Ourland here is an island in the sea. There's no tree-trunk making a bridge from here to the Mainland."

"That never seems to bother you, Marguerite, you've crossed four times, a different way each time. You'll think of something. When you do, I think we should encourage them."

"But it could be dangerous."

"True, but life always has been dangerous for squirrels, that's what keeps us alert – and alive. You'll think of something. *If you think you can . . .*"

*

Either by coincidence or Sun-plan, the dolphins swam in on the evening tide and thought-called to Marguerite as she sat looking up at the giant squirrel that Larch and his family had carved. Some idle tail-wag of a youngster had bitten the tufted ears off, and cut circles round its eyes, so that it appeared to be wearing those glass things that some humans hooked over their ears.

"Marguerite-Friend," Lundy called. "We have come so that Finisterre can thank you for your help. He is much better and we have all recovered from our ordeal. It seems much more than three days ago. How are you? The swans evidently brought you back safely."

Marguerite projected her thoughts and told of the incidents on the flight and the loss of the three Sun-squirrels.

"If we can ever help you, let us know. We owe Finisterre's life to you and your friends."

"We were glad to be able to repay you for all you have done for us in the past," Marguerite said, "but there *is* a little help you could give – if you are not too busy now."

"Our patrol is being swum by others until Finisterre is fully recovered. How can we help?"

"There are squirrels, five altogether, who want to go back to the Mainland to finish off some business there and find what the Greys are up to now. Could you take them?"

"Glad to. When do they want to go?"

"They could be ready at first light."

"Do they want a boat, or can we carry them on sticks in our mouths, that would be easiest. It's not far this time."

"Sticks would be fine."

They discussed the finer details and then Malin asked how the five would return.

"I hadn't thought of that," Marguerite admitted, "everything is happening so fast."

"It's the New Moon in two weeks time. We'll pick up your scouting patrol from the same beach as we drop them at, on New-Moon night. If they're not there we'll come back each New Moon until they come. Rely on us. Until the morning then."

The three dark bodies swam out into the tideway and disappeared under the water.

There was only an hour of daylight left. Marguerite ran off to find Burdock.

"Can you get a message to Sycamore, Bluebell, Rosebay and Willowherb tonight?" she asked breathlessly.

"I'm a News-squirrel, not a Post-squirrel, but yes, I'm sure I can, Marguerite-Ma. What's the message?"

"The dolphins will pick up five squirrels at Pottery Point at first light tomorrow to take them to the Mainland to bury Spindle and the two Greys and to find out what the other Greys are up to."

"You only gave me four names; who's the other?"

"Chip. *I'll* tell him."

"Oak – your son – wanted to go!"

Marguerite thought quickly, one extra squirrel would not make the patrol too large, and Oak needed the experience. "If you can find him, tell him to be ready as well. And . . ."

Burdock stood expectantly.

"A True Message this time. No elaboration . . ."

"Marguerite-Ma – as if I would!"

It was one of those late-summer mornings when autumn

lets you know it is not far away. A certain chill was in the air, and a smell of ripeness, with just a hint of decay, drifted through the woodland to tickle the nostrils of early risers.

At Pottery Point it seemed that the whole squirrel population of Ourland was there to see the patrol leave. The dolphins were just off-shore, each holding a length of driftwood sideways in their mouths. They swam in small circles picking up the sense of squirrelation that was coming from the massed ranks on the beach.

The six squirrel scouts were on the beach, watched by envious youngsters, most of whom would have given their whiskers, if not their tails, to have been able to join the patrol. Marguerite was clearly in charge, pairing the squirrels and allocating each pair to a dolphin.

"Oak, you go with Bluebell, swim out to Malin – that's the biggest dolphin. Chip, you and Sycamore swim out to Lundy; and Rosebay, you go with Willowherb and climb onto Finisterre's stick. You can all swim, can't you? The water's quite warm and you will dry off quickly when you're ashore. Good luck!"

The remaining squirrels watched the scouting party disappear into the early haze as the dolphins swam up the channel. Just Poplar and Clover came to Marguerite's side.

"Can we have a word with yew when the otherz have left?" Just Poplar said quietly.

Chapter 27

"Marguerite," Just Poplar said when only the three of them were left on the beach. "Who iz the zelected Leader of Ourland?"

Marguerite immediately realised the import of the question and felt a rush of concern and regret. She had organised all of this activity without any reference to the Leader, the Tagger or any of the other senior squirrels.

"Oh, Poplar, I know what you are going to say and I am sorry. I just got swept along. All of those young squirrels wanted to go and bury Spindle and when the dolphins offered to take them . . ."

Her voice trailed away. She realised that she was speaking her defence and may have to do so before the full Council if Clover accused her of acting incorrectly. Having been Tagger herself, she knew that she had done just that.

Clover saw the contrite look on her friend's face and reached out a paw.

"It's all right, Marguerite-Friend, we'll call it 'acting on your own initiative'."

Initiative
Is a name for successful
Disobedience.

"Let's hope that the patrol are able to carry out their mission and return safely. They're all fairly young."

"I thinkz it will be good for them," said Just Poplar. "Uz'd have liked to go zcouting on the Mainland when uz wuz young. Too old now though. Being Leader iz tiring enough with all theze troublezome youngzterz. Do yew know what zome did yezterday? . . ."

The dolphins swam steadily westwards, keeping to the deeper waters. Malin explained to Chip, who could follow Dolphin-think, that this way would avoid the mudflats and the boggy harbour shores and they would land at Tallships Point beyond the Long Island.

The squirrels' fur was dry again by the time they reached Tallships. The dolphins cruised along, watching the shore and looking for the best place to land the scouts. There was a Man-drey on the point and, to the south of this, two oak trees grew right on the water's edge, with their roots washed out from under them by the sea so that they appeared to stand on many legs.

"Those are a good landmark," Malin indicated to Chip. "This is where we'll pick you up again at dawn after the night of the New Moon." They turned in towards the beach as Chip thanked them.

Rosebay helped her sister Willowherb, who she knew was a poor swimmer and frightened of water. Wet through once again, the squirrels climbed the low gravelly cliff and sat in the heather watching the dolphins swim down-channel.

"We're on our own now," said Oak the Wary, "the sooner we can get to those trees, the better."

On Ourland Marguerite, Poplar and Clover climbed to the top of the bank and found Rowan and Meadowsweet waiting there.

"We've not really been introduced," Rowan said to Poplar. "I am Rowan the Bold and this is Meadowsweet Rowan's-love. Our daughter, Bluebell, is one of those who has just gone with the dolphins."

"Thiz iz Clover," Poplar said, "but yew will remember her from when yew were all at the Blue Pool, her iz now the Tagger of Ourland, and uz'z Juzt Poplar, the Leader. Uz iz zorry that uz haven't welcomed yew before. Zo much zeemz to be happening all at wonze! Yew'r zizter iz highly thought of here."

Hearing this, Marguerite smiled and her tail rose noticeably.

"Uz expectz that yew will want to rezd after all yew have been through," Poplar continued.

Rowan replied, "I – we are fine. We were hoping to find something to occupy us. We are both experienced teachers and enjoy that. Can you use us in any way?"

"There iz a lot of thingz not right here at prezent. Perhapz yew, zeeing it with new eyeze, zo to zpeak, can zee what needz to be done and teach uz what to do."

Sitting in the areas flattened by the tents of the departed boy scouts, the five squirrels held an impromptu meeting in the grass behind Pottery Point to analyse the problems that were afflicting the squirrel population of the island.

Most seemed to have grown out of boredom. With an abundance of food and no predators, there was nothing to keep the youngsters on their claws.

"That party that went to the Mainland this morning—" Clover said, "if we could organise such scouting patrols regularly, they would provide adventure for the youngsters."

"Would your dolphins help us again?" she asked Marguerite.

"They're not really *my* dolphins, but yes, I think they would."

Meadowsweet said, "All the scouts would need to be taught how to look after themselves and survive in hostile country, *that* could be a job for Rowan and me. We know quite a bit about the Greys as well as about squirrelship and survival."

"We must put these ideas to the Council," said Clover.

"What Council?" said Poplar. "It'z zuppozed to include all the zquirrelz but hardly any com'z nowadayz."

"I don't think you can have a Council with all the squirrels, like we used to at the Blue Pool," said Rowan. "You probably need to have a Council of just a few senior ones and make each of those a guardian of different things."

"Zum zquirrel would have to be in charge," said Poplar. "A zort of King like uz father wuz."

"The problem then, was that *he* made all the decisions, no other squirrel's views mattered," Marguerite reminded him.

"Uz knowz that. That'z why uz abolished it all. Uz wuz King vor a few minutez, remember. That kind of power corruptz. Yew'd make a good Queen, Marguerite-Friend, it would be hard to corrupt yew."

"Me? I'd never be a Queen!"

The scouting party had paused in a tree overlooking some wide fields. So far it had been easy. Humans had made a wooden walk-way through the marshier places and the squirrels had scurried along that, then taken to the trees, mostly oak and birch, all close enough together for them to run and leap from one to the next.

In a state of high exhilaration, they eventually slowed down and halted to regain their breath. A noise like a wasp immediately drew their attention towards a human, tiny in the distance, bent down at the foot of a tree and holding something red. The wasp-sound changed slightly, held steady for a minute, then the human stood up and stepped hurriedly back. The squirrels watched in horror as the distant tree lurched over and fell to the ground. The swish of its leaves and the crunch as the trunk hit the earth reached the squirrels a second later.

Oak, shocked, said, "We must move on, this is a dangerous place."

Chapter 28

Marguerite was with her old friend on a branch outside Wood Anemone's new drey, talking of the time when they had been forced to flee from Ourland together. She wanted to know about the moon mushrooms but felt that it was better to raise the subject obliquely and not rush straight on to it.

"You were called Woodlouse then," she said.

"Zo uz wuz! It do zeem a long time ago."

"It *was* a long time ago," said Marguerite, "and your Spindle was called Spider in those days."

"The Royalz alwayz called zervantz after creepy-crawliez, them did it to keep uz in uz placez, them zaid."

Mention of Spindle made both squirrels think of his body hanging from the Eyeland tree and each wondered how the scouts were progressing with their mission. Five days had passed since Wood Anemone had said farewell to her twin daughters. She had since realised that if they did not come back from what could be a hazardous journey, her family line would end.

"Uz wizhez that uz had only let won go with yew'r dolphinz," she said to Marguerite.

"You know that Rosebay and Willowberb are always together. Sun-knows what will happen when one chooses a mate. It'll be 'take me, take my sister'."

"Marguerite!" said Wood Anemone, shocked at the suggestion. "That'z the zort of thing the Royalz did."

"Poplar suggested that I should be Queen," Marguerite confided to her friend.

"Yew zhould be; yew would make a good Queen," replied Wood Anemone bluntly. "Yew iz vull of good ideaz and all the zquirrelz lovez and rezpectz yew."

"Some call me Miss Hoity-Toity," Marguerite said ruefully.

"If uz hearz any doing that, uz'll pull their tailz," said Wood Anemone. "Yew ignore them. Yew'll make uz a good Queen."

"I'm not going to be Queen. It was only something that Poplar said."

The two sat in comfortable silence enjoying the early September sunshine and watching the people who passed underneath. The human youngsters seemed to have suddenly stopped coming to the island. Only a few days before they had been there in great numbers, now the humans they saw were mostly older and in pairs, or were those men who wore the "Acorn" badge on their green coverings.

"How many squirrels were on the island before we came?" Marguerite asked.

"Yew knowz uz can't count like yew do'z, but there were a 'lot' of Royalz and 'lotz' of zervantz."

"Did there ever get to be too many?"

"Oh no. Uz zaw to that," said Wood Anemone enigmatically.

"How do you mean?" Marguerite asked.

"Uz'z zorry, Marguerite-Friend, uz can't zay."

"Come on, of course you can. We're friends. Whatever it is, you can tell me."

"Uz can't. Uz zwore to keep the zecret. Uz can only talk about it with a King of a Queen, or with their matez. Uz zwore not to tell otherz."

"Tell others what?"

"How to stop zquirrelz breeding too vazd. With the King and the Kingz-mate Zun-gone, only *uz* knowz. Only Woodlouze knowz."

"The Kings-mate was saying something like that to me when she was dying. *She* said, 'Woodlouse knows'."

"What elze did her zay?"

"How the mushrooms of the moon can control breeding. I want you to tell me everything you know. It's very important."

"Uz can't tell yew, unlezz yew'z a Queen."

Nothing Marguerite said could get the old zervant to tell her any more.

The scouts were resting in a hedgerow tree.

"Alert everyone, dogs in sight," Oak said quietly.

They peered between the leaves. Two brown and white dogs had just wriggled under a gate on the far side of the field and were sniffing their way along the hedge. Two men appeared at the gate and the squirrels watched them open it and come through. Each man was carrying a short stick under his right arm with the thinnest end pointing towards the ground.

"Guns," said Bluebell. "Rowan-Pa told me about them.

He saw them when he was on climbabout. Humans use them to kill animals and birds."

"Squirrels?" asked Sycamore.

"I don't think so," said Bluebell, "but you can never tell with humans; they're so unpredictable."

"Keep still and don't show yourselves," said Oak the Wary, parting the leaves carefully.

The dogs were sniffing their way in zigzags across the field when a covey of partridge, two adults and eight young birds, burst into the air and flew towards the squirrels.

The men raised the guns and fired four times. The squirrels instinctively ducked with each report, then ducked again as shot rattled like hail stones on the leaves.

A gap appeared in the arc of birds as two dropped in tumbled heaps of feathers to be seized by the dogs. Two others glided awkwardly into the hedge bottom where they lay, struggling pitiably, the larger of the two trying to escape on its one unbroken leg. The survivors of the family cleared the hedge and dropped into the field behind.

A dog found one of the injured birds and carried it, still cheeping, to the taller of the two men, who pulled its neck. The cheeping stopped. The man grinned at his companion as he put the limp body into the bag slung across his shoulder.

"No squirrel move," whispered Oak.

The shocked squirrels watched the last injured partridge, its feathers stained with blood, fluttering feebly as its life drained away and the brightness faded from its eyes.

Its brothers and sisters scurried noisily along the dead leaves beneath the hedge, then rose again and flew off behind the cover of the bushes.

A dog found the dead bird, carried it to the man, received a pat on the head and returned to the tree, where it sat looking up into the branches. It whined softly and the other dog joined it. The men walked across to the tree and peered up.

A gust of wind caught Willowherb's tail and one man, seeing the movement, raised his gun and pointed it at her. She sat petrified with fear.

"Keep very still," Oak whispered.

The second man joined his companion and they appeared to be arguing. At last the other man lowered the gun, whistled to the dogs to follow him and the two men walked down the hedgerow in the direction that the partridges had flown.

"That was close," said Oak. "This Mainland is a dangerous place. And I still don't know whether humans kill squirrels."

Chapter 29

Marguerite left Wood Anemone and wandered up the island, knowing that her friend held the secret of why Ourland had not been overrun with squirrels in the past, and frustrated because she would not, or could not, confide in her. The secret was in those Moon Mushrooms, whatever they were.

"Greetings, Marguerite the Seeker."

Marguerite looked up to see Heather Treetops and Chestnut the Doubter. She had forgotten that "the Seeker" was her tag. Somehow tagging seemed to be losing its importance. Many of the youngsters had not yet been given tags and those that had, largely ignored them. Youngsters were as often as not referred to by their father's name. She could not remember the tag, if he had one, of Elm Larchson.

She greeted the two formally in the old way, and accepted Chestnut's invitation to see their Woodstock plantation.

In that quiet copse, away from any Man-tracks, Heather and Chestnut had dug up more young honeysuckle plants from other places, replanted them near the roots of several hazel bushes, and were training the growing woodbine shoots around the hazel saplings. Evidence of the earlier raid by idle youngsters was to be seen in the piles of creeper stems, bitten into short lengths, which lay nearby.

Chestnut saw Marguerite looking at these, and said, "I hope for all our sakes that we don't need these Woodstocks too soon. Those Sun-damned young idiots set us back a whole year."

"I hope we never need them," said Marguerite.

"So do we, but I don't trust Grey squirrels not to try and come here, and it is best to be ready," Chestnut said.

> To ensure a Peace
> A wise squirrel will always
> Prepare for a War.

"I don't know that Kernel," said Marguerite. "Who taught you that?"

"We made it up," Chestnut replied. "Do you like it?"

"I think it's a sound idea," said Marguerite, "but it's a pity we have to have words like War and Peace."

She left them and wandered on, her mind back on how to persuade Wood Anemone to reveal her secret. Perhaps if she spelt out the importance of it all to her friend, she would tell. The ex-zervant was no fool.

"Wood Anemone, you *must* tell me about the Mushrooms of the Moon! You don't know how important it is!"

Marguerite went on to tell her friend all about Chip's calculations and his and her concerns about an over-abundance of squirrels on the island.

"But uz *can't* tell yew," Wood Anemone replied. "Uz zwore on uz life and the livez of uz family and uz friendz, not to tell. Only to Kingz and Queenz and their matez.

"Uz could tell yew if yew wuz a Queen," she added, watching Marguerite's reaction.

"You know how I feel about that," Marguerite replied.

"I know how yew feelz about the zecret of the Moon Mushroomz, too," said Wood Anemone. "Yew would make uz a good Queen. Thiz plaze needz won, even uz can zee that!"

The scouting party had escaped from two more dogs and a farmyard cat, had spent uncomfortable nights without proper shelter and had at last reached the North-east Wood near the Blue Pool. They came through the trees cautiously, unsure of their reception from any Greys that might be there. They need not have worried; all the dreytels were empty and cold. They checked each one, but there was no sign of current occupation and no recent scent of Greys.

They circled the Blue Pool, calm in the autumn sunshine, and they fed well at the Hazel Copse, although the nuts were not fully developed. The small nearly-formed kernels were extra tasty and sweet.

The Pool area held mixed memories for them all, except Sycamore, but even he was taken by its beauty and could at last understand why it meant so much to those squirrels on Ourland who had once lived in this demesne.

They briefly visited the empty and forlorn dreys on Steepbank that had once been their homes, then headed towards Rowan's Pool. At the Dogleg Field, Bluebell looked at the twins and said, 'Anyone fancy a ride on a horse?' and smiled.

"Uz iz ztaying on the ground," Rosebay replied, followed by Willowherb's, "On the ground, uz too."

The squirrels dodged amongst the tall thistles as they crossed the field, unseen by the chestnut and the piebald horse and when the roadway was clear, crossed that and were onto the Great Heath.

"Go carefully," said Oak. "It was near here where we met that fox."

They went slowly, scenting the air every few yards, but they were in the belt of trees near Rowan's Pool before they found fresh scent and Fox-dread affected them. Sycamore, who had never smelt fox before, was most affected. They all had to sit in a tree while he composed himself, waiting for the coldness and shivering to stop.

They could not see any sign of the fox below but they moved through the treetops until they reached the edge of the Pool, where they expected to see the three bodies hanging. There were none.

"The vox muzd have vound them," said Rosebay.

"Vound by the vox," repeated Willowherb.

"Voxes – foxes don't climb trees," Oak said.

"Good thing too," said Sycamore.

They descended slowly, watching all about, then, when they were sure that no fox was near, the six squirrels dropped to the ground and scampered across the fallen tree to the Eyeland.

At the foot of each pine was a neat mound of earth and, above each mound, a ⋖ symbol had been cut into the bark of the tree.

"Some Sun-sqirrel has been here before us." Oak stated the obvious.

"And scattered the ground-drey," said Bluebell. "Though the Greys may have done that. I wonder which grave is my Hickory's."

Chip was at the water's edge where the swans had waded ashore. He could see his gold coin in the now clear water but decided that he would not mention it just yet.

"If there's nothing more to do, we should start back. There's still an hour of daylight left," said Oak.

Chip looked round. "I think we should stay the night; we can sleep safely in the trees here. It would be indecent to dash away having come so far and we'll be safe here if that fox is still about."

Chapter 30

Chip was awake at first light and, leaving the other squirrels dozing in the Eyeland trees, he slipped down to the water's edge. From the shore he could see a glinting of gold on the bottom but when he waded in the water again turned milky with particles of disturbed clay. By feeling around with his feet, he located the coin and scrabbled it onto the land. He picked it up in his teeth and was carrying it to the foot of one of the trees.

"Chip, look out, the fox!"

Chip turned and saw the red-brown fur of a large animal crossing the bridge. Still holding the coin in his mouth he leapt for the trunk and ran up it as the white teeth snapped at his tail.

"Sun, that was close!"

Marguerite had, for the time being, given up trying to persuade Wood Anemone to tell her the secret that she felt was so vital to the future of the Ourland squirrels. She was in the Palm Tree Valley, thinking. Wood Anemone was getting older, as indeed they all were. Supposing she were to die and take the secret with her. The knowledge of the moon mushrooms could be lost for ever. It was clear that the ex-zervant wanted to force her friend to become Queen.

A Queen was not necessarily bad because she was called a Queen. What was bad was when the privilege was abused. Supposing that somehow or other she should become Queen, could she hold that position without becoming corrupted by power? Who could tell? The only way would be to hold a Tail-poll each year to ask the squirrels to confirm that they still wanted her to be Queen. That would work. Now, if she was going to ensure the safe future of the island she must find a way to become "Queen".

Marguerite moved up the valley, foraging, not thinking much about the direction she was taking. At the valley head she went through the bracken and the scattered pines to the cliff-edge, feeling that if she could talk with the dolphins they would help her clarify her thoughts. She climbed one of the tallest trees and projected her thoughts seawards, but no matter how hard she tried, there was no response. She consoled herself with the thought that the dolphins must be too far away but were due back in a few days, at New Moon, to return the scouts to the island; and dolphins were always on time.

She recalled what Malin had said when they had first met off Finfast Point and Lundy had repeated:

> *Punctuality*
> *Is vital. Others' time wasted,*
> *Is stolen by you*
> *And can never be returned.*
> *Lost minutes sink for ever.*

That was it. It started as a Kernel but had two more lots of seven sounds. Did dolphins call these "Kernels", or did they have some other, perhaps fishy, name for them? Life was full of questions.

On the shore below her she could see a swan. She watched it for a while, remembering the exhilarating feeling of being "high on a bird's back".

> High on a bird's back
> The Island's Queen flies – bringing
> The Peace of the Sun.

Peace – not *piece*. That was it – *now* the prophecy made sense. If she was the Island's Queen, she had flown high on a bird's back and if she was Queen then Wood Anemone could tell her the secret and there would be the Sun's Peace on the island for ever.

Life was full of answers too, if you thought hard enough. Marguerite suddenly felt very humble.

She looked down at the swan again; there was something wrong with the way it was sitting on the beach. It just did not look right.

Marguerite thought briefly about rushing off to tell Wood Anemone that she had decided to see if the others would accept her as Queen, when she saw the swan shake its head feebly and rest its neck on the gravelly beach. Something was definitely wrong. She climbed down the pine trunk and made her way towards it.

As she got nearer she saw that the normally gleaming white feathers were streaked with some black substance which was also around the swan's beak. It had obviously been trying to clean itself.

Marguerite looked at the bird closely, but could not be sure if it was one of those which had flown her and her friends to the island, but this did not matter. She wanted to help but did not know what to do; the swan looked very sick.

She went up the bank and across the island to look for Clover and the two ex-princesses, Voxglove and Cowzlip, to see if any of these Carers would know how to help the stricken swan.

They could suggest nothing but to ensure that food was brought to it each day and, with the Sun's help, it might recover.

The scouts huddled together in one of the trees on the Eyeland watching the fox waiting patiently below.

"I'm hungry," said Sycamore, having seen that there were no cones whatsoever left on any of the three trees.

"Zo's that vox," said Rosebay.

"That vox iz too," said Willowherb.

"We can't stay here," said Oak in a whisper, as though the fox could understand his words. "We must get across to the land and escape or we won't get back in time to meet the dolphins, especially if we run into more trouble. We must allow at least six days."

They discussed possibilities. Unless a human came to frighten the fox away, or he gave up and left, there seemed only one solution. They would have to leap into the water and swim across to the land, hoping to reach safety there before the fox caught any of them.

They came slowly down to the lower branches, staying just out of reach of the animal prowling below them, and each planned a route along a branch. Chip held his coin tightly between his teeth.

Willowherb whispered to her sister, "Uz'z zcared of the vox, uz iz. Uz can't jump that far and uz can't zwim vast."

"Yew go virzt, uz'z be behind yew."

Oak shouted "Now," and five of the squirrels ran along branches, leapt out into the pool and swam towards the opposite shore. The fox sprang after them and swam strongly towards Willowherb, his mouth only just behind the terrified squirrel's tail.

Rosebay, who had stayed in the tree, ran and leapt onto the swimming fox's head, clawing at his eyes. The two sank in a flurry of scrabbling and splashing as the other squirrels reached the far shore and climbed a tree to safety. Chip, the coin still tight between his teeth, spluttering and coughing awkwardly as he did so.

"Where'z Rozebay, where'z Rozebay," wailed Willowherb.

They watched in horror as the writhing bodies surfaced and sank again, then resurfaced.

The fox swam back to the Eyeland carrying the limp and lifeless body of Rosebay.

"Don't look," said Bluebell to Willowherb as the sound of bones being crunched reached their ears.

Chapter 31

Between the many discussion meetings that were being held, Marguerite did what little she could for the sick swan.

Wood Anemone addressed a special Council Meeting which she had asked Just Poplar to call.

"Vellow squirrelz," she had said. "Uz huz lived on the Mainland for more than a year. When uz left Ourland there wuz a King here, Poplar'z vather, and uz knowz that Poplar won't mind uz zaying that zum of the thingz hiz vather did wuz not *good* thingz. Now, when uz comez back there iz no King and yew iz all trying to do thingz like they wuz done at the Blue Pool. Yew can zee az well az uz can, that it izn't working. Thiz i'land needz a King – or a Queen. Zo uz propozez that Marguerite should be our Queen."

There was a silence as each squirrel considered the likely consequences if the proposal was approved.

"Long live Queen Marguerite," Just Poplar said, at last.

"Wait please," Marguerite held up her paw, "there might be some other squirrel more worthy than me."

"Any other propozalz?" Poplar glowered round at the assembly.

"No? Long live Queen Marguerite. The meeting iz yewrz, Ma'am."

"Please. Do not call me Ma'am. I am Marguerite still, and I accept *only* if you promise to hold a Tail-poll at each Harvest Celebration to see if you would rather have another squirrel to be Queen – or King."

"Long live Queen Marguerite."

Marguerite smiled round at her friends. "I declare today to be a Sun-day in celebration." Then she slipped away to take food to the swan.

"It's your fault," Sycamore said to Chip. "If you hadn't made us stay last night so that you could get your Sun-damned gold thing, Rosebay would still be with us."

"That's hardly fair," said Bluebell. "We all decided to stay, you don't know what foxes are going to do. It might have attacked us last night."

"Voxes iz horrid, eating other animalz," said Willowherb.

"That's not fair either," Bluebell responded. "That's how foxes live. A fox has to do what a fox has to do. Think how lucky you are being a squirrel; at least your nuts don't try and run away when you are eating them."

"Shut up, Bluebell," said Oak. "You're not helping. Oh Sun, it's back.'"

The fox had finished his meal and had come to the foot of the tree where they were sitting. Now he was watching them eagerly, his pink tongue lolling out of the side of his mouth. Willowherb was sure she could see blood on the fox's lips.

Marguerite had asked Rowan and Meadowsweet to take over teaching Kernels, Traditions and Manners to the young squirrels and also to train them in wood-craft and survival. Having seen the difference that a few days of Mainland adventure had had on Sycamore she was beginning to formulate an idea that might stop the mindless behaviour of the island youngsters.

She had already asked Just Poplar to be Guardian of Justice on Ourland, and had made him swear to live up to his Tag at all times and never let anyone, especially herself, influence his judgement.

> *Let Justice be done,*
> *In every squirrel's case,*
> *Though the sky may fall.*

"If expediency affects justice, then we are not worthy to govern," she had told him.

She appointed Chestnut and Heather to be Guardians of Defence and asked Clover to relinquish the post of Tagger which was no longer relevant, and help Voxglove and Cowzlip do all they could to help sick and elderly squirrels. Clover agreed readily.

Then Queen Marguerite sought out Wood Anemone.

"Now, Wood Anemone-Friend, or should I call you Woodlouse? I want you to tell me all about the Mushrooms of the Moon. And don't you dare call me Ma'am!"

They brushed whiskers and hugged one another.

"Can uz be yewr zervant?" Wood Anemone asked.

"No, you can be uz – my friend and companion. I do get lonely on my own. Now, please, tell me about those Mushrooms."

The scouts in the tree were whispering together again.

"If we go back the way we came, we have to come down out of the trees before we have gone very far," Oak said. "We might be able to circle round and go back another way whilst staying safely off the ground."

"If we split up, we can see how big this wood is and whether there is a safe route out," said Sycamore. "Then meet back here."

They each went off in a different direction, Chip lodging his coin in a fork of the tree before he went. The fox prowled about below, keeping one or other of the squirrels always in his sight.

An hour later they were back, Chip returning last. He looked for his coin; it was not in the fork where he had left it, but lay on the ground near the fox's feet. It could not have fallen by itself.

"Who threw down my gold thing?" he asked.

Every squirrel was looking away and none answered.

"More important than that, is there a safe way out of this wood?" Oak asked.

Each scout reported that they had come to the edge of the copse and would have had to drop to the ground before getting to the next clump of trees.

"We're trapped here then until the fox goes away," said Bluebell. "At least there's plenty of things for us to eat – not like on the Eyeland."

Sycamore said, "When I was on the Eyeland with you before, you had a Woodstock thing. I saw one of those growing over there."

They followed him to the edge of the copse where a tangle of honeysuckle enmeshed the top of a hazel bush. Lower down they could see the unmistakable bulge of a Woodstock – but it was low down, possibly within reach of a hungry fox.

"I'll try and cut it out of the stem," said Sycamore. "Call me if the fox comes too close." He ducked as a large brown and yellow insect flew past his head towards a hollow tree across the glade. "Did you see the size of that wasp?" he asked. 'It was enormous!"

Chip edged along the branch towards the disconsolate Willowherb.

"I'm sorry about Rosebay," he said. "But it was a brave thing that she did."

"Her did a brave thing," replied Willowherb.

"Look out," called Bluebell as the fox leapt up at Sycamore but fell just short. He leapt again but could not quite reach the young squirrel as he bit and gnawed at the hazel stem.

When Sycamore's teeth were aching, he handed over to Oak. Between them they cut through below the Woodstock, the fox all the while leaping up at them in vain.

Bluebell and Chip finished cutting the Woodstock clear, and together they pulled it to the top of the mass of honeysuckle, where it lay on the tangle of fine stems while they peeled off the bark and cut the now familiar numbers: 1 Z 3 4 5 6 7 10 X.

The fox prowled back and forth below them.

"What number shall I use?" Bluebell asked.

"Enuff to kill the nazty thing," said Willowherb but the others disagreed.

"A 3 or a 4 should curl its whiskers and stop it chasing us," said Bluebell. "He was only being a fox. And foxes eat squirrels when they can. That's how things are."

She sighted the Woodstock at the fox and scratched a 3.

There was a yelp of surprise but the fox only pawed at his face, shook his head, and continued his prowling below them.

"Try a 4," suggested Oak. This was no more effective. That fox has tough whiskers," Bluebell remarked as another and another of the big wasps flew past towards the distant hollow tree. "Try a 5."

None of the numbers proved effective against the fox. He yelped a little each time the Woodstock was used, but his whiskers stayed as straight as pine needles.

Sycamore was watching the yellow and brown insects as they zoomed past.

"I wonder if those big-wasps have big stings," he said.

"Why," asked Oak.

"We might be able to get them to sting the fox," he replied.

"You won't get me poking a twig in their nest," said Oak. "You can try if you like."

"No, I wondered if the Woodstock Force might stir them up," said Sycamore. "We could do that from here; we're a safe distance away."

They all agreed it was worth a try but that one squirrel would have to tease the fox to keep it near the big-wasps' nest while the others stayed well back. Bluebell drew the short twig and lightly ran along a branch and leapt across to the lower branches of the hollow tree.

From there she chattered insults at the fox, who had followed her. She was careful to keep just out of his reach.

"You're in the way of the Woodstock," Oak called to her. "You'll have to go higher."

The fox sat and watched her climb.

Oak aimed at the hole in the tree and scratched a Ƃ. There was a low rumble from within the tree and the squirrels saw a cloud of big-wasps pour angrily from the hole. The fox turned and ran, yelping and biting at his flanks as hornet after hornet caught up with him and forced their sharp stings through his fur. The yelping faded into the distant sounds of the wood.

Bluebell, unthinking of the danger to her, had watched the scene until she realised that one of the big-wasps had seen her and was coming to attack. She leapt for the next tree, the big-wasp just behind her, raced through the branches and into the next tree. She could still hear the whir of its wings behind her head and ran on towards the pool.

At the last tree she jumped for the water, submerging and coming up under a lily leaf near the shore where her feet were able to touch bottom. Here she stayed, holding the leaf above her head until the frustrated hornet gave up the search and returned to its nest. She crawled out to dry, her teeth chattering with fear, relief and cold.

As soon as the fox was gone and the big-wasps had returned to their nest, Chip climbed down and rushed across the leaf litter to recover the coin. The others followed the direction that Bluebell had taken and found her on the poolside.

"That was well done," said a voice from behind them, and they turned to see a grey squirrel's face grinning at them.

"Zumac! It'z yew!"

"Bluebell, Willowherb . . . where's Rosebay?"

The Grey and the two Reds brushed whiskers, then Bluebell, her chattering gone in the delight at meeting an old friend, introduced Oak and Sycamore.

"Sumac is a Sun-squirrel," Bluebell explained. "Rowan-Pa said he was his best pupil ever."

Sumac looked suitably modest, then asked again about Rosebay.

They told their story and Sumac silently embraced Willowherb.

"Was it you who buried . . . ?" Bluebell's voice trailed away.

"Hickory and Sitka, and your father, Spindle. Yes they're all nourishing trees now, as your Farewell Kernel teaches."

Oak the Wary was listening to Bluebell and Sumac. He was uneasy about the way she was treating him as a trusted friend; after all he was a Grey. He may profess to be a Sun-squirrel but Oak was not going to give him a chance to learn the secret of the Woodstock. He left them exchanging news and slipped back to where the weapon had been dropped when they had followed Bluebell.

Chip was there with his gold disc.

"We must hide the Woodstock," Oak said. "There are Greys about."

"Change the figures," Chip suggested, "Then it won't matter if they *do* find it."

"Watch in case the fox comes back, and listen for the big-wasps."

Oak bit into the wood, tasting the sweet sap of the hazel. His sharp teeth rapidly changed the **1** into **◀**, the **Z** into **◪**, the **⅂** into **ℬ** and the **4** into **✦** The **5** became **ᗺ**, the **Ƅ** : **ᗺ** the **7** : **⅁** and the **10** : **⊕**. Finally he made the **X** look like **✖**, and as he did this he felt the power drain from the Woodstock as the life had drained from the shot partridge.

"Where shall we hide it?" he asked Chip.

Together they pushed the inert stick end-first into the mound of pine needles covering a wood-ants' nest, brushing the ants from their fur and scampering away before they could be bitten.

"It'll be a brave Grey who gets that out, even if they did find it," said Oak.

When they rejoined the others they heard Bluebell say, "Thank you, Sumac-friend. Where is Tumbleweed?"

"She should be here soon. She has been helping old Malachite at the Tanglewood, he's not too well. But he's a Sun-squirrel now, would you believe; *and* so are those other two old puffers. Tumbleweed and I have been doing a bit of teaching ourselves since you all left. Shall I give the three old Lords your regards?"

Chapter 32

Rowan returned to his drey after a day's teaching. Meadowsweet was waiting for him. As they brushed whiskers, he said, "You know young Elm Larchson?"

Meadowsweet nodded.

"Today I said to him, 'I didn't see you at the Camouflage and Concealment class yesterday.' And he said, 'Getting good, aren't I?' Cheeky young thing!"

Queen Marguerite had now learned from Wood Anemone how the old King had ordered all the zervantz to eat one of the tiny mushrooms that grew on Old Wally's wall on the night of each new moon, but had never told them why. It had been Wood Anemone, the Royal's zervant Woodlouse as she had been then, who had always maintained a stock of dried mushrooms from The Wall for the ceremonies. When the King had decided that it was necessary for some new zervantz to be born, he had ordered Woodlouse to give different mushrooms to the selected couples instead. This was the secret that she had been sworn to keep.

"We must *educate* all the squirrels so that they know that if they eat Moon Mushrooms each month once they have had two dreylings we can prevent the island from becoming over-populated," Marguerite told Wood Anemone. "That will be your job. No secrets, no coercion, just *education*."

The swan on the beach was ailing and Marguerite did not know what more she could do to help it recover. Then, early in the morning of the day before the New Moon was due, as a light autumn mist floated through the trees of the island, she was trying to get the swan to feed when she sensed that the dolphins were close. She turned and, through the mist, saw three dark humps rise out of the water and disappear again.

"Malin, Lundy, Finisterre," she called, "I am here."

The answer came immediately. "Squirrel-Friend, we see you. Is that a swan with you?"

"Yes, it is covered with black stuff and very sick. I don't know how to help it."

"Only humans can. There is a poison that they throw into the sea from their biggest boats. It kills many birds and hurts us if it gets into our breathing holes," Malin said. "You must get the swan to the humans, only they can save it."

"Have you heard anything about your young friends who we took to the Mainland?" Lundy asked. "We are due to bring them back at first light tomorrow."

"No, I hope they are safe."

"Try and get that swan to the humans, we will see you in the morning."

"SWAN —

WALK ALONG THE BEACH —

220

ACTION NOW –

ACTION NOW!

Yes you can, yes you can,

ACTION NOW – ''

The swan responded by raising its head but seemed unable to walk. It was obviously just too sick.

Marguerite left it and went inland, looking for a human. She found one just taking off his green covering with the badge of Acorn, the first squirrel in the World. Underneath was another covering which was white with dark lines making squares on it. As she hid and watched, the human fumbled with his square-patterned arm coverings and rolled them up towards his shoulders. Then he picked up a stick with a flat bit of metal on one end and swung it at the trunk of a rhododendron bush. The top of the bush fell off and rolled towards Marguerite who crouched in fear.

Eventually she collected enough courage to hop out towards the man and chatter to attract his attention. He stopped chopping and leant on the axe-handle watching the squirrel. She ran backwards trying to get him to follow her but he did not move. She tried again and again until it seemed that at last he understood. He rested the axe against a bush, picked up his green covering and followed her.

Marguerite stayed on the ground, looking back frequently to see that she was still being followed, but staying far enough in front to be able to leap clear if the human tried to do anything hostile or unexpected.

She led him to the swan, who hissed feebly. The man approached it cautiously then tied a knot in the end of one of the arm tubes on the green covering he was carrying. He

manoeuvred the swan's head into that tube and pulled the
rest of his covering over the swan's body so that it could not
struggle nor peck him. Marguerite admired the firm but
gentle way he had done this and, as he lifted the swan, she
slipped away into the shoreline vegetation. The swan was
now the human's responsibility. She had done all *she* could.
She felt tired and hungry and spent the remainder of that
day resting or feeding listlessly, and the night sleeping
alone in a palm tree in the valley.

Next morning she hurried through the mist across the
island to Pottery Point and joined a group of other squirrels
as they watched the three dolphins carrying the sticks and
the five returning scouts. Five?

Burdock the News-squirrel carried the story across the
island, bearing in mind what her mother, Queen
Marguerite, had told her.

"From now on, you will be as responsible as the Post-
squirrels were. What you say must be the truth, and if you
don't know the truth, find out before you say a word to any
squirrel."

SCOUTING PARTY RETURNS.
ROSEBAY GIVES HER LIFE TO SAVE
HER SISTER
With the return of the scouting party your
reporter learned of the sad death of Rosebay
Wood Anemone's daughter . . .

Chip had been the last one to come ashore; swimming with
the coin in his mouth. He had helped Willowherb up the

beach but then had avoided the group clustered around the other scouts and had carried the golden disc away to his drey. Later he learned from Burdock that Marguerite was now Queen of Ourland.

He waited until he found her alone.

"I've brought you a present," he said. "A present fit for a Queen."

Marguerite took the coin and turned it over. She had not looked at it closely before.

"It's very pretty," she said as the sun glowed on the bright golden metal. "What's it for?"

"It's for you," Chip replied.

"I didn't mean that, Chip-Friend. What does a squirrel use it for?"

"I don't know," Chip admitted. "But Lundy said that the humans think highly of these. There's a little human's head on one side."

"Then I think we'd better give it back to the humans, don't you? It really belongs to them. But thank you for bringing it to show me."

Chip carried his coin through the wood, unsure how to get it to a human. Although none had ever harmed him, he did not know if it was safe to approach one.

He passed many squirrels busy with harvesting the plentiful nuts. Soon it will be our Harvest Sun-day, he thought, as Willowherb, sitting close to her mother, Wood Anemone, waved to him, a ripe hazel nut in her teeth. He had not noticed before what a good looking squirrel she was.

Ahead, the late morning Sun shone on the tower of the

little island church of St Mary, Brownsea. Chip saw this and was drawn in that direction. As he neared the building he could hear the singing of the humans and he hid behind a slab of stone until they all came out.

He was too afraid of such tall creatures to approach closely and so stayed hidden until he was sure that they had gone. The flat wood that the humans used to close the entrance to this great Man-drey was not across the opening, and he was tempted to enter the dark entrance. As he stood timorously in the doorway waiting for his eyes to adjust to the fainter light, he could smell the scent of fruit and newly dug vegetables of every kind. Around him a harvest of human food was piled in heaps on every ledge and in baskets on the floor.

Where could he put his coin so that a human would find it?

He hopped onto a seat and then onto a ledge higher up; he could leave it there. Then, overwhelmed by an urge to hide it out of sight, he frantically looked around for a suitable place to conceal the coin. A closed wooden box at his paw had a slot in it of just the right size. He looked around the church, fearful of being found, rubbed the coin with his paw one last time, enjoying the smooth feel of it, then dropped it through the slot. As he hopped down from the seat he heard it fall with a rattle into the box, on the side of which in human symbols meaningless to him were the words:

FOR THE POOR AND HUNGRY
PEOPLE OF THE WORLD.

Chapter 33

Chip felt strangely relieved as he left the church. He felt too, that he ought to tell Marguerite what he had done and went to find her.

She was sleeping in the warm afternoon sunlight on a branch outside her drey. He sat and watched her lovingly until she awoke. There was something that he wanted to ask her.

"Marguerite-Friend," he began, then paused, embarrassed. Could he address her as intimately as this, now she was Queen?

She looked at the younger squirrel and remembered how he had looked when she first had seen him, an under-fed and sorry looking sqrunt. He had certainly come up in the trees since then.

"Yes?" she said kindly.

"I was – I was going to ask you – ask you . . ." He stopped again.

"Yes, Chip-Friend?"

"I was going to ask you to be my life-mate – but now that you're Queen . . ."

"That would have made no difference if it had been the

right thing to do," she said. "But it would not be fair. I've had two dreylings and you haven't had any. If I'm going to ask all other squirrels to have only two, then *I* mustn't have any more. You must find another mate. But thank you – I do appreciate the compliment."

Marguerite brushed whiskers with him.

"Now go and visit Wood Anemone, there is someone there who needs you."

Chip hopped away, once again surprisingly light-hearted. He found Wood Anemone with Willowherb, both spreading out Moon Mushrooms to dry in the sun, and he watched them from a distance. The sunlight was lighting up Willowherb's ruddy fur and shining through the glossy hairs of her tail. He knew what he should do.

He went across the grass to her side.

"Willowherb-Friend. Will you be my life-mate?"

"Yewr life-mate uz *will* be."

Chipling brushed whiskers with Willowherb, then with Wood Anemone, who appeared to be as pleased as her daughter who was already racing up a tree, giving a tease-call for him to follow her.

Winter passed, with all of the squirrels who had already had two or more dreylings happily joining in the monthly Moon Mushroom Eating ceremonies. March came in gently to the peaceful island.

Marguerite was on her way to choose which of the newly qualified scouts would be selected to be taken, by the dolphins, for the next Mainland Adventure. Hearing the W-wow-W-wow-W-wow of wing-beats overhead, she looked up as a swan, its feathers gleaming white, swept overhead and turned in a long glide to land in the lagoon and paddle over to where she sat near the edge of the black mud of the Zwamp. The bird was carrying a plant in its beak.

It walked up to her, spread its wings and lowered its head in an unmistakable gesture of thanks, then walked to the marsh-edge and pushed the roots of the plant into the mud where the stream ran into the lagoon, above the level of the highest flood-tide. It lowered its head once again, then walked back into the water.

Marguerite waited as it ran across the surface and lifted into the air. She watched it circle above her and fly westwards, the sound of its wing-beats fading into the distance. Only then did she hop over to look at the plant the swan had brought; it was not familiar to her. It had glossy green leaves and hard round buds, one of which showed a trace of yellow where the sepals were just beginning to open.

Each day she made a point of visiting the marsh, and on the day when the humans were celebrating *their* Spring Sunday, Marguerite found the gift-plant covered in a mass of gleaming golden flowers, brighter and more beautiful by far than the metal disc that Chip had spent so much effort in bringing to Ourland.

She would declare *this* day to be the squirrels' Spring Sun-day too. She went to find Burdock, the News-squirrel; her daughter would enjoy spreading the word.

As she passed The Wall the sound of happy young squirrel voices reached her ears. Marguerite climbed the crumbling brickwork until she could see, at the far end, her grandson Hickory, son of her son Oak and his life-mate Bluebell. Young Hickory was playing the part of Leaper in the Wall game. He saw Marguerite and waved a paw, then greeted her shyly.

"Hello, Marguerite-Ma-Ma." Then he turned away and started the chant:

I honour birch-bark
The Island Screen. Flies stinging
A piece of the sun.

Marguerite smiled to herself. Some things never change, she thought.

Epilogue.

Should you be in Dorset, in the south of England, known to some as New America, and take the boat out to Brownsea Island you will, if you are lucky and quiet, see some of the descendants of Marguerite and the United Ourlanders.

The new council tree is there in Beech Valley but the 'Tree that Died of Shame' is now only a grey stump and you will find this a few yards south of the church, often with a royal looking peacock perched on it. The human guardians of the island, The National Trust, have planted another tree nearby.

You will not find red squirrels at the beautiful Blue Pool. This is inhabited by Greys still insisting that they be called Silvers, but they are altogether a gentler breed than the harsh and randee adventurers of the old pioneering days of Marble, his friend Gabbro and their long Sun-gone compatriots.

In the museum at the Blue Pool is the original Woodstock found many years later in the Clay-Pan and now preserved there for the benefit of non-believers.

I searched the North-East Wood to see if I could find the squirrel-shaped mass of metal that remained after Crag's Temple Tree had been struck by lightning but could find no trace of it. Local people believe it was cut up and taken away by gypsies but I did see recently in a London gallery, a vast mass of fused scrap metal, shaped like a squirrel and entitled 'Modern Man's View of Nature'. However as it was valued at several million pounds and had been shortlisted for the Turner Prize it could not possibly have been the one from the North East Wood.

The dolphins still patrol the Dorset coast and the bird-brained swans thrive at Abbotsbury, sharing a legend of small furry creatures that behaved in a way that surprised them all.

Michael Tod.
Llangattock November 1999.

If you have enjoyed reading
The Dorset Squirrels you may also enjoy
Michael Tod's **A Curlew's Cry.**
This is a 'slim volume' of poetry but
also contains **A Bag of Mixed Kernels**
(Haiku) and **Cwm Cadno Days**, short
stories of the author's experiences of
growing up on a Welsh hill farm in the
1950s.

A Curlew's Cry is available from all
good bookshops or by post from
Cadno Books
P.O. Box 34
Abergavenny
NP8 1YN

Price **£3.95** plus **50p** post and packing.

ISBN 1 898225 01 X

Selected poems from A Curlew's Cry

PLAIN JANE

The young men called her plain and went their way
'It's pretty girls we want,' I heard one say
But, once, I saw the love-light in her eyes
And Jane, though plain, was beautiful that day.

KISSING HANDS

Helen,
When first I saw
Your baby hand, born fingerless
I cried and put it to my lips
A vain attempt to 'kiss it better'.

Later I learned to kiss each hand
To show I didn't mind
And let you know that every part
Was just as precious as the rest.

Now, when I watch you play
Handling each problem with such joy and zest
I kiss your hand
From sheer respect

I never notice which.

A DROP OF DOGGEREL

I interviewed a man last night
Who'd just come up from Tooting
Though blind from birth his claim to fame
Was – he loved parachuting.

I asked him how he knew the time
To brace himself for landing
He answered with a ready smile
At my not understanding.

"It's easy, Mike," the man replied.
"I have this simple knack.
I know when I am near the ground
My guide dog's lead goes slack."

ONE GOOD CHURN

Two frogs fell in a bowl of cream
And started swimming round and round.
"There's no way out," the weak one said
Gave up and sank and drowned.

The other frog, of sterner stuff
"I won't give up," was heard to utter
And went on swimming round and round
Then hopped out from the butter.

A CURLEW'S CRY

Hearing a distant curlew's bubbling cry
My heart with hiraeth fills
This sad, lonely sound distils
Sun and wind on Wales' hills.

DOLPHINSONG

'Swimming with dolphins is a life-altering experience.'

Mary O'Connor, whose smile has been stolen by a mugger, learns the truth of this when she swims with Fungie, the dolphin of Ireland's Dingle Bay. His cryptic message in an ancient language leads her to Dorset. From the tower of a redundant church she looks down onto a pool where two captive dolphins and a pilot whale circle endlessly, seeking a way back to the freedom of the sea. Are these the 'three of the race of whales' she had been directed to find? And how should she convey their 'song' to the world as Fungie has instructed?

Michael Tod's latest eco-saga takes us from the blood-drenched shores of the Faeroe Islands, via the West Coast of Ireland, to the holiday beaches of Dorset, returning inexorably to the basalt cliffs and fjords of the isolated Faeroes for a thrilling showdown. Not only do we experience the passions and fears of the human characters, but we enter a fascinating sub-marine society in many ways as advanced as our own.

"A fine novel... It is simply magnificent."
Marc Harshman

"Fantastic book... You have a great talent."
David Bellamy

To be published by Cadno Books in March 2000
ISBN 1 898 22502 8   Price £7.99

If you have ... ...
Ladies Order ... ...

Cabin Press
P.O. Box
...
...

Phone ...

Please allow ... weeks ... payable to
Catalogue.

... New ... Co. ... Blue ...
... Postage ...

... ...

Publishing, ...

If you have difficulty in obtaining any Cadno Books publications they may be ordered by post from

Cadno Books
P.O. Box 34
Abergavenny
NP8 1YN

Phone/Fax 01873 810675

Please enclose a cheque made payable to Cadno Books

A Curlew's Cry Price £3.95
plus 50p Post and Packing
If more than one copy is ordered or if ordered with any other book(s) then post and packing is free of charge

Dolphinsong (After March 2000) Price £7.99 Post Free.